THE SAND TOWER

BY PHIL COLEMAN

ISBN 978-1-300-90108-2

For my Mom and Dad
(Philip and Wyona Coleman)
whose tireless dedication to protecting our environment
inspired me to wonder "what if?"

FORWARD
from the author

One sad September afternoon in the early '80's I stood on the banks of the Gauley River at the scene of a body recovery. Present on this somber scene were state law enforcement officers, dozens of kayakers and raft guides, and the two divers who had found the kayaker in a pool downstream from where he had disappeared earlier that day. Dry eyes were few and far between. As we made our way back up out of the gorge, I diverted off from the crowd and walked instead up the now dry river bed. Water from the dam had been shut off to facilitate the search so I was clambering over damp rocks and boulders.

I wanted to see the rocks that had trapped the unlucky boater, hopefully to learn something about the spot to help in some future similar situation. I had expected to find a few rocks causing a constricted passage but instead found myself in a cave under a massive boulder. It was a perfect trap. I stood in the cave with droplets falling from the roof onto my head. The water was oddly warm, almost hot, Then I felt that I was not alone there. Something else was with me in that cave. It was an evil presence.

I had kayaked from when I was young, My friends and I learned the sport and took it to new levels. We took on the challenges presented by the rapids we ran and took greater and greater risks. As our skills increased, so did a new awareness of the rhymes and rhythms of the water we were paddling. There was something timeless that was speaking to me in a language I did not yet fully understand.

I stood in that cave with the heat and the mist and the dropping water and at that moment this book was born. It would take a dozen years to finally sit down and type it out. I would like to feel that I did a good job spinning a tale that does justice to the feelings that came to me that day, and over a lifetime of adventure on the rivers and streams of our planet.

This book was written on a typewriter before I ever sat down in front of a computer. All of the research was done the old fashioned way: libraries, the postal service, technical manuals and interviews. I feel indebted to the late chief RainCrow of the Shawnee nation for his willingness to help create the mind set his people might have had a thousand years ago. I also would like to thank my parents for their support and help and that of my sister for putting this together. A big thanks goes to Kim Abney for all of her wonderful illustrations.

PROLOGUE
A
THE COIN

July 23, 1797 — Kentucky

"And you would be Christian Katz."

Hearing the strange voice, Christian looked up in surprise. He was not used to being called by name at the quay except by fellow pilots and townsfolk.

A tall thin man held out his hand. "My name is Joshua Spinwall and I am in sufficient hurry to get down over these falls. I understand you to be the best pilot here and want you to run my flatboat for me."

Christian was speechless as he looked at the imposing man towering over him. He didn't look like your average pioneer. His fine clothes were hardly ruffled let alone ragged and dirty from the journey.

"Lad, if you did not hear me, I said I'm in a hurry, let us be off."

"I, I can't go. I've a commitment. You'll have to seek out another."

Anger flashed across the man's face. "Such impertinence will not be tolerated!"

Christian leapt to his feet to sidestep the blow that was sure to follow. Instead the man's face shifted into a broad smile of large white teeth that almost lit the shade below the cottonwood.

Every year more and more settlers were making the perilous journey west floating the Ohio River. They came down in arks, flatboats and broadhorns with all of their worldly possessions. The better prepared were already far downstream. These "late runners" had to hurry toward their winter destinations. And now at this place, something stood in their path. The Falls of the Ohio lay below. The entire flow of the Ohio River dropped twenty-two feet in a mile and a half through a twisting course around islands and sandstone rocks.

"Please excuse me Mr. Katz, but I am feeling tremendous pressure to continue my travels downriver."

"All these folks are in a hurry."

What a fool, like all these others, thought Christian. If they had had a copy of the *Navigator* on board most of them would have stopped on the Indiana side in Jeffersonville, for at this stage of water, the Indian Chute was the only safe way to go.

"I guess you didn't buy a copy of the *Pittsburgh Navigator*."

"No, I did not. Listen to me young man. I will pay you quite well if we can go immediately." With this Spinwall produced a shiny twenty dollar gold piece from his vest pocket. Christian stared, captivated by the large coin. Sanders Stuart had only been gone a half hour and already Christian had been bothered three times with requests to pilot a boat. Each time he explained that he had a commitment and that there would soon be other pilots returning from below. Sanders, his boss and mentor, had told him to wait, but the gold piece said something else. He thought of Sander's metal vault full of one dollar coins. Sanders kept it hidden in the stones below the hearth in his cabin. Once a week he would let the fire go out, brush away the ashes and dig it out to cache his earnings. "Laddie, there be nothing so sweet as gold money."

Spinwall held the coin a little closer. "This is yours when we get below the falls."

Christian, in a flash, snatched it from his fingers and held it.

"You'll pay me now and I'll go."

Joshua forced a smile, smothering fire in his eyes.

"Let us set off then."

Sanders had taught him well, and truth be known, he was as able as any pilot working the rapids. He knew the rocks and ledges, which always stayed the same, but he also was continuously learning and relearning the shifting and changing temporary hazards. His mind was always cataloging the shifting trunks of the huge trees which came floating down the Ohio and imbedded themselves on the bottom. They were an ever changing threat. These came in two classes: planters and sawyers. Planters were always at least partly visible above the surface of the water so one could at least try to give them wide berth when passing. The sawyers rose and fell slowly and sometimes were hidden below the rapids only to rise directly in the path of the unlucky. Christian deferred to Sanders these days out of custom and the sense of security he had with the older man, but he knew the river and knew how to pick a safe route.

Stuart was one of the first of the brave men who had dedicated themselves to guiding boats through the falls. He had arrived just after the revolution, having escaped the indentured servitude he had endured since boyhood in Glascow. To help pay his father's debts, he had become little more than a slave to a merchant from London, sailed across the ocean with the man and made to work countless hours on the docks of Baltimore. It had been a dull existence, with no hope of freedom. Now, he was the master of his own destiny and a highly respected pilot. Recognizing the risks that men like Sanders took, congress in 1796 passed a bill authorizing pilots at the Falls of the Ohio to charge two dollars for a boat guided successfully down through the rapids.

Spinwall turned and walked off. Christian, following him through the crowd, watched Spinwall move easily and quickly. He noticed the muscles of his arms and back ripple through his coat. He would have the strength to row. But Christian felt a growing uneasiness about this strange man.

A fat man smelling of corn liquor grabbed him by the arm.

"Where ye be off to lad? You told my brother here you couldn't run us through!"

Christian pulled away from him and held up the gold piece.

"Yore brother ain't payin' more than this by any chance is he?"

He took off to avoid the man further and caught up with Spinwall as he boarded a broadhorn. Ignoring the scolding of an old woman inside the broadhorn, they climbed over it and down onto a flatboat moored to the far side. Christian noted that it was big; some twenty by fifty feet with sweeps on each side and the stern and a gouger in the bow. The deckhouse sat exactly in the middle. Christian could never understand why so many settlers built their flatboats with the house always blocking the view and preventing communication between bow and stern oarsmen. There were no livestock or people on board. Clothes hung from a line tied to the fore end of the house and the rail.

"Everyone go around by freight?"

Spinwall looked up from the line he was busily untying from the broadhorn. "Excuse me?"

"The others. Yore family and animals."

"Oh, Yes, they have gone overland."

"Where 'bouts you from mister?"

"Baltimore. And yourself my son?"

"Virginia, western counties. My pa and uncle came lookin' for tillable ground and got drowned right here. Been here ever since. I'm goin' back there someday to find my ma."

"Is that so? Loose that other line and we'll be off."

Christian thought he could feel the man's eyes boring into his back as he untied the rope and was suddenly sickened. The deck at his feet was slick with splashes of blood turning black in the mid day sun. From right behind him Spinwall said, "What is the matter lad, have you not ever seen blood before?"

"What's it from?"

"I slaughtered a chicken last night. Now if you would please collect yourself, I'd like to go."

"Okay. Look here, mister. The way I do this, is in the rapids I run the gouger and you the stern sweep. First we turn her around here in the creek, and when we drift out to the mouth, we'll row upstream with the side sweeps in the eddy on this side until it's safe to cross to the Indian Chute."

"You know your art boy. Just tell me what to do and when."

Using the sweeps they turned the sluggish craft into the slight current of Beargrass Creek. Passing by the other boats they came to the mouth at the Ohio. The river was running swiftly towards the falls directly across from their position. Christian pulled hard on his sweep oar and began to turn the flatboat upstream in the eddy. He walked around to the other side of the house and saw that Spinwall had taken off his coat and was rolling up the sleeves of his fine shirt. He was a big man and looked very strong for the dandy he appeared to be. "Okay mister, we've got to work our way all the way up this eddy before we let this current grab us. I'll go back to the other sweep. Just pull steady for upriver."

Christian looked inside the open door of the house when he walked back and stopped in front of it. Plates and dishes were left on the table inside.

Does this fool not know these will be knocked off in the rapids?

He was ready to call out to Spinwall when he noticed a copy of the *Navigator* open amidst the plates on the table.

Sanders was now in the eddy on the Indiana side of the Ohio just downstream of the falls. The broadhorn he had just run through with its owner, a Pennsylvanian named Short, had taken a wave over the side and Sanders felt the ferry back to the Kentucky side would be easier if they bailed most of the water out. Short was below, handing up buckets of water to him, when Sanders saw something floating in the eddy. It was a human body. "Mr. Short, you best come back up we have a problem out here." Sculling with the gougers they manoeuvred the boat close to the victim. It was a woman, skirts washed up over her head, petticoats and one shoe still in place. They each took an arm and as they lifted her up, the skirts fell back revealing a throat cut from side to side. Short gasped and let go of the arm. Falling to the deck he began to retch and vomit. "What devil's mischief is this?!" exclaimed Stuart. "Pull yourself together man for I need to get across in a hurry." Sanders calmed himself with the remembrance of having told Christian to stay put until his return. Hoisting the woman onto the broadhorn however, renewed his concern that something terribly wrong was occurring.

Christian stomped out of the house and around to the land side of the flatboat bent on confronting Spinwall. Spinwall was pulling hard on the sweep and Christian noticed that his strokes were strong enough that the boat was slipping perilously close to the current.

"I thought you said you didn't buy a *Navigator*."

"Boy, why aren't you at your oar rowing? What exactly am I paying you for?"

Christian found himself speechless confronted by the intensity on Spinwall's face. "Get to your oar! We are almost in the river's current!"

He looked out and saw the bow lapping against the eddy line. Running to the bow, he grabbed the gouger and dug in hard with it to pull the bow back into the eddy. Looking over his shoulder, he saw Spinwall still pulling hard on his much longer sweep, edging the boat further into the current.

"Stop pulling mister!"

Spinwall pulled even harder, and staring straight at him, called out; "Call me 'Joshua,' Katz."

The boat peeled out in the stiff current and was carried downstream past the mouth of the creek and the startled onlookers.

Christian stormed over to Spinwall and with one hand on a hip and the other pointing downstream shouted over the roar of the approaching rapid, "Lookee here mister, or Joshua, or whoever the hell you are, now we've gotta run the Kentuck Chute. Don't touch that sweep until I tell you so, and then pull like hell or we'll wreck this boat on Cowlick Rock, you understand me?"

"Whatever you say boy, just give me the word."

Christian went to the stern sweep and pulled a half a dozen strokes to set the angle of the craft to best take the big waves in the first half of the falls. The river was bottlenecking down between islands of rock and dropping over the bedrock shelf. The flatboat creaked and groaned as its length was torqued between the troughs and crests of the powerful waves. The bow slapped hard into a breaking wave top and water shipped onto the deck. Damn, thought Christian, if there's one thing we don't need now it's water on board. The boat cleared the last of the big waves and entered the gathering tongue of water rushing towards Cowlick Rock. He sensed the menacing power of the water driving into the rock like some heavy syrup, slamming into it with thousands of pounds of force, the force being released by throwing the roostertail of water high in the air, the roostertail dancing back and forth like a rattler risen from its coil.

Concentrate, thought Christian. Sanders always ran to the right of Cowlick even though it was the narrower passage. He'd said the water to the left was invisibly shifting right towards the rock and that was why the roostertail was so high. He set the angle once again with the stern sweep and began to run to his side sweep. Spinwall still stood intently at his side sweep.

Christian began pulling with everything he had but the boat began an agonizing spin upstream.

Damn! What the hell is he doing?

He looked over the stern and knew all was lost as he saw the boat heading directly for the rock. He turned just in time to see Spinwall, blood lust in his eyes, running full tilt across the deck at him. He released his sweep and dove for the deck as Spinwall leapt. At this instant the boat shuddered as it struck the rock. Spinwall sailed over him and skittered down the deck towards the rock. Christian tried to regain his feet, but the upstream end of the flatboat sank immediately, and the river rushed over him in a huge torrent. The flatboat was ripped in half with a loud snapping of timbers and he was engulfed and taken down deep. The violence roared in his ears. He opened his eyes to total darkness. This is it, he thought. He slowly regained his equilibrium and looked at what he thought to be up. He saw light in the water that meant the surface. Air. He kicked hard, losing his shoes, broke the surface and gasped for breath. He looked back upriver. Cowlick Rock still spat it's steeple of water high into the sky. Part of the flatboat, mostly submerged, came spinning towards him.

He was coughing and choking when he saw Spinwall break the surface between him and the wreck and begin swimming towards him.

Spinwall screamed in a voice that rang straight into his brain, "You must drown! Now, in this place, with me!"

Christian felt the branch of the rising sawyer against his legs but rode the current over it. The giant tree rose slowly out of the water and Spinwall's gaze shifted to meet it. The face of the man intent on murder changed to that of a man about to meet his doom. He smacked against a crook between two massive branches and had the wind driven from his chest. With his face turning red, he wrestled and struggled to free himself from the current that pinned him to the tree. He never saw the hulk of the flatboat closing on him. It struck his back and flattened itself against the sawyer. As he was being torn in half, blood poured from his mouth. The additional pressure of the boat pinned on the sawyer broke the tree off its mooring on the bottom and the whole assembly sank out of sight.

Christian turned onto his stomach and swam downriver with the speeding current as fast as he could. He flushed out of the rapid and used his last reserve of strength to break into the Kentucky eddy. After what seemed an eternity, he gained the bank and grabbed a sycamore root. He looked up to see Stuart reach down to grasp his wrist. Sanders pulled him up onto the mud bank and let him regain strength. Christian rolled over on his back and looked into the light of the sun. He reached down and felt that the gold piece was still in his pocket.

PROLOGUE
B
TOKEBELLOKE: CLOSING THE GATE

April 9, 1875 — Glenn Ferris, West Virginia

"There she lay, E.B.. Look!"

Sure enough, logs were floating downstream towards a falls, but before they could wash over, they were sucked down into a whirlpool. None appeared downstream of the falls.

"Damnedest thing, eh E.B.?"

Damnedest thing indeed, he thought. E. B. Honeycutt was watching the winter harvest of timber, the future of Stockton's lumber company, and his job, dropping into a hole.

The idea to run timber down the Meadow and the Gauley rivers to Stockton's mill had been E.B.'s. Opponents claimed that the rapids would cause interminable log jams. "That's why we have dynamite," he had said, and took pleasure in thinking how the rapids would pound and shave every scrap of bark from the logs.

But now his men were confronted with an impossible situation. He had never seen or heard of such a thing -- three fourths of the current sucking into a hole and carrying all the logs with it. It must be a giant cave, but no cave acted like that. If he didn't stop this giant drain from flushing his logs, his entire season's work would be gone. The men had tried throwing sticks of dynamite into the hole, but nothing had happened. Now, it was time for him to try a bigger blast. He took three of the roughnecks down onto the flat rocks lining the river by the falls.

"Start drilling here," he said, pointing down to the stone. E.B. took a handful of dynamite sticks from the metal box and led his foreman to the edge of the falls. Retrieving a safety match from the inner pockets of his coat, E.B. hovered over a stick of dynamite to protect it from the rain, and lit the fuse. He watched the fuse burn rapidly, and with only a few seconds to go, lofted the stick into the whirlpool. The water took it down and he braced himself for the blast. It never came. He tried again with the same result. Meanwhile, the logs continued to disappear into the vortex.

"See what I mean, E.B.?"

"Yes. I do."

E.B. was at a loss. The water went in. The logs and dynamite went in. Water was rushing out from the bottom of the falls, from behind the curtain of water falling from above. No logs appeared below. No dynamite exploded. It seemed to defy physics. He had now personally witnessed close to one hundred thirty-foot logs drop into the hole. He estimated there couldn't be enough room for half of them to be lodged under the falls.

Starting at the edge of the water, he carefully counted his paces until he reached the spot where the men were drilling a hole in the shelf rock. Thirty seven paces. He added ten more to make up the difference from the water's edge to the center of the whirlpool. He now directed the foreman, Walt, to supervise the mounting of the iron rod into the drilled hole while he and the other roughnecks stretched the chain upriver along the bank. He went back to the rod and measured off forty seven paces. Two roughnecks carried the strongbox upstream to him, and he fastened one of its handles to the appropriate chain link with some bolts. E.B. told the roughnecks to snag a passing log and soon they succeeded in piking one into shore. They lashed it to the midpoint of the chain with some hemp rope to serve as a float. Now they bolted the other end of the chain to the ring at the end of the iron rod placed in the hole.

"Walt, we're about set. When I ready the charges and light the fuse, I'm going to shut the strongbox and shove it into the water. When I do that, you and the other boys pike the float log out into the current. Understand?"

"Yeah, I got it. It's a good plan. Ought to blow that sonavabitchin rock to hell."

Yes, it ought to, thought E.B.

In ten minutes, all was ready. He was striking a match to light the fuse when a cry came up from downstream. The roughnecks were pointing to the river by the whirlpool. E.B. stood up to see what was happening. There, on the other side of the river at the edge of the falls stood a little man. E.B. brushed the rain from his forehead. It was an old Indian. Walt came running up the bank to him.

"You see 'im, E.B.?"

"Yes. Where in the hell did he come from?"

"The hell if I know. We ain't had no Injun sightin's here for thirty, forty years now. What ya gonna do?"

The Indian was standing by the river's edge, and looked to be chanting something while he stared down into the swirling waters. He moved his feet in a slow dance. He was dressed in a ragged fur robe and seemed to be oblivious to the freezing rain.

Logs continued to flow into the hole.

"I'll tell you what we're going to do. We're gonna blow that rock now, before we lose more logs."

"But you'll kill him!"

"To hell with him! He's just a damned Indian. Stockton's is losing its ass in that falls. Now do as I say and get back down to that float."

Walt stood looking at the younger man for a moment. He had seen enough loggers killed in his years, many in the name of haste. But this would be murder.

"I said now, Walt! Get the hell down there!" Walt grumbled and moved off. The old Indian continued to chant by the water's edge.

E.B. bent down and opened the box. There were twenty sticks of dynamite bundled together, with a fuse running out of one of the center sticks. He lit the fuse a foot and a half away from the dynamite and quickly closed and padlocked the strongbox so that it couldn't open accidentally while floating out in the river. He pushed it out into the water and, taking a pike, shoved it into the current. The roughnecks piked the float log into the current, and the entire length began to swing slowly downstream towards the falls. The roughnecks ran for cover into the forest, but E.B. remained. The old Indian remained also, chanting by the far side and now extending his arms towards the hole in the water. The strong box was taken by the current into the swirling waters and dropped into the hole. The chain went taut and E.B. feared it would snap under the strain. Then the entire mass of rock of the falls shuddered with a sickening thud, and a huge geyser of water shot upwards from the whirlpool. With a great cracking and moaning sound, the whole shelf of rock split and collapsed. A wave of water washed up on the far bank and carried the old Indian over the edge and into the tumult created by the blast and falling rock. The unrelenting force of the river carried several of the broken sections of rock downstream, and all that remained was a big flushing rapid. The arriving logs washed through with ease.

E.B. expected a cheer to erupt from the men, but none was forthcoming. They slowly emerged from the forest and began to gather their tools. He worked his way downstream to where the end of the rod protruded from the shelf. It had bent under the stress, and the chain had broken from it and disappeared.

"Pull the rod out."

Try as the roughnecks would, the rod didn't budge; it was wedged into the bedrock.

While they struggled with it, E.B. thought proudly how another obstacle had been removed from Stockton's path to fortune, and how the log running venture would carry him to a secure future. The roughnecks shared glances and a common thought: it had been wrong to kill the old Indian. They gave up in the attempt to free the rod and started making their way upriver.

Within the year, E.B. Honeycutt would be dead from an accident suffered near Gauley Bridge. Log runs soon would be replaced by winching logs uphill, and later, a rail line through the Gauley River canyon. The mysterious old Indian had been killed, and the riddle of the whirlpool was silenced forever. All that remained, was an iron ring set in the stone.

PROLOGUE
C
MISTAKEN IDENTITY

August 14, 1984 — Nepal

"I repeat: no sign of Jacques. Do you copy? Over."

Roberts looked at the raging river in front of him and then over to Wettman and Cravetts as they stood at the ready with rescue lines. Cravetts shrugged and looked back down into the torrent, not wanting to miss any telltale piece of boat or gear which might bob past. Wettman glared at him and shouted over the roar of the rapids.

"We've got to do something! It's been too long!"

Roberts keyed the mike and yelled into the radio.

"Camera Two, this is Safety, what can you see?"

Wilson, the operator of Camera Two and expert kayaker himself, felt for his Motorola without withdrawing from the eyepiece of his camera.

"No sign of Jacques."

Damn Jacques. He should never have been allowed to come along, much less permitted to be on the river team. Bleeding primitive kayaker if I've ever seen one. Sure, the lanky frog is strong as an ox, and fearless, but we're out here in the middle of the Himalayas to make the ultimate kayaking movie, not a bleeding snuff film!

"I've got to keep pasted to this eyepiece until something happens. You blokes had better check on Frenchie from shore. Over."

Mike Clark heard all this crackle over Foster's radio as he sat in his boat. He was in a micro eddy just above one of the Dudh Kosi's countless Class VI rapids.

The Dudh Kosi River is the drainage basin of the Southeast flank of Mount Everest. By the time the team had descended from Everest Base Camp to where they were now at 14,000 feet, the river had gathered dozens of tributaries and was flowing at a rate of over two thousand cubic feet of water per second. They were well on their way to filming the most spectacular whitewater documentary ever, and he, Britain's preeminent kayaker, was in charge. He was the expedition's founder, coordinator and leader. Now something had gone wrong and it was his fault. It had been he who had allowed DuBois to come along. In his twenty odd years of kayaking he had never seen a paddler as strong and fearless as Jacques, but others argued his style was deficient. Mike had overruled their protests and insisted on the inclusion of the cordial Frenchman.

"Foster, radio down that I'm going."

Clark realized that his expedition, film, reputation, and possibly his life and that of Jacques hinged on what happened next. Taking a few careful paddle strokes, he slid out of the eddy and onto the upstream face of a large standing wave, riding it out into the middle of the river before turning off of it to head downstream. Big waves continued to the sharp turn to the right at the start of the rapid. The canyon walls here were so vertical that they had only been able to guess on the best route through this part to where the river again bent to the left and the camera team could pick up the action. He knew that the best probable route was up against the left wall where the force of the river at flood stages in the past would have blown through all but the biggest of rocks. He paddled hard for the wall and mentally prepared himself for the violence that was sure to ensue. The water slamming off of the wall threw him to the right and almost flipped him. The water cleared from his eyes and he realized he could see nothing in front of him which meant he was about to go over a big drop. He felt the bottom drop out from under and suddenly slammed into the reversing water at the drop's base. The frothing water cartwheeled the kayak repeatedly. Mike had been through this type of punishment hundreds of times before and even the ice water of the Dudh Kosi couldn't break his concentration now. Finally he was spit from the trap and rolled upright just in time to drop into a sharp crease forcing the water into the right wall. He instinctively leaned hard to his left and braced into the diagonal hydraulic. It shot him across to the right and into a boiling eddy against the wall. There, at the upstream end of the eddy, DuBois, still in his boat, clung to an outcropping of the rock.

Fighting for breath in the thin air, Mike called out to him as he surged up and down with the turbulence in the eddy.

"Jacques, are you okay?"

Jacques only leered back.

"Jacques. Answer me, are you all right? What happened?"

"I have been waiting all of my life on this earth for this moment."

Clark stared back in utter confusion and realized DuBois no longer spoke with a French accent. The churning eddy started to carry him upstream.

"I believe it is you who would destroy my father's greatest work."

"What in bloody hell are you talking about?"

In an instant Jacques ripped his spray skirt from the cockpit rim, stood up in his boat and leapt at the shocked Clark. Locking him in an iron grip, he flipped him over and held tightly to his neck. The grappling mass was swirled in the eddy and grabbed by the downstream current. Together they were pulled out into the rapid below. Jacques, though quickly losing consciousness himself, maintained his hold on Clark and the kayak. Moments later, the overturned boat rushed past the horrified camera team and the safety crew and around the next bend and out of sight. Search as they would for the next four days, the expedition members would never find a trace. It was as if the two had been consumed by the river.

CHAPTER 1 -- SAHARA

June 24, 1998
Algeria

Pete Dornblaser removed lead-lined gloves from his rucksack and slid them on. They came up almost to his elbows and were hot. He kept them in the rucksack to shield them from the sun, but that didn't help much, and his sweat and the dust were making slimy soup inside them.

Damn, they're hot.

He looked up and Salil was looking intently at the heavy lead box with the dangerous contents.

He liked Salil. Salil was cool. He was also the only outsider working with them. The only one they had a chance of being able to trust. The Bedouins laying cables on both sides of the wadi sure weren't trustworthy. They were a nervous, shifty bunch.

Kneeling on the baking ground, he lifted the dropper-top off the large bottle wedged inside the box. With a steady hand he held it over the paint mark.

"Howard, I'm ready." The Tyvek mask muffled his voice a bit, but his headset transmitted it clearly to the man who stood a hundred meters away, calibrating a computerized transit.

Calibrating it for the fifth Goddamn time in the last hour.

"Sorry Petey. Hang on for a second."

Howard was a stickler for accuracy. It had to be exact. Exact.

"I know Howard, 'if it's not exact, it won't work. And if it doesn't work, we'll have to do it again.'"

Spatial dimension. A three dimensional grid. An invisible cage. A method for analyzing the flow of invisible water. Invisible water flowing down a real river bed.

Pete respected the meticulous detailing that Howard demanded. His friend was a genius. He had proven it over and over again working for prestigious firms around the world. However, this project was Howard's. Howard's idea. Howard's brainchild. Financed with Howard's money. It was costing him a bundle. Pete wanted it to work. It would work, if the surveying was exact.

"Chill, Salil."

He cast a sideways glance at Salil. Salil relaxed a bit and even managed a smile. He had heard Pete say 'Chill' enough times so that now it was their little joke. Nobody "Chills" in the Sahara. Not in daytime anyway. It was broiling. Not even back at the compound, in the computer trailer with the air conditioners running, did one really "Chill."

"Okay Petey." Howard's voice came crackling over the headset, "from the center of the paint circle, point three centimeters towards me. Point five centimeters to the inside."

There was a paint circle every meter. All of the paint circles had a center mark and penciled marks radiating out every millimeter from the center. Pete and Salil had done the penciling at night, to avoid the heat. That phase alone, had taken weeks to complete.

It had taken two months to get this far. First they had done the "rough survey," extremely accurate by anyone else's standards. Then, with the paint circles stenciled to the stone, they were going back through with the "truing survey." Twenty Algerian locals, Bedouins, were laying computer and power cable along the cliff tops on both sides of the river bed. Once laid, Howard, Pete and Salil would install the data recorders, sensors and monitors along the walls. Then, the river would flow once more, with invisible water: gamma rays. The flow would be ray-traced, and slowed down by the computers to real-water-time. Then the computers would use the data to achieve the "magic equation." The equation would explain, once and for all, how water flows, crashes, tumbles, responds to gravity, and is pushed by its own fluid force. The equation, via computer software, would have myriad uses all over the world, ranging from simple municipal water projects to advanced weather forecasting based on predicting the patterns of ocean currents.

Pete had counted out from the center point on both axes and found his target. He gently squeezed the dropper and a drop of plutonium released from it. Pete watched as it fell to the ground. It seemed to freeze in mid-air. The drop was speaking to him. His sight became dim, as if a dark cloud was cloaking the sun. No, it wasn't a cloud, it was something rising from ground and the sun was behind it. The drop was warning him. It hit the rock and he felt as if he was going to pass out.

"Petey. Are you all right?"

The voice in the headset seemed to be speaking to someone else.

"Pete, put the dropper in the bottle."

Howard was running towards him. Slowly he came out of it. Salil was looking at him. Worried.

He placed the dropper top back in the bottle and closed the lead box. Howard stopped at his side, breathing hard.

"Petey, what happened?"

"I don't know what happened. I'm okay."

Howard knelt down beside him. "Salil, hand me the Geiger counter, quick." Salil removed it from his backpack and handed it to Howard, who turned it on and passed it over Pete. Nothing. As a control, he waved it over the paint mark and it whirred loudly.

"Must be the heat. Let's take a break."

"Let's keep going. I'm fine."

"That's some real deadly shit we're working with Petey. You almost passed out with the dropper in your hand. You want to talk about it?"

"We'll talk back at camp. I'm okay, man. Let's keep going."

Howard walked back towards the transit. The sun was baking him.

The project was important, but so was Pete. He needed Pete. Not someone like Pete (because there wasn't). Howard had known him since Pete was a rebellious teenager and the best kayaker he'd ever met. On the water, Howard was the technician, but it was Pete who was always fluid, always understanding the water. He liked to think of Pete as a cursor, moving effortlessly about the most complex program. But Pete was more than that. Howard knew that the world had never seen anyone who understood moving water as well as Pete. He needed him. Only Pete's misfortune had made it possible. Poor Petey.

Pete had let a student climb up onto the roof of the van to load kayaks and he fell off. Result: broken back. And a lawsuit blaming Pete.

Pete had lost, and he couldn't afford an appeal. It would have been useless anyway. The legal system was so screwed. His lawyer had told him that a good defense was no match for a plaintiff in a wheelchair. He'd been right. It didn't matter. In this day and age you couldn't sell Wonder Bread without somebody eventually suing you. Pete's assets, including the kayak school, now belonged to the plaintiff, and Pete still owed over half a million. Without the school, Pete's only skill was as a whitewater guide, and no raft company would hire a guide convicted of negligence.

It could be worse for him, thought Howard. At least he's making great money working on the project. He'll get back on his feet with it. And besides, I know he's fascinated with this place.

The "place" was a dry riverbed; a wadi, in central Algeria. It had been "found," by an old associate, Anders Lieb. Anders, a semi-retired cartographer with connections in the aerospace industry, had been receiving the reviews of LandSat photos from Bell Labs.

Heavier than normal Serengeti rains had generated strong sandstorms far to the north in the Sahara. They had exposed part of an ancient river system that had not been known to exist. This aroused Anders' interest. After he reviewed the next pass of photos, he called Howard to tell him that what he'd been looking for had been found.

It was perfect for Howard's project. Not only was it a totally dry riverbed, it was a good one. Even more importantly, the work could be done in relative privacy, far from the prying eyes of government.

Neither Howard nor Pete had seen anything like it. The steep walled canyon was a masterpiece of creation. Swept free of the sand which had preserved it, the riverbed was a perfect laboratory for the project, while at the same time an enigmatic and foreboding place.

Later, as they ate their lunch, consisting of slightly too warm kabhouleh, Pete thought out loud: "I'd hate to have to run this thing with a lot of water in here." Howard had determined that the average gradient in the metered section, "the grid," was 32 meters/kilometer. Gradient, in whitewater terminology, is the loss of altitude that a given section of a river or stream undergoes in the course of a mile or kilometer. Gradient is measured in feet per mile or meters per kilometer.

"Steep, eh Petey?"

"Yep. And judging from the height of the scour line, it looks like it was in the five thousand plus, cubic feet range."

The volume of water in a whitewater river is measured in cubic feet per second or cubic meters per second. A whitewater river abrades, or scours, the rock walls and boulders lining it. The lower parts of the rocks are scoured more, because even when the water is low, it is still smoothing those parts of the rocks. The highest reach of the water on the rocks is called the scour line.

They sat in the shade of an overhang, looking at the canyon wall on the far side. Damn, Pete is good, thought Howard. It took me an hour on the computer to come up with an average volume of 5,750 cubic feet per second.

In Howard's mind kayakers were special and Pete was the creme de la creme. He thought about the difference between kayaks and jet boats. Any healthy kid could rent a jet boat and in an hour fool himself into believing he was an expert. He needed no strength or stamina. The boat provided that. He needed no knowledge of water or waves. The boat powered through whatever he aimed at and aiming at it wrong just added to the excitement -- up until he crashed into another jet skier or hit a wake dead wrong and went flying. Kayakers earn every bit of their fun. They power themselves, and they must understand water and waves to get anywhere, no matter how strong they are. They play all day, and to outsiders seem to be mindless about it. But every stroke, every wave mastered, is a celebration.

Howard had read an article in an ornithology text about chickadees flying south in winter. The author had calculated the weight of the chickadee in calories and had concluded that flying over the Caribbean the little bird would consume its entire weight. Its journey was physically impossible. But Howard knew that any kayaker could understand the chickadee. He would know that there were waves in wind currents and that a wind wave could be surfed like a water wave. Chickadees ferry wind waves and glide to Yucatan. He knew that when he kayaked he was in tune with extraordinary forces, and however much he was in tune, Pete was a dimension beyond.

At 2:30 in the afternoon they heard the telltale sound of an approaching helicopter. Howard blew his whistle as a signal to the Bedouins to knock off for the day. Pete and Salil packed their rucksacks and Howard shouldered the transit. Together they started up through the grid towards camp. Though his pack was heavy, Pete carried it easily. He was a big man, six feet tall, 190 pounds. Howard was slightly smaller; 175 pounds and five foot ten. They both made Salil look small.

They rounded a curve in the canyon and started to climb the sand dune that spilled from above. They could now hear the helicopter departing.

"I wasn't aware of any deliveries due today. You?"

Pete couldn't hide his grin. "I think it might have been the computer I ordered."

"Dornblaser, you are so full of crap. You never touched a keyboard in your life."

They reached the top of the dune and walked across to the camp, a circular compound consisting of seven mobile office trailers. All had been airlifted in from Algiers by a Sikorsky Sky-Crane helicopter. There were two computer trailers, two dormitory trailers for the workers, a kitchen and mess hall, an equipment trailer that was equipped like a hardware store, and a trailer for the security staff.

In charge of security was an Algerian from Tinnhert named Khalem. He was a serious man in his fifties who had served in the French Foreign Legion. He was in charge of the camp when Howard was conducting field work in the canyon. Helping him were three of his sons.

Khalem met them as they walked into camp. "A helicopter has delivered another computer," he said, pointing to the plastic-wrapped crate in front of the main computer trailer.

"Khalem, would you please have some men move it inside the auxiliary computer trailer?"

"Oui, Monsieur Pete."

Pete caught Howard looking at him.

"What's in the crate, Dornblaser?"

"A dozen cases of Budweiser."

"Well, what are you waiting for? Get in there and get a couple of those cases in the freezer, ASAP!" Howard smiled.

"Yes sir!"

Beer was against Islamic law, but they would hide the drinking from the others. Besides, they had spent an exhausting ten days dyeing the grid. It was almost completed. Why not celebrate a little?

An hour later Pete slipped into the main computer trailer with a twelve pack hidden in a backpack. Howard met him as he entered, blood-pressure cuff in hand.

"Have a seat, Petey."

"Aw. What is this, Calvert?"

"You almost passed out today. Just want to check you over before you start drinking."

Pete knew he was defeated and gave in.

"134 over 85. Not bad. Stop smoking Camels and you'd be superman."

"You, know, Howard, I didn't almost pass out. It was different. Time slowed down. That drop took forever to fall three inches. And I just sat there watching. And then it was as if I was somewhere else. I was kayaking and headed for a dropoff and a huge boulder was blocking the sun. Am I going nuts?"

"No. Just an everyday hallucination." Howard hid his concern.

"Can we drink beer now?"

"You bet."

A while later, Howard turned serious again.

"Pete, I've been thinking about something. Soon, we're going to be ready to flood the grid, and we're going to need the Bedouins to help out. But I'm afraid it's going to spook them pretty bad."

"They seem to respond to cash bonuses."

Pete was right of course. He would have Khalem announce a 5,000 Dinar per man ($90.00) bonus for the upcoming night-time shoot. Though he hadn't really liked any of the Bedouins, Howard was thankful for the work they had done. Partly because of them, his project was becoming a reality.

They're all right guys, thought Pete. But now, when camp security was most important, they were going to freak out with the shoot. After that, who knows? Hell, half of the Arab world would, literally, kill, for the plutonium they had locked in the security trailer.....

శ్రూ ళ్ళి

"Okay, Pete, sensor check three."

They were behind a barrier made of sand-bags. Howard was standing by two tables covered with computers and monitors. Pete was beside the tables, kneeling in front of a huge assortment of cables and switches. All the lights on the switches were green.

"Sensor check three is a go."

Damn if Howard didn't have to do everything three times.

That's okay now, he thought. The last thing I want to do over again is a night shoot with all one hundred gamma ray tubes glowing and humming with Howard running around like a maniac, computer monitors lit up like the Fourth of July.

This is going to scare the shit out of the Bedouins.

"Monitor check three."

All ten T.V. screens were showing their perspectives of the grid.

"Monitor check three is a go."

"Recorder check three."

The data recorders lining the grid were linked into the red switches. All forty-eight red lights were on and blinking.

"Recorder check three is a go."

"Computer system check three is a go."

Why even say it? thought Pete. Like you'd really trust me with the computers.

"Okay, let's get everybody behind the barriers!" Howard shouted over the noise of the gas generators.

Howard was really ready now. Salil had yelled something in Arabic and all of the Bedouins followed him to the shielded area behind the other sand-bag barrier. All of their field work had been for what came next. Miles of computer cable now fed in from all the sensors and recorders on the grid perimeter. Each sensor had a recorder unit. Each recorder unit had its own power cable and computer cable. They all converged where Pete was stationed and then fed into the bank of computers on the tables.

"Power up the tubes!"

Oh God, here we go.

Pete flipped the big switch on the thick power cable at his feet.

"Tubes have power."

All conversation amongst the Bedouins stopped as the gamma ray tubes started to hum in concert. Soon the noise drowned out the sound of the generators. Howard and Pete looked at each other as the roar reached proportion totally unexpected by either. It bounced and echoed off of the canyon walls. The Bedouins, those legendary fearless macho men of the desert, also looked at one another in what was fast becoming abject fear. Now a pink glow of the gamma tubes lit up the canyon walls and illuminated the hasty upstream retreat of the workers. Salil had remained and gave them an amused smile.

Salil had been through all phases of the project side by side with Pete and Howard and wasn't about to leave now. Both he and Pete were now looking at Howard, who was glued to the computer monitors.

A steady stream of gamma rays was now pouring through the length of the grid. Howard had wanted to do a real-water-time conversion of a sample of the grid but was horrified of the thought of losing any of the information being collected by the recorders.

All sensors were reporting the swirl of particles down through the ancient riverbed. Howard would let it run another eighteen minutes before shutting down the recorders and then the tubes.

The fieldwork was coming to an end. Now he would sequester himself in the trailers for God only knows how long trying to put it all together.

The gamma rays flowed down through and out the downstream end of the grid. There were no sensors to notice them, no recorders to mark their passage. But they continued, rebounding their way through the dry canyon for two and a half more kilometers before plunging off of the lip of a bowl-shaped dry waterfall. They drained into the pit in the center of the bowl.

Within, something woke from a timeless hibernation.

☙❧

Tassile N'Ajjer means "plateau of rivers." Three or four thousand years ago, the Sahara had been a hospitable place. Rivers flowed with an abundance of water, supporting herds of the largest mammals. Lush vegetation covered the river banks, aiding in the erosion of the beautiful sandstone walls of the shallow canyons. Then, climatic change brought drought. The cave paintings of primitive inhabitants reflected the change for the worse; fewer and fewer species appeared in their art. These last, contained only elephant and giraffe. Then the sand took over.

But history repeats itself. This had already happened several times before. The difference with "Wadi Nouveau," as they were calling their canyon, was that it had been buried so deeply in sand eons ago that it had only partially emerged at times, only to be buried again. It had not had water flowing through it again as had the other wadis further to the south. Its walls had been perfectly preserved by the sand. Both Howard and Pete had become entranced by the super smooth curves of the water-shaped stone.

A little more than a kilometer upstream of the grid, the canyon was still buried in sand. The dune was their access ramp down into the riverbed. The camp sat on the southern rim of the gorge on flat, wind-weathered rock.

Pete walked back upriver and trudged up the dune to camp while Salil waited with Howard at the grid.

Howard was reviewing data files and summary tables. All had apparently gone perfectly. He was pleased with the night's work and dreading the bulk of computer work that would follow. Collating, analyzing, programming. There was still plenty that could go wrong.

When Pete reached the camp, Khalem and one of his sons ran to meet him at the perimeter.

"Monsieur Pete, there is trouble. The workers are leaving. They say the project is against the will of Allah."

Uh oh! Now we've done it.

"My sons and I will stay. The cooks will stay. These are just cowards. That is why they leave."

Pete wondered if Khalem and his boys would be leaving, too, if they'd been down in the canyon to see the show. Khalem read his thoughts.

"We heard the sounds and we saw the lights. I know how important is this work to Monsieur Howard. We will stay. In the morning I will send for more workers from Tinnhert to help recover the equipment."

Khalem caught him off guard, but he was relieved. Still, he could not help but notice the fervor with which the Bedouins were saddling up their horses to leave in the middle of the night.

I've got a bad feeling about this.

"Khalem, I have an idea. I'm going to go back down to the grid. Call Algiers and have the chopper come first thing in the morning to lift out the equipment. I don't think the men from Tinnhert are going to work out."

"Oui, Monsieur Pete, this is well thought. I will radio Algiers tonight."

"We are going to need some new men, maybe from a little further away. Think you can arrange it?"

"I have an associate in Tassile. I will radio him tonight also and discover if he can help us. I believe there will be no problem."

Pete packed a rucksack with blankets and a large thermos of coffee. He then went to his room in the auxiliary computer trailer and unlocked his footlocker.

Underneath his clothes was a series of plastic bags containing a forty-five long barreled pistol he had bought before flying over. He had hidden the gun in one of the computer crates. The computers had received special clearance from the Algerian government because the project was of a scientific nature and because of the hefty bribes Howard had paid to the right people. Nothing had been searched by Customs on the way in.

Pete had the gun in case things got ugly. At the very least, things were getting strange. He thought about the last weeks. A new worker had joined them. The others had seemed to accept him readily, almost as a leader. He was big and strong, and a good worker, so Pete hadn't said anything. He had noticed however, that Khalem looked at the man with a hint of contempt. Frank Zappa was the nickname Howard had given him.

स•स

"What's going on back there?" Howard was still buzzing with excitement, but realized that none of the workers had come back to help pack up.

"Look, we've got a problem. The Bedouins left camp and I don't think they're coming back. Not to work anyway. Khalem is a rock, and he and his sons are guarding the compound. So basically, we've still got the kitchen staff and security. Khalem is going to call in a chopper to lift this stuff out. Until morning, we've got to sit on it."

Howard noticed the forty-five in Pete's belt and looked suddenly drained. "You've got a gun?"

"Relax Howard, it's just in case."

Pete hated to see Howard like this, just hours after he'd been so up with the success of the shoot.

"Want a cup of coffee?" he said, pulling the thermos out of the rucksack. "Yeah. That sounds great."

As the three of them drank under the brilliant stars, Howard laid out the new plan for getting the gear organized. Now that it couldn't be carried by the Bedouins, it would be airlifted in several short trips by the chopper and had to be packed accordingly.

Pete and Salil spent a couple of hours unmounting and packing up the gamma tubes. Even if they had to do another shoot, the tubes were too expensive to leave out in the elements. The orientation mounts would be left bolted to the riverbed, just in case.

Then Pete and Salil worked their way down through the grid disconnecting the sensors, recorders and cameras. Pete took the south wall and Salil the north.

They found themselves making a bit of a competition out of it to see who could go the fastest. Salil won and was jubilant. They carried the equipment back to the head of the grid, making several trips each, and Howard boxed it up. Then they coiled the power cables and switching cables. The computer cables laid along the canyon walls would be left in place for the moment in the event another shoot was necessary. By dawn the packing was complete. They were thinking about stretching out on the blankets when they heard the approach of the helicopter.

Howard went to camp with the first load and sent back the airlift pallet with the chopper. Pete and Salil stayed behind to send off equipment in the order Howard had laid out, and Howard off-loaded it and packed it away in the computer trailers as it arrived. By noon, everything was back in camp and Howard went right to work unpacking the computers and the recorders in the main computer trailer.

Later in the afternoon, the new men arrived in a truck from Tassile. Salil set about orienting them to the camp and their duties. Pete offered his assistance to Howard who politely declined, citing a need to do everything by himself.

Pete, suddenly with nothing to do after months of hard work, retired to the auxiliary computer trailer and a couple of cold beers.

He began thinking about the hasty departure of the workers. They were going to talk about the plutonium and that scared the shit out of Pete. But he didn't want to get Howard worked up about it. The computer work had to be done right here in case they had to do another shoot, or if Howard had to cor-relate recorded data against measurements in the grid.

No, now it was his job to make sure everything was as secure as possible in camp and down in the canyon. This wasn't his field at all. The forty-five was the first gun he'd ever owned. He knew how to shoot and certainly wouldn't have a problem with his conscience if he had to kill some Arabs to defend himself, Howard, or anybody from camp. But if someone came after the plutonium (which wasn't even supposed to be there), Pete would be outgunned. Khalem and his sons were armed with old M-1 carbines, not exactly the arms of choice in a firefight.

As he popped another beer, he began to map a new defense plan for the camp.

The exposed section of the next wadi to the south was the crossing point of the rough trail the trucks used to come in from Tinnhert Oasis. They would set up a sentry post hidden in the rocks, and rotate pairs of guards in and out in twelve hour shifts. With radio communication, the camp would thus have at least twenty-five minutes notice of intruders from the south. This was definitely the only access route for vehicles. He would oversee the briefing of the guards.

But what if they came in on horseback? How many more access routes existed? The fact remained that trouble, if it came, would probably come from Tinnhert, and the truck trail was the only direct route.

He finished off the can of Bud in the air-conditioned comfort of the trailer. Through the dust-covered window he was witness to yet another spectacular Sahara sunset.

Pete caught himself thinking what a beautiful place this was and how he would actually miss the desert when they left. He'd never spent any time in deserts before. They were so contrary to the environment he was used to. West Virginia, his home, was so lush and wet in comparison. Hillsides covered with hardwood forests and rhododendron. The Tassile N'Ajjer was incredibly flat except for the canyons of the wadis. And no vegetation anywhere.

But there was something about Wadi Nouveau. It must have been such a beautiful river. The canyon was special, so enigmatic. There had been something echoing in his mind since they had arrived. A strange feeling of deja vu. Like he had been there before.

He left the trailer and headed across the compound to talk to Howard, feeling a bit of a buzz from the beer. Going outside had been a good reality check for him. He had been spacing out. That was a luxury he couldn't afford at the moment.

As he walked through the door, Howard swiveled in his chair to greet him. "My boy, good news. By tomorrow, I should be able to bring up images on the monitor of what the wadi would look like with water in it. What water level would you like to see?"

"No shit? That was quick." Pete was at once excited and relieved.

"Actually, it took more than a year to get to this point. The data collected in the shoot is inserted into parts of the program I developed back at Davis. Now it's a matter of using the data and the program to achieve the equation that says, 'why' it flows that way." Howard paused for a moment and then looked up at him

"Pete, I've been thinking about something."

"What?"

"Do you remember when I was playing around making helmets?"

Pete did remember. For Pete, a kayaking helmet was a kayaking helmet. If it looked good, he'd wear it. Howard, however, was always the perfectionist. He wasn't satisfied with the helmets on the market and had plunged head first into designing, developing, and testing his own. The results had been amazing. The helmets he made were pressurized: Two thin laminates with compressed argon injected into the space within. Super light and super strong.

"Well, I think I can engineer a device into a helmet with a face shield, a visor. The visor would be a screen. The device, using the equation, will be able to look at any section of moving water and determine what the bottom and the sides look like. It would also have the capability to display what the rapids would look like at any given water level, recommend routes through it, etc."

"Howard, if you can really make something like that, I want one."

"Pete, you're the only person I know that I can truly say would never need it. It would be redundant technology. Your brain already functions that way."

"I guess I'll take that as a compliment, Doc. Hey, how 'bout a cold beer?"

"No Petey. Look, I've got to concentrate. Don't even try to distract me. I need a couple of solid days to work on this."

"Howard, when are you going to get some sleep?"

"I'll catnap when I need to."

"And what should I do then?"

"I tell you what. I'm pretty sure we're not going to have to do another shoot. Why don't you and Salil get the new men started pulling the cable out of the grid, and then you can take your hike down to the bowl. Take Salil with you."

"I thought you wanted to go?"

Howard swept his hand past the bank of computers. "My work is here. You go. Have a good time. You've been working hard for months. You deserve some time off."

Howard had intentionally not included the lower part of the river in the field work.

Below the grid, the gradient picked up appreciably and the canyon twisted and turned. Surveying would have been exponentially more complex and tedious. Further downstream lay the bowl. They had overflown it a couple of times and Pete was dying to see it from the ground. He had never seen anything like it, even in pictures. The bowl was strange.

Pete almost copped an attitude about Howard's implied suggestion he get out of his hair. But he realized that Howard really did need time alone with the computers.

What the hell.

He found Salil in the mess trailer eating falafel and drinking a coke.

Poor devils, he thought, by their religion can't drink. They didn't even know enough about it to give me a sideways glance when I came in smelling of beer. Sure doesn't keep 'em from getting stoned though.

Howard had forbidden Pete to use any drugs during the field work. But if he could get Salil to go with him down into the canyon, they could make an adventure of it and smoke some 'kif.'

"Hey Salil, tomorrow we're going to get the new workers started on removing the computer cables and I thought that we could go from there and hike down to the bowl. Want to go?"

"As you wish Monsieur Pete," he replied with his usual smile.

Pete liked Salil. He had found him during their first week in Algeria. They had been in Algiers arranging equipment and he had met Salil when he was renting desert trucks from the Mercedes agency. Salil was bright and energetic and spoke excellent English. He also seemed to be trustworthy, something they hadn't seen very much of that first week. Pete had told Howard about him and, as usual, Howard trusted his judgment. They desperately needed a translator for the project; also, there were going to be sensitive phases of the project that demanded help from the "outside." Pete and Howard both knew that trusting potentially violent Muslims with plutonium would be like asking a room full of drug addicts to guard some cocaine.

They had hired Salil the next day.

"Pack for an overnight trip. I don't know exactly what it's going to be like on the ground."

From the air, it appeared to be a short distance. But that was from the air. Pete knew the canyon below was steep and that the bowl was an ancient waterfall. They would go armed for bear: ropes, prussics, carabiners, lights, etc.. Salil was young and strong; if Pete could handle it, so could Salil. It would be a good adventure, as close to a vacation as you could get in the Sahara.

Leaving the mess trailer, he caught up with Khalem who was making the rounds with Mektar, his youngest son. Pete took him aside to run past him his new plan for camp security.

Khalem, as usual, didn't bat an eye. Pete was sure he realized that the risks were heightened since the mutiny of the workers.

"Monsieur Pete, your plan is well ascertained. When I radioed my associate in Tasile, I asked him to also look for more men to work with me. He has found three. They will arrive tomorrow."

"How do we know if we can trust them?"

"They will be examined carefully."

"Sounds good. Khalem. Salil and I are going down below the grid for a couple of days. Howard needs some time alone to work, so I'm taking a vacation."

"Very well. Do not be preoccupied for him or the camp. I will make things secure."

"Thanks Khalem. Thanks for doing a good job. I really appreciate it."

"You are welcome, Monsieur Pete."

"Good night Khalem." He turned to go.

"Monsieur Pete. One moment please." Khalem looked him dead in the eye. "The sand in Sahara flows with the winds. It covers many things. Things that are sometimes best covered. Now the sand is laying bare relics of the past. The place you go tomorrow, it is a bizarre place. Always full of sand until now. No one ever goes there. It is thought that spirits dwell there."

Pete wasn't sure what to think of this. "I'll be careful."

"Take your revolver tomorrow."

The next morning Pete looked in on Howard before leaving. He was still occupied plugging the digital information from the recorders, one by one, into the data base of the main computer.

"Howard, you been up all night?"

"I slept a little. I'm too excited to really stop. You and Salil taking off?"

"Yeah. We're out of here. I'm taking my camera. Show you the pictures of what you missed."

"Sounds good. Now get out of here, will you?"

"Okay, okay. Bye."

Salil was in the mess trailer packing food.

"Ready Salil?"

"Let's go boss"

At the dune, Salil divided the workers into two teams, one for each side of the canyon. He explained to them that all they had to do was pull the computer cables and power cables and coil them up. They were then to be hauled back to camp. Though they were now to be discarded, Howard was adamant about not leaving debris from the project in the desert. It would be flown to Algiers and sold as scrap.

Pete and Salil headed down the dune. The sun was blazing. They were instantly drenched with sweat. They were dressed in light cotton pants and shirts, wide brimmed hats and hiking boots. Salil eschewed the traditional Arab robes for the western style of dress. He was, after all, a city boy and disliked the nomadic garb. The robes of the Bedouins were more effective against the heat. They essentially insulated the body from external heat, but the trade-off was that, inside the robes, the temperature was always at least 98.6 degrees, body temperature. The robes were also a bit bulky, and it was hard to move around when hiking over rough ground.

Better to take the trade-off of mobility and the opportunity to enjoy the cooling breeze when passing the occasional overhang.

They headed down the wadi. The grid, so familiar to them both, took on a lonely cast now that the fieldwork was done.

The riverbed within the grid was steep but had no drops or falls that were river-wide. Pete had been down the canyon another five hundred meters and knew it became increasingly steeper. Soon, he and Salil were scrambling down ledges higher than they were tall. It was easy to see why Howard had not wanted to include this section in the grid.

They paused behind an enormous boulder in the wadi to take some shade. Pete noticed Salil marveling at the beautiful curves the water had carved into the rock. Pete wondered exactly how many millions of years it had taken the water to create them.

Pete looked down at his feet and a revelation hit him like a brick. The riverbed was absolutely bare except for some swirling grains of sand. Here, behind this enormous boulder was no debris such as smaller rocks or gravel. There they were, standing in what was definitely the flood shadow of the boulder, and there was nothing there but smooth bedrock. Pete realized he hadn't seen any debris in any other flood shadow either.

Why hadn't he noticed it earlier?

Looking up at the vertical walls towering over them in the canyon he noticed that here also there were no signs of erosion from vegetation; nowhere from which debris or smaller rocks could fall from above.

But what about from upstream? Certainly the river would have carried rock down with it. Unless, of course, the water had come out of the top of a lake. Or a sea. Interesting.

The wadi he and Howard had checked out to the south of Tinnhert had had debris in the flood shadows, but it was of a much younger geology, and was forty miles away.

"Everything okay Monsieur Pete?"

"Sorry Salil, I was just thinking about something."

They continued downstream, descending through the ever steeper riverbed. Pete thought to himself, this thing is like an animal that wants to kill. It gets deadlier with each turn.

The wadi truly was getting mean. It was now dropping in elevation over forty meters per kilometer. Pete could just imagine 5,000 plus c.f.s. jamming down through the narrow gorge. And it wasn't just that. The wadi was taking some wicked curves.

To Salil, it was just a hike, but to Pete, with his whitewater background, it was something more. He could imagine the true hell a kayaker would face trying to descend through there. No kayaker had ever had to deal with it. After all, kayakers had only been running rivers for forty years. Wadi Nouveau hadn't had water flowing through it for who knows how many thousands of years. But he was one of the best, and he knew he wouldn't feel very comfortable at all on this type of water.

The curves of the wadi would throw a boater high to the outside of the turns, where awaited the inside of the next turn.

The next bend of the canyon, however beautiful, yielded an even more sinister prospect.

The wadi curved left, dropping steeply and divided evenly against a convoluted pillar of sandstone. To the right, the water would have passed through a perfectly round hole in the rock, emerging some ten meters downstream. The tunnel was about twenty feet in diameter. To the left of the pillar, the river would have shoved the unlucky chooser of the apparently safer route under an overhang in the river left cliff. Smaller pillars of rock descended like stalagmites from the ceiling of the undercut cliff, forming a strainer effect. They were relatively delicate, to the point of being fragile.

But they're strong enough to really fuck up the boater who decided to go left instead of through a tunnel full of water, thought Pete.

He caught himself and laughed. Why think these things? It wasn't like he was previewing the canyon for an upcoming run. It wasn't like anyone had, or would have to run it. No. Just enjoy the scenery.

They continued around the next bend, past exquisitely carved pillars buttressing the wall on the outside of the turn. To the inside, the water would have poured three meters over the top of a shelf of rock jutting out from the river left wall. The water had carved a large pothole into the wall below the pour-over, indicating to Pete that a strong recycling action had existed there when water had flowed.

Immediately below, the next rapid contained a more serious death threat yet. The wadi dropped over one ledge of about two meters in height, and then over another ledge three meters high. Just downstream of the first drop was a big pothole in the sandstone which would ensnare anyone running the middle of the first ledge. The kayak would be trapped like dropping a pencil into a jar. Pete had seen a similar formation on Overflow Creek in Georgia. It was called Gravity Falls, but this was much more severe. This was on a river, not on a creek.

I'm going to have some bad dreams about this.

Pete's problem was that he had hiked down several semi-dry creek and riverbeds before kayaking them. Afterward, he had hypothesized that it was important for the success of the run not to see the riverbed without water before paddling it. It was something psychological. Whenever he thought it remotely prudent, Pete preferred to kayak drops "blind." Sometimes, it is better to let the body do its work by itself than to let one's mind take over and screw things up.

They descended onward and downward through the gorge. It was an altogether new experience for Salil. He was becoming ever more fascinated and enthralled with the beautiful sculpting of the stone. It was a new concept to him: that water could have carved the stone in such an intricate manner. Pete, however, had a strange feeling. A premonition of danger. Something was telling him to turn back. Return to camp. Ridiculous. No. Not ridiculous. Go back. No. Shrug it off. What is wrong with me?

As a nervous symptom of his discomfort, he started to put the camera away into his rucksack.

"Monsieur Pete, if you please, I would like to photograph the rocks." Salil's enthusiasm gave him some relief. "Sure Salil. Go ahead, knock yourself out." Salil looked at him.

"Just another American saying, Salil." They both laughed. It helped to take a bit of the edge off of Pete's nervousness.

He noticed Salil taking some rather impressionistic photos of some of the more complex curves carved into the stone walls. Almost like the body of a beautiful woman.

They now encountered something Pete had noticed from the air: The wadi began to divide into smaller channels. These in turn, also divided, fanning out in all directions.

"Salil, I'd like to check out several of these routes, but I'm too tired. How you doing?"

"I am also tired, but I can persevere."

"Okay, let's stick to one of these center channels and see if we can't push on to the lip of the bowl."

"Comme tu veux, Monsieur Pete."

Judging from the diminished size of the channel they chose, Pete calculated that it would have carried only about five percent of the water of the river. How odd that a river would divide so.

Howard had said the sandstone was Precambrian, very old. No plant fossils. No Trilobite fossils. Just very fine, very old, sandstone. It had been formed when Africa, South America, Australia, and Antarctica were all joined in the super-continent; Gondwanaland.

Water formed the sandstone by depositing layers of sediments. Then water formed the canyon through the process of erosion. Pete always pondered the creation of different river canyons and rapid formations such as waterfalls. There was always reason in the rhyme, he thought.

And there was some reason behind the formation of this also.

After less than five hundred meters, they arrived at the lip of the bowl. At the edge, the channels' sides widened and dropped in height down to nothing, in effect fairing the channel into the channels on either side. The sight from the lip was breathtaking. The bowl spread out below them in a beautiful panorama. Around the circumference, they could see the other channels entering at even intervals.

The other predominant feature was a round hole in the middle of the floor of the bowl.

Pete thought out loud: "Why didn't I notice that from the air?"

"Maybe it has only recently been uncovered by the shifting sand," conjectured Salil.

Pete estimated that the channels to the south had to be wrapping around the bowl before they entered, as their mouths were evident almost to the eastern side. The channels to the north entered at the same intervals all the way to the north-east. At that point, the wall of the bowl seemed to have been eroded away and a large dune spilled from above to the floor below.

Salil dropped his backpack and let out a whistle of appreciation and wonder. It was spectacular.

The bowl itself, thought Pete, was really shaped like the bottom two-thirds of a hemisphere. When the water flowed, it must have been a fantastic sight.

"Monsieur Pete, where would have gone all of the water? Into the cave in the middle?"

Pete focused on the dune. From their vantage point, he could see that the plane of the earth seemed to angle slightly downhill to that side.

"The water could have drained into that cave, but it's possible that there might have been an exit under the dune. That dune, Salil, is our ticket down to the bottom. Let's go."

"Yes. It is arriving to be late."

They walked around the circumference of the bowl to the dune and started to descend. The wind was carrying sand up the dune and it stung and burned at their faces. Pete found himself holding his hand in front of his face to block it. Suddenly he froze in his tracks.

"What has passed, Monsieur Pete?"

He was looking to the side, where the dune abutted into the wall of the bowl. Though very weathered, there were unmistakable marks in the sandstone. It had been cut. Removed in large blocks.

What the fuck? Something is going on here. He looked through the blowing sand to the far side of the dune and could make out similar marks there as well. "Look Salil. The stone. It was cut."

"Why would someone have cut it?"

"Good question. I don't know, but I'm still thinking about it. Let's go, this sand is killing me."

They descended the dune to the floor, and found themselves staring at the walls of the bowl all around them and also down into the cave.

"Well worth the hike, eh Salil?"

"Yes, it is fantastic."

The cave was more like a pit. It was about fifty meters across, and it was filled to within ten meters of the top with a conical pile of sand. The sand spread out into the darkness such that they could not tell how deep the cave really was from where they stood. The rim of the cave was surrounded with uneven fragments of sandstone layered into the floor of the bowl.

"This broken rock. I think it came from the cut in the bowl," Pete said, pointing back towards the dune.

"It is all making me feel very strange."

He knew exactly how Salil felt. There had been some kind of construction. But why? It was fascinating, but Pete felt his enthusiasm for their field trip waning once again. Replacing the enthusiasm was the feeling that they were intruding somewhere they were not welcome. But, there they were.

"We'll camp here."

"I knew you were going to say that, Monsieur Pete."

The sun had dropped behind the rim of the bowl, and soon a cooling breeze prefaced the cold night which would follow. Pete looked forward to the relief it would bring. They dropped their packs and sat leaning against some of the broken rock.

Salil produced a pack of tobacco and a small ball of hashish from his rucksack. He cut the hashish into thin slivers and mixed it into the tobacco. He rolled the kif in a rice paper, lit the cigarette and took a long draw. Smiling, he passed it to Pete.

It's been a long time, but I'm ready to get stoned.

They sat and talked about the day's events as they watched the colors of the sunset. Salil was mellowing out, and spooky thoughts no longer dominated him. Pete, however, was running a boatload of troubles and worries through his head. They drifted off to sleep in their bags.

➊⧸⧹

Pete was dreaming. He was bent over a paint marker. The drop of plutonium was falling towards it. It fell and fell but never hit the ground. How can it not hit the ground? It's not like it's not moving. Then he knew why. The drop was his life. When it hit, he would die. Lawyers bent over him as he watched the drop, pinning him down with their questions. The same questions in different forms, over and over. Taking turns questioning him, twisting everything he said. The lawyers were wearing Arab robes. He was in a cage. They were stabbing at him through the bars with shiny swords. He lay on his back in sand, the sun blazing in his eyes. Pain. The drop was going to hit the ground.

A voice: "Father, help me."

"I'm coming, Simon."

He woke with a start. He was soaked with sweat and shivering. Salil softly snored nearby. Looking at his watch, it was 2:35 in the morning. The stars shone overhead. He pulled a T-shirt from his rucksack and mopped the sweat from his face and neck. Digging deeper into the pack, he retrieved two instant cold packs and a can of Budweiser. He popped the cold packs and wrapped them around the beer can in the T-shirt. It was a wasteful way to chill a can of beer, but he had had a feeling that he'd need one on this trip. As he drank the beer, he thought about the dream. Suddenly, the end of it came back to him. His son calling out for help. The cry had been so urgent and desperate. He finished the beer as a sad-looking half moon began to rise over the rim of the bowl. The cave was exhaling a steady warm breeze.

Pete had never had any children. Simon? Simon.

ഹൈ

The Arabs stole into the camp by the light of the half moon. More than twenty in number, they swarmed into the tents and began to drag the startled people out into the common area by the quonset hut. Soon someone resisted, and the shooting started. Automatic weapon fire and screams of terror and pain shattered the night and echoed off the stone walls. Then some bedouins gunned down the women. This enraged the others who had wanted to rape them first. Soon, the entire dig team of French archeologists was dead, their blood mixing with the sand of the Sahara. A tall Arab directed the removal of the stones from the quonset hut. They were loaded onto the back of one of the dig team's trucks and were driven away into the night.

ഹൈ

Salil woke Pete from a sound sleep as the sun began to rise over the rim of the bowl.

"Bon jour, Monsieur Pete. You slept well I hope."

"I had a bad dream, but I'm fine. You?"

"I feel well rested. Pete, what is the plan?"

"Give me a few minutes to wake up and we'll figure it out."

They both felt scroungy and used some of the precious water to clean up. Then, Salil walked about fifty meters away for his morning constitutional. Pete gazed over at Salil squatting down and had a twinge of guilt for his partner defecating there, as if they were in some kind of temple. He started to laugh at himself for the thought, and resigned himself to walking off in the other direction to do the same.

After a breakfast of day-old falafel and some bottled juice, they once again peered down into the pit. Without speaking, Pete pulled the seven millimeter climbing rope from his rucksack. He anchored the rope to one of the jagged remnants of rock at the edge of the abyss. He readied himself with a climbing harness and then packed his other gear: lights (his and Salil's), two climbing ascenders and prussics, his camera and a liter of water. Salil would remain up top. This was fine with Salil.

"Comme te veux, Monsieur Pete."

This adventure in the desert merde is getting out of hand, thought Salil. Pete took the forty-five out of his rucksack and handed it to Salil. "Just in case." Salil wasn't smiling and just looked around the rim of the bowl.

"Look, just put it in your pack, okay?"

"Okay, Monsieur Pete."

Pete began to rappel into the pit. As he went down, he saw that the cave was much deeper than he had thought. His light came nowhere close to illuminating the recesses that spread out in all directions below the ceiling. As he touched down on the sand pile, he looked around and felt as if he'd dropped into the bottom half of a giant hourglass.

Salil was lying on his stomach peering down at him.

"It's pretty wild in here Salil. I'm going to unhook myself and walk down the dune."

Pete walked down the sandpile to the floor below. Although his light became lost in the vastness of the cave, his eyes were adjusting to the ambient light coming in through the pit. The cave seemed to be round on the bottom and rose like a cone to the ceiling. All around the bottom of the cave were smaller caves that seemed to intertwine like Swiss cheese or worm holes. He began to walk around the perimeter of the floor and found it to be alternately clean sandstone and drifted over from the sand pile.

When he reached the northernmost radius of the cave, he encountered an opening close to thirty meters in diameter. He entered it and noticed dozens of the worm hole-like smaller caves entering from the sides. Less than fifty meters in, the tunnel was filled to the roof with sand. He stood casting his light about, thinking. This must have been a subterranean drain for the wadi.

The scale of it all began to sink in. He decided to take some pictures. The flash was being lost in the vastness of the cavern. Pete moved over to the side and started to take pictures of the worm hole tunnels, when something reflected the flash back at him. He jumped back in surprise.

Damn, there's something in there.

He entered the twisting tunnel only to realize that whatever it was, he couldn't get to it from the crawlway he was in. He aimed his light through the opening and once again came the brilliant reflection. It seemed to be some sort of transparent crystal, but it was reflecting the light too much to be clearly seen. He retreated back into the drain cave, and after four tries, finally found the tunnel that led to the object. Pete crawled through the spiraling tunnel and raised his light.

"Ho-ly Shit."

కింళ

An hour had passed and Salil was thinking that it was too much time. Something had happened. What would he do? Suddenly, he felt a slight jerk on the rope and almost leapt to his feet in shock. "Monsieur Pete, you have frightened me. What took you so much time?"

"I'm getting ready to come up. Everything is just. . . Everything is okay."

Pete jumarred up the rope and soon stood beside Salil. As he started to pull the rope up he turned to him. "I found something down there."

"What?"

The slack came out of the rope and Salil realized that Pete was pulling up whatever it was he had found. He leaned over to take a look.

"It is, some kind of boat?"

"It's a kayak, Salil."

"Is this why we came here to this place? You have known that this was in the cave?"

"No Salil, I had no idea. I was as surprised as you are now."

"But how does this come to be here?"

Pete was now sweating hard in the mid-morning sun. Good fucking question. "I don't know."

Pete had tied two loops in the rope and slipped them over the ends of the kayak. Then he had tied the two loops together so the boat couldn't slide out.

Salil now lent his assistance in pulling on the rope. As they lifted it more, the boat hit against the ceiling of the cave, emitting an almost musical tone. They looked at each other in surprise. They pulled it the rest of the way up and laid it on the stone at their feet, staring at it, speechless.

What a beautiful creation.

Pete turned it over to look at the hull. There wasn't a scratch on it. It was a river kayak, very similar to the types he used. It was also absolutely perfect in form and was made of what appeared to be transparent crystal. There were no dents, no breaks, no scratches, anywhere.

This thing is indestructible.

He looked inside the cockpit. The seat and foot braces flowed into the rest of the inside of the boat. No rough edges. Pete removed his boots and slipped into the seat. The foot braces fit him perfectly.

What the hell!?

He stepped out of the boat and put his boots back on.

"Pete, this is all so strange. I am afraid."

So am I.

"Look Salil, I don't know what's going on either, but I didn't know this thing was down there. I don't know how it got there, but I bet this kayak has been down in that cave for a long time.

"Something else. This thing couldn't be made anywhere I know of. I've been kayaking for over twenty years, and I've never seen anything like it. This material is totally unknown to me."

They both stood and looked at it a while before Salil said exactly what Pete had been thinking: "It seems to have some kind of resonance."

This damn thing is alive.

"What will you do with it?"

"We'll take it with us... I found it. I guess it's mine now."

i have always been yours

The boat was getting really hot in the sun. Pete looked up at the rim of the bowl and thought about what a long afternoon and evening it was going to be ascending the wadi back to camp. He stepped back and snapped a picture of the kayak. As he took the shot, neither he nor Salil noticed the change in color in part of the deck or the strange markings that rose from within the blotch of the light green. Unnoticed, the color faded again to transparent crystal.

Now, how best to carry the boat? He had an idea. He slid their sleeping bags over the ends of the kayak so that they met in the center. Then he wrapped it all together with the climbing rope. They would each take an end on a shoulder and carry it home.

Pete finished off the roll of film taking shots of the mouth of the cave and a shot of every sixty degrees of the radius of the bowl. They repacked the rucksacks and Pete stuck the forty-five in his belt.

Salil, being shorter than Pete, would take the lead as they headed up the dune out of the bowl. Pete thought about how tired he was of walking uphill through sand; always one step forward, half a step back. He also thought about something else.

This is going to totally blow Howard's mind.

He knew Howard. Always so pragmatic, practical, logical, realistic. Howard's sense of reality was going to have a hard time dealing with this. Or would Howard have some practical explanation? No. He could not.

As they walked up the dune, Pete's mind drifted back to another time.

When he first met Howard, he was nineteen and Howard was twenty-seven. They were kayaking the Cheat River during the spring rafting season and had pulled over at Coliseum rapids to wait for several rafting groups to pass through. Pete had lit up a joint and Howard was aghast.

"How can you smoke that shit and paddle?"

"All depends on what you're used to, I guess. For me, it opens my mind to what I'm doing."

"I'll stick to reality if you don't mind."

"Reality? What is, reality, Howard?"

"Well, it's what you see. All this," he said, waving his hand at the river that lay before them, "is reality. What goes on in your mind, when you're stoned on marijuana, is not."

"Is that so?"

"Yes, it is."

"Okay then Howard, I've got something for you."

"No thanks. No drugs for me. Some other time maybe, but not out here."

"Not talking about drugs Howard. See the waterfall over there?"

He was talking about Conner Run Falls, a scenic highlight of Coliseum Rapids. The slender falls crashed from above onto the shore rocks, not far from where they sat.

"Yes, of course I see it. It's real isn't it?"

"Okay Mr. Reality, pick out one of the cracks in the rock behind the curtain of falling water. Stare at it. Don't move your eyes from it."

"Okay, I'm doing it."

"Don't blink. Don't move your eyes with the falling water. Don't turn your head."

"Okay, okay, I'm doing it for Christ's sake. What's this all about, Dornblaser?"   "Just wait. Keep looking at the rock behind the water. Ready?"

"Ready for what?"

"Ready for a wrinkle in your sense of reality. Now look at the cliff off to the side of the waterfall."

Howard shifted his gaze to the rocks. A swath in the center leapt upward, while the sides remain fixed. Howard flinched.

"What the hell!?"

"Uh huh! Got you Calvert. What's the matter? You on drugs or something?"

"Okay. Okay. That can be explained. The optic nerve works overtime, looking at something fixed behind the moving water. It fools the brain so that it can look at the fixed object and then needs a moment to re-adjust when you look away."

"But you admit that you saw the rocks move?"

"Yes, but. . . Okay Petey, I get your point. I guess I just spend too much time dwelling on the physical aspect of things."

"Don't worry Howard. You could still explain what just happened on the blackboard."

"Shut up and pass me that joint, will you."

They had laughed and laughed.

≋

Neither noticed as they sweated and grunted, climbing the dune with their load, that they were being observed. From the south side of the bowl, 'Frank Zappa' and one of his cronies from Tinnhert were watching them. The crony was wondering what it was they were carrying. 'Frank Zappa' had seen enough, and together they sneaked over the sand to a third, who was holding their mounts.

CHAPTER 2 — VIRUS

Virus! God Bless America. These programs were guaranteed clean.

All the data from the shoot was being erased before his eyes. The computer virus had infected the hard drive he was using to merge the data from the shoot with the program he'd created back at Davis.

He just shook his head and let it go. After ten painful minutes, all the data was gone. He shut down the computer and went to the fridge for a beer.

Why would someone want to ruin his work?

Howard was no dummy. He had copied the data from each recorder used in the shoot, onto disk. Not once, but four times. Hell of a lot easier than doing another shoot, he had thought.

Where are Pete and Salil?

Howard was tired of being alone with the computers. He walked across the trailer with his beer and replayed the computer mock-up of Wadi Nouveau from the perspective of dye marker 17N plus 3M, his favorite so far. If he squinted, it was as if he was standing on the side of the river, watching it rage.

Man, what a cooking piece of water it must have been.

Over the past night, while the other computer was copying the recorded information, he had plugged some of it in with his program and plotted eight perspectives. It had worked perfectly. His program was based on metric holographic correlation. After slowing the gamma ray tracing to real-water-time, the computer analyzed the bottom left forward cubic centimeter for vector and speed. Simultaneously, another program analyzed the entire cubic meter, of random cubic meters, within cosine-triangulated marker perspectives.

With his program, this was relatively simple for the computer to do. This data was then transposed into BLOBs: binary large objects. These were fed into a third program, located in a third computer, which perspective-extrapolated vector and water speed. This was the most space-demanding portion of the equation. Once the random cubic meters correlated water speeds and vectors (as they related to movement of water volume), the computer would choose, at random, another cubic meter within the ray-path of the analyzed cubic meters as a control.

The computer had analyzed two hundred cubic meter sets, with all control cubic meters responding positive.

Howard had been pleased, but not surprised. He had done his homework.

Then the data had begun to erase. The virus must have been in one of the space-saver-slave programs he had acquired from BiDyne. The SSS programs had been a necessary evil. Without them, there wasn't enough memory in his computers (or anybody else's for that matter) to do what needed to be done.

The virus was malicious. It only surfaced when data was fed into it and only erased that data.

Who would have wanted to do that to him? Probably some hacker whiz fresh out of some top school making triple figures at BiDyne with nothing better to do than screw up his million dollar research project. Now he was going to have to print out the SSS programs and go over each line until he found the virus. That might take as much as a week.

Howard was exhausted. He had slept a total of six hours in three days. A computer scientist, however, had to be capable of that type of endurance.

He thought back to the time spent at West Virginia University. He'd spent the majority of his nights alone in his little office in the computer center, working in front of a screen until he couldn't see straight. Many of those nights, that wild man Dornblaser, fresh from an escapade, would sneak in through the basement doors. Depending on the hour, he would then drag Howard out for beers or early breakfast at Eat'nPark. He chuckled to himself. How he missed those years in West Virginia, kayaking with Pete.

Before that, he had been working for a big computer consulting firm on the Jersey side of the Hudson. Every week, they'd fly him somewhere to work, and he was free to fly wherever he wanted for the weekends. He had started flying into Charleston to go kayaking in West Virginia. He'd bought a cheap car and parked it at Chuck Yeager Airport with his kayak chained to the top. Every Friday night he would drive up into the mountains and join other kayakers to run the rivers. Some friends had told him about a crazy, acid-boater, Dornblaser, but he wasn't sure Pete was somebody he wanted to paddle with. One Sunday he was on the Cheat, eddied out in Tier Drop Rapid, when here came this guy slicing and dicing all the moves with speed, grace, and style. His friend turned to him and said: "That's Pete Dornblaser." They had been friends ever since.

Pete was the kind of guy that would prefer to hang out at the take-out and get stoned and drink beer than pack everything up and get on home. Hell, Pete would live on the river and never go home if he didn't have to.

Howard's daydreaming came to an abrupt end. A whistle was being blown out in the compound. Shouting followed and he looked out the window, to see what appeared to be Khalem trying to talk one of the new guards out of shooting Pete and Salil. The two of them were carrying what looked like a kayak cocooned up in sleeping bags towards the computer trailer. He opened the door and they carried their load right in and set it in the middle of the floor.

"You're not going to believe this."

"Please excuse me Messieurs, I will go now to take some rest."

"Okay Salil. Thanks, buddy."

Once the door swung shut, Howard looked at Pete who was already kneeling by the boat, untying knots. He pulled the sleeping bags off, revealing it to Howard.

"Jesus Christ Almighty!"

⁓

Pete was into his second six-pack, and Howard had still not stopped going over the boat. Inside and out, front to back, top to bottom. While Howard examined the kayak, he had had Pete thoroughly recount the voyage of its discovery. Howard was taking it better than Pete had thought he would, but he wasn't saying much either. He did say something that worried Pete.

"It looks like one of yours."

"Howard, this thing," he said pointing at the kayak, "has weirded me out. I've been thinking about it all afternoon, and, well, it just seems like too much of a coincidence. I mean, I can't believe that I came to Africa, to the Sahara desert, and took one fucking day off and I find a crystal kayak."

"Pete, I feel that the 'coincidence' is limited to the fact that a kayaker, you, found it. And you found it because of your interest in seeing a river, albeit a dry one, but a river nonetheless. Right place, right time. We're here because of the project. Nobody else found it first because the bowl was covered with sand until now."

Howard could tell he wasn't convinced.

"Listen to me Pete. I don't think I have to tell you that this thing couldn't have been made with any technology I'm aware of. You know that too. This kayak is an incredible find. And not just because of its make-up. Its origin is a mystery we have to unravel." Howard noticed that Pete looked weary and stressed. Stressed or not, Howard thought, I'd better fill him in now.

"Don't get me wrong Petey, I am fascinated by it, but.. But, we have pressing problems. I've run into a nightmare with the software. A computer virus. We obviously have another problem as well. Today some new guards arrived. Khalem is beefing up security. You knew about it, didn't you?"

"Yes, I knew."

"We've got to get out of here, fast. We'll take this thing with us, and when there's more time, I'll check it out and see what I come up with."

"This virus, you going to be able to get rid of it?"

"Yes, but it might take some time. That's what I'm working on now. Look Petey, I want you to get some serious rest. Your only duties for the next couple of days are going to be working with Khalem on this security thing and getting the workers to ready all equipment for extraction. As soon as I get this program up and running, we pull the plug and leave, understood?"

"Yes sir."

"Okay, get some sleep."

When he left, Howard gave the crystal craft another looking over, and then turned back to the monitor. He had one of the SSS programs up and was going through it, line by line, looking for the virus. At the rate he was going, he knew that it would take until morning just to get through that one program. He was beat. Soon he started to doze off in his chair.

He was suddenly startled. Someone was there, watching him. He pivoted around in his chair. He was alone in the trailer. There was only the hum of the computers, and the crystal kayak on the floor behind him. He got up and locked the door. He went back to the monitor where he lasted only about ten more minutes before falling fast asleep.

❧❦

Pete slept in. He rose at eight-thirty, feeling refreshed.

As he showered, he spent a couple of luxurious extra minutes letting the water pound on his neck and back. He closed his eyes and was entranced by the sweet sensation. When he opened his eyes, he was looking down at his feet, water dripping downward. The droplets began to slow in their fall. Began to hang in mid-air. The light in the shower stall began to dim.

He jerked himself out of it, back to reality.

What was that? Forget it. It was nothing. Get out of the shower.

Water.

The water was expensive. Ridiculously expensive. It was brought in by truck from Tinnhert Oasis. For Pete and Howard, it was worth it. One had to be able to take a shower after a day in the desert. All of the trailers had showers, fed by the large tanks mounted on a platform made of telephone poles. Between cooking, cleaning, bathing, and evaporation, they were using over four hundred gallons a week, at three dollars a gallon. "Part of the cost of doing business," as Howard said.

Pete was looking forward to a huge breakfast, and was heading across the compound when Khalem intercepted him.

"Bon jour, Monsieur Pete."

"Bon jour, Khalem. The new guards arrive okay?"

"That is why I have come to speak with you. Four men came. Three are family of my colleague in Tassili. The fourth, however, has preoccupied me. He approached the truck as it took on fuel in Tinnhert, and offered his services. I feel he may have intercepted my call on the radiophone to Tassili. Very much a coincidence if not, will you not agree?"

Pete grunted and continued to listen.

"He is called Hasef Ben Rabat. He comes from Tunis. The driver radioed to me about him. I told the driver to tell him he had work here, and to bring him. I called Algiers on another frequency. Hasef appears to have worked in security in Tunis."

Pete didn't like what he was hearing, at all.

"We have established the checkpoint at the wadi crossing. I told Hasef that he would be stationed here at the camp. I thought we should watch him closely. If you wish, I will send him away, today."

"Good work Khalem. Look, if this guy is here for anything else other than the job, no, we don't want him here. But before we send him away, I'd like to know what he's up to."

"We are then in accordance. Monsieur Howard is well I presume? I have seen little of him these two days."

"He's okay, just real busy. We need to take care of the camp so he can work. You've got to keep a handle on security, and I need to get the new workers busy, getting stuff ready for extraction."

"Bien sur, Monsieur Pete. In anything else also, I am at the service of yourself and Monsieur Howard."

Howard. I better get over there and check on him.

Pete forgot about breakfast, and grabbing two cups of coffee instead, hurried over to the main computer trailer.

"Howard, open the door! I've got coffee!"

No answer. He must be asleep. Pete set the coffee on the steps and fumbled for his keys; then Howard opened the door and motioned him inside. Howard was acting strange.

"What's up?"

"Pete, sit down."

Uh oh. Here we go.

Howard looked him in the eye and then with a pause and a sigh, looked up at the ceiling of the trailer. Pete had no idea what was running through his head, but Howard had had his world turned on end since they had bid each other a good night twelve hours earlier. He felt he could not, and would not tell Pete about any of it. What had happened was this: He had awakened in his chair once more and was aware of a glowing orange light coming from behind him. Swiveling about in the chair, he saw that it came from the deck of the kayak. Rising to take a closer look, he made out a series of patterns in the light. When he rubbed his hand over them he could feel that they were raised above the surface much like braille. They had a crystalline like lattice shape, each being different. He knelt partially to get a closer look and partially in awe of what was happening. Feeling he had to record the shapes, Howard grabbed a pen and paper. The figures faded away and the color did too. Then a blue glow appeared near the stern and he could see the same series of shapes rising out of the crystal surface. He rushed to the end of the boat and the color began to fade. Quickly, he laid the paper over them and rubbed the side of his pen across the paper. He could see the pattern of the glyphs raise in relief. Then, they and the light, were gone. Howard was at a total loss about what had just happened and the meaning held in the little symbols in the magazine. It was causing a paradigm shift in science as he knew it and also took him out of his comfort zone. It was starting to freak him out.

He had organized everything down to the tiniest detail for this project. Hell, his whole life was organized. Then Pete had been acting strangely -- narcoleptic fits with unexplainable visions, then the discovery of the crystal boat, and now this. But those things were not what freaked Howard out. What freaked him out was that he knew it was all leading somewhere further beyond the parameters of what he had called reality until a short while ago.

No new light came from the kayak, so Howard sank down in his chair and studied the series of symbols. There were 17 shapes in all with 5 that repeated within the series 3 times. Upon a more minute inspection, he noted subtle differences in the 5 that appeared to be repeating. This is an equation, Howard thought to himself. He was going to copy them onto a sheet of blank paper but sleep got the better of him.

He had a dream. In the dream Pete was leaving and he knew he would never see him again. Pete said that, no, they would meet up but Howard knew better. He was worried for Pete and wanted to give him something to help him on his journey. Then he felt that Pete was in grave danger but instead of being afraid was doing all that he could to help another: someone younger than he. Then the dream shifted and he was kayaking through a narrow canyon behind Pete. The canyon abruptly opened up and a horizon line in front of Pete signaled a big drop off. Then looking up, he saw it, a dark tower coming from below looming high into the sky. Pete dropped off of the lip of the falls and disappeared.

Then Howard shot awake. The kayak was there. It had been aglow with a white light that was quickly fading.

"Mihalis." The crystal had a name and it had come to him the moment he awakened.

Howard looked at him. "We've got problems. Khalem doesn't trust one of the new guards, does he?"

"No. How did you know?"

"I try to pay attention. You and I could have big time troubles if the plutonium is taken."

"We both knew that coming here."

"Now we have something new to worry about," he said pointing to Mihalis.

ॐ❦

"Yes, Marge. What is it?"

"It's Elliot Carlson, Sir."

"What does he want?"

"He says it's the Algerian thing, Sir."

"Show him in."

The young commander walked in, looking crisp and sharp as usual. Standing five foot ten, he was trim and muscular. His jet black hair bristled in a slightly outgrown buzz-cut.

"Okay, Elliot. What's the latest?"

"Well, Sir, as you know, we've been monitoring them from space for two months now."

"Would you please get to the fucking point."

George Mitchell was director of Islamic Affairs for the C.I.A., a post that didn't officially exist. He was stressed. He was always stressed. He was one of those bureaucrats who conceal their true natures by lacing their speech with profanity. He was impatient and rude with agent Carlson. Carlson was just doing his job, and doing it well, as always. He was actually upset with the situation. This guy Calvert, where the hell did he get off? Taking a kilo of weapons-grade plutonium out of the country, without clearance, to Algeria of all goddamn places. He was tempted to send in an extraction team and drag Dr. Calvert and the other asshole, Dornblaser, back with the stuff and slap them with espionage charges. Yes, they'd been checked out and were looking pretty clean. Nothing at all on Calvert. Dornblaser had recently lost his ass in a lawsuit and had been on an eighties list as being involved with L.S.D. But other than that, he was clean too.

But right now he didn't give a crap. If something happened and the Arab world got its hands on that plutonium, he'd have them both burned at the stake.

"Sir, we received a classified cable this morning. Two nights ago, a French archeology team was massacred twenty five miles west of Calvert's research site. Our people feel this thing is getting too hot to sit on any longer."

"What 'French team'? I didn't see anything in the dailies about anybody being anywhere close to Calvert."

"Apparently, their dig was hush-hush. We hadn't noticed anything from the surveillance photos because their camp looked like any other Bedouin camp. Then they put up a quonset hut and we started to wonder. We noticed archeological activity only three days ago. There is a large complex of ruins that has recently been uncovered by the shifting sand, and they were removing some stone blocks.."

"Carlson, why in hell wasn't I kept up to date on this? Do you realize how fucking bad this is going to look for us if. . . Never mind. I want the last two months' photos gone over again, starting right now, Dammit."

∽⧸

Hasef had seen the way Dornblaser looked at him. He also noticed him following him surreptitiously. He had figured out that the plutonium must be in the security trailer. There was always one of Khalem's sons on guard duty by the door. He had seen Khalem and Dornblaser talking. Khalem had made the slightest mistake of looking his way during the conversation. No problem. He could take them all out if he had to. But he was supposed to wait. After sunset, he would walk out into the darkness and radio Barkoui again. Odd, Barkoui asking about the water tanks. Whatever. The plutonium was as good as in their hands.

Foolish American Dogs.

Hasef was as surprised as everybody else with the arrival of the helicopter.It was a customs chief from Algerian government named Omar Boixel. Pete had met him in Algiers when they came in. The meeting had been, "arranged." Boixel had been one of the two officials who had been bribed to make sure 'certain things' slid through customs without being inspected. The crates had not been opened. One of them had contained the plutonium. When Pete had handed him the hush money, Boixel had been happy. Today he was not happy. He was trundling toward him behind a man who was looking extremely businesslike.

This other was some sort of officer. He looked like he hadn't ever been happy.

The grim-looking man was dressed in a Spartan uniform, but his insignia, and the way he carried himself revealed his importance. Khalem met them at the pad and led them over to Pete. The pilot and an armed soldier remained with the helicopter.

"Monsieur Dornblaser, may I present Colonel Humeau, French Foreign Legion. There has been some trouble. Might we speak?"

Khalem was already rushing to clear the staff out of the mess trailer so they could talk in private. The three of them went in.

Khalem now went to Hasef and asked him to stand guard with his son Isaac at the security trailer. Good, thought Hasef. His mind began to race. This was the golden moment. He could take the camp and force the pilot to fly him to Algiers at gunpoint. He could double-cross Barkoui, cut him out of the action, and up the price with Kriouche. He looked around, formulating a quick plan. First he would kill the man beside him, then the soldier, then Khalem...

☙❧

Khalem excused himself for interrupting the meeting. He had entered the mess trailer through the back door. "Monsieur Pete, may I have a moment."

"Excuse me gentlemen, won't be but a second." He stepped out with Khalem. Laid out on the bare rock were an Uzi, a nine-millimeter pistol equipped with a silencer, and a Motorola HP600 hand-held radio.

"These were in Hasef's duffel."

They agreed on a plan and Pete went back into the mess trailer.

"Pete, I trust Dr. Calvert is well?"

"Yes Omar," he said nervously, not knowing what the colonel did or did not know about the plutonium and the bribes, "he's over in the computer trailer, working away."

"Good. We will not need to disturb him. Now, I have some unpleasant news. Two nights ago, a group of scientists from the University of Versailles were murdered by Bedouins forty kilometers west of here."

Upstream, thought Pete.

"They were conducting archeological research."

"I had no idea that there were any digs going on anywhere near here. What exactly was it they were doing?"

"They were surveying the ruins of an ancient city. It had only recently been exposed by the shifting dunes. Now the sandstorms are covering it once again.

The sand has also covered the tracks of the guilty. We are very concerned."

What sandstorms? It's been clear as a bell here.

Boixel continued. "Tomorrow, a government team is coming from Algiers to investigate. The French are demanding an accounting of what has passed."

The colonel leaned forward in his chair and looked at Pete. "Monsieur Dornblaser, it has come to my attention that you have been using radioactive materials in your work here..."

God, get me out of here.

"We want no problems of this sort, in our jurisdiction." Humeau cast a disgusted look towards Boixel, who now stared at his clasped hands on the table. "I understand that you have a capable security unit here. I trust that they do their job well and that you leave, soon, with everything you came with. Am I clear?"

"Yes sir. Very much so, sir."

"Thank you for your time, Monsieur Dornblaser. We will be leaving now." Pete looked out the window and saw Khalem in position at the end of the security trailer. Pete needed to give him a little time.

"Gentlemen, could I offer you some lunch?

"Merci, but it is getting to be late, and it is best to complete our flights in the light of day."

Pete thought to himself: Well, maybe I can kill some time finding out about something I'd really like to know.

"Before you go, could you tell me more about the killings?"

"Yes, I suppose so."

"Please, I'd really like to know."

Pete stood with his back to the window and scratched his head.

Colonel Humeau began to summarize what he knew about the dig to the west. Over the past year, a massive dune had shifted, revealing some very well preserved stone walls. Legionnaires on patrol had stumbled on it. Humeau himself had flown to the site with an archeology professor from Algiers. The professor in turn called on old associates from Versailles who had come to look it over. There had been much debate over the origin of the stone in the walls. Apparently, they were not of any stone endemic to the Sahara. What was interesting was that attempts to date the site with carbon-14 dating had proved futile, which meant the site was more than thirty-five thousand years old. But such antiquity seemed impossible.

According to notes found after the attack, in the past month vicious sandstorms had come out of nowhere and had begun to shift the dune back over the site.

A dozen stones had been removed with intention of sending them to Versailles for analysis. Before they could be shipped out, a revolt of the workers had left them short-handed. The workers had claimed the removal was against the will of Allah. The last journal entries had mentioned sightings of Bedouins on horseback.

Everyone at the site had been slain. Dead were eleven French and four Algerians, the worst attack ever on archeologists. There had been no security force.

"The Sahara can be a deadly place, Monsieur Dornblaser. The nomads respect neither authority nor political boundaries, and rationalize each act of violence only with Allah."

The Sahara can be a deadly place.

Boixel interrupted: "Pete, we really must be going. Give my regards to Dr. Calvert. I assume he is quite busy with the computers?"

"Yes he is. With luck, we won't need to do any more field work and can prepare to leave within a week."

"For the benefit of all, I hope you are correct." The colonel rose to leave.

∂∽⟨͡

Khalem's middle son, Ryak, came around the other corner of the security trailer. He approached his brother and asked for a light. Isaac lit the cigarette and Ryak offered one to Hasef. Hasef disdained Gauloises and instead reached for his pack of Marlboro. That was when he felt the gun barrel against the back of his head. Khalem politely whispered to him to step into the security trailer. He was led to a room that was empty other than for a freshly installed eye-bolt sticking out of the floor. Isaac handcuffed his right hand to the eye bolt while Ryak trained his M-1 on him. Khalem wrapped his head and mouth with duct tape and offered him two options: Keep quiet, or take a ride with the French Foreign Legion. He chose the former.

As the chopper lifted off, Pete went to the security trailer. There Hasef was handcuffed to an eyebolt, newly installed in the floor. His head was bound in duct tape. Khalem had carried out his plan.

Pete went to the computer trailer, only to find Howard and Salil packing up equipment. Howard was handing drives and discs to Salil and Salil was wrapping each in old newspaper and masking tape. Howard was then writing notes on the tape with a magic marker denoting which grid sector, etc.etc. that the disc corresponded to.

"What are you doing?"

"Pete, Salil told me what just happened with the new guard. I'm going to have the sky crane lift me and this trailer out of here tomorrow. I'm going to count on you to get everything else out in the days to follow."

"And you're positive we won't need to do any more measurements in the grid?"

"I found the virus. I woke up after a catnap in my chair and there it was, the virus, right on the screen, just waiting to be cut out and deleted."

"It was on the screen by chance or you didn't notice it when you were falling asleep or what?"

"Don't ask."

"What do you mean, 'don't ask'?"

Salil was shuffling around nervously between them.

"I mean, I'll tell you later, okay?"

"I guess. This thing is giving me the creeps."

"It scared me."

"Why? What did it do?"

"Last night, part of the kayak deck began to glow. When I got close to it I could make out a series of symbols that stuck out from the surface. Then they disappeared but came back, on a different part of the deck a minute later. This time I snagged it", with this he held up the sheet of paper with the rubbings of the shapes.

"They look like snowflakes", Pete said, staring at the paper.

"At first I didn't understand them at all. Then I thought, 'this is some kind of code.' It was. It took a while, but I was able to, 'break' the code. Simply speaking, the symbols are two, different, 'programs.' Turns out that each individual symbol was a differential equation. They build on each other, tear each other apart, and then, once changed, rebuild on each other again. Now they're scaring the crap out of me. They deal with a lot of holographic quantum physics. The first is very complicated but very short. The program is multi-track and creates additional tracks as it progresses, but, through compression, uses very little storage. The decompression algorithm is unique in that it retrieves only specific information from each track and simultaneously discards the rest from memory, and then repeats the process."

Pete and Salil were both looking lost.

"To cut to the chase, the program is designed to synthesize energy."

"I thought energy couldn't be created or destroyed."

"So did I and everybody else. The energy created cannot be stored, however, and is applied directly into the second program. This is even more fascinating. The second program is a combination tracking mechanism and teleportation unit."

"What?"

"You heard right. It is a four dimensional gps."

"But what is it for?"

"For you to be able to rendezvous in time and space with the crystal boat. By the way, it has a name. It came to me as I woke from a dream. It is called 'Mihalis."

"Mihalis. . . . I need a beer."

"I'll have one with you."

Leaving Salil behind, they stepped outside into the Saharan sunset, beers hidden in coolie cups.

They saw two of the workers jabbering in Arabic and pointing to the east. A dense cloud was moving in from the south over the vicinity of the bowl. It was a sandstorm, and it was dumping its charge.

Time to get out of here.

They spent the night sorting and packing and drinking. Howard would inventory each category of item to be packed, decide how and in what it would be stored, and then turn the job over to Salil and Pete. Each item would get wrapped in old newspaper, taped and labeled. Pete was working in a beer each time Howard stopped to inventory. They no longer hid the drinking from Salil, as he seemed not to care.

Khalem stopped in at midnight with a FAX that had come in. The cover sheet was addressed to Howard with no return address, and the message was in Arabic.

"That's weird," Howard said, passing the FAX to Pete.

Pete looked at it and handed it to Salil. "What's it say?"

Salil studied the page for a moment and looked up at them.

"I think it has come from Boixel. It reads that there are Americans in Algiers asking many questions. It then reads only that they are not scientists."

ॐ✧

"Sir, I have something to report."

Agent Carlson was seated in Mitchell's private office. The two men were separated by Mitchell's expansive desk. Carlson spread several large photos across it in front of him.

"Sir, as per your orders, we've gone over the satellite intelligence for every day they've have been in there. The guys down in analysis did a little playing around with them too and we've a better idea now of what Calvert's been up to. This first shot is May tenth, when they started to move in. Nice resolution. You can read Sikorsky on the rotor blades of the sky crane."

"Where did they get the fucking chopper?"

"It was contracted from an outfit called..," Carlson thumbed through a file and pulled out a report. "Yes, here it is. Med Construction International. It's one of the biggest construction firms in northern Africa. They did some building in Tripoli after our '86 strike on Kadafi, but they're clean enough. Calvert paid $9,500, each, to have the trailers flown in. The price also includes their eventual extraction. There are seven trailers: $66,500. Not cheap. Dornblaser arranged the leasing of the trailers from a construction equipment rental agency in Algiers called..."

"All right already, go on."

"Sorry sir."

Carlson pointed to another picture.

"They seemed to be surveying a dry riverbed by their camp. Then this." The photo was larger scale, shot at night, and showed a rectangular pattern of little blotches of light. "This seems to back up their story sir. Andresky in Space Surveillance and Analysis did this for me. This is where the plutonium comes in. Those little specks are hot. Real hot. According to Andresky, if they can show up with an ultraviolet photo scan like this, it has to be almost pure plutonium. We got one other interesting photo at night. This one shows the riverbed all lit up from one side to the other. This was about a week ago. We had to be careful talking to Calvert's associates at USC Davis, but we know he rented 125 gamma ray tubes. Andresky thinks that's what this light was."

"Basically sir, Calvert checks out. He's just your average mad scientist with a bunch of money to throw into some secret research project that just happens to involve a kilo of illegally obtained weapons-grade plutonium, illegally taken out of the country and slid into an Arab stronghold."

Although he didn't appreciate the cynicism, Mitchell knew Elliot was right. Calvert was on the level. But he could not deny the risk to national security and his responsibility in the matter. It was times like this when he wondered why he hadn't left the agency for the easier life in the private sector.

"Sir, there are some other things that have come to light that I think you should know about. One, as you have ordered, we put stringers as close to their site as possible. We lost the first two men we put in Tinnhert Oasis about a week ago. M.I.A. They were good plants too. We've got another guy in there now with his ear to the ground. Our man in Tassili reported that Calvert recruited more guards after a worker revolt disturbingly similar to the one the Frenchies had before the massacre. Two, there is another Ph.D. working in Calvert's old department at U.S.C.. He's from Tunisia and his name is Farid Kriouche. Maybe you recall the F.B.I. bust down in Melbourne Beach, Florida a couple of years back? They uncovered a racket involving Palestinians operating a stolen phone card scam. The card numbers were sold in the Arab-American black market."

Mitchell nodded but said nothing.

"Well, we cross-checked the computer records and there was a call put in to a hotel in Algiers from a pay phone on the Davis campus using one of the stolen numbers, the day after Calvert received the plutonium from Northern Diversified Dynamics."

"Oh shit."

"Possibly a coincidence, sir."

"Right.."

"Three. Now this is really confusing. We have known for some time about a terrorist named Barkoui from the Hezbollah Liberation Front."

"I recognize the name."

"Yes, of course sir. Well, it appears he showed up to work on Calvert's project..."

"What!?"

"That's the easy part. This guy seems to be fanning the fires of Mujahadin with the Bedouins as we would imagine. But according to sources within the HLF, Barkoui was not sent there. Actually, he came up missing a couple months back. And, the Barkoui in Tinnhert doesn't match the one picture we had on file.

One theory is that this guy murdered Barkoui, and is an impostor.

"But why?"

"Plutonium is big business."

"Goddamit! Quit joking!"

"Sorry, sir. Four, there are some other people running around in Algiers claiming they're ours, showing some lousy fake I.D.s and talking to some of the same people we've been watching. No coincidence there, I believe. Sir, it's time to move in and get what's left of that plutonium."

"Do it, Carlson."

Elliot rose to leave. "One other thing sir. Just for fun, I had S.S.A. go back a year with the photos of the research site."

"And?"

"Sir, it didn't exist. It was a sand dune."

☙❧

"Pete, we talked about this before we came down here, and I want to see if you still agree. I'm going to go out as clean as I can and you're going to carry the plutonium back like we thought. Is that still okay?"

"Yes, of course it is."

"I know it's looking hairier than we thought it was going to..."

Pete cut him off. "Don't worry, Howard. I know what could happen and I accepted that before I agreed to come. If somebody tries to take the plutonium, they'll have to do it over my dead body. I've been thinking about a plan for getting it out, and I think it will work. While the sky crane is lifting out the other trailers, I'll drive to Tasili in one of the trucks with Salil. We'll charter a plane to Algiers, and I'll surrender the plutonium and the dropper log at the U.S. embassy. Then you contact your pal Bradshaw and hopefully I'll only spend a couple of months in the pokey."

"Hopefully less than a week."

"We've got to be realistic, Howard. We don't know how they're going to react."

Pete had indeed made up his mind to die before he parted with the plutonium. At this point in his life, when he was as far down as someone could be, it certainly wouldn't help to be known as the guy who had let plutonium slip into the hands of people who wouldn't hesitate to use it.

By 1 a.m., the packing of the main computer trailer was complete. Howard went over his "to do" list with Pete one more time and then they called it a night. Howard fell fast asleep on the couch with Mihalis at his side on the floor.

Pete went to the security trailer to see what Khalem had or hadn't learned from their guest.

Nothing. The duct tape was now off, but Hasef wasn't talking. That was no surprise. In addition, Pete had made it clear to Khalem that they would not torture him to acquire information. No, they wouldn't drop to that level.

જ∽⑥

Mitchell picked up the phone. It was Carlson.

"Sir, things are happening. Last night, Kriouche boarded a flight in San Francisco, bound for New York. We have a confirmation from immigration that he flew out of New York on Air France, bound for Paris. He will arrive there in an hour. We've got a tail ready to pin to him in Paris."

"Good work, Elliot."

"There's more sir. Calvert is having a trailer lifted out in the morning."

"I want a full welcoming party for Calvert and that trailer the second they touch down in Algiers. And, By God, I want it kept quiet."

Mitchell's mind was moving a mile a minute. He was tempted to pull some strings and have an A.W.A.C.S. plane trace the flight of the Sikorsky from the camp to Algiers. No. Too many questions would be asked and relations with Algeria weren't that good to begin with.

"Do we know where the trailer is supposed to be dropped?"

"Last time I tried to tell you, and you cut me off."

"Carlson, don't fuck with me right now."

"Don't worry sir. Believe me sir, we'll be there."

☙❧

Pete's alarm went off before dawn and he looked out to see Howard already running around giving orders. Soon everyone was up and in action, readying the airlift stanchions on the main computer trailer.

When Pete walked out, he could see that Howard, though showered and shaved, obviously hadn't had much rest.

"You've been up all night, haven't you?"

"Yeah."

"You were almost asleep when I left. What happened?"

"Mihalis."

"What now?"

"I can't tell you."

"What do you mean you can't tell me?"

"It's best, it's best that I explain, later."

"Why not now?"

"Because, later's better. There's too much to do right now. I need your help, ASAP. The chopper is on its way."

Salil was already inside. He was wedging crates against each other on the floor for stability on the flight out. Howard had slipped Mihalis back into the sleeping bags.

"Pete, pull the stake bed up out front so loading Mihalis doesn't get too much notice."

"I'll keep it in my trailer till I leave tomorrow or the next day."

"You're going to leave today, okay?"

It was more of an order than a question.

"Why today? What about all the other equipment?"

"I made a bunch of arrangements last night. It's all going to be taken care of.""What is going on Howard?"

"We're being watched from space. There's less time than I thought."

"And how do you know?"

"I put 2 and 2 together, okay?

"All right already. I'll get the truck."

"Then we have to do the quarterback sneak with the plutonium."

"Got it."

After loading Mihalis, Pete went to the equipment trailer and pried apart the casing of one of the extra truck batteries. He removed the cells and thoroughly rinsed the shell free of battery acid. He put the casing in a cardboard box and headed for the security trailer.

Hasef looked a little worse for wear chained to the floor.

"Anything you'd like to tell me, Hasef?"

"Fuck you, American dog."

"We're quite sophisticated for a security guard, aren't we?"

Pete knew from his limited experience in Algeria that you could bounce 'Fuck you' off of the Bedouins all day and none of them knew what it meant. But, if you told one he was 'bullshit,' he'd go ballistic.

"Hasef, guess what? You're going to take a little nap now, and when you wake up, you're going to sing like you never sang before."

Hasef just glowered.

Pete went to the first aid room and opened the refrigerator.

He rooted through a box of drugs until he found one of the vials of sodium pentothal. Taking a new syringe, he drew thirty millimeters from the vial. Holding the syringe behind his back, he returned to Hasef. The man tried to resist, but between being bound and Pete's overwhelming size, he was quickly pinned to the floor on his stomach. Pete sat on his back and injected the 'truth serum' into Hasef's buttock, right through his robes. Hasef's curses changed from English to Arabic and then to an ever slowing, slurred babble. Soon he was unconscious on the floor.

"See you around lunchtime, sweetheart."

Pete inserted the lead case containing the plutonium into the empty battery casing. He stuck foam in around the lead box so that it couldn't shift, and snapped the top back onto the battery. It weighed about the same as the battery. Now he took an assortment of hardware and loaded it into a small wooden crate. After nailing it shut, he slapped HazMat stickers on all four sides. Feigning extra care and caution, he slowly carried the crate across the compound to Howard's trailer. All eyes were on him and the crate. That was good. They wanted everybody to think the plutonium was leaving with the trailer. To complete the act, Howard opened the door and stepped out of his way as he carried it inside.

"Pete, the sky crane will be here in less than an hour. We need to talk."

"About..?"

"There's been a slight change of plan."

"Well you better explain it to me then."

"I think that as soon as you get back to the states you should get some things together and put that South American plan you told me about into high gear.

"Relax bro. We will get out of here, straighten out the mess with the plutonium and all will be cool."

"Petey, I have a hunch that there is a lot more going on than you could ever imagine. There are other parties and, and things involved here."

"What do you mean by 'things'? You mean that kayak?"

Howard looked like he wanted to say something. Instead, he bit his tongue.

"Look, Howard, the project is almost over. Everything's going to work out. It's going to be a big success. Big. As beautiful as this kayak is, I don't want it. It's dangerous. Don't let it fuck everything up. Let's leave it here. Forget about it. I'm looking forward to partying down when you get your Nobel prize."

"I'm sorry Petey, I've made up my mind. You've got to trust me."

The two stared at each other.

"Okay, Howard. It's your experiment we're fucking with." Pete had always trusted Howard. He knew that Howard was steady, sane. He, Pete, was the crazy one. He was the one who would go out of his way for a kayak. And this beautiful kayak fit his body like a glove. There was no sense in changing things now.

⊱⋅⋅⋅⋅⊰

"Sir, as you know, we're getting photos every 25 minutes. The Sikorsky took off from Algiers a half hour ago, heading south."

"Are we all set?"

"Yes. The men in Tassili moved out overland at 0300, local time. Our man in Tinnhert left on horseback last night with the Bedouin group we infiltrated, We're assuming Barkoui is leading them. We have a space shot of them, thirty two in number. They're holed up in some rocks near a dry river crossing sixty klicks south of the camp..."

⊱⋅⋅⋅⋅⊰

"Fais gaffe Mujahadin!"

The man was tall and thin, with a hawk-like beak, moustache and goatee. When he opened his mouth, his narrow face was nearly all teeth.

"Today, we make the will of Allah. Our people will have the power to burn the American Satan in his own land. We are part of the second coming of our god!"He believed none of it. His mind was focused on something else. He raised his AK to the sky.

"We must wash ourselves clean of those who do not believe."

With this he lowered the machine gun and pumped a stream of bullets into the CIA plant. The man looked surprised as he lay on his back, his life running out onto the Sahara sand.

☙❧

When he heard the shots, a Bedouin stationed near the wadi crossing lowered the cross-hairs of the high powered rifle. As Mektar reached for the Motorola, he was slain with the shot. Dropping another bullet into the rifle, the marksman could see through the scope that the other sentry was stunned by the sudden violence. He then blew his head in half.

CHAPTER 3 — MAELSTROM

Salil pulled the Mercedes stake-bed truck in front of the security trailer to load the"extra battery." Only he and Pete knew what it really was.

Pete and Howard emerged from the main computer trailer. Howard was carrying a sealed cardboard box and had a duffel bag slung across his shoulder. He set them down beside the truck and shook hands with Khalem.

"I can never thank you enough, Khalem."

"It has been my pleasure, Monsieur Howard. Do not be preoccupied for the extraction. We will maintain vigilance here."

They could now hear the approaching drone of the sky crane.

"Petey, I'll be in touch before you know it."

"Okay, Howard, whatever happens, you just hang on to that data and try to talk your way out of this when you get to Algiers."

Howard again bit his tongue. He looked at Pete. The man was his best friend. He reached out and locked him in a bear hug.

"Be careful boy."

The massive helicopter slowly circled the camp before beginning its descent to the pad. Sand swirled about the compound as it landed. With a wave, Howard climbed into the aft cabin with his box and duffel. Lifting off once again, the sky crane dropped the lift cable, and a couple of workers hitched it to the airlift stanchions of the trailer. The workers climbed down, and, the trailer was lifted into the air.

Pete watched as the helicopter sailed away, the trailer dangling below. So Howard was leaving. The project was coming to an end. Now if they could just wrap it up to the satisfaction of the two governments. Pete thought about having money to get back on his feet. He wasn't sure what he would do, but things would change for the better.

He walked past the Mercedes and stopped. He could feel something. It was the crystal kayak. Even cocooned in the sleeping bags, it would not allow the power of its presence to be contained.

"Don't you go fucking things up now. Be good."

He felt a sudden wave of energy pass by him. "What the hell?"

Looking around, he guessed that he was the only one who had sensed it. He had a premonition of impending danger.

Shake it off, Petey. There's too much to do.

Hasef was snoring away on the floor. Pete gave him some rough shakes and he began to stir.

"Hasef, wake up. It's me, Pete."

The drugged captive rolled over and let out a low moan. He opened his eyes and looked up at Pete. Then his eyes seemed to roll around the room. "Oh... I fly. I feel so very good in this place."

Yeah Hasef, that would be my idea of heaven on earth too. Handcuffed to the floor of an office trailer in the Sahara. "Hasef, can I get you something to drink? You must be thirsty."

"No. I do not have thirst. I am feeling good."

"Do you want to call your friends?"

"Yes. Yes, I want to call Kriouche, for to tell him I am flying."

Kriouche? I know that name.

Then it came to him all at once. Kriouche was the professor from Tunisia that had been riding Howard's coattails at West Virginia University. Pete remembered him because of something that had happened. He had just arrived at WVU and hardly knew any English. He was a genius, but because he didn't speak or read English very well, he had bought a can of Crisco with a picture of fried chicken on the label, thinking there was chicken inside the can. Then he made the mistake of telling Howard about it in front of Pete. Pete had rolled on the floor laughing at this idiot with a Ph.D. who had thought fried chicken came in a can. The man had become enraged at Pete's impertinence and had screamed something in Arabic. Pete of course hadn't understood what he had said, but the look could have killed. He would never forget that look.

It all fell into place. Kriouche was in California at U.S.C., undoubtedly knew all about the project, probably knew about the plutonium, and was an Arab. He had probably arranged the computer virus too.

Pete had to warn Howard. He got on the radiophone and put in a call to Filasi Equipment. A man's voice crackled through the phone. "Bon Jour, Equipage Filasi."

Strange that it was a male; there had always been a female receptionist when he'd called before.

"Bon Jour, this is Peter Dornblaser. I would like to leave a message for Dr. Calvert. I believe he will be arriving via helicopter in about an hour with the first of our trailers."

"Ah... Oui, Monsieur Dornblaser. What is the message that you would like to give to Dr. Calvert?"

"Just a name: 'Kriouche.'"

"Monsieur Peter, I must tell you, that there were Americans here two times, asking many questions. They too asked for this man Kriouche. The name is Tunisian, is it not?"

"Yes, I believe so."

"We are afraid here. I sent the secretaries home. We don't want any trouble."

"Why do you think there could be some trouble?"

"Because, the first Americans asked questions about when you were coming back. The second ones were different men, and asked about the first group, and about you. They also asked about this man Kriouche."

"Okay, I understand. Would you please just have Doctor Calvert call the camp the moment he arrives?"

"But of course Monsieur, Dornblaser."

"Thanks. Good bye."

ȣ.ȣ

"Sir, Dornblaser just called Equipage Filasi. He confirmed that Calvert is on that chopper. He wanted the manager to give Calvert a message when he arrived: 'Kriouche.' I got the impression that they're worried about him. We're all set in Algiers to pounce on Calvert the second he steps off that bird."

Mitchell was pondering his options in the event they didn't recover the plutonium. Cover-ups were a dangerous game, but his ass was really in the sling if the boys upstairs found out he'd let the situation go as far as it had. He made his decision.

"Look Carlson, I want a full operation, starting now. I don't dare be discreet any longer. I can't risk that we lose that stuff. Detain Dr. Calvert in our safe house and fully interrogate. As soon as we have Calvert, the ground team moves in and takes the camp. I want Dornblaser interrogated there, immediately."

"Yes sir, I'm on my way back down to the ops room right now to take care of it." As Elliot was hanging up, Mitchell screamed into the phone:

"And No Fuck-Ups!"

ȣ.ȣ

Pete threw his duffel into the bed of the Mercedes beside Salil's. Salil was topping off the tank with diesel fuel when Khalem rushed over. Khalem looked shaken. Pete had never seen him like that. The guards at the wadi crossing hadn't made their hourly radio check and attempts to raise them had yielded nothing.

"Who were the sentries?"

"Mektar and Ali."

Oh God, not the man's youngest son.

Pete knew that there was no use saying perhaps the radio had just gone out. Their eyes met and locked.

"Khalem, we're leaving now, do you want to go with us?"

"My charges are here. I will stay."

Pete was tempted to order Khalem to accompany them. No. That will just draw more attention to the plutonium, he thought. The stuff is well camouflaged as a battery. I'll chance it.

Pete scribbled a quick note explaining the Kriouche revelation to Howard, and handed it to Khalem. "Howard should be calling within the hour. Khalem, your job, after I drive out, is to protect the people here. If the Americans come, tell them the plutonium is with Dr. Calvert. If they want to take anything, let them. We're going to drive past the checkpoint. I'll see what's up with Mektar, and radio from there. By the way, when the dust settles, let Hasef go."

"Comme te vieu."

Pete was thinking that he couldn't drag any more human lives into their mess. He had to have Salil with him to make it to Algiers, but the plutonium was his responsibility.

"Khalem, it's been a pleasure to know you and your family. I wish you the best." "You and Doctor Calvert are good people. You will always be welcome here." "Thank you Khalem. I will come back here someday."

Pete buckled his seat belt and placed his Motorola on the dash. He put the forty-five in his lap. They drove out of Wadi Nouveau heading south. The 'road' was hardly discernible in most places, with the recently shifted sands obscuring the track across the flat bedrock. They had mounted posts, four meters high, every kilometer, all the way to the next wadi. One could see the next post from the last, and thus navigate across the plain without getting lost. It would be twenty minutes to the wadi crossing. He found his thoughts drifting to what would happen next. He was running logistical strategies through his head: what he would do when they reached Tinnhert, then the flight to Algiers, what he would say to the police if they questioned him....

Salil was softly crying and beginning to tremble. "Salil, what is going on? What is the matter?"

"Monsieur Pete, I am going to die."

"Salil, calm down. Everything is going to be fine. Certainly for you at least. Wait till we get to Algiers and you'll see."

"No, I will not make it to Algiers, I am going to die now."

"What are you talking about?"

"Ever since I touched the little boat, I have dreams. In the day and the night. I know you do too. And Monsieur Howard. The boat comes to me. It has shown to me what is going to happen to you. The ugly tower in the river. And to me, it has spoken that I will pass before I leave here. It says it laments this. But, that I do not believe."

Pete was speechless. He knew Salil was right.

⋙⋘

The sky crane gently set the computer trailer down in the fenced compound of Equipage Filasi and two yard hands disengaged the lift hook. The big helicopter then maneuvered over the pad and landed. As the pilot killed the rotors and started systems-shut-down, they looked up in surprise at the three Ford vans barreling towards them. The vans screeched to a stop just outside the rotor radius and a dozen men armed with Uzis jumped out and circled the Sikorsky. An American-looking man in a blue windbreaker approached the crew cabin and threw the door open. Pointing his Uzi at the pilots, he shouted: "Where is Dr. Calvert?"

"Don't shoot! He's in the aft cabin!"

Agents entered the rear cabin from both sides.

Howard Steven Calvert, P.H.D., was not in the helicopter.

⋙⋘

The bandits had mounted up and begun to ride out of the wadi, when one of their own came at a full gallop back to them. He rode right up to the tall, thin leader and blurted out that a truck was coming.

"Only one?," questioned Barkoui.

"Oui, just one."

This new development took him by surprise. They were prepared to make a post-sundown raid on the camp. After finding the radio with the bodies of the sentries, he was afraid he'd been a little hasty with the gunfire. Now they'd sent someone to check. That was okay. They could take the truck, no problem. Yes. They would kill the driver and use the truck in the attack. His hands were as good as around Dornblaser's throat, holding him down in the water tank. He formulated the attack plan and positioned the band in the rocks.

❧❧

"Sir, I think you'd better get down here right away."

"Carlson, what happened?"

"Calvert wasn't on the chopper, and a truck just left the camp, heading south."

"Godammit! I'm on my way."

❧❧

Four unmarked Apache attack helicopters lifted off of the deck of the U.S.S. John F. Kennedy. Practically skimming the wave tops, they sped toward the coastline west of Algiers. Once over land, they stayed low, on a beeline for Wadi Nouveau.

❧❧

Salil tried to pull himself together and attempted radio contact with Khalem.

Nothing.

What the hell? These things work better than this.

"Monsieur Pete, do you want me to try to call to Mektar on the other channel?"

"Better not, Salil. If there's trouble there, it's better not to announce our arrival."

They were driving down the ravine to the wadi crossing. Suddenly, gunfire erupted all around them. Instinctively, Pete hit the brakes. In half a moment he thought better of it and tried to get the truck moving again, but they were surrounded by Bedouins wielding machine guns. An AK47 was thrust through the window into Pete's face.

"Donnes nous Vos Armes!"

They both froze. A hand reached in the window and took the radio from the dash and the forty-five from Pete's lap. The passenger door was thrown open and there stood a familiar face.

Frank Zappa of the Sahara.

He dragged Salil from the cab and took a few steps back. As he raised his gun, Salil called out in anguish. "Ho! Mondieu No! Aiole Moi!"

What followed was nightmarish. Barkoui fired the AK and Salil was thrown back against the Mercedes, his blood splattering across Pete's face.

Barkoui stood over Salil's body and fired a coup de grace into his skull.

"Infidel!" The other Bedouins shouted their approval. Pete's head was spinning. He had never seen anyone killed before. From where he sat, he could only see Salil's feet and legs on the ground. His friend was dead. The bastard had killed his friend. He could feel the truck shift around as Bedouins climbed into the bed. He watched through the rear-view mirror as two of them dumped the contents of Pete and Salil's duffels out onto the sand. Another cut away the rope holding the sleeping bags around Mihalis. The man let out a cry of surprise and called Barkoui to see his discovery.

Barkoui looked startled, then triumphant: Dornblaser is the one. The pilot. We will get him to water. Drown him. The water tank at the camp. He has a debt to pay. Revenge for my brothers!. He climbed into the passenger seat of the truck and jabbed the barrel of the AK into Peter's cheekbone, drawing blood.

"Turn the truck around, we will return to your camp."

Complying, Pete pulled the Mercedes forward and swung a wide 180 in the sand. Driving past Salil's lifeless body, Pete felt rage.

The Bedouins had mounted their horses and filed out ahead of the lumbering truck. In the mirror, Pete could count four remaining in the bed. They were pointing at Mihalis and speaking rapidly. So far, they had totally ignored the battery. He could feel Barkoui's eyes pouring over him. The man kept his gun trained on Pete's temple.

He had to do something.

They rounded a bend in the narrow defile and Pete noticed the men on horseback shift left around a refrigerator-size block of sandstone. On his way in, he'd had to swing the Mercedes out around it.

Okay, Motherfucker.

He turned to Barkoui and spit in his face. "You know what you are? You're just another bullshit Arab coward. Real, true, bullshit."

Barkoui went off. He struck Pete again and again with the gun barrel. Blood began to stream down into his right eye. The rock was twenty meters away. Barkoui didn't notice that the truck was picking up speed.

The warning shouts from the back came too late and Pete rammed the rock head on. The impact threw him hard against the shoulder belt. Barkoui went right through the windshield. The four in the back were launched forward and landed in the same cloud of dust as Barkoui.

Pete jumped from the truck and ran to the pile of men. He grabbed up an AK and fumbled with the safety. Barkoui was rising from the pile, blood running from the gashes in his face. He knocked him onto his back with a burst from the rifle. Barkoui looked up at him, hate burning in his eyes. "You should always wear your seat belt you cocksucker!" Pete let him have it with a sustained blast from the AK. That's for Salil you bastard.

The men on horseback wheeled their Arabians around and started charging back towards him, firing as they came. Bullets plowed into the sand all around him and he ran for shelter behind the truck. Suddenly a strange voice came into his head.

touch me

The first Bedouin to make it to the truck dismounted and came running around the passenger side. Pete discharged the clip of the AK and the man went down in a mist of blood.

touch me

Two more had now dismounted and were cautiously approaching from each side of the truck. Pete threw the AK at the one on the driver side, breaking the man's jaw. They now charged their defenseless prey.

touch me now

He stared through the wooden slats of the truck bed. The bow of Mihalis stuck out from the cover of the sleeping bags and gleamed in the sun. It was calling out to him. It was going to protect him. He reached for it through the slats. Flame projected from the gun barrel of the Arab closest to him and stopped. The burst of flame was frozen. There was no sound. The man's face was glaring his hatred and intensity, but it was frozen. Pete could now see the bullet. It spun it's way ever so slowly towards him through the flame. It was like the reverse of the dream. It was no longer a drop of water falling from him to the floor. Now it was a bullet, coming towards him. Its approach was slow to the point of being comical. But the danger was real. He could sense it. He just wished that he had never come here. He wished that he was home.....

now

He put his hand on the bow of Mihalis and had the sensation of falling through a plate-glass window. He was falling. Falling with broken glass all around him. No. The glass was him. He was breaking. Into a billion pieces. Suddenly a giant flash went off from where he had fallen.

Then, nothing.

The pilots of the approaching helicopters were blinded by the flash. Even before they regained their vision they knew there would be no outrunning the shock wave. They were twelve kilometers from ground zero. As fast as they could, they set the birds down in the sand. The special forces operatives leapt out before the landing was completed, ran towards the blast and hit the ground on their bellies. They had their heads toward the choppers. When the shock wave hit them, they saw it topple three of the four Apaches. Twenty seconds later, it hit the camp at Wadi Nouveau. Khalem and the others watched the ground ripple in concentric waves as the fireball rose into the sky. They knelt facing the east and prayed to Allah. Then they took Hasef out behind camp and hacked him to bits with their swords.

The Legionnaires and the government inspection team saw the fireball turn into a huge mushroom cloud before they too were hit by the shock wave.

The man's shirtsleeves were rolled up to his elbows and he was short of breath. "Major Mitchell, sir, you'd better take a look at this."

He removed a large photo from an oversize manila envelope and laid it on the table in the Ops room. "Sir, S.S.A. says this is an atomic mushroom cloud, fifty plus kiloton range."

Holy God. Mitchell turned to Elliot who was loosening his tie.

"I'll be in my office. I want an update every fifteen minutes, new developments or not. Understood?"

"Yes sir."

Mitchell had to make a phone call. He wasn't looking forward to it.

Time to face the music.

CHAPTER 4 — WEST VIRGINIA

Esmeralda Dornblaser was running late. Her 28 students would be on time. She would be late.

Damn.

It was all because she always tried to do too much. Always had too many commitments. This particular morning she was late because she had been making phone calls on behalf of the West Virginia River Coalition. It was important work. Somebody had to stay on top of it.

Esmy was a tall good-looking woman in her late fifties, with the extra pounds that always seem to come with middle age. Streaks of gray peaked through her dark hair. Every time Ben noticed more gray hairs, he joked that she must be worried about her youngest.

She had risen at six, bathed, dressed, and had coffee and toast. She had begun making calls at seven thirty. She had started with the people she knew would be getting ready to leave for work. As the minutes rolled by, she switched over to those who would be just arriving at their desks.

Benjamin, her husband, had Tuesdays off and didn't have to go into his office. Esmy, however, had a nine o'clock Art History class to teach. It was across town at the Creative Arts Center.

She was going to be late.

Esmy and Ben lived in South Park, an old residential neighborhood in Morgantown, West Virginia. They had lived in their home for what now seemed a lifetime. It was a big, rambling brick house, half a block off of Grand Street. They had bought the old place back in the sixties, restored it, steadily improved it, and raised their children in it. It was too comfortable to ever leave. It was home.

Their oldest child, Jonathan, had graduated from WVU and gone on to medical school at Georgetown. He was now an orthopedic surgeon in Connecticut.

Their second, Elizabeth, had been more the artsy type and after a stint in Denver with a theater group, had settled down somewhat and was managing a computer graphics production house in San Francisco.

Ben was content with his administrative duties at WVU. And she was happy enough teaching. They had both accepted long ago that this was all there was to be to their lives.

Esmy caught herself running through this last again. Modern people in a modern world, acquiring a status quo in the rat-race. Content with an achieved level of success. No longer desiring to ascend. Secure enough not to have to worry about dropping one single rung back down the ladder. People who would live out their lives in such a manner.

Then there was Peter Simon, their youngest. So wild and crazy.

So often Esmy almost broke into tears at the merest thought of him. Just when it seemed he had actually started to settle down, had married Angela (how she had battled with him to stop running around and finally marry that sweet child), and at last had his paddling school up and running, the lawsuit had blown it all apart. Pete's world had fallen like a house of cards.

What a nightmare it had all been. Angela had dropped him like a hot potato, and had never spoken to her or Ben again. Peter Simon had lost everything, including so much of his spark. And now he was away in Africa.

At least he was with Howard. Thank the Lord for Howard. He was by far the sanest of Petey's friends.

Briefcase in hand, she headed for the carport. "Ben, I'm leaving. See you at six."

As she reached for the door handle of the Subaru, she saw something out of the corner of her eye. Looking up, she saw a man, covered with blood, lying crumpled in the drive behind the car, beside him, a kayak wrapped up in a sleeping bag.

Peter Simon!

He woke with his mother's hand stroking his hair, her tears falling onto his face. His head was throbbing. He couldn't see anything but a dark blur.

"Salil!"

He heard his father. "Jesus Christ. I'm going to call an ambulance."

"No, Dad. Wait. Don't call anybody."

"Peter, you're all bloody?"

"Yeah. I'm, not really sure. But don't call anyone."

While he showered, his mother cried in the living room and his father stood in the bathroom doorway asking him questions. The blood washed away. He felt around his face. There were no cuts. He stepped out of the shower and looked at himself in the mirror. He recalled the pain of being hit with the gun barrel, but the mirror revealed no wounds. Studying the reflection of his face, he realized that all the old scars were missing too.

"I'm waiting, Peter."

So, as best he could, he told his father what had happened. When he got to the part about the attack, there remained the mystery of his arrival in Morgantown.

"How in the hell did you get here? You've got the dates mixed up or something. According to your story, all this happened around two thirty in the afternoon, Algerian time, today. That means it all just took place. An hour ago. This is crazy, Peter. It doesn't add up."

"So what do you think, Dad? That it really happened a couple of days ago? That I got on some plane all covered with blood and flew back here?"

Ben was running it all through his head. Peter was in trouble. Big trouble. And he was giving him some horseshit story.

While Pete shaved, Ben gathered up his blood splattered clothes, and headed for the basement. He put them in the washing machine and started it. His son had been involved in some kind of violence. Like it or not, he had to cover Peter's butt. Destroy any evidence. He picked up Pete's boots. One slipped out of his hand and fell to the floor. Grains of sand slid from the boot onto the carpet.

ॐ◆ॐ

George Mitchell sat at a large conference table. Present were his boss, Warren Savitsky, an undersecretary to the Director, and James Rainforth from the State Department.

Warren was a very low-profile person. Almost as though he didn't exist. He never had, and would never have to do anything like testify in front of the Senate. He was a professional career spook.

Rainforth had made a quick trip across the Potomac for the meeting. He was Mister Plausible Deniability. He would take the news personally to the President. Neither yet knew what was up. But they both knew that it wasn't good.

"Gentlemen, we have a crisis to deal with." Mitchell laid the photo on the conference table. "At 2:17 P.M., local time, there was a nuclear detonation in the Sahara Desert in central Algeria. We were trying to recover some plutonium that had been illegally removed from the country. Something happened. We're not sure what, or how, but there was this explosion," he said pointing to the photo. "It was a Damn big one."

Mitchell's words weren't coming out the way he wanted them to. He wondered to himself: Are there any small nuclear explosions?

"George, are we linked to this?"

"I'm afraid so, Jim. We've got our frigging hands in the cookie jar. There are three company Apaches down, close to ground zero. The Algerian government, I should say the French Foreign Legion, has fourteen of our people and a lot of questions. We flew out as many people as we could on a fourth chopper. I believe we can count on those left behind not to talk. But, we have a lot to explain to the rest of the world."

Warren wasn't saying anything, as if he knew that Mitchell had not yet let the real cat out of the bag.

Rainforth thought for a moment and said: "It seems fairly straightforward to me. Some Islamic faction takes some plutonium from us and we try to get it back, and it blows up in their faces. We were just trying to get it back, right?"

"That's the problem. No. It was two of our civilians that took it out."

"What!?" Rainforth was incredulous. Savitsky smiled grimly.

"Let me explain."

⊱•⊰

Pete slept most of the afternoon. Esmy cried. Ben went over his son's story, again and again, looking for some logical explanation. There was none.

Pete woke at six and went downstairs. While Ben prepared some snacks and drinks, Esmy clicked on the ABC evening news. She liked Peter Jennings and tuned in every day, even in the summer.

"Good evening. There was a nuclear explosion in Algeria today, and there is evidence that the United States is somehow connected to it. We go now to Algeria for this report."

The picture shifted to an aerial view of the Sahara shot from a moving plane. The tape showed a huge crater of blackened sand and little else. The voice had a French accent.

"This is the site of what was estimated to have been a fifty kiloton, above-ground nuclear explosion. Although details at the moment are still tentative, there seems to have been some American involvement."

The image of three helicopters lying on their sides, rotors bent, now filled the screen. Several trucks bearing French Foreign Legion insignia surrounded the choppers. Armed soldiers were standing guard.

"These helicopters were encountered less than ten miles from the site of the explosion, and have been identified as U.S. Apache Attack Warships. Fourteen U.S. special forces are being detained by the Algerian government."

Peter Jennings came back on. "We now go to a taped statement by spokesperson Felicia Lourdes, from the U.S. State Department."

Ms. Lourdes appeared to be a very serious-minded woman in her late thirties. She was wearing a navy blue vested suit. She read a prepared statement, rarely looking up at the cameras.

"At approximately two-thirty P.M., local time today, in Algeria, there was what we suspect was an above-ground atomic event. The U.S. Central Intelligence Agency was in the early stages of the finalization of recovering an unspecified amount of weapons grade plutonium at the time of the detonation. The bomb grade material had been illegally exported to Algeria by two Americans, presumably to be employed in a private research project. Due to the anomaly, the extraction team was compelled to make a controlled flight into terrain which resulted in the uncontained blade liberation in three of the four reconnaissance vehicles utilized in the operation.

"Although the mission is being viewed as an incomplete success, the repatriation of American personnel is expected within hours, and on-site collateral damage appears to have been limited to the death of one of the two Americans. This statement will be amplified when additional details become available."

The news program now returned to Peter Jennings at the news desk. "The American in charge of the research project was Dr. Howard Calvert from the Davis campus of the University of California. Dr. Calvert reportedly parachuted from an airplane to avoid arrest in Algiers. A massive manhunt for him is underway in the Sahara. The other American involved is a West Virginia man named Peter Dornblaser. Dornblaser is presumed to have been killed in the blast.

"Anti-American protests caused authorities in Algiers to impose an eleven P.M. curfew in Algiers a short while ago. Larger protests are expected tomorrow.

"In Sarjevo, the war crimes tribunals of ...."

Ben clicked off the T.V. and gulped down the rest of his drink.

"Well, son, this sure seems to have topped all of your other misadventures. What do we do now?"

The phone rang.

"I'm not here."

❧

Elliot Carlson already didn't like Algeria and he'd only been there for twelve hours.

Damn Mitchell. It wasn't like this mess was his fault. He had done everything he was supposed to have done. It had just gone critical too fast.

Elliot was 32. He'd been recruited by the C.I.A. his senior year at Dartmouth. Every year when the agency came to recruit, there were student protests. However, he found the idea of serving his country in such a manner highly stimulating. He hadn't been disappointed.

His first two years had been spent working as a Foreign Service Officer. He'd been stationed in India, Korea, and Peru. Then, as a field agent, he had risen steadily through the ranks. He had seen crises come, and pass by. Communism was less and less of a threat to national security. He had decided to specialize in Islamic affairs. To Elliot, and many others at the agency, Islamic fanaticism was the predominant threat to world peace, and would remain so for a long time to come.

There were thousands of agents working in the Islamic division. There was plenty to be done. They were always trying to run down leads on individual terrorist cells before they struck. When Mitchell had handed him the Calvert case, he had jumped at the opportunity. It was a backwards affair. It wasn't like most cases: when would the kids play with the matches? It was: when would the kids realize there were matches to play with? And which kids?

Now he wasn't a happy camper. He was playing "chambermaid." It was up to him to clean up the mess. Damage control. Bring the guilty to face justice. Dornblaser was vapor. Calvert was his prey, and was proving elusive.

Elliot had started by analyzing the statements of the Sky Crane pilots. There was little doubt that Dr. Calvert had been on that chopper. He had had with him a box and a duffel bag. Either could have contained a parachute. The pilots had been a little spooked. Both swore they had never seen the 'door open' light flash on in the cockpit. Both had stated that it would be extremely risky to jump with the trailer dangling below. Agency sources concurred on that. A quick check had revealed that Calvert had no traceable parachuting experience. The pilots stated that the mean altitude during the flight had been a little under a thousand feet; pretty low for a jump considering the trailer. Nothing had come up in the ground search. He was running out of leads.

Then he'd gone to Equipage Filasi. His driver had taken a circuitous route through the outskirts of the city to avoid protests. Two more trailers had been airlifted in and impounded.

Upon arrival, he'd been prevented from entering while the police checked his diplomatic credentials with the embassy. After the credentials had been verified, they made him wait another half hour for good measure. The compound was swarming with Algerian officials, soldiers, and police.

Elliot was introduced to Major Antoine Mahklouf, who was to let him look, but not touch. Mahklouf led him to an outer office. As they entered, a slender man in his fifties rose stiffly from a chair and extended his hand.

"Dr.Anders Lieb."

"I'm Elliot Carlson, U.S. Embassy, protocol attaché."

"Mr. Carlson, I have something I would like you to read."

Lieb handed him a document with a Federal District Court letterhead. It was an affidavit sworn by Calvert in front of a district court judge named Clemens in Sacramento. The affidavit authorized Lieb to administer the disposition of all contents of the trailers upon their release by the two governments. It was dated April 28, 1998; three months ago. There was another sheet on which Calvert had inventoried the contents and identified the owners in instances where equipment had been rented.

Elliot's mind was racing.

He recognized Lieb from a report he had received on Calvert's source of the plutonium. Lieb had been the main contact Calvert had used to get through the chain of command at Northern Diversified Dynamics. But how did he get here so fast? Was Calvert planning to disappear? And the date of the affidavit; just before Calvert and Dornblaser left the states to come here. How did Calvert know then that he would need the type of assistance that Lieb was now here to lend?

"What is your relationship with Dr. Calvert?"

"We are good friends. I headed the physics department at Davis before Howard arrived. After I retired, I assisted him in some of his research there."

"You were aware he was using plutonium in his project?"

"Yes, I was."

"I don't see the plutonium listed in the inventory."

"Howard was concerned with all the equipment being seized if the plutonium was in the trailers. Mr. Dornblaser was to bring it overland and hand it over to your people here."

"Dr. Lieb, as we both know, plutonium doesn't just blow up. Do you have an explanation?"

Anders sighed and looked down at the floor. "I've been thinking about that from the moment I heard about the explosion."

"And?"

"I have no idea."

"What would you say if I told you that I am not alone in thinking that Dr. Calvert built a nuclear device, and it blew up in his face, or to be more specific, Dornblaser's?"

"That is impossible."

"Nothing's impossible, and under the circumstances, I would say it's probable. I want to have a look inside the trailers. Come with me. Please."

Major Mahklouf accompanied them, eying them both suspiciously. They first examined the main computer trailer. It was meticulously organized. Elliot's eyes immediately locked on the small crate with HazMat stickers. "Major Mahklouf, would you please open this?"

The major had one of the guards bring a hammer and pried the top from the crate. Inside it was only an assortment of hardware. "What do you make of this, Dr. Lieb."

"Most likely a ruse. They must have wanted the personnel in their camp to think it held the plutonium."

There is plenty this man is not telling me, thought Elliot.

"When was the last time you spoke with Dr. Calvert?"

"Mr. Carlson, you haven't jurisdiction to place me under arrest here. My answers to your questions will be at my discretion. I do not wish to answer that question."

"You are correct, Dr. Lieb. I don't have the jurisdiction to arrest you, here."

Elliot looked around. Everything seemed to be in place. They would go over all of it with a fine toothed comb the second they had it in the states.

Next, they inspected the auxiliary computer trailer. Compared to the other, it was a mess. They filed down the narrow hallway, peering into the various rooms. The second was a bedroom. Elliot was guessing that it was Dornblaser's. A quick scan of the room's contents gave him the impression that the occupant had packed quickly. On the shelf by the door were dozens of what looked to be the foil tops of cigarette packs twisted up like little candies, jet fighter planes, or birds. A nervous habit, though it revealed an ordered and disciplined trait. More like Calvert than Dornblaser, thought Elliot, based on what he'd read in the briefs. But Calvert didn't smoke. It was Dornblaser's room all right. Then he noticed the three rolls of film amongst the wrapped pieces of foil. Mahklouf and Lieb had their back to him as they continued down the narrow hallway and he quickly scooped up the rolls and slipped them into his blazer pocket.

The third trailer hadn't fared well on the flight in. A refrigerator had tipped over and vials of drugs were broken and spilled out on the floor. In one of the rooms there was an eye bolt sticking out of the floor. Elliot found that odd, but said nothing. Anders occasionally glanced at his inventory but didn't say much during the inspection of the trailers.

They stepped outside into the blazing sun and Mahklouf motioned two guards back in front of the door.

"Very few clues, Mr. Carlson."

"Yes, I'm afraid there's little to go on here. Dr. Lieb, what do you think about the possibility that Calvert committed suicide by jumping from the helicopter?"

"Absurd. Howard was very dedicated to this project. It is his life's work."

"Maybe he just couldn't face dealing with espionage charges."

"Howard isn't afraid of that. He knows they won't stick. Besides, he is fearless. You know he's a kayaker? And a very good one at that. The type of rivers that Howard descends are no place for the timid."

"We have done thorough background checks on both Calvert and Dornblaser. Yes, I know they are both kayakers, for what it's worth."

"Mr. Carlson, 'for what it's worth,' never underestimate a water man, a true kayaker. There is something about them. Something they learn, something they glean from the currents. They will run circles around you."

"Well then, what do you think happened to Calvert?"

"I'll tell you what I think. I don't believe that either one of them is dead."

Elliot laughed. "Surely Dornblaser. All the people in camp confirmed that he was driving the truck. We have photos from space of the truck nearing ground zero, minutes before the blast. Dornblaser is dead."

"Very well then. You seem to be sure of what you know to be the truth. Mr. Carlson, let's speak frankly for a moment. You are not who you claim to be. Our government wouldn't send someone from the embassy to head the investigation of an atomic explosion on foreign soil. What are you really? CIA?"

Lieb was sharp, thought Elliot. That was okay. Sometimes with people like him you had to let it all hang out if you wanted to get anywhere.

"Yes, I'm from the agency. Look, this thing is really bad for our image. Calvert makes us seem to be out of it. I believe that his project was legit and that he had no intention of letting the plutonium slip into hostile hands. But still. Mainly, I'm here to make sure that it all went up in smoke. To do that, I have to talk to Calvert."

"I am sure that when that moment arrives, it will be of Howard's choosing, and not yours."

"By the way Dr. Lieb, does the name Farid Kriouche ring any bells?"

"Yes. Kriouche is a Tunisian working at Davis in the same department as Howard. Not very dedicated, either, if I might say so. Sort of a nasty fellow. Why do you ask?"

"Just curious."

∂❧

The phone rang constantly. His brother and sister had both called. All their relatives and many friends had called. All offered condolences and asked hesitant questions. Ben and Esmy fell into a pattern of saying that nothing was confirmed and that there would be no memorial service planned until it was. Esmy was crying enough to ward off any suspicions.

Pete thought about what had happened. The surreality of it all began to sink in. Then he remembered those last seconds in Africa.

While his parents were still on the phones, he slipped out through the kitchen door into the back yard. It was a hot, sticky, West Virginia summer night. The cicadas droned away in the trees. Although there were houses to either side of theirs, the back yard sloped away and merged into the forested hollow below. Outside of the reach of the porch light, it was dark. Though the stars shone brilliantly above, little of their light pierced the canopy of trees. He needed to think. There was a spot at his parents' house that he was always drawn to for moments like this.

Pete walked out to the kayak rack he had built so many years before. Kayaks weren't allowed in front of the house. Esmy didn't want the place looking like "Tobacco Road." So many memories of days on the river were held in the old kayaks lining the rack. Most were battered to the point of being unusable, but to Pete, they were treasured relics. Ben had dragged Mihalis, still wrapped in sleeping bags around back and deposited it on the ground by the kayak rack.

the sand tower must be destroyed

Pete felt a sensation like an LSD flashback. He was kayaking. A raging current hurtled him forward. Looming ahead of him was a dark obelisk. He was too harried by the rapids to look up enough to see its highest reaches. The water forced him to concentrate. The kayak was Mihalis.

He couldn't believe it. It wasn't real. Something inside him told him that it was. He had to run, escape. The cyclone was drawing him in. There was no way out.

❧

It was a short hop from Wadi Nouveau to the dig site. In the air, Elliot had a different perspective from what he had seen in the SSA photos. It was big, about a thousand meters across. To the west, flat table tops of bedrock protruded from the encroaching dune. The encircling wall of the ruins abutted into the table tops. The dark color of the stone in the wall contrasted with the lighter colored natural rock. Within the perimeter of the ruins were several large structures that he imagined were the tops of some larger complex, buried in the sand. It was wrong, he thought, to call it a ruins. Everything seemed perfectly preserved, but the sand was in the process of shifting back over the site. There was a perceivable difference from the photos that had been shot only days before. Soon, it would be totally concealed. The security man at Calvert's camp had said that sandstorms were now arriving daily after dusk, each stronger than the last.

The Legionnaires looked up from their posts at the circling helicopter. Elliot didn't want to deal with them today. He wouldn't land. Instead, he took advantage of the opportunity to study as much as he could of the ancient city below.

❧

The phone had rung all evening and Ben and Esmy had never had to lie so many times in their entire lives.

On the eleven o'clock news, Channel Four in Pittsburgh had run the atomic blast as its lead story. It also ran taped footage of Islamic demonstrations from around the Arab world, denouncing the great Satan, burning American flags, promises of vengeance. Now there were claims that dozens of innocent Bedouins had also perished in the explosion. Pete thought to himself that this could never be confirmed. There would be absolutely nothing left of his attackers at ground zero.

A West Virginia University faculty photo of Howard flashed on the screen with the report that he was still on the run.

"Also presumed dead in the blast is a Morgantown, West Virginia man named Peter Dornblaser who was working with Dr. Calvert. Dr. Calvert purportedly knew Dornblaser from his years of teaching and research in Morgantown at West Virginia University.

"The U.S. State Department is downplaying the incident, claiming it was an independent research project of which the department had no knowledge.

Only when it became known that the project involved weapons-grade plutonium, illegally removed from the United States, did the C.I.A. attempt a recovery mission which has been termed an 'incomplete success.'"

The phone rang again. Esmy picked it up and said hello. After listening for a few seconds, she covered the mouthpiece and handed it to Pete. "It's Howard."

"Listen, I'll call you tomorrow at nine, where I used to get you in the evenings." He hung up.

"What did he say?"

"Howard is going to call me tomorrow somewhere else. I've got to sneak out and get the call."

"Peter Simon, where is Howard?"

"He didn't say. Look, Mom, I'm in trouble. It's best that you and Dad know as little as possible. People are going to ask questions and it will be easier to protect us if you and Dad don't know the details."

Ben looked perturbed and sank deeper into his chair.

"Son, it would be an understatement to say that Esmy and I are upset about all of this. I think if the circumstances were any different, we would insist that you go to the authorities. It is not easy to accept the reality of what happened, but it has happened. Now we have to react as rationally as possible. It sounds to me like you could end up spending the rest of your life in jail. None of us want that. I think that if the authorities get wind that you are here, they will come for you immediately. I anticipate that the paper is going to send somebody over for a story in the morning. Friends and neighbors are going to drop in. I don't like the idea of you going out to receive this call either."

Esmy was getting more upset listening to Ben.ss "It's true Peter, there is going to be some slip up and you're going to get caught. It's just a matter of time."

"Mom, all I need is a few days to let the dust settle and see what's going to happen. I'll be careful. I promise."

"Let's hope so son," Ben said. "I'm going to call it a night."

కుండ

The chopper dropped Elliot off at the helipad on the roof of the embassy. Running down two flights of steps, he entered the hastily arranged Ops room. Several agents were glued to the T.V., and one pointed at a chair. The news story, broadcast in French, shifted from a videotape of Islamic protests in downtown Algiers, to a live press-conference. At the podium was General Pierre Monserrat of the French Foreign Legion. He read a prepared statement into an array of microphones. Elliot's French wasn't fluent enough to follow what was being said.

"What's he saying?"

"Good news for us. The F.F.L. is saying that after a thorough investigation, they have determined that the Bedouins killed in the blast were the same ones that massacred the dig team. It's going to defuse the protests from all but the hard-line fundamentalists."

"That's where our problems always come from, but this is good news anyway." Elliot turned to an envelope on the table with his name on it. He pulled out three packages of color prints and started going through them. After looking at a dozen or so photos he exclaimed to himself that they were nothing but pictures of rocks. They were interestingly shaped rocks, but rocks nonetheless. Continuing, he came to some flash shots. These were of a cavern. Then there was a shot all washed out by something reflecting the flash back at the lens. Next were shots of a canyon wall, shot from a distance. At first Elliot thought they were of the same cliffs and then noticed the different orientation of the sunlight. They were shots of the bowl to the east of Calvert's camp. The next photo revealed a surprising sight. There was a kayak on the rocky ground. A man knelt beside it. He recognized him as Salil DeLys, the young Algerian working with Calvert and Dornblaser. The kayak looked strange. It was transparent. He knew very little about kayaks, but he'd never seen one you could see through.

Why was this kayak there? There was nothing in his intelligence reports that Calvert had taken any kayaks to Algeria with him. There was nowhere to use it. There wasn't any water. They must have found it. Found it in the cave.

Elliot put in a scrambled call to Langley and asked for all photos of the bowl from the past two months to be reviewed for human activity.

Twenty minutes later Andresky called back. There was indeed a space shot which showed two men at the mouth of the pit, with what looked to be a kayak. The same photo pass revealed two men in Arab dress at the southern lip of the bowl, with a third tending their horses eighty meters away.

Elliot put in another scrambled call, this time to Mitchell.

"Sir, things are wrapping up here. I think I should pay a visit to West Virginia."

"Why West Virginia?"

"I have a hunch that Dornblaser, if he wasn't killed, will head that way."

"You're thinking Dornblaser is alive?"

"I'm starting to, sir. I think we should have a P.I.C.S. run on both of them."

"Color it done. By the way, we've gotten hold of a couple of the stones removed from the ruins. I had a call from the lab man we sent over. What he said spooked me a little bit. The stones apparently are made of an unknown element and are more or less indestructible." Mitchell wasn't prone to such strong statements.

"Indestructible, sir?"

"You heard me right, dammit. The lab man is Chapman. That's what he told me. We'll know more later. He's flying out with them tonight. All I can say is that Goddamned city was built to last."

"Do we have anybody inside?"

"We've a Frenchie in there now with the F.F.L.. He's getting all the pictures he can, but at the present rate, the ruins are going to be covered by the dune in less than a week."

"Maybe that's for the best, Sir."

"I know what you mean."

❧❦

Farid Kriouche walked out of the lobby of the Hotel Ejecutif and into the evening breeze. Throngs of people bustled by in both directions, heading home after a long day in the streets of Algiers. Car horns blared everywhere in the snarl. He merged into the mass of people and started to make his way down the street. Though still trembling nervously, he felt safe for the first time in two days.

Everything had gone so terribly wrong. Howard should still have been in the desert, trying to untangle the computer virus, unable to leave. Hasef should have killed them all and delivered the plutonium to Barkoui. He should have had the other half million in his pockets and be heading for Thailand. He would have been a Muslim cult hero, idolized forever. But no. It was all a huge fiasco. The C.I.A. was hunting him and his only hope was that they found him before the Hezbollah Liberation Front did. There would be no returning to Davis, or even Tunis. The H.L.F. would hunt him for the rest of his life. If only he hadn't spent their money, he might have been able to beg their forgiveness. No. He was screwed.

He never knew that the assassin was slipping through the crowd behind him. The silenced pistol made little sound as it pumped the nine-milimeter slug into his brain. He dropped to the pavement as his killer ran into the crowd.

❧❦

Pete slept incredibly well in his old bed and dreamed of kayaking. He had never passed so much time off the water. His dreams told him how much he yearned to return to the rivers.

Wadi Nouveau had sparked his imagination. West Virginia also had a very old sandstone geology, but nothing like Wadi Nouveau. The stone there had been so smooth, so perfectly rounded. What a rush it would be to kayak, full of bounding water.

He awakened to the sound of the phone ringing. Friends of his, and of his parents had been calling continuously. How rich to have people so concerned about your death without having to die. He thought of Tom Sawyer and Huck Finn, watching their own funeral.

He walked downstairs and had a cup of coffee with Ben while Esmy talked on the telephone. It was the same story she'd told a dozen times. Nothing was confirmed, and there would be no service until it was.

The Today Show ran photos from space of the mushroom cloud, the photo of Howard, videotapes of Islamic protests and the news that the protests were subsiding with the revelation that the Bedouins killed had been the murderers of the French archeologists. There was also an interview with an atomic physicist from M.I.T., a Dr. Arthur Barnes. He was saying that the plutonium could not have simply exploded. His theory was that Howard had made a bomb, and that Pete was in the process of delivering it when it went off.

Pete felt himself starting to sweat.

Ben looked at him. "Son, tell me again, if you would please, that that is not what happened over there."

"Dad, even if you don't believe me, you know Howard. Howard wouldn't do anything like that, would he?"

Ben looked worried and relieved at the same time. "No. Howard wouldn't have done that."

CHAPTER 5 — HOWARD'S YEAR

Howard sat in the aft cabin of the sky crane. He had a tight grip on the box and the duffel bag. A million things ran through his head. He was in trouble. Pete was in trouble. Somehow he had to fix everything and get back to his lab at Davis to finish up the project. But how? Everything had become so messy. Then a terrifying thought: what if the authorities seized his hard drives and destroyed the data from the shoot? Even if he made it back to Davis, they could raid his lab at any moment. Thoughts of peaceful days at Clemson came to mind. He turned to the window and was trying to look back at the camp when he suddenly felt himself dissolving into a billion pieces. Then everything went dark.

Howard lay dreaming. The dream, however, was more of a nightmare vision. He was just an observer. He, the observer paddled behind Pete. Pete was in Mihalis. Pete looked different; he was shorter and had brown skin. He was wearing a paddle jacket make of animal hide of some sort. The day was dark and grey and cold. Wisps of snow fell into the river. Pete kept looking back, but not at him. Now another boater appeared beside him, passing him, gaining on Pete. The other boater was tall and slim. Slim yet powerful, breathing hard though his mouth. Now he was practically upon Pete and took a swing with his kayak paddle, the sharpened blade tip opening a gaping wound across Pete's shoulder blade. Pete was stunned by the blow and resulting cut and could hardly lift his right arm to paddle. The rapids sent Pete crashing into the left wall of the canyon and against a river level outcrop of the stone. Dropping his paddle, Pete clung to the cracks in the outcrop and was able to stop there while his attacker was borne downriver cursing, yelling and screaming. A surge in the water carried Mihaliis and Pete up onto the outcrop. Ever weakening from the loss of blood which streamed down his back onto the rear deck of Mihalis, painting the crystal a crimson red, Pete died.

Now Howard's vision shifted to a different time, but once again observing Pete in Mihalis. He was much further upriver, before the city, yes, there was a city in sight downstream of them. A beautiful black woman strode across the rock to the water's edge, and beckoned him to stop. Pete stepped out of Mihalis and pulled it up onto the stone ledge. Pete was tall and black, a gilded sword scabbarded across the back of his reed life vest. Mihalis seemed to be calling out to him but Pete paid no heed. The tower must fall, it cried in muted voice that fell on ears deafened by the black siren now disrobing on the rocks. The tower was bad, created by evil will for an evil deed. It could only be taken down by ramming into it with the boat, the crystal boat. He was kayaking behind Pete in the canyon. The canyon opened up and the tower loomed ahead. Pete was now Pete again and he was paddling for all he was worth, but he was not in Mihalis....

Howard awakened in a grove of pine trees. Everything was a blur. When he tried to sit up, he was restrained by the shoulder strap of the duffel and had to wrestle free of it. He felt the box against his leg. It was raining and windy. He had a splitting headache and his vision was blurred. He fumbled with the duffel bag and removed a water bottle and drank deeply. He waited for his head to clear and his vision to return. He started to make out cars and trucks passing by, a hundred yards away. Now soaked by the rain, he turned to gather his load and brush off the pine needles. He made his way through the trees and saw an interstate. Howard was dumbfounded and in shock. He was obviously back in the United States. What in the hell.... The only explanation was one that made him sick to his stomach: Mihalis. The vision replaying in his mind, he found himself utterly depressed and confused.

Looking down the road, he could see a green and white sign that told him he was a mile from the Orangeburg exit on Interstate 26. So he was in South Carolina.

Howard climbed over the fence and walked down to the shoulder of the interstate. The noise of the passing traffic hurt his still throbbing head. He could see the tall sign of a Texaco truck stop near the exit and started walking. Aware that he probably looked like a common bum, with his cardboard box and duffel bag, he worried about being spotted by the state police.

Have to stay low-key.

By the time he reached the truck stop he was sweating hard. His guess that it was summertime was confirmed by the newspaper vending machine outside. He stared at the USA Today through the glass. He couldn't believe what he was seeing. It was June 28, 1997. It must be a typo, he thought. No the USA Today doesn't get the dates wrong. He rubbed his eyes and looked again. The date clearly read 1997. Mihalis had taken him exactly one year back in time. He tried to take it all in when he became aware that an older couple was staring at him through the window of the diner. Time to act casual. But acting casual while totally stressed out was not exactly Howard's forte.

Inside, he asked a rather tough looking woman at the fuel desk about the showers.

"You're not a driver, so it'll be six bucks."

He paid with a crisp, hundred dollar bill. While she made change, he reset his watch. It was 9:40 a.m.

The shower felt great. All the water pressure he could want. And hot. As he shampooed, he noticed that he couldn't feel the old scar on his temple. He'd received it kayaking years before. The scar was something he was accustomed to feel daily as he bathed. Now it was gone. Interesting.

Digging into the duffel, Howard retrieved some fresh clothes. Inspecting himself in the mirror, he realized that he still looked out of place; he was still dressed for the desert. Returning to the duffel, he dug deeper until he found a T-shirt to replace the desert khaki button down shirt he had on.

Howard needed a plan and he needed it fast. His encounter with Mihalis had caused a radical shift in his sense of reality and world view. He was in sheer awe of the power it had displayed. He, the scientist, had just been given a front row seat to a practical demonstration of travel through time and space. Now as he sat in a shower room in a truck stop, he was forced to deal with it and all of the complications that came with it. He halted that train of thought. Complications yes, but, grand opportunities as well. Where to start? The beginning.

It came to him that it had been no coincidence that Wadi Nouveau had been swept clean of sand at the time he was looking for a dry riverbed for his project. He had been lured in. Something had had the ability to see and feel across time and space and seek him out.

Mihalis had the myriad abilities required not only to control the weather near it's resting place in the bowl, but also to divine the participation of Pete in his project. There was a link between them. A timeless connection. It all made sense. He could believe it. There was no other explanation. It was fascinating: A link between the environment, technology, and the soul of a man. A contest between good and evil. A game of the highest stakes, where the rules were subject to attrition with each subsequent round that was played. Now Mihalis had called upon him to help even the odds.

But he needed time, and now he had it: an extra year. It would take money too, and lots of it. Howard couldn't use his own money. The"other" Howard would know something was happening if his bank statements suddenly revealed unexplainable withdrawals.

He felt himself coming out of the block of deep thought. One step at a time, Howard, he thought to himself. He turned in the towel and the shower key to the lady at the fuel desk and asked if a taxi could be called out from Columbia. The burly woman gave him a contemptuous look, until she remembered that he had paid her with a hundred dollar bill.

"Nice T-shirt buddy." said the man behind him in line at the register.

"Excuse me?"

"Your shirt", the man said, I guess I won't have to watch any football this fall."

The T-shirt that Howard had put on said"Denver Broncos Super Bowl Champs 1998." The man behind him had been reading the list of all the Bronco's games of the '97/'98 season and post season, complete with the opponents and final scores; none of which had yet been played. Snappy comebacks were Pete's specialty, not his, and he felt himself turning red in the face. He sucked it up and turned to the man, a tough looking guy who was pretty obviously a truck driver."Sometimes you just have to reset your parameters of what you believe to be reality." The driver looked lost and let it drop.

The taxi driver was a young black man, who tried to strike up a conversation by asking questions. Howard fended off curious questions with one word answers. Soon the young man stopped asking.

The scenery was lush and green compared to the Sahara. It was pretty until they reached the outskirts of Columbia with its attendant signs of modern American civilization.

"Where exactly you headed mister?"

Howard looked up in time to see the sign of the Hampton Inn above the coming interchange."Right over there."

Hamptons are rather upscale for an off-the-interstate motel chain and the desk man noticeably raised an eyebrow as Howard entered with his duffel and cardboard box. He paid in advance for two nights with hundred dollar bills. He checked into his room, showered again and had the desk call him another taxi.

The driver this time was a semi-retired Carolina cracker named George. Howard asked him if he knew of a mall with a mens' clothing store, and he took him to Fine's at Columbia Outer Circle. While George waited, Howard spent an hour and close to two thousand dollars on a new wardrobe including a couple of three piece business suits.

During the ride back to the Hampton, Howard made a mental accounting of his remaining cash. He had a little less than eleven thousand dollars. He was going to need a lot more.

"George, excuse me but, what do you know about sports betting here in Columbia?"

ॐॐ

Howard searched through the newspaper wrapping hard drives and discs looking for the sports sections. He laid them out in chronological order and chuckled to himself. He had a nearly complete history of the '97 baseball season.

In the next weeks, his fortunes skyrocketed. He wagered moderately, but constantly on major league baseball. Using due caution, he made several losing wagers with each bookie. Nonetheless, there were a couple of sore losers and one even tried to tail him. Howard lost him by jumping out of his taxi at a mall entrance, and after quickly buying some different clothes, exited the mall in disguise after calling in another taxi from a pay phone. He laughed and thought how Pete would have loved that. He would have to wait almost a year to tell him about it.

Now it was time for a new identity. He couldn't afford to have himself, still working away at Davis, catch wind that there was another Dr. Howard Calvert running around in South Carolina. There was much that would need to be done that required a signature, a driver's license, a social security number, etc.

Working his way through a chain of slick and shifty characters, he was introduced to a young computer whiz named Mouse. The deal was straightforward: $10,000 in advance, in exchange for a systems-accepted, perfectly counterfeited South Carolina driver's license. Howard played computer-dumb, but marveled at the deftness displayed by the diminutive hacker. Via modem from his apartment, Mouse skillfully penetrated the computer system of the South Carolina Department of Motor Vehicles. While they waited for a suitable status change to be entered, Mouse photographed Howard.

Then it came up. A Walterboro man named Joseph Patrick Morton had been killed in a car wreck in Kentucky. His date of birth was listed as 08/14/54, a year younger than Howard. His height and weight were similar and his eyes were blue, like Howard's. It was perfect. At 12:15 P.M., while the D.M.V. was closed for lunch, Mouse deleted the status change. He then put together a genuine looking driver's license.

"Mr. Morton, congratulations. You're ready to enter society."

Howard was now ready to get down to the business at hand. His destination was Clemson. He had done a year of grad work there before taking the job at Intel. The head of the Computer Science Department was James Harrington. Jim had been also worked at Intel, back in New Jersey, but 2 years before Howard had signed on with them. Howard knew that he wasn't the kind of guy apt to ask a lot of questions. All he would have to do was approach him, explain that he was developing an esoteric program and offer to pay for computer time, and Jim would gladly grant him modem access to the powerful IBM system under his control.

Howard was ready financially as well. He now had over $300,000. He would need it. The helmet project was going to be expensive. He needed to buy his own computer system, install it in a workshop, and buy all the components. All the hardware, microchips, shock-hardened CCDs, etc., that he required were very, very pricey.

It was time to get out of Columbia. Joe Morton paid cash for a new Ford Explorer, and the same afternoon left for Clemson.

He checked into a hotel and the next morning began the search for a suitable workshop. He found what he was looking for twenty minutes away in Liberty. Under his Joe Morton identity, he leased a 4,000 square foot metal pole building. It was equipped with a bathroom and shower. He had a four line phone system installed and extra wiring rigged in. He bought a fridge, stove, bed, TV, and office furniture. He made a trip to Atlanta and bought a powerful IBM system with ten million gigabytes of memory capability and supplemental hard drives.

Howard didn't want to pass any more time without kayaking, so he bought a Perception Overflow and a full set of gear at an outfitter shop in Clemson. It wouldn't be the same as kayaking with his custom equipment, but it would be far better than nothing. He knew that the ability to recreate was important to the project. He would need diversion if he didn't want to go stir crazy in the workshop.

Mid-August found him designing the circuitry for the device. The work flowed smoothly for the next several months. He fell into a rhythm of rising late, drinking coffee for a couple of hours while watching CNN, and starting to work around eleven. He would work until four in the afternoon and then take off for a kayak workout until dark at one of two Pickens county fall-line whitewater segments; the nearby Blythe Shoals or Tamassee Slides. Then after dinner out, usually fast food, he would head back to the shop and work until the early hours of the morning.

Throughout this period, he had almost no social contact. He didn't mind. He was thoroughly enmeshed in his work. It was also for the best; he had to lay as low as possible. The only person he spoke with on a regular basis was the UPS man.

He was living in a vacuum. In one sense it was a luxury. He was living a year over again, with all the freedom and privacy to work undisturbed, but it was living in a vacuum nonetheless.

There were no surprises. Each morning he would recognize several of the news stories on CNN from memory. Dark blotches of deja vu. He stopped watching. Howard was also limited in his choice of whom he could talk to. At times he spoke with Harrington, but those conversations were kept to a minimum. Jim was a very busy man and never pressed Howard for details of the project. That was good.

Living and working in such a manner gave him lots of time for deep concentration, mental focus, and long range thought. This was key to the success of the helmet project. The technical demands were immense. But such thought also led him to consider what he was doing.

A year is a lot of time for one to hold an internal moral debate. He believed what Mihalis had told him by way of the visions he had had. There was no reason not to. His very existence there in South Carolina, reliving an entire year, was plenty.

He had concurred with Mihalis that it was not yet time for Pete to know what was going to happen. Pete was rebellious. And as intense and cosmic as he was on the water, his senses would revolt against Mihalis' revelation of his true identity and purpose in life.

But Pete was his best friend. He owed him. Often he would flash back to a time when Pete had saved him: peeling out of his safe eddy on the Upper Blackwater, Pete giving him the stern grab loop of his kayak and battling the current to tow him to shore after a nasty swim, another Class V rapid, studded with death-traps, lurking immediately below. Besides that, he remembered all the good times, all the technical discussion of different facets of the sport, and water itself. So much of what he was now, he owed to Pete.

The visions continued, though most often as waking dreams in the mornings. It explained much of Pete's nature, instinct, and being. Whenever a moment of doubt would come about the truth behind the visions, he merely need remind himself of where he was and what he was doing. Considering that he was there to begin with; back in time a year lent all the dedication and perseverance necessary to complete his task. Pete however, was not there, not back in time a year, without the luxury of time to think out what lay ahead, without a choice. Howard was convinced that he was helping Pete to fulfill his destiny. But did that excuse his silence? And was silence betrayal?

These internal conversations usually took place late at night, the only sound, the steady hum of the computer, the workshop retreating into the shadows from the solitary lamp on the workstation. He realized he was freaking himself out with his thoughts, and always tried to tear himself away from them and concentrate on the project phase at hand.

Howard was pleased with the progress he was making. Mihalis had provided him with what he needed for energy synthesis and teleportation theory. It had recorded the programs for him that last night at Wadi Nouveau.

But as he dug into the programs, he realized that the information they contained was directly limited to its application in altering the space time continuum relative to the perspective of the user of the helmet, and delivering the user to Mihalis, via a signal from Mihalis, in time and space. The program put Mihalis in control. Howard tried several avenues to circumvent this control and each time came to a dead end. At first he didn't understand them at all. Now they were scaring the crap out of him. They dealt with a lot of holographic quantum physics. The first was very complicated but very short. The program was multitrack and created additional tracks as it progresses, but, through compression, used very few megabytes of storage. The decompression algorithm was unique in that it retrieved only specific information from each track and simultaneously discarded the rest from memory, and then repeated.

He felt his respect for Mihalis grow as he realized the quantity of knowledge it was certainly withholding from him. But a burning question remained: Was Mihalis planning to leave Pete? And later call him forth? If that wasn't the plan, then the track and transfer function was a failsafe mechanism. Either way, he had become more determined to find a way to place more control in Pete's hands.

It was obvious to him that he did not have the programming information he needed to give Pete ability to transport himself at will through time and space, and try as he did, he could not find any way to attain it. Maybe it was an attempt by Mihalis to control his movements, and location in time. Maybe that was for the best. Time travel had its dangers.

One night as he sat at the computer, working on the programming which would integrate the three functions of the unit, something came to him, something that would really complete the Moving Water Analysis unit within the helmet. He nicknamed it, the Lazarus function.

The Lazarus function was an override mechanism that would initiate when the unit sensed a potentially dangerous whitewater situation and the"vital signs" sensors in the helmet sensed a prolonged absence of oxygen to the user. The override initiated the teleportation program, but wouldn't transport the user to where Mihalis was in time, that being the location where the danger of drowning existed. Howard already knew he didn't have the programming available to vector the override in space, but estimated that the unit would choose a different, and hopefully safer, time in which to deposit the user. It had to be at random. There was no way to preselect the time. Mihalis simply hadn't given him enough to work with.

As Howard worked through the different phases of the program, a profound question remained echoing within him: What, or more precisely who, was this God that had created Mihalis? Mihalis was so perfect in form, and the life form within so different, intelligent, and magical. Its creator was surely more than a genius: it would have to be a true master of knowledge.

Howard had never doubted the existence of a God, at least in the respect that there must be a higher form of intelligence, shepherding mankind. So many of his contemporaries and colleagues however, did not share his belief. So many held the conceited belief that science was the domain of mankind and mankind alone.

Science. It seemed more and more that science was closing in on so many answers to questions which not so long before had been unattainable. Howard had a theory that so many scientists, working on so many previously unfrontiered scientific questions, would someday soon yield a cumulative result much larger than the sum of individual parts. This would yield a holographic effect, where a small piece of the big picture could yield a solution to many other scientific investigations.

To Howard, what made Mihalis so fascinating was that it could not only synthesize its own energy, it surely had the capability to apply it as needed. And yet it wasn't a life form such as man, or a form of intelligence such as computers. It had no genes, no circuitry. It was crystal – crystal with an actual and undeniable resonance. It was alive, but neither mortal nor capable of reproducing, so it wasn't life as humans know it.

With December came the winter rains, and Howard felt drawn to the rivers. Liberty was less than a two hour drive from the Chattooga and he began to spend the weekends kayaking the river and its tributaries. He continued to boat throughout the winter, and kept himself in good physical condition. By spring, Joe Morton was becoming a well known fixture on the rivers of the Southeast.

Most of the time, he would join a party in setting up a car shuttle in the morning and give an excuse for wanting to get off the river late. He would leave his car at the take-out. In this manner, he limited his conversations with other paddlers to river talk while on the river, reducing his chances of letting too much be known about himself.

By March he had a completed prototype of the helmet. He had tested the moving water analysis program at the Tamassee Slides. It worked perfectly. However, testing the Mihalis track-and-transfer function, let alone the override function, horrified him. He didn't test those functions at all. The controls were voice activated, and he had already decided to add voice fingerprinting to Pete's unit so that only Pete could use it. Then he would disassemble the prototype.

In mid-April, Howard had an encounter that shook him. It was the season when he and Pete were readying themselves to depart for Africa, from California and West Virginia respectively, and the Southeast was verdant with spring growth. Seasonal rains had filled the rivers and the paddling was excellent.

This day, Howard headed for section four of the Chattooga and ran shuttle with some boaters from Knoxville, a loose knit club called"The Wheats." He left the Explorer at the take-out and ran down to Five Falls, as the last five big Class IV rapids are called, with the group. At Soc-em-Dog rapid he bid them farewell, saying he wanted to take in some sun and relax on the riverside.

As they disappeared down over Shoulder Bone rapid, he took out his dry bag and removed a small vial containing a dose of LSD. He was looking forward to an intense, multi-layered meditation. It was a form of mental vacation for Howard. A freeing of his mind to wander and play, much as the river trip had been for his body.

He placed the minute piece of amber gel under his tongue and felt it slowly dissolve. The use of LSD. was something that wasn't practiced by any of his colleagues. More exactly, it would shock them. Society condemned it. Heinous acts perpetrated by drug-crazed delinquents didn't help society to comprehend the magic it held.

At Pete's urging, Howard had researched it thoroughly. Within the human brain, a chemical substance called M.A.O. wipes clean the neurons after each synapse so as to ready them to receive the next impulse. LSD blocks the M.A.O., creating an overload of impulses in the neurons. The user can develop the ability to use this overload as a tool for thought, and more. The tool opens the senses, taking them beyond preset realms and parameters. Howard found that it enabled him to look within himself, review the mental paths that he had utilized in his recent project work, and strategize how he would clear the hurdles that lay ahead.

For him, the acid trip would be a refreshing experience, as long as he had the tranquility and solitude with which to enjoy it. Howard reclined on an angled surface in the rock and began to soak up the sun.

Other groups of kayakers came down over Five Falls, and as they passed by, he would wave or call out a greeting. The river was crowded for a Sunday afternoon, but he saw few boaters that he recognized.

Soon the river cleared out and he began to feel the effects of the acid. Bird life seemed to return now that people were gone. Kingfishers chattered up and downstream over the surface of the water. Their blue and white plumage contrasted with the greens and grays of the foliage and the rock. Only the water reflecting the blue of the afternoon sky matched their color. Looking about, he realized how alive the world had become after its long winter sleep.

There was such a difference between a place like this lush river gorge and Wadi Nouveau. The Sahara had been such a stark and barren reality. As he looked around, the forest seemed to breathe. He began to think about his place in the world and the role he played. Though he knew that his work was potentially important to all of mankind, he suddenly felt very small and insignificant. The ecosystem of the river was complex and vigorous. He was only an observer and not a participant. It did not matter whether he was here or not. It would all go on without him.

He thought back. Pete had at times expressed this same sentiment to him. But Pete was always in tune with the real world and the forces that rule it. None of us are just observers.

This was the last thought that ran through Howard's mind before he heard a whistle being blown from upstream.

He stood up and saw a boater, at first pinned vertically on the river left side of the main drop of Soc-em-Dog, and then shake loose, only to fall over and be pinned again broadside on the rocks at the left side base of the drop. Howard grabbed his throw bag from the stern of his boat and began to work his way upstream over the shore rocks.

The boater in trouble managed to wriggle out of his pinned kayak, but was drawn up into the recycling water at the base of the drop and began to be tumbled in the foam. Now one of the two other boaters in his group paddled over the drop but was carried swiftly downstream of the cauldron which held his companion. The third followed suit but also was carried downstream before he could react.

Howard was now in throw bag range and tossed the line out to the man being tumbled in the recycling water. Somehow, the man sensed the rope and grabbed hold. Howard felt the tension on the line and with a hand over hand motion, pulled him free. He pulled him across the current rushing out from the bottom of the rapid and leaned over to grasp his outstretched hand. The man's face was ashen from lack of oxygen and the fatigue of fighting the currents that had held him. He looked up at Howard and seemed to be about to pass out.

"Thank you Joe."

Howard looked up to see that one of the other boaters had ferried over into the eddy where he was holding on to the hapless kayaker. The man had recognized him and called out his name. How had the other boater crossed over to them so fast? His sense of time must surely now be distorted by the LSD.

"Great rescue Howard! Should have known it was you."

Howard looked into the boater's face and recognized him. It was Bryan Rogers, an old paddling buddy from West Virginia whom he hadn't seen in years.

"What are you doing here? I thought you were in California?"

Howard paused for a moment, at a loss for words. Now the third kayaker had ferried into their eddy and started to climb out of his boat and onto the shore rocks. Howard began to pull the swimmer up onto the rock he was on and the third paddler joined him in the effort.

Howard's mind reeled. This was the first time that he'd been recognized by anyone as Howard Calvert, and worse yet, at the same time as Joe Morton.

The man lay at their feet shivering, clearly unable to get up.

"Paul, are you okay?"

Howard now recognized him as one of the guys he'd run shuttle with a couple of months back. He was an inexperienced paddler out of Atlanta named

Paul Benson. Howard remembered that he'd asked him a million questions about kayaking. Most likely, he had probably just hooked up with Rogers and this other guy.

Howard started to panic, his cover was about to be blown straight to hell."Paul, are you going to be all right?" Bryan asked.

Paul was starting to come around."I'm okay. Just give me a couple of minutes."

Bryan put a comforting hand on the man's shoulder."Just relax buddy. Take all the time you want. There's no hurry."

"This guy's had quite an afternoon, eh Howard?"

It seemed to Howard that he could see the blood pulsing in the capillaries in Bryan's face. In fact, everything seemed to be moving; animate. His carefully planned afternoon of solitude and deep thought had come to a crashing halt with this unforeseen encounter.

The third boater now stepped over to them. Howard picked up negative vibrations from the man who now was extending his hand to him."Franklin McCafferty. And you are?"

"Howard Calvert," he replied, taking his hand and shaking it once.

Paul, now slowly recovering, looked up at them but said nothing.

Howard felt himself withdrawing within his consciousness. He was analyzing the situation thoroughly, but wasn't reacting properly to those around him. He tried to snap out of it.

Time to get it in gear Howard. Come on."So Bryan, what are you doing here? The last time I saw you, you were working for ELKem back in Charleston."

"I took a new job down in Atlanta back in '93 and been there ever since. The boating here's not quite like back in West Virginia though. We have some long dry spells down here."

"I know the feeling. In California we have some long dry spells too, but there's always something to run."

"So what brings you here Howard?" queried McCafferty.

Howard had already started to dislike him.

"I decided to get away for a while. I'm working on a little project down at Clemson."

"What kind of project?" McCafferty inquired further.

"I do a lot of computer programming."

Rogers chimed in, "You have to excuse Frank. He works for the State Department and feels it's his duty to be nosy all the time."

Oh shit, thought Howard, State Department.

Benson had now regained his feet. "I thought your name was Joe Morton?"

"No, it's Howard," he said looking him straight in the face.

Bryan laughed and said: "I guess you must have hit your head up there Paul." Everyone was now laughing except for McCafferty, Howard a bit too giddily. He wondered if he had the glazed look of someone tripping. Once again he found himself drifting, this time looking around at the trees swaying in the gently breeze. This time it was Bryan who snapped him out of his trance.

"Hey everybody, it's getting late. Paul, if you're up to it, I think we ought to get going."

Howard quickly weighed his options. Was it better to let them go without him, and talk, or to be there to help steer the conversation away from him. He decided, for better or worse, to go with them.

A short distance below the next rapid, Shoulder Bone, the Chattooga river merges into the still waters of Lake Tugaloo. They paddled into the setting sun and a cool breeze. Howard was at once enjoying the sensations and dreading the consequences of what had happened.

Paddling across the lake, he had positioned himself well to control the conversation. McCafferty was to his left, and Rogers and Benson off to his right. With the rather swift pace he was setting, Benson was trailing slightly, and due to his lesser skill level, was using a greater amount of energy to keep up with them. This effectively put him out of the conversation. Howard and Bryan filled each other in on what had been happening in their lives and Howard was careful of course, to omit everything about the upcoming project in Africa. Though Frank was excluded from the conversation, Howard could feel him trying to listen in.

As they neared the take-out, Howard considered trying to get Benson to ride out with him and then decided against it. It would be too awkward, and perhaps obvious. He was tiring of this game anyway. Was it acid that made him dislike McCafferty?

On the drive back to Liberty all he could say was "Shit!" There would be no more paddling trips for him. It was time to finish up his work hidden away in the shop and cover his tracks on the way out.

He was quite upset with himself for the slip up. He could justify it by telling himself that it was just an unfortunate coincidence, him running into two people at the same time who each knew one of his personages, Howard knew better. Putting himself in a river, slash, social situation, the odds of something like that skyrocketed. If by any chance the more pragmatic pre-Sahara Howard Calvert were to be affected by the knowledge that something was going on, it could set off a chain of events which could result in a divergent parallel reality, in which he could be stuck for the rest of his life. It could also expose Pete to danger, and his mission to failure.

As he worked it all through again and again in his head it started to rain.

He found his thoughts falling into cadence with the windshield wipers and then fell into a trance. The rhythm of the wipers now became paddle strokes. He was following behind Pete down through a desolate river canyon. Pete was wearing the helmet he had made for him but wasn't paddling Mihalis. Instead, he was in an Augsburg. Pete seemed to be looking for something as he went. They ran a tough rapid and then eddied left behind some huge boulders. A flock of vultures was on top of and tearing at something on shore. Mihalis lay half sunken in the eddy. At their arrival, the buzzards reluctantly took off with a great beating of wings. There on the shore was what was left of Pete. But it wasn't Pete. Pete was in the Augsburg still and cried out.

"Simon!" Howard snapped out of the trance with a great blaring of horns and bright lights flashing in his face. He had crossed the center line of the highway and it was all he could do to regain control of the Explorer. Breathless and sweating, he pulled off of the road and shut off the engine.

My God, what have I done? That was when it hit him. Mihalis was using Pete. Mihalis was willing to sacrifice a yet to be born son for a chance at the tower. No. It can't be so. He slowly came back to reality and found himself staring straight ahead through the windshield with an iron grip on the steering wheel. He decided not to think about what had happened and the vision. Have to stay focused. This proved to be too hard to do. Howard started to wrap his brain tightly around the vision and what it meant. It was the acid. The prolonged period of coming down off of an acid trip. Few things lend themselves more to Monday morning quarterbacking than coming down off of LSD. The acid had helped his mind break through Mihalis' motives that presented themselves in the visions he had been experiencing. Mihalis had been hiding its plan to involve an unborn son in the game at the tower and now he was the holder of that knowledge.

It was a long and sleepless night back at his workshop. In the morning he searched out some extra passport photos of Pete and drove to Columbia. He found Mouse and had him create a new identity for Pete with corresponding driver's license and passport. The new Pete was named Duane Singley. He bought an open date first class ticket to Rio de Janeiro and sent it all by private courier to Patch. What he really had done was something to ease his own conscience.

April 25th found Howard flying to Sacramento to swear out the affidavit before Judge Clemens that would empower Anders Lieb to administer disposition of his Saharan equipment. He returned on the 29th and resumed work on Pete's helmet.

In both units he had used hard-to-get special components. All CCD's were shock hardened and epoxy coated with Epon 868 for added water resistance. The photovoltaic charge system was of up-to-the-minute military aerospace specs, and was used as the initial charge for lithium batteries in a parallel system. The main power supply was Mihalis' energy synthesis program. The Moving Water Analysis portion of the circuitry used a tremendous amount of energy. To display everything going on in whitewater the unit required sixty MIPS: million instructions per second. The unit had two terabytes of memory to be shared between three main functions. To make this possible in such a small unit, Howard had used Gallium Arsenide super conductor chips. These in turn had to be super-cooled with heat pipe technology. Howard used nine micron pipe with lithium working fluid and Beryllium screen.

This was all expensive, but tough and durable.

The face shield/screen was green tinted polycarbonate with user aspect orientation and full L.E.D. display. All circuitry was contained within the pressurized inner and outer skin laminates of the helmet itself. Total weight was 836 grams per unit. It was true state of the art. It was more than that. It contained programming far more advanced than anything yet created.

Built to last, and ready to go.

Time was flying for Howard. He and Pete were finishing up the project in Africa. His work in South Carolina had come to an end. He found it interesting to think of himself re-entering his life in its sequence with the wrinkle of having spent an extra year working on something so esoteric.

Howard now had to concentrate on his return. July 28th, he had to pick up where he had left off. There was plenty to do first.

On the 10th of July, Howard went to Atlanta and sold the IBM system to the dealership that had sold it to him. He had to take a big loss on it, but he didn't care. Anything was better than nothing. While there, as Joe Morton, he sold the Explorer to a dealership and checked into a hotel.

Two days later he checked out, with a new identity. He went to an Isuzu dealership and bought a new Rodeo.

Once back in Liberty, he began the work of cleaning out the workshop. All the computer paper and notes that he didn't want to save were shredded and burned. He sold or gave away everything except for the refrigerator and his bed.

On July 18th, Howard called Anders and spent an hour explaining what had happened, and about the affidavit and the need to have someone in Algiers to administer the equipment and to spring Salil. Anders accepted. Howard wasn't surprised. They were more than friends, and more than a year ago, Anders had shared a dark personal secret with him. Anders had nothing to lose in the process of helping him.

On the 26th, he started driving north. He was traveling light. He made a stop at Greenville at the Yellow Freight warehouse to pick up his kayaks and gear that Anders had had crated and shipped from the west coast. He continued northward on Interstate 77.

His destination was Washington DC.. He needed to be there before everything went down in Africa. He had a day and a half to get there, so he took his time.

Six P.M on the 28th found him sitting at the bar in a Mexican restaurant at Tyson's Corner Mall, just outside the D.C. beltway. After ordering another Budweiser, he asked the bartender if he could switch the T.V. channel from ESPN to the ABC evening news.

After obliging him with a fresh beer, the bartender hit the remote control. Peter Jennings appeared at the news desk in the New York City studio.

This is it, thought Howard. The moment he'd waited for, for an entire year. Hopefully everything had gone smoothly with Pete, Salil, and the plutonium. If there was no news story, everything was probably okay.

"Good evening. There was an atomic explosion in Algeria today and there is evidence that the United States is somehow connected to it. We go now to Algeria for this report."

Howard sputtered and choked back his beer in mid gulp, but the bartender didn't notice. He was looking up at the set as were the three patrons sitting at the bar. Howard set a ten dollar bill on the bar and hurried out into the evening gloom. Things had not gone right. Now he would have to ad lib.

Five minutes later, and six hundred miles to the south, Franklin McCafferty-was making a phone call.

CHAPTER 6 — PREPARATIONS

July 29, 1998

The Dornblaser residence had been a hectic place. Friends of Pete's and the family called constantly. Numerous concerned neighbors had stopped by to offer their condolences. A reporter from the Dominion Post had come by for a statement.

CNN carried the atomic blast as its lead story all day. The U.S. government remained elusive in its press releases.

His mother had come upstairs and knocked on his door.

"Peter, with all of the excitement, I almost forgot about this box that came for you last week. It was a bit odd because it wasn't UPS or anybody of that sort, but some private courier service. Very nice man, and he said I didn't even need to sign for it."

She left him to open it alone. It was from C.A. Jones. It took him a couple of seconds but he realized that was one of Howard's joke aliases. If you took the periods out it read "cajones" or big balls in Spanish.

Once in his room, Pete ripped the box open. Surrounded with packing material and encased in bubble wrap, was a helmet. A helmet like he'd never seen. It was a marvel of technology. He turned it in his hands several times, examining each feature with the glee of a kid at Christmas. He slowly slipped it on over his head. He pulled the green tinted visor down and felt it lock in place. Something inside the helmet made a slight clicking sound, and the word: READY appeared on the upper left corner of the screen. Nervously, he lifted the helmet off of his head and set it down. There was a note sticking up through the styrofoam peanuts in the bottom of the box. The note read: "I have been working on this for a year and will explain soon. The money is for the patch option.....

Only then did it hit him that something had happened to Howard. Mere days and hours before they had been talking and joking about such a helmet and now he held it in his hands. The implausibility was absolute: Howard had had time, and lots of it, to make something so elaborate.

Pete turned his attention back to what he'd seen beneath the bubble wrap in the box. He withdrew an oversize manila envelope stuffed full to bulging with its contents. It was money. Cold, hard cash. Pete counted it out on the bed. $30,000 in hundreds, fifties and twenties. It was more than what Howard owed him. Howard had paid him twenty thousand dollars, against his protests that it was too much, before they had even left for Africa. That had gone into paying off all of his debts.

Brazil. It was looking better all the time. This was the "patch option." Patch was his friend. He was a special kind of guy. Patch had been a union steel worker who had retired up into the hills. He had a really nice, yet unassuming farm compound up on Chestnut Ridge. What Patch actually was though was the gatekeeper for a community of ex-pats that had disappeared into the Atlantic coast region of Brazil south of the big cities. Patch had always liked Pete and when the crap had gone down with the lawsuit and the closure of the kayak school it was he who approached Pete with the idea of leaving. Patch assured him that he would take care of all of the logistics and once there, the group would orient him into their new world. Before going to Africa Pete had his doubts if that was what he really wanted, but now, it seemed more and more the best option. He had discussed it with Howard. Howard, always analytical, agreed that given Pete's lifestyle and present circumstances, he might be better off with a fresh start in that distant land.

He looked out the window. It had started to rain, hard. Strange, the weather channel had predicted continued hot, humid, and no rain in sight.

Then he saw it. A van from the phone company had pulled up just down the block and a lineman was scaling the pole beside it. Pete noticed that their phone line ran from the pole to the house. What a coincidence, he thought. There was no doubt, they were about to be tapped. The man descended the pole with a thin wire in hand and then retreated into the van with it. They sure weren't being very discreet about it. But the shit was getting deeper.

❧❦

Four late model Suburbans turned off of the highway into the Liberty Industrial Park, a cluster of metal pole buildings that housed small businesses and repair shops. They braked to a stop in front of one of the metal buildings. The building sported no signs identifying the character of its business. The double garage doors were rolled down and padlocked shut.

The men who leapt from the Suburbans wore black bulletproof vests and black caps that said FBI across the front. Taking a ram, they bashed in the office door. Guns drawn, they ran inside.

They found an empty workshop with a living space at one end. Whatever had been there, it was now meticulously cleaned out, its occupant obviously long gone. The only sound was coming from the small refrigerator. An agent opened it carefully. Inside was a twelve pack of Budweiser and a note that read:

Better luck next time boys! Have a cold one on us.
Howard & Joe

ॐॐ

With the carport lights off, Pete slipped into the back of his father's Caravan and lay on the floor Twenty minutes later, Ben turned on the lights, walked out, and started up the van. Without speaking, he turned down the street going the other way from where the telephone van was still parked. Ben looked in the rearview mirror as he pulled onto Grand street and started down the hill towards downtown. Lights turned onto the street behind him. As they had suspected, wherever they now went, they would be followed.

Ben pulled into the parking garage on University Avenue and began to slowly spiral upward. Two levels up, Pete practically rolled out of the sliding side door and ran alongside as he slid it shut. He ran and hid behind a parked car seconds before a dark blue Ford sedan slid up the ramp behind Ben. He pulled up the hood of his parka and ran into the stairwell of the garage. Emerging from the street level exit, he walked swiftly across to the alleyway leading one street up to High Street. A handful of Asian students made their way laughing through the rain, but otherwise the sidewalks were nearly empty. The street, however, was full of cars passing by.

Pete checked his watch. Five till nine.

He opened the door to the Met Pool Hall and walked down the worn marble steps into the basement of the old building. Reaching the bottom, he kept his hood up and stole a glance over at the bar as he headed for the pay phone in the back corner.

Old Al was there, as he had always been, handing out racks of balls and serving beer. Pete stood by the phone, waiting for it to ring, his back to the tables and the townies playing pool.

"Hey Petey, thought you might be wanting one of these."

He turned around and Al was standing there with a long-necked bottle of Bud and a Fed Ex envelope. Shocked at first, he asked, "How did you know it was me?""You gots to be able to trust somebody sometimes Dornblaser. Howard told me you'd be here. This came today Federal Express." Al handed him the envelope. "Howard told me to give it to you. Said it was real important. Hope you guys know what you're doing. And don't worry, I don't know nothing."

Recovering from the surprise, he took a big slug off of his beer and examined the envelope. It obviously contained a videocassette.

The phone rang.

"Hello.."

"Hey, it's me. No names, understand, no names. You okay?"

"Yeah. I'm all right. How are y...?"

"What the hell happened over there?!"

"Look Sal..., our friend, is dead. We were driving out with the plutonium and Mihalis when we got ambushed at the Wadi crossing. They killed him. It was that asshole we were calling Frank Zappa. I wrecked the truck to get the jump on them, and . . . I . . . killed some of them with an AK-47. I killed people! At least I think I did. Next thing I know, I'm waking up at my parents' house. The kayak is here too.

There was a silence on the other end of the line. Howard had been quite fond of Salil, just as Pete had. This was very personal collateral damage that he wasn't prepared for. The costs were piling up. The whirlwinds were growing ever stronger and appeared to be set to land on them again and this time stronger yet.

"You there?"

"Yeah, just thinking about our little buddy. I don't know what to say."

Now, more silence.

"Dude, where are you?"

"You remember when I got on the chopper and took off? Do you remember anything about that moment?" It came back to him: he had jokingly said to the kayak in the truck something about not causing any more trouble when there had been a burst of power or a wave of energy.

"That was as far as I made it in the chopper that day, and for me, that was a year ago." Pete said nothing as he stood there taking it all in but not really understanding it at all. It took me back in time, exactly a year back in time. The kayak has a name; it is called Mihalis."

As if dumbstruck, he remained speechless, Howard's words echoing around in his skull, they made no sense, but this was Howard talking. Of course they were true.

"I was in South Carolina building you the helmet. You received the box, didn't you?"

The one thing that started to add up in his mind was that Howard had obviously needed, and had had a lot of time to build the helmet. The helmet that had arrived before he had even left Africa. "What the fuck is going on?"

"My friend, what is going on, is something much bigger than I ever imagined possible. But, it is all about you. Search your thoughts and your dreams. You know and have known, without acknowledging, that you have had past lives. You have been sent over and over again to destroy this, this tower, with the kayak, Mihalis. Sometimes you succeeded, and others you failed. Now, it has come for you again. What I have done with the helmet is to give you a tool, and advantage, and just maybe an ace in the hole I explain more on the video cassette"

"The one he just gave me?"

"It's also a training manual for using the helmet."

"And why did you send me so much money?"

"The money is to buy the things you're going to need if you choose to run with the P option. I wouldn't blame you a bit if that was what you decide to do."

Pete sighed. "People are after us. That's for sure. But fuck that kayak. The goddamned thing is bringing me nothing but trouble heaped on more trouble. What if I tell you. . . what if I say I want to get rid of it?"

"Knowing you, part of me could believe it and part of me says you want that thing. All the mystical part aside, I know you want that boat just for the boat itself. You have got to make a decision. If you go with the P option, you have to get rid of it to be safe from it. Either way, our government is going to go nuts trying to track us down. When they find you, they are going to try to crucify you or at least make you suffer for a long time. Why waste yourself like that? You have an opportunity here with Mihalis. An incredible experience. The only other option is to get out of here fast, and, getting as far from Mihalis as you can to be outside of its sphere of control".

Pete thought about it.

"Where are you?"

"I'm at a pay phone. It's a safe call, more or less. Everything is recorded and computerized. Even this call can be isolated and accessed later if they figure out enough to check it. Al isn't going to tell anybody though. The chances are slim to none that the Feds will ever hear this conversation."

"I hope not. My dad's car was followed here when he dropped me off."

"Then the chances just went up to 'slim.' We need to talk though, you're in for a wild ride, and I'm not talking about legally either."

"Well start talking then."

"Okay, that last night at Wadi Nouveau, I had vision-like dreams. Mihalis is an 'angel,' created by God. The only difference is that it is in the form of a kayak. It was created by God to serve a special purpose."

"Destroy the sand tower."

"Exactly. But it can't do it alone. It is you who must paddle it. You have been chosen. It seems that God had a master plan for the earth, with geologic and climatic schedules. Conditions had to balance out for the existence of life. One vulnerable link in the plan was for the Atlantic to drain underground. The devil built the tower over the drain in the bowl and used it to divert the water out through the cut you saw. The water floods out over Africa and disrupts the world ecology enough to screw things up royally."

"But this is what I don't understand. The tower is not there. It's gone."

"Yes, I know. It's gone because you destroyed it. Time is linear, but apparently our place in time as participants is not fixed. Mihalis has the ability to make leaps through time. Forward and backward. It arrived through time to be found by you."

"Now I'm really confused."

"Well, I've had a year to run it through my head. It plays. Your whole life now adds up to me with this. You were born for this. It will be the wildest thing you have ever done. Besides, if you don't go, we've got another problem."

"And what would that be?"

"I don't want the Feds or anyone else getting hold of the technology in the helmet. It would be way too tempting to use it and the result could be catastrophic. The helmet can do what Mihalis does and take you forward or backward in time.

"What about them getting hold of Mihalis?"

"Never happen. They try to grab Mihalis and, poof! Gone. I've already shredded everything on paper and burned all the disks and drives. All that's left is your helmet and the prototype. The prototype is well hidden. I'm keeping it around just in case."

"Just in case what?"

"I don't know. Just in case."

"Yeah, like 'just in case this crystal kayak decides to leave my ass dumped in some Godforsaken nowhere time.'"

Howard was at a crossroads; he felt that to be true to his friend he needed to reveal his suspicion about Mihalis's plan to utilize a yet unborn son. Though he had little doubt that that was what the crystal intended to do, he wasn't sure what Pete's reaction would be and which course of action he would take. For better or worse, he said nothing of it. Instead, he gave the best warning that he dare:

"The crystal is alive. It thinks, it can interact with us and our thoughts. If you want to be safe from whatever it might have for you as a plan, you have to get away from it. Understand?

"This can't be real."

"I remember when you showed me that what we see, hear or feel is not necessarily reality. This is all real. The future isn't what it used to be. Think about it. Okay?"

૨∞૭

Pete walked through the pouring rain. He headed over Decker's Creek bridge into South Park.

Decker's Creek was now running high.

"Okay kayak, tomorrow we go to the river and talk."

The voice, somehow distant, came into his head.

very well

He returned home using his childhood route: through the little park with the basketball courts, down through the woods to the little creek, walking hunched over through the culvert under Ogle Avenue, continuing up the creek to the split, up the right fork and finally up his little trail to his back yard. His parents were in the kitchen drinking coffee and were obviously relieved at his safe return.

"What did Howard have to say, son?" Ben asked in a hushed tone.

"Mom, Dad, I think I am going to have to leave for a while. A good while. I've got to think out a plan. Let's talk in the morning, okay?"

His parents just stared at each other.

Pete grabbed a Bud from the fridge and headed for his room. He placed the envelope with the VHS cassette on top of his TV set saying to himself that he would watch it in a few minutes. He stretched out on his bed to think about it all. Soon, he was asleep.

He awoke and noticed a figure silhouetted in his bedroom doorway. He had left his light on, and now it was off. His door had been closed, now it was open. Slowly the figure came into focus through his sleepy eyes. It was a tall man, but not a man. Horns protruded from his hair on his head. A tail swished and twitched to one side. Shit! It's the fucking Devil!

It turned to look down the hall and its teeth flashed in the hallway light, framed by the beard and moustache on its long angular face. Pete wanted to spring up and flee, but was frozen with fear.

Bullshit. I'm never frozen with fear.

But it was true, he simply could not move. He was paralyzed. He couldn't even turn his head, shut his eyes, or utter a scream.

This is a dream, just a dream. No it's not. I'm awake. Why can't I move? Go away you bastard. Got to get up. Got to do something. Can't move. Can't move at all. What is happening?

It was still raining hard and lightning flashed outside. The light illuminated the face momentarily. He knew that face. The figure didn't move from the doorway. It looked down the hallway as would a child fearful of being discovered where it didn't belong. It held something small in one hand. Something shiny.

Lightning flashed again. This time close by and followed immediately by a booming thunderclap. The devil glowered at him for a moment more and then turned and clopped off down the hall.

He still couldn't move and lay in his own sweat. Soon he calmed down and started to rationalize. Things like this only happen in dreams. Yes, it was just a dream.

Later, wide awake, he couldn't recall anything but the feeling of being numb.

☙❧

"Sir, excuse me, but we've spotted Dornblaser. He left his parents' house in Morgantown, West Virginia fifteen minutes ago."

"What? And we have him?"

"No sir. What happened is his parents left together in one vehicle and were followed by the tail car. Twenty minutes later Dornblaser rolled out in another vehicle with a kayak tied to the roof. The guy in the phone van was cabled to the pole and couldn't roll fast enough. We lost him for now, but he's there." Elliot thought smugly to himself that Mitchell couldn't fault him for Dornblaser's escape. He had insisted that they budget two tail cars for the surveillance operation and Mitchell had overruled him, saying it was highly improbable that Dornblaser was alive, much less that he would arrive at his parents' home. Mitchell had further argued that a dangerous criminal like Dornblaser if he was still alive, would not be trying to re-enter the United States. He would be sheltered in some Islamic state, revered as a hero for his efforts to deliver the bomb that had gone off.

"Just like I told you, sir, somehow I knew he'd be there."

Elliot had mentally profiled Dornblaser's psyche. The man simply did not have the ethos of a criminal, spy, or traitor. He was a hedonistic, self-centered, outdoor sports nut. He was a kayaker. He lived and breathed kayaking.

"Damn, Elliot, I can't believe it. How in the hell did he get there so fast? And why there? Don't tell me he had to see his parents that badly, the kind of trouble he's in."

"I know what you're saying sir, but it is like that Calvert raid yesterday."

None of this adds up, Mitchell thought.

"Elliot, how in the hell did they get into the country? If I'm to believe that fucking FBI report from South Carolina, Calvert's been coming and going every couple of Goddam days. This shit is impossible. They are priority one. We were looking for them everywhere. They must have walked through Miami International. The whole shitty place is run by Cubans. They were probably chasing a skirt while two guys who'd just popped off an A-bomb casually waltzed through the turnstiles. How? Goddamit, How!?"

Something is up, that's for sure, Elliot thought to himself, but he just bit his lip and turned to leave.

Mitchell bellowed after him, "Dammit! Run another P.I.C.S. I want answers!"

∾∾

Pete dropped Mihalis into the water and it skipped lightly across the surface, as would a new fiberglass boat free of scratches. Taking a last look, he saw that there was still nobody around. His mother's car sat parked in the field. His parents would retrieve it the next day. It was safe. There was not much in the way of car thieves in Sang Run, Maryland.

The day had dawned clear and bright, but the river was running high with muddy brown water from the rains.

They would be the only ones on the Upper Youghiogheny today. The rafting trips would have to be run on some other river. The Yough was way too high. The Friendsville "Hardcores" would be on the Upper Blackwater with summer water like this.

There were lots of people he would have liked to see just one more time. Most everyone probably thought he was dead. He hated the idea that his buddies didn't even know he was around. He paddled downstream under the Sang Run bridge, the brown water smelling of soil. As they rounded the first bend, a Great Blue Heron took flight, leading him downstream from its nest in a timeless ritual. The Appalachian hardwood forest boasted a deep dark green hue given off the water from the unexpected summer storm. Sunlight sparkled across the wave tops in the riffles.

Pete looked down and through Mihalis and could see his legs refracting through the facets of the deck. He marveled at the being that was transporting him now in such a concrete and literal sense.

The rhododendron was beginning to bud and in a few weeks the river would be lined with large white blossoms. Shit, I'm going to miss the flowering of the rhododendron this summer. His panic was borne of something greater than missing the blossoming of a flower.

☙❧

Esmeralda Dornblaser was crying again. Driving and crying. She had a strong feeling that she would never see her son again. Peter Simon had told them it was just going to be a matter of months or at most a couple of years, but somehow a mother knows. She was in Ben's Caravan, headed for Friendsville, Maryland. She was taking a back route. Peter Simon had insisted that they all take different routes. She had dropped Ben off in Kingwood at the Ryder Rental Truck agency and now she was headed north on Rt. 26 to the Pennsylvania line. There she would turn onto Maryland Route 42 and meet Ben in Friendsville. Ben would be driving east out of Kingwood to Oakland, Maryland. Then he would drive north on 219 and 42 to Friendsville. They would leave the Ryder by the river and head back to Morgantown. Never to see her son again.

☙❧

Pete had a hundred things running through his head. Tomorrow morning he would leave. He had to get everything ready. Then, there was the hastily arranged plan with his mom and dad. Then there was the reason why he had to leave: they were after him, whoever 'they' were. And if they were, which they certainly were, what was he doing here now? Something for myself, he thought. What I really need now, is time lone. Time to think. Here on the Upper Yough, at a super high water level. Blue sky, a helmet from outer space and a kayak that's a messenger from God. It could be worse. Or could it?

it could

They rounded the last bend of the flatwater section and Pete could see the waves of Warm-Up Riffle leaping higher and stronger with the increased volume of water. Twenty, Class IV and V rapids awaited him downstream. At today's water level, they might as well be one rapid; there would be no flat water between them, only rushing current.

He turned Mihalis upstream and dropped backwards into the trough of the first wave, his power strokes coming somewhat rusty. Pete was feeling a bit off from his three month hiatus from paddling. It had been the most time spent without river running in his adult life. Shake it off, Petey, he thought to himself. Mihalis took to the wave and he felt the hull glissing about on the wave face, responding to every lean of his body and touch of his paddle blades. He allowed Mihalis to drop upstream into the trough of the wave and as it turned sideways, he leaned back and, with his downstream blade, dug into the water with a prying motion. Mihalis responded with a sweet pivot off the wave, bow high in the air.

"Okay, here we go Mihalis."

Man and kayak were carried downstream towards Gap Falls, the first major obstacle. Pete had the helmet visor up, wanting to enjoy one new toy at a time. He was feeling good mentally. Feeling relief from the stress that had dominated him over the past few days. The attack in the desert now seemed as if it had occurred in a past life. He was feeling a rebirth, brought on by the anticipation of confronting danger. The type of danger he was used to confronting.

Gap Falls normally consists of a river-wide sloping ledge of sandstone, covered by the water sliding downwards, ending in a powerful hydraulic. The water level this day, however, was much higher than normal. Today the rapid would be one huge hydraulic wave stretching from the right bank to within three meters of the left bank. Pete knew that the left was the only passable route. The problem was a large plowshare wave guarding the approach to that line. Hitting it wrong would send him to the right; and into the hydraulic; a five foot high, wall of whitewater.

As he crested the wave upstream of it, he saw the plowshare splitting the water. He leaned to the right and planted a right side power stroke deep into the wave trough. Mihalis reacted, rocketing up, and to the left. Newton's laws in motion, he thought. As Pete crested over the plowshare, he was already shaking the water from his eyes and he began powering down the backside of the wave and shot the gap between the left bank and the hole.

Though at this water level the next mile was fairly intense big water Class IV, Pete was running his proposed lines through his head for the monster Class V's that would be coming up soon.

❧❦

Ben eased the Ryder truck down the steep grade of Blue Goose Road and parked it by the river underneath the overpass of the Interstate 68 exit ramp. The river was rushing by, the water high and muddy. That wouldn't be a problem for his boy Petey.

Making sure nobody was around to see, he slipped the keys into the exhaust pipe. Ben climbed up the concrete bridge apron and over the guard rail. Esmy was waiting in the Caravan parked on the shoulder of the exit ramp and they started driving back to Morgantown on the interstate. Esmy was no longer crying, but she looked drawn.

"Talk to me Ben."

"I don't know what to say."

Esmy couldn't look at him and just stared ahead at the road. "Peter Simon was always my baby. He was always so sparky and inquisitive. But he never wanted to be like other children. I never felt like he was born under a dark cloud or anything like that, but I was always worried that something like this was going to happen. Not this of course. I never imagined this. It's as if I knew someday he would be punished for his wild streak. And now it's happened and I've lost him."

"Pete is special, Esmy. Remember when we fought about him dropping out of school? I tried to tell you then that he was more than just an expert in the field of whitewater. He has a way of relating what he knows to a higher level." Ben paused for a moment, looking straight ahead through the windshield. "He might be going away, but he's not going to perish. No impediment will stand in his way for long. He's a survivor."

In Langley, Mitchell was running everything through his head over and over again. Why couldn't Calvert and Dornblaser have had the decency to die in Algeria? Now all these blatantly contradictory reports. Calvert in California. Calvert in Africa. Calvert in South Carolina. Dornblaser at ground zero. Dornblaser at home in West Virginia. In all of his years of working in intelligence, he'd never been confronted by such quick and unexplainable movements. These two were amateurs, but they were running circles around him. It was time to do something. He pressed the intercom on his desk.

"Caroline, send Carlson up here and call Spork and tell him I want Customs, Espionage, and Interstate Flight written on both Calvert and Dornblaser."

"Sir, Elliot left the grounds via helicopter with instructions to have a car at his disposal at the Morgantown, West Virginia airport at two this afternoon. He's apparently called a meeting there with the FBI."

"All right, Dammit! Call Spork and have the warrants readied for them there. I'll be here if he has any questions."

"Yes sir." The intercom clicked off and Mitchell found himself staring at it.

He realized he was losing control of the situation. Carlson had never taken off like that before.

What is really going on here?

໑ﻪ৹ﻬ

The "Upper Yough," as the Youghiogheny River in Maryland is known, lies amid ridge and valley, farm and woodlands in the Appalachian mountains. Despite its twists and turns, it flows in a northerly direction three miles east of the West Virginia line. It is an impressive pocket of wilderness. The gorge is deep and rugged, the river confined in a narrow defile of enormous boulders shaded by towering stands of hardwoods and hemlock. Normally during the summer months, the only water comes from hydroelectric releases from Deep Creek Lake, six miles upstream of where Pete was at the moment. Today, rains had tripled its flow.

Pete was concentrating hard. The river was fast and pushy in its urge to carry such a large volume of water downstream through such a steep a canyon. The warm-up rapids end suddenly at a rapid affectionately named Bastard Falls. Frustrated and beaten kayakers had named many of the Upper's drops in a similar manner back in the seventies. Bastard's main flow was coursing down the river left side and was blocked by several large pourovers, mini waterfalls over individual submerged boulders. Pete knew that it was the kind of place where one mistake got you trashed, with no hope of gaining the side of the river swimming. He headed off towards the river right through a maze of smaller pourovers and holes. This side ended in a high ledge that he boofed off of and found himself re-entering the main current with a crisp peel out. Now he was back in the big action, with diagonal waves slapping at him from both sides. But he had already made it past the crux of the rapid and they only served to help him get in time with himself and the power of the now steeper rapids.

Charlie's Choice was next and he found himself tensing as the current carried him into this yet more intense rapid.

Though he started down the easier, river left side, he found himself having a hard time keeping track of where he was, as all of the landmark boulders were now underwater. For the final series of drops he moved more towards the center of the river to avoid the large pourover on the left. Two meter high hydraulic waves pummeled him one after the other and then he was through. He wanted to grab an eddy and rest a moment to strategize for the next two rapids, Triple Drop and National Falls, which would be the most dangerous segment to today's run, but there was no time. He reached up and pulled down the visor screen and heard it lock into position.

READY and FUNCTION? appeared in the upper left corner of the screen. Nervously, he said: "Helmet, river screen on."

Immediately a vibrant overlay of the river in high resolution graphics bounded by data filled the visor. He was flowing quickly toward the nearly washed over boulders guarding the entrance to Triple Drop and simultaneously plotting to run around to the right side, all while watching the screen compute the route for the greatest percentage of success. A small rectangle began to grow out of the center of the screen and soon filled the visor with what amounted to an advertisement. WELCOME TO THE HSC MOVING WATER ANALYSIS AND SPACE-TIME COMMAND UNIT.

His entire field of vision was now blocked by the message.

THE FOLLOWING TWELVE MINUTE INTRODUCTION AND ORIENTATION TO YOUR UNIT'S FUNCTIONS SHOULD ANSWER ANY QUESTIONS YOU MAY HAVE. AFTER THIS INITIAL USE, YOU MUST RECALL THIS INTRODUCTION WITH THE COM-MAND: HELMET, INTRODUCTION. YOU WILL FIND ALL SYS-

TEMS ARE VOICE ACTIVATED AND FREE OF…

The message continued to scroll up the screen, totally blocking Pete"s vision of the rapids. Panicking, he tried to raise the visor, but it was locked down.

"Helmet, Exit introduction, Return to river screen."

It worked. Instantly the screen returned to the computer overlay of the river. Water pillowed hard off of the right side of the right guardian boulder and a green X appeared on the pillow. He paddled hard for it, as it was indeed the best choice. To avoid the pillow to the right would put him dangerously close to the angry shore rocks. He rose high on the pillow and took advantage of the moment there to take a quick glance down through Triple Drop and the heavy water leading towards National Falls. National looked to be totally blocked by a maze of holes, waves, and certainly, several hidden pourovers; some of which could be lethal. He fixed his gaze back on the water in front of Mihalis but a red WARNING flashed on the screen with a green arrow pointing to the bottom of the screen at PROBABILITY OF SUCCESS. In red, above that area appeared: NAVIGATION QUESTIONABLE. Pete rode out the last two clean waves and then slammed into a wall of whitewater. It stalled him for a second but let him slide over its top. He had a second of clear vision as the water rolled down the face shield. The hole had robbed him of his momentum and he was dropping sideways into the huge gaping hole at the bottom of National Falls. NAVIGATION QUESTIONABLE now was enlarging in a translucent overlay across the screen.

No shit, Howard.

NAVIGATION QUESTIONABLE continued to grow and when it touched both sides of the screen, Pete felt two pieces of curved composite pop out of the bottom edge of the helmet and lock under the ridge of his jaw. Mihalis hit the foam and started to be tumbled violently. Pete tucked his paddle tightly under his left arm and pinned the right blade to the deck of Mihalis. He knew that in this manner the hole would have less leverage to rip the paddle away. Although he was mostly submerged, the boat was cartwheeling on several axes at once. Pete opened his eyes to a dizzying display of the rock structure of the hydraulic as displayed by the helmet. Now in another red overlay came a new message: COUNTDOWN TO OVERRIDE: 60 SECONDS

Mihalis was squirted out of the foam and was thrown down into the vortex of the hole. It now began to "ender" right in the trough, and after a few such revolutions was shot into the air. As it came back down, it speared deeply into the converging waters. Mihalis was sent down and caught the exiting water below the hydraulic. It was carried free of the grip of the hole and slowly rose to the surface. Pete rolled up in the rushing foam. Exhausted, he looked for an eddy.

Yes. River right.

Using returning strength, he paddled hard for the eddy and with some difficulty crossed the boiling waters separating safety from the rushing current. As he paused to catch his breath the composite chin grips slowly retracted into the helmet. Pete was mentally kicking himself for not having watched the instructional video that Howard had sent.

He looked at the river charging past. A Kingfisher swooped by, chattering as it flew upriver. Sunlight piercing through the trees played patterns on the surface of the flow. He was alive. Really alive. From here down, the river would be a blast. There would be danger spots, but there were safe routes around them. It was going to be fun. In fact, he was having the time of his life in the most perfect kayak he had ever paddled.

They continued downriver and Pete found himself jumping waves, whipping in and out of eddies and pulling off sweet wave turns. Pete had been taking sneak routes through some of the more intense rapids to avoid the immense hydraulic traps they were sporting today. Now he was approaching Powerful Popper. At this level the sensible route was far to the left of the main chute in the middle. The main chute normally dropped a meter as it passed between two boulders. Today, however, was not normal. The river piled high on the boulders and dropped over two meters into a foaming cauldron. Pete knew that he could leap the kayak off of the left hand boulder and skip across the foam below, escaping the grip of the hole. But it was risky. He arrived to the point where he needed to veer left, but found himself saying: "Why not?" and began his charge for the center chute. He aimed for the boulder on the left, almost covered with water, and took a big power stroke on the right while leaning back, to throw the boat up and to the left. The bow didn't rise enough to clear the curling wave coming off of the rock and instead pierced through. Pete braced himself for the coming impact with the boulder but instead heard and felt the crack and splintering of rock. Mihalis sailed through the air and a piece of the sandstone bounced hard but harmlessly off of his helmet. The kayak skipped across the foam and they continued with the flow towards the next rapid. Pete only had time to think of what had happened as he cleared through the tail end of it. The rock didn't break from the impact from the kayak. Usually, it was the other way around with the kayak breaking from a rock impact. No, there had been an actual burst of energy from the crystal boat that broke the rock. The "new reality" hit him like a bucket of cold water. The boat he was paddling was there for only one reason. He felt the narcolepsy sweep over him, and in a single instant he was paddling towards a falls with the tower nearly blotting out the sun. He came out of it and shook off the dizziness and confusion. He continued on down the river but he wasn't there, he was thinking about what it all really meant. The crystal kayak was far and away the finest boat he had ever paddled. It felt like his to be and yet there was a tremendous current of danger in even being close to it. There was a gnawing sense of denial and at once, a solemn realization that all Howard had said was true. The visions and dreams he was having became harder and harder to dismiss

Pete paddled on down the last few miles and reached the exit ramp bridge above Friendsville at 1:15 in the afternoon. The water was so high that he just paddled Mihalis up onto the long grass bent over by the current. He ripped the skirt off of the crystal cockpit rim and stepped out into ankle deep water. Looking down at the boat he felt a twist in his gut. This was the moment. Just push it out into the current and let it float downstream. He would be free of it. Free of its curse. Free to choose his own destiny. The boat would sink and never be seen again. But what if somebody found it? Somebody else would paddle it. Hell no. He was Pete Dornblaser and that kayak was his and his alone. For better or worse, Mihalis was going with him.

At least for now, he thought.

Pete pulled the keys from the exhaust pipe and opened the back doors of the rental truck. As he slid Mihalis inside, he noticed several boxes stacked against the side. One contained the money from Howard. One of the others held clothes, and two were full of books. There was the entire edition of the family's Encyclopedia Britannica and an assortment of other reference books. His Mom. She had certainly been the one to send the encyclopedias.

Pete changed quickly into dry shorts, a T-shirt, baseball cap and sneakers. A pair of dark sunglasses topped off his summertime casual look. The helmet was carefully packed into the box containing the clothes, and his wet river gear was unceremoniously dumped in the cockpit of Mihalis.

Time to go shopping, he thought, as he closed the doors on Mihalis, but first, time for a couple of cold bottles of Budweiser!

He drove down Water Street under the interstate overpasses with their wide concrete aprons and on past the row of houses on the other side of the street from the river. Nobody was out and about in the summer heat; business as usual for Friendsville. At the stop sign, he pulled slowly across the highway and into the parking lot of the Riverside Lounge. He slid inside and had a hard time adjusting to the nonexistent light of the barroom. Three drunks were parked at the far side of the bar and didn't even look up at him. Pete knew the barmaid. Paula was thirtyish, blonde, and good looking. He often wondered why she had never married to escape the drudgery of the Riverside.

"Excuse me Ma'am, but you ought to be babysitting your kids and not these pickled livers."

She quickly hushed a gasp and walked over to him. "What the hell are you doing here? You're supposed to dead over in Africa."

"It's a long story Paula. We'll get blasted some day and I'll tell you all about it. How about a six of Bud in cans and a pack of Camel's?"

As she rang up the sale and he zipped the cellophane off of the Camel pack, pulled the foil from the top, rolled the plastic in the foil and twisted the ends: one into a long graceful neck head and beak and the other into a flowing tail. He dropped the foil swan into the ashtray on the bar. He popped a can of Bud and took a long drink. The first slug after the river was always the best.

Paula looked at him enjoying his beer. Pete had never been like so many of the other kayakers. He often stayed late into the night, never in a hurry to get out of town after running the river. He was a regular guy. He must be in a shitpile of trouble. "You been out runnin' that river by yourself, ain't you?"

"You know how it is. Sometimes a guy just has to get away from it all." The wink was readable over the sunglasses.

"Oh Pete, you are crazy. You know that?" Paula paused for a moment and looked up at him. "You're on the run, Pete?"

"Yeah, and matter of fact", he glanced at his watch, it was 1:38, "I'd better get going."

"You take care of yourself. And don't worry, I ain't seen you."

"Thanks, Paula."

He slipped out into the afternoon sun with the five remaining cans in a paper bag and started down Maryland 42 heading for the Pennsylvania line.

Paula pulled back the curtain from the window and watched the Ryder truck disappear around the curve of Route 42. A couple of the drunks grumbled about the ray of light streaming into the barroom. She poured each of them a double whiskey on the house and heard the approach of a helicopter.

❧❦

The pilot tapped Elliot's arm and pointed below to a river sweeping past a small town. They had been flying to the west above Interstate 68, heading for Morgantown. "Youghiogheny River. Friendsville, Maryland," shouted the pilot over the thunder of the rotors.

Elliot knew this was one of two dozen places that Dornblaser could be. Damn those imbeciles in Morgantown. Dornblaser was alive and back on his home turf. Incredible. Tricky this man was. It was time to bring him in once and for all. Ten more operatives were on their way from Pittsburgh and would meet him at the airport.

They circled the small town once and Elliot pointed the pilot westward. He didn't want to be late. The cellfax beeped and he read the transmission as it slid out of the machine. The Dornblasers had returned home in the Caravan. No sign of the Subaru. Warrants would be waiting at the airport.

Elliot tapped out a Fax transmission and sent it off. Moments later, agents would swarm the Dornblaser residence. Good. Hold those people till I get there. Below was another, but slightly smaller, river.

"Big Sandy Creek, Bruceton Mills, West Virginia."

Elliot recognized these place names from the intelligence packet he'd read on Dornblaser including the man's own kayak school brochure. It was piquing his interest to actually see them for himself. So this was Dornblaser's domain. It was all coming alive.

They cruised over Cheat Lake and set down on the helipad at Morgantown airport at 1:56. Elliot was rushed into a borrowed conference room in the terminal building. Outside the door an F.B.I. agent was talking to half a dozen West Virginia State Police officers and as many Morgantown city cops. He wasn't introduced. Overtly at least, he didn't exist. Once inside, and with the door shut, Mark Shreve, the C.I.A. chief in Pittsburgh handed him a Photo I.D. badge that said Justice Department. He was still Elliot Carlson but J.D. took a bit of the edge off of his presence.

"Mitchell wants you to call him. Damn, that man has a foul mouth!" Shreve said, staring at him.

"I want to get over to the Dornblaser residence."

"I think you'd better call now. This line has been secured." He pointed at the phone on the conference table.

Elliot dialed and Mitchell himself answered.

"Dammit, Carlson, Why the fuck did you take off like that?"

"Excuse me, sir, but you do want Dornblaser brought in, don't you? I felt I could be much more effective here and it is our two heads on the block on this one. Isn't it, sir?"

"Shit! Okay, Elliot. Look, as long as you're there, see to it no one talks to Dornblaser's parents but you. And that goes triple A for Dornblaser when you get him. Understood?"

"Yes Sir".

"Okay. And call me, Dammit!"

With that Mitchell slammed down the phone on his end.

Elliot could imagine the sparks and steam flying in Langley.

"Take me to my car." he said to Shreve, this time in a demanding tone.

It was a white Jeep Cherokee with West Virginia tags, unmarked. The drive down into town took ten minutes, winding down the Willey street hill and passing through downtown. Shreve said traffic was light compared to when the WVU school year was in full swing and there were another twenty thousand students around. They crossed the Deckers Creek bridge and climbed Grand street into South Park. Elliot noticed that it was an old neighborhood of large homes shaded by ancient hardwoods. They turned off Grand onto Maple and parked in front of the Dornblaser residence. A U.S marshal stood at the door and let them pass inside where another marshal stood beside the couch where a middle aged couple, not too unlike his own parents, sat looking sad and weary. It was not like he had expected. He'd expected the Dornblasers to be a bit on the rough side, but here were two very civilized, community pillar types in a middle class, well cared for home. He forgot about being the threatening government agent, making threats to get the information he needed . Instead he felt a flash of empathy.

No. This can't be. Empathy doesn't go with this job at all.

Speaking in a voice that seemed not to come from himself, he said: "Mr. and Mrs. Dornblaser, my name is Elliot Carlson and I'm from the U.S. Department of Justice. I think you know why I'm here."

"Mr. Carlson, with all due respect, just tell me whether or not we are under arrest."

"Well, Mrs. Dornblaser, not yet. And it depends on what happens next."

"As in what?" asked Ben.

"As in how well you cooperate with us for one thing. I need to have a look around."

"The search warrant was served when we arrived, sir," the marshal chimed in.

"Have your look, Mr. Carlson," said Ben.

"Does your son have his own room in the house?"

"Upstairs, first room on the left."

Elliot entered Pete's room feeling that he was violating personal space. Kayaking photos hung from all four walls. There were shots of kayaks running waterfalls and standing up vertically on waves.

What a life this guy's had.

Otherwise, the room looked as if it hadn't been occupied for some time.

Or somebody wants it to look that way.

The drawers of the dresser each had a smattering of clothing but held no clues. The bookcase held a range of fiction and nonfiction but no books on kayaking. Most of the shelves were littered with various kayaking trinkets. An ashtray held a few cigarette butts and some foil twisted up like a little fighter jet. As he turned away from the shelves, something caught his eye behind the TV set. It was a padded manila envelope with no markings. He picked it up and an unmarked video cassette slid out. Taking a look out into the hallway first, he turned on the television and quickly lowered the volume. He pushed the tape into the machine and pushed play. Howard Calvert appeared on the screen. He turned up the volume enough to hear and watched the tape. Howard appeared on the screen holding the helmet.

"Hi, Petey, I hope you find this entertaining. Please watch and listen carefully. I've tried to make this as simple to operate as possible. This unit is a combination of the latest technologies. The three main functions are: Moving Water Analysis, using the equation I worked up after our work in Africa, time and space transfer, using Mihalis' program, and a tracking locator for Mihalis. Two additional functions are a vital signs indicator and an override function. These two functions are interconnected, as I will explain later."

"All controls are voice activated, and only your voice can activate them. Only you can use this helmet.

"The computer technology is all super advanced, and the total cost of this unit including all expenses was $278,000. Don't worry about that, though. It was all financed with a SuperBowl T-shirt and some old newspaper financial sections. The only bad part about that is that there are some pissed off bookies and stockbrokers in Columbia, South Carolina. They'll get over it.

"Back to the unit. River Analysis uses relatively little energy. The Mihalis tracking system almost none; it merely receives a signal from Mihalis. The time and space transfer function uses a hell of a lot of energy, and has some noticeable side effects that we'll talk about in a minute."

Now the video shifted to Howard beside a computer monitor.

"This monitor will simulate what you see inside your visor." Howard had now assumed his more serious, professorial manner.

"When you put the helmet on you will notice that the word 'ready' appears in upper left corner of the visor."

READY

"When you don't want any function, feel free to say whatever. To initiate any function, you must first say, 'Helmet.'" Now the screen changed and read:

FUNCTION?

"Let's say you want river analysis. You say 'River Screen On.'"

RIVER SCREEN ON MATRIX AMP. ANIMINAMIN RATIO ME-
TERS U.C.

0	0			
0	0			
0	0			
0	0			
0				0
0				0
0				0
0				0

AVG. GRAD. NEXT 10 MTS./50 MTS. CFS RECOM. ROUTE
PERCENT SUCC.

"As you can see here, the screen is bordered with zeros. That is because there is no whitewater river within sensor range right now. You will be amazed the first time you use it. On the water, there will be no zeros. The screen will overlay exactly what you are looking at. Shifting your eyes without turning your head will give you a slight tracing effect, but you will quickly get used to it. I did.

"Next is Matrix Amplification. If you want a lighter screen, call out: 'Matrix lighter.' Darker overlay, 'Matrix darker.'

"The Animate/Inanimate Ratio is an analysis of the riverbed's rock structure derived from moving water analysis using my equation. Anything under five and you should use extreme caution."

"Meters Under Craft measures the depth of water under your kayak. This will change constantly in most river situations."

"Now at the bottom of the screen you will see gradient analysis. When you see the two figures converging with any number over three meters you know you're in for the steep stuff. Cubic feet per second was used instead of cubic meters per second to be more exact and because we are more accustomed to that system."

"Now the Recommended Route and Percentage of Success. Pete, I know what you're thinking: 'I don't need a computer to tell me where to go.' Part of the concept of this part of the helmet unit is to simulate what any given piece of water would look like at different water levels. The computer automatically analyzes the rock structure based on moving water analysis and records it. You can eddy out above a given rapid you feel is potentially threatening and say, for example: 'Helmet, record Aquatarkus.' Then, if you find yourself there with super-high water at some other time, you can simulate the Aquatarkus with the day's water level by saying: 'Helmet, simulate Aquatarkus at 4,000 c.f.s.'. The screen will then display that rapid from the perspective you had when you said 'record.' The unit will then give you the recommended route and the percentage of success. This is something directly derived from our work at Wadi Nouveau. There, we took absolute measurements of rock structure and simulated water with gamma rays to verify the flow as defined by that structure. My equation allows the reversal of that process with 92% accuracy, minimum.

"Now, Petey, I'm going to explain something very important about this helmet. I think that Mihalis wanted you to have this unit, to help guarantee your survival until the completion of your mission. You are my best friend, and I, too, want you to survive."

Howard now turned away from the monitor and looked more directly at the camera.

"I have built an override function into the helmet. One triggering mechanism is based on oxygen availability. If the unit goes under water for more than three seconds, it begins a sixty second countdown to override, which will be displayed prominently on the visor. If the moving water analysis reveals a percentage of success of under fifteen percent, or the vital signs sensor that monitors your pulse at your left temple, indicates a more complex situation than oxygen deficiency, the override can be automatically triggered and accelerated by the unit. In either scenario, if the unit feels that your survival quotient is compromised, it takes you out of there by time transfer. You will be dropped in a different time and your survivability will be monitored until it becomes viable. In other words, until you regain consciousness."

Howard continued: "The Mihalis tracking function works like this: if you are separated from Mihalis, you can transfer to the same time and approximate space by saying: 'Helmet, Mihalis track and transfer.'"

"You must of course be ready for the physical side effects that we have both experienced: temporary loss of consciousness, temporary vision loss, and headache. Also, any space/time transfer from the helmet requires so much energy from the unit, in the form of heat exchange, that you need to be prepared for some hot and cold sensations from the helmet. I have calculated that these will be tolerable, but not pleasant. Don't touch the outside of the helmet if you can avoid it.

"One thing that the unit cannot do is allow you to transfer through space and time on your own. Mihalis did not provide programming for that, and even after a thorough review of each algorithm, I can't figure out how it works. All I know is that it does."

Now the scene shifted to what looked like Howard in a hotel room.

"I had wanted to explain all this to you in person, and the tape would have been something you could watch a couple of times as a sort of review, but it looks like that won't be possible now.

"None of us know what will happen in the future, not even Mihalis. Time is very linear. From my examinations, we can revisit past times, but we cannot change past events. If we do so, we risk setting a divergent path for time to flow. It is a holographic concept; where a small piece of the whole is removed intact, still containing all the parts that existed before. What happens next, however, is a separate reality from what we know. I am convinced now these realities do exist and can be created anew. Be careful Pete. You are about to experience that which no one has experienced. It is going to be very different from the soft lives we have led. I hope you know what this means.

"One last thing, Pete. I sometimes use the terms 'angel' and 'God" to describe Mihalis and what you are being asked to do. I don't know any better terms. Mihalis' God is different from the Big Guy in the Bible. And Mihalis is no Gabriel. Nevertheless, I'm sure that Mihalis is a vital force for good and for human life as we know it. You and I are very different, and you are the one that this is all about. I doubt that you and I are receiving this in the same light, and I don't blame you for having incredible doubts. I have one myself. It has to do with a son you will have. I, I just think that Mihalis is capable of involving him against your wishes. I would tell you to be careful but that never worked before so instead I will just say, 'follow your instincts'. Good luck little brother."

The screen went to snow.

Jesus Christ Almighty

Elliot thought for a moment and slowly reached for the remote control. With a sense of detachment from what he was doing, he rewound the tape and pushed record. Confident that the tape was erasing, he turned off the TV and had a last look around. No more clues. Jesus. Wait a second, I'm not telling anybody about that tape I just erased. What is happening to me? Have I gone crazy? Hell, nobody would have believed that tape anyway.

But why did I erase it?

Elliot walked back downstairs and received the blank stares of the Dornblasers and the Marshal.

"All clean up there," he said, more for the benefit of the marshal than Ben and Esmeralda. "You two are under house arrest until further notice. The marshal will read you your rights and whether or not you are formally charged will be up to the U.S. Attorney's Office. Any questions?"

Instead of responding to him Esmy took Ben's arm and pointed with her free hand at the mantle.

"Look Ben, the coin."

All eyes shifted to the mantle but Elliot saw no coin, only an open glass frame with a faded red velvet backing. In the center of the velvet was a circle of unfaded velvet where obviously something had been removed. Esmy had already stood and crossed to the mantle as Elliot asked: "Something missing?"

"Yes" Ben said. "It's an heirloom that's been in Esmy's family forever. It was a twenty dollar gold piece from the eighteenth century that, as the story goes, an ancestor of hers won in a wager with the Devil..."

☙❧

Elliot had not learned anything from the Dornblasers. They both had simply stated that they wanted to speak first with their attorney and as he pressed further they only stared at him.

His call to Mitchell had left him feeling uncomfortable. He had mentioned nothing of the video tape. He had committed the unpardonable to his superior. Worse yet, he was worried that perhaps Mitchell had detected nervousness in his voice. The omission. The infidelity.

Calvert and Dornblaser had hooked on to something in Algeria. Something big. From the perspective of the C.I.A., it didn't add up. It wasn't logistically possible. "Logistically possible." Yet it had happened. The company didn't like it when things didn't match its view. These guys were two steps ahead. Now he was privy to part of the explanation. Time and space transfer. Creating energy. The company would want all that. He was holding back. He was implicated. Would he also soon become an outsider? As soon as they found out he had done something against them . . .

Them.

I'm already starting to think of the agency as them! . . . they'll get it out of him.

But what is the solution? Find the pair before the company finds them. Then what? Who the hell knows? I've taken the first step. Any further and I can't turn back.

Interstate 68 runs east from Morgantown, West Virginia to Hancock, Maryland. In its course it passes Bruceton Mills and Friendsville. He was racing the Cherokee over the mountain past Coopers Rock State Park. He was surprised at the beauty of the area. It had seemed so flat from the air, hours before, but now it was steep and mountainous.

Minutes later he rolled off the highway at the Bruceton Mills exit and began asking questions about Pete Dornblaser. Nobody had seen him for months. He'd lost a big lawsuit, right? You looking for Pete? He blew himself up with an A-bomb in Africa, didn't he?

Innocent answers from simple country people. A few more questions and he was informed that there weren't any kayaking businesses in Bruceton Mills. Plenty in Friendsville. Back onto the interstate. Fifteen minutes later he was across the state line and rolling to a stop in front of the kayak store. A stocky man in shorts and a ragged T-shirt was sitting on the curb talking on a cordless phone. Elliot stepped out of his Jeep and walked over to him. The man finished his conversation and beeped off the phone.

"Yes sir," he said, "what can I help you with?"

"I need to ask you some questions about Peter Dornblaser."

The man stared at him.

"I don't talk to guys in suits."

"I don't think you know who I'm with."

The man stepped up on to the street and looked at the back of the Cherokee."Well, you're from West Virginia which tells me you're out of your jurisdiction, and as far as I'm concerned, you can shove it up your ass. Any questions?"

"No. Thanks a lot."

"Glad to be of help."

Damn, thought Elliot as he climbed back into the Jeep, that guy probably knows Dornblaser, and I'm not getting anywhere.

The rest of the people he talked to in Friendsville gave him the same sort of cold shoulder. He started to roll out of town and stopped for a second on the bridge over the Youghiogheny river. The river, that hadn't looked like much from the air, now had the look of an awesome force. Here it was almost flat. Yet it was full of brown water, moving relentlessly past. Elliot remembered from his readings of the briefing packet that upstream was a canyon with Class IV and V rapids. What would those be like on a day like this?

I want to know.

He started to accelerate across the bridge when he noticed the Riverside Lounge on the right and braked to a stop in the parking lot. He walked in and when his eyes adjusted to the dark, he saw the barmaid, an attractive blond. Across from him were three drunks. One was out cold with his face on the bar. The other two gave him unfriendly stares.

I've got to change clothes.

"Get you somethin'?" asked the woman.

"I need to ask you some questions."

"I ain't real good about answerin' questions. You some kind of cop?"

"No. Do you know Peter Dornblaser?"

"You look like a cop and sound like a cop."

"Trust me. I'm not. I really need to talk to Peter."

"Look mister, I don't know why you come here askin' about him. Don't you know he's dead over in Africa?"

This is hopeless.

He had lowered his head to think of another angle of questioning when he looked at the ashtray.

A little foil bird.

Thanks Ma'am. You've been a big help."

By the eleventh cart at Walmart, Pete had started to draw a small crowd of store employees. He rolled the sixteenth and final cart out to the parking lot and loaded its contents in the truck. The truck was piled high with camping gear, hiking boots, warm clothes, knives, generators, electronics he wasn't sure he would ever use. Who knew what you could get ahold of easily in Brazil and what not. Anyway, he had the cash and it sure wouldn't hurt to show up with everything he could possibly need.

He rummaged through the hundred-plus bags until he found the bolt cutters and set them off to the side close to the door. Pete rolled down the door and placed a huge new Master lock on the hasp.

But the sad truth was that Pete Dornblaser was feeling hollow. He was going away for a long time and wouldn't be seeing his friends or family. He was shocked that people like all of the other shoppers in Walmart were the kind of people he wouldn't be seeing anymore. Suddenly he was feeling nostalgia. After so many years of rebelling against society, either overtly or covertly, he was after all, an element of society. He had despised these people's humdrum lives. But now he was going to miss them.

Shit! I've got to buy food!

On to Giant Eagle. It was now 7:45 and not getting any earlier.

Elliot wasn't really sure where he was going next. He was on Interstate 68 heading west and at Bruceton Mills he would either go north to Ohiopyle, Pennsylvania, or south to Albright, West Virginia, where Dornblaser's paddling school had been.

The cellphone beeped.

"Carlson here."

"Elliot." It was Mitchell. "We computer isolated the last time the Dornblasers used one of their credit cards."

"And..?"

"They rented a Goddam Ryder truck right after they left their house this morning."

"Did we have it checked out?"

"Yes. That fucker had double tanks and a range of 400 miles without refueling. S.S.A. is working overtime but we only get one damn pass every 48 minutes over your area. He could be anywhere by now. We're going to have every Ryder truck east of the Mississippi stopped. You turn up anything?"

"Nothing Sir."

"Okay, Carlson. Got to go. Keep me informed."

He clicked off.

So he's in a Ryder truck. That helps.

Elliot pulled over to the side of the road and spent the next two hours studying and absorbing the maps of the three-state area and correlating them with the river information in the briefing packs. He changed into jeans and a golf shirt. He still had black shoes. Oh well.

If he was going to find Dornblaser, he had to think like Dornblaser. 'Pete,' not Peter, was a man of casual intensity. Elliot also was an intense man, and now he felt more casual without the suit and tie. Maybe people would actually talk to him.

He decided to go south. At the end of the ramp at the Bruceton Mills exit, he turned left onto WV 26 and drove eleven miles to Albright. He pulled into Cheat Canyon campgrounds and there was Dornblaser's Paddling School. A large truck trailer was parked outside the rustic building set to the east side of the campground. The campground was a large field between a row of houses along the highway, and the Cheat River. There was a white cinder block building at the gate which was obviously the campground headquarters. He remembered that the peak rafting season on the Cheat was already past for the year. In other years, Dornblaser would have been operating his school here until late October. There would be students camping in the campground. Now the camp looked closed. The gate was locked with a heavy chain. The grass was high in the field. The sun was ready to set between the mountains downstream where the Cheat entered its canyon. The river, running unseasonably high, shimmered in the evening light. It was a beautiful sight but directly west across the river, was a huge strip mining project.

The paradox of West Virginia. West Virginia is a state rich in bituminous coal and rich in natural beauty. The two do not mix and natural beauty is losing out to progress.

Elliot walked over to the paddling school and looked in through the windows. All was neat and tidy. The front door was padlocked with an ugly hasp bolted right through the rustic door frames. The windows on the door were plastered with IRS stickers warning against entrance and spelling out all potential criminal complications for doing so. The trailer was also padlocked and stickered. There was no sign that anyone had been there. As Elliot walked back to the Cherokee, he felt a flush of sympathy for Pete. It was bad enough to have the IRS on your case.

అ≪

Pete pulled out of the Giant Eagle after spending over a thousand dollars on food. He had stocked up on a huge assortment of dried and canned food as well as a cartload of junk food. He had drawn the same sort of looks from the staff of Giant Eagle as he had in Walmart.

Next, he pulled into a gas station and filled all twenty of the plastic five gallon gas jugs he'd bought at Walmart. The gas station was self-service, but the owner came out to help.

"You going where there aint any gas stations buddy?"

"Oh no. I've got a construction project up in the hills. This is for the generator."

The man took a look inside the truck and saw all the grocery bags.

"Guess there's no food where you're going either."

"Got to feed the workers you know."

"Okay buddy. Is that all of 'em?"

Pete said, "Yes sir," and set the last of the jugs into the back of the truck. "How much?"

"Hundred forty nine bucks. By the way, this is a Ryder truck, isn't it?"

"Yeah. So?"

"Came over the scanner a little while ago that they're pulling over all Ryder trucks."

"Here, in Uniontown?"

"No. Everywhere. Looking for some guy with a strange sounding name. Dunheiser or something like that."

"Well, nothing to do with me."

Nervously, he slid out into traffic.

Shit! Got to make one more stop.

He pulled around to the side lot of Grampies and walked inside.

Grampies was the last place in town to buy case beer. He paid the woman at the register for twenty cases of Bud and twenty four cartons of Camels.

"What you driving sonny, a truck?"

"Yes Ma'am."

"Kenny there will load you out on the side dock."

"Sounds good, that's right where I'm parked. Thanks a million."

"Thank you, sonny. Have a good evening."

Pete rolled out of Grampies and headed down through Hopwood and onto Route 40 heading east. He had to climb Summit Mountain. It would be the last four miles of possible highway contact with cops.

It was nine o'clock. He turned on the headlights.

How I love these long summer days.

As he neared the top of the mountain the last rays of the setting sun broke through the clouds and glinted off of the red light on top of a Pennsylvania State Police cruiser.

Instinctively Pete clicked on the high beams and between his bright lights and the angle of the sunlight, the westbound cop sailed past the eastbound Pete without seeing the Ryder truck.

Pete crested the summit and hung a right on Summit Road. The road ran south along the top of Chestnut ridge almost to West Virginia.

Some miles down the road, he turned into a long driveway. It was the farm of an old friend, Patrick "Patch" Majewicz. Pete parked in front of the barn as Patch stepped down off the front porch, beer in hand. Pete stepped out of the truck.

"Patch! What's going on?!"

"Well look what the cat dragged in! Great God Almighty. If it ain't Peter S. Dornblaser. You know I was just saying to myself last night, if you weren't dead, it was just a matter of time before you showed up here."

Patch Majewicz stood about six feet tall, had coarse black hair and the broad shoulders and toughened hands of an Appalachian farmer.

"Pete, you're a hot boy. First thing is get that truck in the barn. Let me roll out the tractor."

Patch took a long look straight up in the evening sky and hastened to the task of starting up his aging John Deere. Once he had driven it out, Pete pulled the Ryder in. They shut the barn doors and Patch put an arm around Pete, leading him toward the farmhouse.

"Let's have a drink Pete. I want to hear all about your trip to Africa. Hah! This is going to be a good one."

Several beers and several shots of moonshine later, Pete had explained as best he could to Patch all that had happened. Together, they half staggered out to the barn so Pete could show him Mihalis. Patch was a kayaker and weekend warrior rafting guide and, with his background, knew about kayaks. They waded through the hundreds of bags in the back of the Ryder and Pete pulled Mihalis up into view.

"Holy Jesus" was all he could say at first, and then as the astonishment subsided: "Well Petey, you finally have all the toys. Don't you?"

"Yeah, but this one makes me nervous."

"Nervous? Ya think? Shit son, this thing has bad juju written all over it."

"Maybe you could get rid of it for me."

Patch reached out to touch the crystal and it let out a huge static spark with a loud snapping sound. "Fuck! Sorry son but I think it says it's yours."

Pete was almost shaking with uneasiness. "Patch, I am flipping out."

"Look Petey, you oughta know that there's a whole lot of people that think there has to be a logical explanation for everything, but that is just not the case. Let me give you an example, my uncle was telling me about this classified mission into Laos they pulled. Seems they got sent this big black kid to help hump the gear. Black kid wasn't even 18, wasn't even 'sposed to be there, but the thing was they figured he'd keep his mouth shut. Well, the squad got stumbled onto by an NVA company and got just about wiped out in a firefight. Just a badly wounded sergeant, some ass hole Lieutenant who was really CIA and the kid made it. So the kid goes out and slits the throats of a dozen nips who are still alive. The Lieutenant gets the kid court-martialed for killing enemy wounded and the kid, get this, says when asked if he felt bad about it, that he never feels anything, that he has no conscience, just somebody else's soul inside of him that tells him when, and when not to do shit."

"So what happened to the black kid?"

"He's still in the Army, the one that freaked was the flaky lieutenant, ran around told the story and then just came up missing out of Bangkok while on leave, never to be seen again. Point is Petey, when the crap don't add up, they've got a way of dealing with the problem and in your case, it probably wouldn't end well for you."

'So it's a good thing that I'm going to Brazil."

"Yes, it's a good thing."

"I think I need a gun."

"That, my boy, will be no problem. Let's go back to the house."

Once inside, Bruno led him down into the basement and clicked on the lights. As always, it was totally organized and immaculately clean. He gestured toward the coal chute beside the furnace and said:

"Spread out this old tarp on the floor. We've got to get this coal out of there. We'll shovel it onto the tarp."

Twenty minutes later, shirts off and sweating, they cleared the last of the coal away from the floor. Patch took two angled pieces of steel rod from a drawer and inserted them into holes in the cement and lifted a section of the floor up and set it to the side.

"Come on down here Petey," he said climbing down a ladder into the hole. Pete descended into the secret sub-basement and Patch turned on a battery powered lantern. Shelves holding wooden crates with stenciled writing in several languages lined three sides of the room. The fourth wall was lined with automatic weapons in a long rack.

"Haven't been down here for years, Petey."

"Christ, Patch. I knew you were heavy into this shit but I had no idea. I was just going to ask you for one of your pistols."

"Pete, we don't send guys where you're about to go without more serious protection. You might well need this."

Patch lowered a crate to the floor and pried the top off.

"Pete, these are Claymore mines. They are an unequaled perimeter security system. Bet you didn't know I've got 'em all around the house and the barn."

"Claymores! You crazy? You mean trip lines and all that?"

"They don't have to be trip line activated. Three smacks on the trigger handle and any unwanted guests are met by a wall of C-4 powered ball bearings. No more problems, and it's pretty hard to goof up. To hit the trigger hard three times by accident is next to impossible."

"Where in the hell did you get all this crap?"

"My two uncles were in Nam, remember? They figured they weren't over there risking getting blown apart and not going to get anything out of it. They had connections and sent all this back, bit by bit. I've got it all, Pete. Just about. You name it, I have it. I figure two rounds of these Claymores, eight units. One of these SKS Chinese carbines with the aftermarket folding stock, a thousand rounds of 7.63 ammo on speed loader clips. A pump twelve gauge, and a pistol I've got upstairs, and you will be set."

Patch spent some time going over the placement and activation of the Claymores with Pete, and they moved everything up to the basement and sealed the coal chute back up with coal. They moved over to the gun bench and Patch took Pete through the steps of dismantling and cleaning the SKS and the shotgun. Patch was always meticulous, and went into painstaking detail explaining how the weapons functioned and had to be cared for.

Once finished, they moved everything out to the truck and packed it in the back.

"Pete, are you sure you want to go through with this?"

"Hell. I don't know, Patch. Seems like lately, I just take whatever life throws at me. I'm a little afraid, but all this shit I bought today makes me feel more secure."

"Yeah, I noticed all the Budweiser."

"Patch. Let's go back to the house and have another drink."

"Okay Petey, but it's almost two A.M. Look, you have to get all this into the container at your paddling school. I can't risk it. Too many people down there count on me. They will take care of you when you get there. The container will get picked up and an identical one, more or less, left in its place. I have your new passport and your ticket to Rio in the house."

Pete stared at him.

"Howard sent it by private courier two weeks ago, Mr. Duane Singley"

Everything would have been different had they not been standing and talking next to Mihalis.

❧

Elliot Carlson had been within eight miles of Pete at nine P.M. as he was crossing Route 40 heading north to Ohiopyle, Pennsylvania.

Ohiopyle was one of the most famous river towns in the world and this time he hadn't made the mistake of asking about Pete. He had found his way instead to a bar called "Dogwood Acres" and was surprised to find himself sitting in on what amounted to a wake for his fugitive. The parking lot had been full of cars with kayaks on the roof racks.

Elliot had looked at himself in the rearview mirror; he needed a shave. His golf shirt was now not so crisp and his black shoes were scuffed and muddy. That was good. He had walked up on the front porch and noticed that the bar wasn't there but down around to the side. Oops. He walked down the side steps and there were two dozen kayaker types sitting around the picnic tables drinking and talking. He walked inside and noticed the predominating beer was Pabst Blue Ribbon. He caught the attention of the barmaid.

"I'll have a Pabst please."

Although most of the crowd had been seated outside, the chill and mosquitoes were chasing them in. Soon the talk returned to where it had obviously been outside as well: Peter Dornblaser. The bulk of the sentiment was that he had perished in the atomic blast, but there were a vocal few who did not believe it and were sure he would soon reappear. After midnight, most of the people started to drift out. Elliot was on his fifth Pabst and was starting to feel drunk. He had had his back to them most of the night and hadn't aroused any visible suspicion.

He hadn't called in to Mitchell. Mitchell was going to be pissed.

The diehard crowd hadn't even hinted that any of them knew that Dornblaser was in the area. What had come of their conversations were a wealth of Dornblaser anecdotes and tales: on the rivers and off. Pete was a legend.

Now there were only five men left in the bar, all drunk. Elliot asked for another beer and decided to try to talk to them.

"You guys mind if I sit here?" he said, moving over to their table.

"Not at all. Have a seat buddy," said a slender, fortyish, sandy haired man, gesturing to a chair.

"You up in the mountains for some rafting?" asked a younger man with long black hair.

"Yes. I'm really interested in whitewater. I've never done it, but it sounds fascinating. Who is this guy you have all been talking about all night?"

"Pete? He's the guy that blew up all them Ayrabs over in Africa the other day."

"No kidding? That guy? And he was from here?"

"He was from Morgantown, but Pete was everywhere. You never knew where you'd see him next."

"He's not dead, he's not dead. I'll bet anything he's back here running around somewhere," said a cherub faced, blue eyed man.

"Yeah, Kid, I'll bet you're right. None of it adds up. And that shit they said came over the scanner this afternoon."

"That Pete is somthin else, ain't he?"

He sure is, but where the hell is he, thought Elliot glancing down at his watch. It was almost 2 A.M. Closing time. Time to go.

"Well, I am going to call it a night. Nice meeting you guys. Good luck with your friend."

"Hey, so you runnin the river tomorrow?" said the long haired man.

"Yeah."

"Careful buddy."

"Why's that? Is it dangerous?"

"No. Addictive!"

They all continued to laugh and giggle drunkenly as he walked out the door. Now those are real people. They don't waste an hour a day on the beltway. They wear comfortable clothes. They may be crude. They drink too much. They laugh too loud. But, what a life. And, what a life I have. Where am I going? I'm going to be in big trouble with Mitchell for one thing. I better call in. At least Mitchell will probably be home asleep right now.

Wrong. Mitchell was in and he was cranky.

"Carlson, what in Hell have you been doing?"

"Sir, I've been driving around the area trying to find out as much as I can about Dornblaser."

"Well why have you been in a bar for the last three and a half hours?"

Shit. there must be a GPS tracker in the car. They located me by satellite.

"Do you know how much agency time, technology, and effort it took to determine that our Goddam number one man on the case has been drinking beer in a fucking hick bar?"

"Sir, sometimes you have to really try to blend in if you want to get somewhere with people." He cringed.

"Well get this Elliot. We've stopped over six hundred Ryder trucks in the last six hours and nothing. However, a Pennsylvania State Trooper 'thinks' he maybe saw a Ryder heading east on Route 40 around nine o'clock. By the time he could get turned around to pursue, he found nothing. We've established checkpoints at all major intersections. We're going to intensify the search at daybreak, and I want you to stay on top of it. But stay low profile. The second Dornblaser is in custody, move in and grab him. Understood?"

"Yes sir. I'm going to drive back to Albright, West Virginia on the off chance he shows up at his kayak school."

"And Elliot . . ."

"Yes, Sir?"

". . . don't drink anymore, Goddamit!"

"No, Sir."

Elliot rolled down the road into Ohiopyle and stopped at a state park sign which read: "Falls Parking." The lot was closed with a padlocked cable. He parked the Cherokee at the entrance and walked down to the falls overlook with the roar of the waterfall building in his ears.

He'd seen much higher and more spectacular waterfalls in his life. It was certainly no Niagara. But now his perspective had changed. Everything was changing. What he saw was the domain of river people. The thrill, the risk, the control needed to ply such water. Building within him was a respect for these people and even more for his prey. Dornblaser had mastered the sport; helped create the sport. But now he was on the verge of something bigger. Much bigger. Why him? What was the real connection between Dornblaser and Dr. Calvert? The video tape he'd seen in the afternoon kept rolling through his head. He had to find him. Not stop him. No. Find him.

Elliot had been staring into the falling water, hypnotized.

Dornblaser wasn't really a dangerous criminal. If anything, he was a victim. And Elliot realized that he himself was no longer a field agent for Central Intelligence. No. He was a rogue, using the advantage of the agency to locate a fugitive for his own gains. But what could those gains possibly be?

As he walked to the car he thought: this will all become clear. I know it. But a fatalism seemed to hold him. He had always believed in free will. He still did. But he seemed to be drawn. And he didn't know why.

He drove through the night, south on a back road called Pennsylvania 381. At one point he crossed the Mason Dixon Line into West Virginia. Dark forests hung over the twisting road and crickets and frogs added their constant accompaniment to the drive. He turned left onto West Virginia 26 at the end of 381. In less than two minutes he was driving into Bruceton Mills. A dense fog seemed to be rolling across the road. It must be coming from Big Sandy Creek. Blue flashing lights were piercing the fog and he realized he was approaching the junction with the Interstate. West Virginia State police were on the overpass and down on the divided highway below. He rolled to a stop and two officers peered into the Cherokee from either side with Maglights. They had black and white prints of Dornblaser's high school yearbook photo on clipboards. He was ready to reach for his Department of Justice I.D. badge when they waved him through.

Shit. Why should I go to Albright? Dornblaser could never get through this roadblock. Yes he could. He just wouldn't come through here. He would take back roads.

Twenty minutes later, Elliot pulled into the entrance of Cheat Canyon Campgrounds. He trained the lights of the Jeep on the gate. It was padlocked just as it had been in the evening. Elliot had a flash. He could wait across the river high in the strip mine where he would be able to watch the paddling school.

This is stupid. He's not coming here.

Yes he is. I know he is. I feel it.

Elliot drove another mile south into Albright and crossed the bridge over the Cheat River and turned right into the open gate of the strip mine. The road ran uphill, angling its way to the top of the ridge. Finally he reached the open area which he had seen earlier from below. Spread before him was a perfect panorama of the campground across the river. He pulled the Jeep to a stop pointed straight towards the paddling school building.

It was 3:30 A.M. He settled back in the driver's seat and thought of what a long day he had had. How little sleep he had had. How tiring the last week had been. He hadn't yet shaken off jet lag from the Africa trip. *Can't rest yet, not until I catch up with Dornblaser.*

Patch held out the grip of the pistol to Pete.

"Smith and Wesson, nine millimeter. Including the bullet in the chamber, you've got twelve rounds. Press the release, clip drops out." The clip thunked heavily on the carpet in the living room. "Don't think about catching it, slam in the next one." The clip made a definitive clicking sound as it locked into the grip of the gun.

"This is your best friend in the jungle my boy. If the shit gets heavy, just keep moving and keep pulling the trigger. And never let it away from your side until it's 'pried from your cold dead fingers,' as they say."

"That's exactly what happened in Africa."

"When they killed your friend. What was his name again?"

"Salil. He was a good dude. And it's my fault that he's dead."

"That sucks Pete. Look, I've got a feeling that might have just been the beginning. You've got to stay sharp. You can do it."

"You do know better than to drive through Bruceton."

"Yeah, I've got the route, I've got to get going."

"I know."

They walked out to the barn and Patch gave him a bear hug before he climbed into the truck. He put the pistol and the heavy bag of loaded clips on the passenger side floor. With a mock salute he rolled out of the barn and down the drive. Patch stood and watched as the taillights disappeared into the darkness.

CHAPTER 7 — READY, SET...

Pete drove cautiously down Summit Road. Crossing the West Virginia line, he detoured down a dirt road into the upper Big Sandy valley. He crossed an old iron bridge over the creek and wound his way upward until he came out on 381. At its terminus with Route 26, he turned right and began driving toward Bruceton Mills. Entering the village of Brandonville, he took a left on Brandonville Pike, heading towards Terra Alta. He had to pass over Interstate 68 and, as he started onto the overpass, he could see blue lights strobing the hillside below.

Shit. There must be a roadblock in Bruceton.

He hurried over the bridge and drove onward. He hadn't passed any cars, but he changed his mind about the route. It was too risky to finish out the last leg by dropping down Woolen Mill road from the Pike to Route 26. He decided to continue towards Terra Alta and take the old dirt road down Roaring Creek. That would put him right across Route 26 from the campground. He had a stab of anxiety.

What if they're waiting for me at the campground?

Too late for those kind of thoughts. The plan is set.

Pete nervously glanced at his watch. It was 4:12 a.m. He knew he was cutting it perilously close to daybreak. Finally he came to the turnoff for Roaring Creek road and carefully worked his way downhill. It was a steep and narrow dirt road for the Ryder truck and he had to creep down. Finally, he arrived within a quarter mile of his destination. He stopped the truck and turned off the lights. He stepped out and stretched his legs. He lit up a Camel and tried to relax.

Damn, the bolt cutters! Better get them out now.

Pete removed the bolt cutters from the back and placed them on the front seat. Driving without lights, he crawled down the road to the stop sign. There, across the highway, was the campgrounds.

The place had always felt like home, and there it was, same as ever. Not quite the same. The grass had grown and it had a forlorn, empty look. No sound but crickets. He decided to go for it. He pulled up to the gate and hopped out with the bolt cutters, sliced through the chain which fell to the gravel with a clatter. The gate creaked painfully loud as he swung it open. He climbed back into the truck and eased it across the high grass to the school trailer. Hopping out again, he chopped the IRS padlock off of the back doors. He swung the doors open and then backed the Ryder to within two feet. He killed the engine and left the keys in the ignition. Pete now bent to the task of transferring the contents of the Ryder to the trailer. The trailer had most of the paddling school kayaks and equipment stored in racks on the side walls, but the floor was cluttered with everything the IRS had taken from the headquarters building. It was a mess. It took the better part of an hour to move just the bags of purchased items, the gas cans and the weaponry. Finally all that was left were the boxes of books from his parents' house, the box containing the helmet. And, Mihalis.

It was 5:36 a.m. He stuffed the boxes and Mihalis on top of the huge pile. Tired and sweaty, Pete rummaged through the load until he came to the Budweiser. He grabbed a couple of the warm cans and popped one open. Turning his back on the task at hand, he walked across the campground to the banks of the river. This was the moment of truth and he knew better than to be next to Mihalis as he thought it through. It was time to leave Mihalis behind. He would walk back to the container and pull the crystal kayak back out and stuff it into the Ryder. Then he would close the doors and walk away. This of course was the rational decision, but for Pete, the kayaker, a very difficult one. Leaving the most incredible kayak in the history of the sport behind and walking away from it somehow did not seem rational.

The first rays of the sun were lighting the tops of the canyon downstream. How long would it be until he would see this again? Or would he? This last thought saddened him. The Cheat river had been his home all his adult life.......

❧❦

Elliot's cell phone beeped and he woke with a start.

"Carlson here."

"Elliot wake up! SSA just handed me a photo of the campground with the Ryder truck backed up to Dornblaser's trailer!" Mitchell's shaken voice was reverberating in his head. Elliot leaned forward and looked.

Jesus Christ. There he is, walking towards the trailer.

"Affirmative sir! I see him. He's right there."

❧❦

Pete's calm was shattered at the sound of tires hitting gravel. He looked up and State Police cars were streaming through the open gate. He immediately ran to the trailer and leapt into the back.

"God dammit, the pistol!"

He jumped out of the trailer and ran to the cab of the Ryder. The first of the State Police cruisers was almost on him.

જ⁓

"Sir. We've got a problem! There are West Virginia State Police cars in the campground."

"God bless America, Carlson, get down there quick before those guys cap our boy."

Too late for that thought Elliot. Another squadron of cruisers was charging down from the north on 26, lights flashing and sirens howling. Somebody must have called.

જ⁓

Pete grabbed the gun and the bag of clips from the floor as the closest car slid to a stop in the grass, officers jumping out of the doors, drawing pistols.

"Freeze!"

Pete bolted towards the trailer.

"Blam!" The bullet smacked into the side of the Ryder, splinters catching Pete in the cheek. He hit the ground and crawled at gator speed under the truck towards the trailer.

"He's got a gun!"

More shots rang out and resonated on the metal. Air blasted out of the tire by Pete's head as he was slashing his way through the grass under the rear end of the truck.

"Sir, shots are being fired."

"For God's sake Carlson, do something! Get down there! I want that fucker alive!"

"Might be too late, Sir. Sounds like a battle!"

Pete threw the bag of clips up and into the trailer opening.

Bullets were clanging off metal all around him.

Time to go.

He launched himself upward and into the trailer. Bullets were now ripping through the sides. He looked around and he was right in the middle of gas jugs and crates of Claymore mines, and rifle bullets.

Man am I getting tired of people shooting at me.

There were State Troopers crouched behind cars on three sides of the trailer now firing into it. Elliot at first couldn't believe his eyes. The trailer seemed to be shrinking and then suddenly it expanded, and as it did, it rammed against the Ryder truck and shoved it several feet forward. Then in a brilliant flash, the container disappeared. A glowing kayak hung in the air for a moment and then disappeared in another flash. The trailer was gone. The Ryder truck was still right there, but the trailer was gone. A few troopers fired into something on the ground and liquid sprayed into the air. The firing stopped and the liquid continued to spray into the air.

Now all firing stopped and the officers slowly began to rise from behind the cars. There were no longer any sirens, no more lights flashing. Elliot's cell phone was dead. The Cherokee was dead. Two officers moved in to where the trailer had been, guns still drawn, but there was nothing. One reached down and picked something up. Elliot reached into the back and grabbed up his binoculars. The officer was holding a six pack of Budweiser.

He had to walk back down through the strip mine to the bridge. At the gas station in town he called Mitchell.

"Elliot, what the hell happened?"

"Dornblaser is gone."

"Dead?"

"No. Gone. Vanished. He and the trailer vanished in a flash of light."

"Another explosion?"

"No, like Doctor Calvert, like a David Copperfield act. Vanished into thin air."

"Carlson, are you calling me from a public telephone!"

"Sir. Relax. With all respect, I'm in Podunk West Virginia. The cell phone went dead when the trailer vanished. Everything went dead. My car is dead. There are ten State Police cruisers that shut off down there. I imagine any second they're going to be walking in here to call, too."

"Jesus, I don't believe it."

"I know it's hard to believe, but I saw it with my own eyes. There's a bunch of West Virginia State Troopers that can't believe it either, but it happened. Check out the next pass of photos from SSA."

"Okay, I will. Look, Elliot, you haven't talked to anyone there have you?"

"No sir, of course not."

"In that case, we're almost clean. The West Virginia State Police can have the job of explaining this fuckup. Meantime, dammit, I want you back here this afternoon. We need to talk. Understood?"

Yes sir. One thing, sir..."

"What now, Elliot!?"

"Could you please send me another car?"

ᏽᏽᏽ

Elliot didn't go straight back to Washington. Instead, when his car was delivered from Morgantown, he back to Ohiopyle and went on a raft trip. It was crazy. In the midst of all he had seen that he couldn't understand, something made him indulge his wish to raft. He knew that Mitchell wouldn't understand, but he couldn't make himself care.

He had been assigned a space in a black rubber raft with a family of three in a group of over a dozen rafts, each holding four people. He recognized a couple of the guides as people he'd seen outside the bar the night before. One of them was a very good kayaker, doing tricks in the water in every rapid. Elliot alternated watching him and watching the whitewater and what it did to his raft. At the end of the trip, he cornered the kayaker and asked him to recommend a good kayak school.

"Where are you from?"

"Washington, D.C."

"Okay. There's a good school there called Adventure Schools. I'm sure they're in the book. Give them a call."

On the drive to Washington, he felt refreshed. He couldn't explain why he was enthralled by whitewater. But, he was. Captivated. This was more than just getting to know Dornblaser. And it was different from just having a blast doing something different. Something was making him move in a certain direction. What was it? What compelled him?

Throughout the drive he mulled over the past week's events. So Dornblaser was gone. There would be no catching up with him now. The disappearing act had been otherworldly but matched the pattern of unexplainable movements. Actually it provided clues to the others. They had certainly been moving about faster than jets can travel. Was there really such a thing as space/time transfer? That could explain Calvert's various appearances, Dornblaser's rapid return from Africa, and now, his departure. The video tape had said it was all possible. And all this was only preliminary to Dornblaser's "mission." Jesus. What could it be? The answers could only be found with Howard Calvert. He now had to find the good doctor. But how? And if he did, would Calvert pull a disappearing act?

The other thing he had to do was learn to kayak.

❧❦

He rolled into CIA headquarters in Langley a little before 8 p.m. and Mitchell was there.

"I guess you didn't see the Goddamn evening news, did you Elliot?"

"No, sir."

Mitchell popped a video cassette into one of the V.C.R.s in the wall console. A news correspondent stood in front of the Ryder truck in the campground.

"In a bizarre follow-up to the Algerian nuclear incident involving two Americans, one alleged suspect, a West Virginia man named Peter Dornblaser, was killed in an explosion. Trapped by West Virginia State Police officers in a truck trailer here in this campground, the suspect apparently detonated some kind of explosive device. The resulting blast left no trace of the trailer. Oddly enough, no one was injured, although more than a dozen officers were surrounding the trailer at the time. The blast also rendered ten West Virginia State Police cars inoperable."

The scene shifted to show a cruiser being hooked up to a tow truck.

"Although the CIA, which had been investigating the Algerian tragedy, has declined to comment on this latest incident, the FBI stated this afternoon that this 'closes the case' on Peter Dornblaser. Emphasis will now be shifted to the capture of the other suspect, Dr. Howard Calvert."

The scene shifted again to an old man dressed in a plaid shirt and worn gray pants. He was speaking rapidly into the microphone held before him.

"The only other known eyewitness to today's actions was this man, a lifelong resident of Ruthbelle, as this row of houses by the campground is known. His version contrasts vividly with that of the West Virginia State Police statement:"

"I don't know what them troopers think they saw, but what I seen was just a big bright light, and then a 'poof' and that trailer was gone. Then there was this thing hanging in the air for a second, and it was gone too. But there weren't no explosion. Take a look for yourselves. There ain't nothin' burnt down there, no busted windows. Nothin'."

"This eyewitness account is being treated here by the authorities as what amounts to the ramblings of a mentally ill old man. His neighbors here, however, say he only lies to strangers. And as you can see . . ." The scene shifted to the grass behind the Ryder truck. "This certainly doesn't look like the scene of an explosion. The only thing that is certain here is that this case is a long way from being closed. From Albright, West Virginia, Bob Fielder, ABC News."

Peter Jennings appeared seated at the news desk, rear projection of Howard

Calvert on the screen.

"The saga of these two men has taken another turn. But every new development brings another round of contradictions. An unnamed State Department source has termed the movements of these two men as 'logistically impossible' and today's events were no exception. Our source suggests that both men must have stand-ins intended to confuse authorities."

"In other news the World Health Organization...."

Mitchell shut off the tape with the remote and turned to Elliot.

"Jesus, Carlson, this craziness seems to be contagious, and I'm afraid it's starting to spread to you."

"Sir, I can explain eve..."

"I'm going to explain something to you, Elliot! Do you by any chance have any fucking idea how close you are to a 'review'?"

A "Review" was agency slang for a complete, involuntary debriefing. It amounted to an interrogation where no stone was left unturned and any method necessary to drain the candidate of intelligence was within the parameters of agency rules.

Elliot shuddered within but showed nothing of his fear to Mitchell. For years he'd considered Mitchell a friend. Now he wasn't acting like a friend. Elliot was holding back. If you held back intelligence from the agency, you were an enemy of the agency. Mitchell had sensed that Elliot was holding back. Granted, his actions had been strange enough to arouse suspicion. But he couldn't afford a review. What he knew, he alone knew, and he wanted to keep it that way. He was on the trail of something that truly captivated all of his interest. He needed Mitchell. He needed the agency. He needed to get Mitchell off his back. He needed to win back Mitchell's confidence. He was going to have to show some cards, but not the entire hand.

"Okay sir, I think a big part of the problem for you was my taking off yesterday morning, going to that bar last night, missing a few phone-ins, and showing up late tonight."

"Fucking A right!"

"Sir, the key to this thing is, in a word, kayaking."

"Kayaking? Ridiculous. Kayaking is just a stupid childish hobby shared by Calvert and Dornblaser."

"Wrong, Sir."

"Explain."

"What did Dornblaser pull out of that cave in Algeria? A kayak. What was that kayak doing there?"

"Look Carlson, this isn't about a Goddamn kayak. It's about the Goddamn unauthorized removal of plutonium from this country and a Goddamn atomic explosion."

"Yes, I know. But don't underestimate the importance of that kayak. Everything mysterious that happened, happened after he found that boat. Dornblaser dies in the A-blast. No. Dornblaser immediately, immediately, shows up in West Virginia. And where does he go? I'm ninety nine percent sure he went kayaking yesterday. I'm willing to bet he was in that very same kayak. You analyzed the space photos of that campground, and you've seen enough explosions to know that trailer didn't blow up. It's gone, but it didn't explode. Calvert's project in the desert was in a dry riverbed. They didn't take any kayaks there. That boat was there. The question is, why was it there? I've got a hunch that that city in the sand lies upstream of where Calvert's project was and that bowl in the riverbed where the kayak was found. Sir, we're on to something really big here. We may be talking about something as big as the meaning of life."

"Christ, Elliot. What the hell is wrong with you? I've got my tit in the wringer, and you're standing here talking to me about the meaning of life! What does that have to do with National Security? I want a logical explanation, not some fantasy."

"Sir, please, looking for logical answers isn't going to get us anywhere. These guys are going to remain two steps ahead of us if we continue to operate as usual. That is why I have been trying to immerse myself in Dornblaser's world. If I'm going to catch up with Dornblaser, I've got to be able to think like Dornblaser."

"Oh, Christ!" Mitchell sighed. "Just don't hold anything back from me, Elliot. Anything. Understood?"

⊱⊰

As Elliot drove back to his McLean townhouse he breathed a deep sigh of relief. He was okay for now, but he would no longer enjoy the comfort of Mitchell's trust. He had to keep everything locked deep inside. Every word he said might be listened to. Anything he wrote might be read. He had to be careful.

Once home he poured himself a whiskey on the rocks and sank down into his couch.

Got to assume I'm being listened to and possibly also being watched on hidden video. Can't go looking for the bugs either or they'll think I'm trying to hide something. Nothing goes on paper either, but now is the time to think this out.

What is the "mission?"

Elliot began to draw a mental outline. Using his near photographic memory, he placed everything in order in his brain When it was done, he reviewed it and had a few glaring questions about the holes it contained. Who was Mihalis? None of the intelligence work done on the research site staff revealed anyone by that name or anyone who could have fit that role. Although the Arab named Khalem, who had been in charge of security, had remained tight lipped about Calvert and Dornblaser, many of the others had told everything they knew. Calvert had worked alone on the computers and was aided by Dornblaser mainly in the fieldwork. Elliot came to a startling conclusion: Mihalis was the kayak!

Now I'm getting somewhere, he thought. It was all fitting into place. But where and how do Calvert and Dornblaser come into all of it? Calvert was used by Mihalis to make the helmet. Dornblaser's only skill seems to be kayaking. Mihalis has the ability to make space/time transfer occur. So why the helmet?

Elliot felt an uncomfortable feeling growing within him that for some reason, Mihalis was going to take Dornblaser back to the city in the sand. He would have to work on that.

Elliot felt sleep coming over him. He didn't have the energy to get up and go to his bed. How sweet it was to relax, sleep.

CHAPTER 8 — GONE

He was hunched over, watching the drop of water slowly fall to the floor. It was close to the floor, but slowing in its fall. Slowing more and more. Never totally stopping but now hardly moving. It had to hit the floor, didn't it? Now he felt the burning pain. He turned onto his back, and unable to close his eyes, he was blinded by the light of the sun.

He woke slowly, first lifting only one eyelid. The world was dark and out of focus. Sunlight streamed in through small holes in the wall, particles of dust tumbling in the thin rays. He heard the sound again. Tok tok tok tok tok tok.

Fuck. They're still shooting at me!

Pete now practically jumped up, looking around for the Smith and Wesson in the process.

Tok tok tok tok tok.

His vision began to clear, but he took a step and tripped over something and landed in a heap on top of some boxes. He looked up and stared out at the green light which was quickly turning into a forest.

Tok tok tok tok tok.

He slowly climbed down out of the trailer and stepped into deep moss growing amongst ferns. All around were immense trees. He looked up and couldn't see their tops. Sunlight filtered through the trees and lit the ground in patches.

Tok tok tok tok tok.

He walked toward the sound. Fifty yards from the trailer a large pileated woodpecker was drilling a hole high on the trunk of a dead tree. He moved closer to the tree, and the bird heard him and stopped it's labors to look around for the intruder. It wasn't a pileated at all. It was too big and had no red on its neck or head. The bill wasn't black either, but a bright white.

It came to him that he was looking at a live, ivory billed woodpecker, commonly believed to be long extinct.

Where am I?

The immensity of the forest surrounding him began to sink in. It sure didn't look like Brazil either.

He found his way back to the trailer and took stock of his situation. The trailer had "landed" nicely among the huge trees. There was no apparent damage to the outside. Climbing back in Pete looked around. Mihalis was not in the trailer. Neither was the Budweiser.

Well, I guess this is it. I'm on my own.

He turned back to his new surroundings. The forest was beautiful. Hickory, White Oak, Sycamore, and a tree whose leaves he couldn't identify. Pete walked over to one of the mystery trees and notice the ground covered with the broken round nutshells. He looked up again.

"Damn, Chestnut."

Chestnut trees had been wiped out by a blight in the 1920's.

Where am I? More like, when am I?

Pete had an idea and climbed back up into the trailer. He took the helmet out of the box and put it on. The screen came up and said:

READY

"Helmet, date and time."

Instantly, 6/16/906 2:35P.M. appeared in the center of the screen. Then, the instructional content of the helmet began to play, ending up with Howard's warning about Mihalis being willing to sacrifice an unborn son to destroy the tower. He felt sick. So basically he was in exile, incommunicado with all he had known, but certainly within grasp of the claws of the crystal boat at its whim.

Holy shit. "Helmet, off."

The screen clicked off and he carefully put the helmet back into the box. He looked around in the trailer. Everything was just like he had loaded it in. the exceptions were Mihalis and the beer. Pondering it further, he remembered that when he had popped from Africa to his parents house, he had been touching Mihalis, albeit through the sleeping bag wrapping it. He climbed down out of the trailer and made a circuit around it. Even pieces of gravel stuck in the tread of the tires had been transported, but nothing else. Mihalis evidently could well control what was transported and what not.

Pete started to walk further and further from the trailer, looking for some telltale sign of where he was. Squirrels leapt about in the high branches of the trees and scurried around on the ground. Game trails seemed to be crossing the entire forest floor. He checked the compass on his watchband and the trails were mainly running north and south. Pete now started to walk due west and had to pass through some rhododendron. He saw a clearing ahead and rather suddenly came out to the bank of a river. Crystal green water flowed swiftly by. A kingfisher swooped chattering past. A great blue heron rose into the air from the far side of the river and began to fly downstream. As he followed its flight, he noticed a familiar silhouette, the steep walls of the Cheat Canyon. Mihalis had taken him back in time, but he was in the same place. It had always been a dream of his to see the Cheat, his favorite of all of the rivers, as it must have been before the ravages of logging and strip mining, and now here he was experiencing the dream. It was much like he had imagined, but there were some surprising differences. The river was narrower than the river that flowed past the campground. There were also some large boulders with inviting sand-bars stretching out downstream of them. Looking down into the water, he saw schools of rainbow trout darting in and out of the shadows.

Pete sat on the rocks for the rest of the afternoon and felt a full range of emotions. Happiness, wonder, sadness, loneliness, and fear. The sun set between the canyon walls and he began to find his way back to the trailer. He suddenly realized the source of his present fear. Surely he was not alone. There must be Indians in the area. How would they react to him? He spent a fitful night as he slept in the trailer. The next morning dawned clear, and he felt more at ease. He decided to begin the difficult task of organizing the trailer. Pete took all of the smaller items outside and laid them out in an orderly fashion. He was taking an inventory when he looked up from his clipboard and saw people. They came walking past in single file and even though they certainly saw him, they only looked straight ahead They were six in number. First walked an old man. His hair was graying and his red skin wrinkled on his face but otherwise one might not have known he was old. His chest and stomach muscles still rippled against his flesh. A slight paunch hung above his loincloth. Three osprey feathers hung down behind his head from a buckskin thong. He wore buckskin leggings from below the knees down to a pair of worn moccasins. Behind him strode two strapping young men. Between them they carried a pole from which hung dozens of huge trout, split open and dried and smoked. They were dressed like the old man, but their hair was plucked out leaving only a round patch of long hair at the crown which hung down behind in a pony tail. They wore no feathers but had large copper earrings. The first had a strong but unattractive face. The second, however, was handsome and appeared to be slightly younger than the first.

A few paces behind them came a young woman in a beaded buckskin dress. Her straight black hair fell across her back and the side of her face. Hanging down in her hair were several bright green feathers held in a piece of painted bone. Behind her marched two young boys of eight to ten years, dressed only in loincloths. Pete just stood there while they walked past without looking at him. Pete found himself staring at the woman when she brushed the hair from her face and shot an upward glance at him. As he made contact with her brown eyes, he felt a ripple down his spine. She looked forward again and they disappeared into the forest.

࿇

Line three buzzed on Mitchell's desk. It was Andresky.

Carlson wanted access to the space intelligence from Africa.

"Go ahead, let him see everything. I'm glad you called me first."

Mitchell pressed some buttons on the wall and had a video and audio feed from SSA come up on a monitor. Andresky pushed a button on his desk and with a buzz, the door clicked open and Elliot walked in. The two men shook hands and Andresky began to lay out photos on a large table.

"Elliot, as you can plainly see, things have taken a serious turn for the worse over there since last week. Hundreds of feet of sand have drifted over the wadi and the site of the old city. I would say further excavation is out of the question for now, and that bowl downstream is almost full of sand, too."

Damn. "Okay Herb, let's go over everything we shot over the last months."

"Well, you've seen most of it, as far as photos go, but there is something else." He started picking through a pile of large envelopes. "Ah. Here it is. It's some sonar shots. Fairly revealing. Before, we were much more interested in what was going on on the surface, and these didn't get much notice. It is about the most low tech of all of our surveillance techniques. As you can see, this pretty effectively strips away the sand and gives you a clear layout of the city."

Elliot pored over the sonar photo. The city was a series of concentric rings, with some walls much thicker than others. The outer ring was the dam, or dike, which surrounded the city.

"What is that dark circle near the center?"

"I wondered that myself. I do have a detail of that somewhere." He started through the envelope again and pulled out another photo. "Yes, here it is." The photo was a blowup of the dark ring.

"Why wasn't I shown this?"

"Nobody has seen it but me. Once everything shifted over to West Virginia, no one showed any interest in this Algerian stuff."

Elliot stared intently at the photo.

"Why does it show so much darker than the rest of the city?"

"Density. My thought on it is that it is some kind of metal."

"Metal? But it's huge."

"Forty seven meters outside diameter, thirteen meters inside diameter."

"Wait a second Andresky, that city is ancient. There was no metalworking going on back then and certainly not on that scale."

"Elliot, there isn't any metalworking going on today on that scale. Look, archeology is not my field, I'm just telling you what the photos tell me. And there is something else about this cylinder. If you look, you can see the faint outlines of what looks to me to be some kind of fins radiating eight meters out from the base."

"What's that all about?"

"Your guess is as good as mine."

Elliot took a long look at the two sonar shots.

"Thanks, Herb."

As he walked back to his office, he recorded the photos in his mind. When he entered, his secretary motioned toward the phone.

"Elliot Carlson here."

"Yes Mr. Carlson, Allen Marks from Adventure Kayak Sport returning your call."

橾❧

Pete had spent eleven days in his new home. The trailer was organized. He had sketched out plans for a log cabin and had felled a stand of straight poplars on the hillside to the east. He had cut a white oak into two and a half foot sections for the roof shakes, but was dreading the work of splitting them. He had explored the river as far downstream as Even Nastier rapids and attained, with a few carries, back up. Ranging further and further on foot, he had explored much of the surrounding forest and had found the hiking to be easy, owing to the openness of the forest understory beneath trees, some of which were ten feet in diameter. However, the entire time he had not been able to get the Indians out of his mind, especially the beautiful eyes of the Indian woman.

On the eleventh night, it rained heavily for hours and as he listened to it pound on the trailer roof, he concocted a plan to run the Big Sandy. He would walk up the Muddy Creek valley and cross over the divide to the Little Sandy. After the junction with the Big Sandy, he would attain back up through the Cheat Canyon to the trailer. Pete figured he would be gone three days but, what the heck, it was summertime and he could camp without gear. He would take a dry bag with food. Drinking water was everywhere. And a beer was nowhere to be found.

Early the next morning he padlocked the trailer and set out. He shouldered his boat, a fiberglass and Kevlar Augsburg I selected for its attaining abilities, and headed through the tall trees for Muddy Creek. By nightfall, he had walked upstream some ten miles along the creek, climbing up over the divide and down the other side to the Little Sandy. The solitude of the unbroken forest was overwhelming. He had seen deer, otters, and a badger.

Exhausted, he stretched out on a bed of pine needles by the rushing waters. Morning came quickly, and he set off downstream. Soon he was in familiar territory and figured he had now passed below where Route 26 would someday cross the Little Sandy.

Or would it? Would history still run the same course? Yes, he thought, unfortunately it would. His being back in time would not affect anything. In another six hundred years, white men would arrive and devastate the natural beauty he was experiencing.

Soon the excitement of the rapids overrode these thoughts and he began to enjoy the timeless thrill of kayaking. Slice out of the current into an eddy and fire back out and launch across a curling wave to the far side and repeat the process. After entering the Big Sandy, his play shifted to wave surfing and side surfing the broad hydraulics. Passing the future site of the Rockville bridge, the Big Sandy changes character as it readies for its plunge to the Cheat River. The streambed narrows and begins to drop much more steeply over sandstone ledges. Pete arrived at Wonder Falls, a seventeen foot vertical drop. Paddling hard to build up his speed, he launched off the lip and splashed to a flat landing in the foam below.

Yeah!

After lingering in the richness of the negative ion-saturated air for a few minutes, Pete continued on downstream. Several big drops awaited before he would arrive at the next falls, Big Splat. "The Splat" was a complex, cascading drop of twenty five feet. Lots of kayakers routinely ran it but Pete did not, mainly out of respect. Not only was it dangerous, it was also a "cosmic place" for him and brought forth strange feelings which he had never been able to control or understand.

As he cleared the last drop of Little Splat, the rapid upstream of Big Splat, he looked downriver and saw dozens of Indians crowding the rock ledges on river right. Pete saw several quivers bristling with arrows hanging from the backs of the men. But they didn't look up to see him. They seemed to be focused on something out in the river. Then he saw them. Two boys clung to the rocks immediately above the entrance to the Splat. If they lost their grip, they would certainly wash over. He paddled down into the eddy by Indians gathered on the shore, and they saw him. He looked up to their shocked expressions. Pete looked out to the boys and saw that the current would soon tear them off the rocks. It would be risky, but he had to do something. He ferried out of the eddy and over to the rocks to which they clung, He bounced into the rock and grabbed hold with one hand and held his paddle aloft in the other. The boys looked at him with terrified faces.

"One at a time, get on the back of the kayak!" Pete shouted over the roar of the falls, but of course they didn't understand.

He looked at them again and realized they were the boys he had seen walk past the trailer. The larger seemed to have a better grip than the other, so he quickly laid his paddle across his deck and with the now free hand grabbed the smaller boy and pulled him across the rock and onto his spray deck. Pushing away from the rock, he grabbed up his paddle and ferried back to the shore, almost flipping in the process. Several hands reached down and grabbed the child. Suddenly the Indians let out a collective shriek, and Pete looked up just in time to see the other boy lose his grip and be swept away. Now there was no time to lose. Pete hammered back out of the eddy and ferried around to the far side of the pinnacle rock in the center and ran the first two drops of the cascade. He looked about in a frenzy and saw the boy trying to clutch the shelf rock as he came sliding toward Pete's new position. He tumbled off of the drop and landed in the tiny eddy just above the main drop of the falls. Pete charged across the current to him but the boy's body was being sucked down in the eddy line. The boy popped up in the current and Pete peeled out in a last ditch effort to save him. As he reached out, the child went under again and Pete realized that now they were both going to go over the falls, and he was backwards, still pointing upstream.

Oh Shit!

Pete felt himself not only falling, but flipping over backwards as well, as he went off. At the same time he knew he was way too far to the right and was going to land on the splat rock. He hit the foam at the base of the falls and went deep and began to tumble in his boat, with the full force of the water beating him. Finally the roar abated and he felt the current carry him away from the fall's base. He'd never hit the rock! Rolling up, Pete took a breath and opening his eyes found himself looking upward and seeing the splat rock high on the cliff. It hadn't yet fallen into the river. Looking frantically about, he saw no trace of the boy.

There he is!

The boy bobbed up, face down in the foaming water below the falls and came floating downstream towards him. Pete tried to slow his backwards motion by paddling hard upstream towards him. The motionless form floated up to his boat and he grabbed him up and flopped him up on the deck. The current was now carrying them quickly towards the next rapids, AquaTarkus. He had to eddy out. The boy was unconscious and was turning blue. He grabbed a shore eddy and tossed his paddle up onto the rocks. Peeling off his spray skirt, in one quick motion he grabbed the child and jumped into waist deep water. The kayak swirled out of the eddy and was gone. Throwing the boy over his left shoulder, he climbed up out of the river and laid him on his back on a rock. The boy was motionless and blue. Pete knelt down and put his ear to the child's mouth and felt no breathing. He tilted the boy's head back and covered the boy's lips with his and gave him two breaths. Placing two fingers to the carotid artery, he counted to twenty and didn't feel any pulse.

"Oh God, help me now."

Clasping his hands together he began chest compressions on the child. Now there were moccasined feet on the rock. He continued the compressions and then shifted and gave two more breaths.

The boy coughed and gasped and opened his eyes. Pete put his fingers to his neck and now felt a strong, rapid pulse.

Pete stood up and was face to face with four astonished Indian men. All five of them were speechless for some seconds and finally one motioned downriver and two of them took off running. One of the others began talking to him and all Pete understood was that they were thanking him. The old man he'd seen walk past the trailer emerged from the rhododendron and stepped out on the rock with them. He knelt down and picked up the boy. The boy put his arms around the old man and began to cry. The old man also began to cry. The next moment, the young woman appeared. She took the boy from the old man and looked him over. She looked up at Pete and said a few words. Pete felt himself melting inside. He wanted to run, to hide, to be somewhere else. Now, the two men who had gone downstream came climbing back up with his kayak and laid it on the rock. The old man spoke to the four men and they all began speaking and pointing to Pete and the boy, and the old man looked at Pete and said some things to him.

Pete didn't understand anything and didn't respond. He was aware of those brown eyes boring into his back. Now the old man pointed to Big Splat and said: "Apu Tokebelloke. Apu Tokebelloke."

Then he reached out and touched Pete, tentatively at first as if to see if he was real and then more firmly as he realized that, yes, he was human.

The old man continued to speak and he continued to not understand a word. He didn't want to be impolite but he felt a nervous attack about to explode from within.

"Excuse me, but I have to go now." and he pointed at the kayak. They seemed surprised to hear him speak and said nothing as he climbed into the boat and put on the spray skirt. He slid into the water and turned the boat in the eddy to face them. He raised his arm in a salute to them, and they waved back. As he turned to go he stole a last glance at the woman. She was looking at him. She was beautiful. Pete felt himself blush. How long had it been since a woman had caught his eye?

A good while.

He thought about what had happened all the way down the Sandy and all the way up the Cheat to Pete Morgan rapid where he ran out of daylight. Who were these people? Surely Shawnee. Pete had read a bit about early Indian cultures, and he knew that archeologists thought tenth century Indians were still fairly primitive. But, these Indians looked like pictures of Shawnee he had seen. And, they definitely had bows and arrows. Where was their home, their village? Good question. What were they doing at Big Splat? Better question yet. Who was the woman? Got to find out. Was she the mother of the two boys? No. Impossible. She was way too young. What did they think of him? Take a guess. Strange looking man in strange clothes paddling strange boat brings drowned boy back to life and takes off. Well, at least because of the act of resuscitating the boy, they knew he didn't mean them harm. That was good. They had him outnumbered.

Pete made it upstream through the canyon to his camp late the next day. He took the following day off to rest and daydream and then applied himself to get somewhere on the cabin project. With the advantage of the chainsaw, he had the logs cut to length in a day. The hard part was dragging them to the site. He made a harness so that he could really lean into the pulling. It took two days of hard work to get all the logs to the cabin site by the trailer. He positioned the cabin site itself so that there was a big tree on all four sides and as the walls went up, he used a z-drag from high on the tree on the opposing side to roll each log up an inclined plane consisting of other logs leaned up on the wall. As the walls went higher and the inclined planes became steeper, he had to substitute come-alongs for the z-drags. In a week he had the four walls up, all nicely notched together at the corners. The cabin was eighteen feet by twenty four feet on the outside, It had two window openings front and back and one on each end. The one and only door faced south, towards the trailer. At the top of the walls he notched in smaller logs across the width of the cabin for ceiling joists. Now was a good time to split the shakes for the roof, so he spent two long days with axe and adz. Pete had split shakes before, helping a friend during his exhibition at the Mountaineer Festival at WVU. He made these a bit on the thick side to make them even more durable than those exhibition shakes. A good shake roof was known to last fifty years or more without replacement. How long would he live in the cabin before Mihalis called on him?

Next came the job of building up the gable ends of the cabin and bracing them into the ceiling joists. As his labors continued, he took more and more pride in his work. After all, winter was coming, and he would need a nice tight cabin for himself, and the woman. He couldn't get her out of his mind. He thought about her the entire day that it took to mount the ridgepole across the gables.

Pete had not lived with a woman since his marriage fizzled. His wife had been the only woman he had had a long term relationship with. They had begun as a typical river couple. She showed up one day wanting to raft and learn to kayak. Unlike most river groupies, she had stuck around, had become a good paddler. They had started sleeping together, then living together. They had been passionate and Pete thought they were in love. But after marriage, something happened. She wanted comfort, and he had never settled for comfort or worked for it. She complained. He defended himself. Soon they were at odds. Then the accident left him bankrupt. She knew that he would never afford the comforts, the stability she wanted. And she was gone.

Pete wondered if this Indian vision of the forest would settle for less. Her notion of comfort didn't include cable TV or a car. Maybe to her, he would represent comfort. Pete rationalized in his reveries.

By the time he had run the roof rafter poles and the cross poles, he had just about decimated the entire stand of poplars. It was easy to see how the pioneers had impacted on the environment each time a cabin was built. It also bothered him that every time he fired up the chainsaw it seemed to be an obscene gesture directed against the spiritual solitude of the forest.

Once the roof was shaked and the cabin safe from the rains, he turned his efforts to splitting poplars for the floor boards and making windows and doors. Now came time to build the hearth. He carried flat shale blocks from beneath a cliff on Roaring Creek. Carefully laying them, he built a massive hearth into the back of the cabin with a chimney that reached above the ridgeline.

By mid-August, the cabin was done. As he stood back admiring his work, he realized that the cabin was in exactly the same space occupied by the headquarters building of his paddling school. Pete chuckled as he thought about the quarrels he'd had with the contractor, and how he'd finished his cabin in the same amount of time it had taken the construction firm to build the headquarters.

He began to worry about the amount of food he'd gone through in the last two months. Winter was coming and he would need to prepare. The land, however, could provide. The branches of the hickories and chestnuts were drooping under their load of nuts. He would have to battle the squirrels and chipmunks for his share. There were plenty of deer and the river ran thick with schools of trout. He'd be okay.

Once again the rains came and Pete found himself yearning for adventure. He decided he would portage up Roaring Creek and across the Laurel Hill divide into the Yough drainage. He would run the Yough to Ohiopyle and then portage up Meadow Run and cross over the divide to the Big Sandy. He calculated the trip would take a week to complete, but he had worked hard, and there wasn't much good paddling weather left before fall.

He padlocked the trailer and cabin both and set out. Two days later he found himself on the banks of the Youghiogheny River in Sang Run, right across the river from where he'd put in with Mihalis two months ago, and right across the river from a large Shawnee village. After some trepidation, he decided to go across and introduce himself. He had better get used to it; he would probably encounter more villages all the way down the river to Ohiopyle.

The Shawnee saw him as he got into his boat to paddle over and were waiting on the bank when he landed on their side. They seemed surprised and excited to see him, but not shocked.

Has word of my arrival traveled this far?

Pete climbed out of the Augsburg and, surrounded by Indian men, women and children, carried it up the bank into the village. Four older men walked together toward him. Using hand gestures and smiling faces, they beckoned him to follow them. The village consisted of eight or nine tipis and as many shelters that resembled tiny quonset huts with skin coverings stretched over a series of poles, bent over and stuck into the ground. He was led to a ring of logs placed around a fireplace in the village center and urged to take a seat. Behind him, a gaggle of children were gathered around the Augsburg pointing at it and talking and laughing. Innocence filled the air, and he felt his apprehensions lifting. The logs filled quickly with men and women. They soon realized that he could neither speak nor understand their language. He was however, obviously the center of attention.

One of the older men said something and all fell silent. The man turned to Pete and tapping his chest, said: "Hawapiti." He was saying his name. Pete tapped his chest and said: "Pete." Raising his hands, Hawapiti seemed to be asking, where did you come from? Pete drew a diagram in the sand of the Yough, and Laurel Hill, and the Cheat. His audience seemed puzzled. Pete pointed up to the sun, and standing up, made a circular motion with his arm, trying to symbolize the passing of time.

Hawapiti nodded but looked concerned. The communication was getting nowhere fast, but at this moment, some women brought forth sizzling meat on wood skewers. Hawapiti cut off a hunk with a stone knife and handed it to Pete. They all stopped to see if he would eat it. He ripped into it ravenously. When he looked up, he could see what seemed a sigh of collective relief. As they all partook, he noticed what a happy and family-oriented people they were. Now everyone was sitting on the logs and small children were climbing about on the laps of their parents who would rip off small chunks of meat for them.

Pete drew a picture of a deer head with antlers in the dirt and pointed to the meat he was eating. One of the braves shook his head no and produced a buffalo skull. This surprised him, and he gestured: where? The brave continued the map of the Yough in an upriver direction and at one point drew a line across the river. Then he said, "Apu Tokebelloke," and gestured even further up river.

He had heard this before, yes, at Big Splat. He pointed to the line and said: "Apu Tobelloke?"

The brave shook his head no and said again "Apu Tokebelloke".

Pete was puzzled, but wanted to know what it meant. He made it obvious that he didn't understand and that he wanted the brave to explain.

Through a series of hand signals he came to understand it as a place where water fell and spoke to humans. Pete nodded understanding and decided it must be Swallow Falls, which lay some five miles upstream. And he did understand. He had often lingered on the riverside rocks beside waterfalls, staring into the cascading waters, absorbing the sounds, trying to work his way through their riddle.

Pete decided it was time to go and gestured so. The entire village followed him to the water to see him off. Hawapiti made a circle in the air and pointed at him and then at the ground. Pete understood it to mean, "come back someday." Pete gestured that he would. Hawapiti reached into a buckskin pouch and handed a large ginseng root to Pete. Pete thanked him, and thinking for a moment, unclipped his Spyderco river knife from his life jacket and handed it to the old man. He opened it up and looked with wonder at the shiny steel blade. Pete waved goodbye from the kayak and they all waved back.

He had similar experiences with Indians in their villages in Friendsville, Selby's Port and Confluence. Three days later he arrived in Ohiopyle and spent the night there in a village. In the morning he rose early and entertained the villagers with a run of the falls.

No rangers to fine me now.

At the mouth of Meadow Run, he left the river and started hiking. He slept that night at the headwaters of the Sandy near the summit of Chestnut Ridge.

With daybreak, he began hiking downstream, looking for navigable water.

It was a long day. He had to carry around what seemed like a hundred downed trees. It was dark before he reached Bruceton Mills, but the water was flat and the moon bright, so he decided to continue.

҂ఄ

She wondered why the strange thoughts and feelings came so strongly to her. She had shared them only with her mother. Her mother was wise, almost as wise as her father. It wouldn't have been correct to discuss woman things with her father though. She had done well to hide her thoughts from him and her brothers. But her mother had not been able to give her any advice, only cautions. The strange intruder was a sign of the beginning of a dangerous time. He was best avoided, no matter that the men had been impressed with his actions at Apu Tokebelloke. Feelings of attraction to him must be repressed. Nothing good could come from him.

She had prayed to Kijemoneto for understanding, for the feelings of desire that were rising into her woman's body, from a mind that had only recently awakened from the innocence of youth. Kijemoneto had offered no sign, good or bad, in answer to her prayers.

Each night, she walked the trail from the village down to the river to bathe. She could no longer bathe with her brothers in the light of day. They would see the changes in her. Her breasts had become large and full. Her body covered with flesh where before had only been brown skin and bones. Bathing became a time to be alone and meditate.

As the light from the campfires filtered less and less through the tree branches, her eyes adjusted to the darkness of the forest at the river's edge. She slipped out of her buckskin dress and laid it across a rock. To the concert of frogs creaking and cicadas droning, she waded into the cool dark waters and dove below the surface. The blackness engulfed her but for some reason she did not feel it's comfort. A strong feeling of impending danger rushed through her.

Coming to the surface she looked around, though with the moon behind a passing cloud darkness cloaked the source of her worry. Then she saw the flicker of paddle blades in the gloom. What would a canoe be doing here? Would invaders have carried it over the divide? Not knowing that impassable rapids lay soon below?

The realization came as a shock. It was not a canoe. It was not paddle blades. It was the double bladed paddle of the strange boat. Piloted by the strange man. The man so different. The man who was not beautiful, but was beautiful in his essence so mysteriously unknown to the Shawnee sphere of reality. Her man. Yes, confront the truth. Confront the hidden thought. She had known from that first moment. Something deep inside of her had known before it had told the rest of her being. This strange man was to be hers.

These thoughts alone were not enough to erase the sense of fear she was now experiencing. Using a trick long before explained by her father, she swam back to the river's edge as would an otter: her body and extremities sunk down in the water, her head raised only enough that her eyes and nose appeared above the surface. The man was not fooled. He had stopped paddling and was straining to see what was swimming across the river before him. She swam to a rock next to the bank and stopped, still low in the water. He had seen her. But did he know it was her? Did he remember her? Or had he already taken up with another? This last thought stabbed like an icy knife. There were others. This she could not allow. He must become hers and hers alone. She could not let the moment pass. He had come to a stop in the eddy on the far side. He was honoring her space. He could have come to her but had not. But he wasn't leaving either. Slowly she stood up in the waist-deep water. He stared at her, as if not knowing what to make of her. She felt shame. Would he not be pleased with her body?

It was too late now for such feelings of regret. He slowly paddled to the far bank and climbed out of the boat. He pulled it onto the sand and began to remove his strange clothes. Now he was naked, the parts untouched by the sun a pale white in the moonlight. He waded into the gentle current and stopped in the middle of the river. She began to wade towards him. What am I doing? He was tall. They stood facing each other. The water came to his ribs but was deep enough to almost cover her breasts. She felt them floating a bit and was almost overcome with the self-consciousness of her body. His eyes were not pouring over her body as she had thought they would but instead were studying her face and eyes. She thought she noticed a wave of relief and joy pass over him as he realized that it was her. She reached up and put her hand over her heart.

"Sana"

He awkwardly mimicked her gesture. "Pete."

"Pede," she gently said, as if questioning the strange new sound of his name. "Peter Simon."

"Simon," she said with ease. A smile came to her face.

Slowly, they reached out and touched, and then kissed. He carried her in his arms to the sand.

≈≈≈

In the morning, she was gone. He debated looking for her and decided not to. He bathed in the river, put on his equipment and headed downstream.

Pete reached his camp, exhausted, late the next day. It had been an unforgettable trip. He'd kayaked the Upper Yough and the rest of the Yough all the way to Ohiopyle Falls. Then, he had portaged overland and kayaked down the Big Sandy. He finished the trip off by attaining up through the Cheat Canyon. He'd also walked through magnificent forests and met and made new friends. He would have to make that trip every year.

He rested a day and lazily daydreamed of his newfound love.

When would he see her again?

It was time to get to work and prepare for winter. Out of small poles and straight branches he built a frame for a smoke house. Inside was a series of shelves made of even smaller branch sections. Pete then lined the outside and the roof with rushes which grew along the river. He spent the mornings fishing trout out of the river, and the afternoons cleaning them. He chopped up hickory branches left over from building the cabin and built three smoldering fires under the fish in the smokehouse. He continued for a week until the smokehouse was brimming with drying fish.

Once the fish were totally dry, he wrapped them in brochures from the paddling school and packed them in cardboard boxes.

The nights were now getting cool, and deer were starting to come more and more into the bottom land by Roaring Creek to browse. Taking the SKS, he shot a fat buck just before dark. The rifle blast shattered the silence and echoed in the hills. Pete realized that it had been the first shot he had fired since his arrival. He field dressed the buck, and laid it in the cool waters of the creek. Pete hung it by the cabin and skinned it the next morning. He cut the meat into narrow strips and placed them in the smokehouse Remembering what he'd read as a youth about tanning deer hides, Pete made a frame to stretch the hide and treated it with a solution of water and the deer's brains He didn't really need buckskin for anything, but he felt it wrong to waste it. Over the next days, he killed two more bucks and processed them. He was kept busy tending the smoldering fires of the smokehouse and cutting the leftover treetops from the construction of the cabin into firewood, stacking it under the trailer to dry.

The days and weeks were flying by. Pete alternated passing his time paddling down to Decision Rapids and collecting chestnuts and hickory nuts. The skies were full of huge flocks of migrating birds. He inventoried what remained of the food he had bought and calculated he had barely enough to get through the winter. The next year he would have to seek other solutions.

Next year.

Pete was beginning to feel the effects of his solitude. How long would Mihalis leave him here? Forever?

Fuck Mihalis anyway. I'm fine here. No one to bother me. No taxes. No lawyers. No law.

He missed his parents. He missed Howard. He missed his friends. Their lives were continuing without him, all around him, over a thousand years into the future.

And what of Sana? He hadn't seen any Indians since he returned from his trip. It was as if they were giving him space.

Pete shifted his energies toward fixing up the inside of the cabin. He made a big counter out of poplar boards which he sanded smooth. He made large cabinets of chestnut boards, and fashioned a couch out of springy sassafras poles. He fashioned a big, comfortable bed with the frame of poplar and crosspoles of hickory. He had split straight grained hickory into two by two's and then hand-planed them round. He fit them across the frame with half inch spaces between the rods. Once he'd laid a foam pad upon it, it was as comfortable as the Holiday Inn. Then he made a bookcase out of chestnut and a large hickory mantelpiece for the hearth.

The lethargic, but beautiful time of fall came and went and then winter arrived. In mid-December three feet of snow fell in one night. It remained for months. Only after it packed down could Pete get further than from the cabin to the trailer. He tried to exercise as much as possible and paddled a mile upstream through the flatwater every day at noon. He spent his evenings reading by the light of a Coleman lantern.

Pete found that these months tested his ability to be alone more than any other period of his life. He missed little things -- casual conversations with clerks, banter with waitresses, swapping lies with fellow boaters. In Friendsville he was on such good terms with the ladies who owned the Old Mill Grill that he poured his own coffee, cleaned tables when they were rushed, even washed dishes on occasion. Now, with no one to talk to, he embarrassed himself when he heard his own voice. He wondered how long he would have to live a hermit.

One late afternoon in February, as the sun began to set. Pete ducked out of the cabin to grab up an armload of firewood from beneath the trailer. As he turned back towards the cabin, he was startled to see three Indians approaching through the forest. He recognized the first two as the young braves he'd seen walk past the camp the second day after his arrival The third was Sana. She did not look up and just stared down at the snow. He saw that she was pregnant. The braves signed a greeting and seemed to be thoroughly checking out the cabin, which hadn't existed the last time they were there. One of them unslung a large buckskin pack and laid it at Pete's feet. Now Sana looked up at Pete, as if waiting for a response. He found himself overwhelmed with emotion. He set down the firewood and brushing away a tear, nodded yes to Sana and put a hand on her shoulder. The braves said something between themselves and then each said something to her. They were off, into the forest.

Sana seemed nervous and a bit unsure. He picked up her pack and took her hand, leading her inside. He could tell she was surprised by the cabin and she began to look around the inside. She took off her deerskin robe and revealed an ornately beaded buckskin dress which was a bit tight around her midsection. Sana now looked him in the eye, and he took her into his arms and held her. He knelt down in front of her and took her hands and kissed them.

"Sana, I love you."

❧◦❦

They were happy together. She brightened his days and filled his nights. They spent the rest of the winter side by side. He taught her English, and she taught him Shawnee. They bathed in the river every morning, some days breaking through the ice to do so. She had instructed him in the construction of a sweat lodge and tried to explain that it was about more than the cleansing of one's body. It was also the method for ridding oneself of evil thoughts and spirits.

They spent their evenings learning about each other. She explained that the two braves were her brothers, as were the two boys he'd rescued at the falls. The old man was her father. Her mother was in the village and surely missed her. Her family had been deathly afraid of him the first time they had seen him. They had been upstream fishing and had passed through the day before his arrival, and then, when they returned, there he was. However, after he had saved the boys he had gained widespread respect within the tribe.

On reflection, he wondered at the chances of pregnancy after one time together. It seemed to him that Mihalis might have managed their meeting. But he soon dismissed all questions. He was overjoyed with the companionship she brought him.

Sana was, as he had thought she would be, a sweet and caring woman. It was with some difficulty that he told her the tale of why and how he had come to be there. She seemed to accept the story. To her, what better explanation could there be for his appearance in her world? To Pete, the words sounded as if they were a great lie. He was living in denial of the truth of what had happened and his reason for being there. He left out everything having to do with his yet unborn child. He hoped that the child she carried would be a girl and swore that Mihalis would never take him should it be born a son.

In early May, with spring well established, her mother, Shawana, arrived with all four of her brothers. They had brought a tipi and erected it near the cabin. With his new understanding of their language, he was able to talk with them in simple terms. Her mother was friendly and witty, and they got on well.

On the twentieth, Sana went into labor and retreated to the tipi with her mother. Shawana came out and told the men to get lost for the day. They went up Roaring Creek and Sana's oldest brother, Kiri, expertly brought down a buck with an arrow. They returned at nightfall, and Shawana beckoned Pete into the tipi. She then left him with Sana. Sana lay on a bed of pine boughs covered with a buffalo robe. In her arms was a newborn child. She held the boy up to Pete and he took him in his arms.

"Simon."

Holding the sleeping infant, Pete cried out of joy. There would be time, later, to worry.

CHAPTER 9 — ELLIOT

He had improved every time on the water. He had made every instructor push him hard. The first was surprised when he learned to roll in less than half an hour. He rolled in whitewater the first day on the Potomac, and his skill level was spiraling upward every time he went out. His final instructor at the kayak school was the owner, Allen Marks. "Teach me everything you know Allen," became his daily greeting.

The days became shorter as they entered autumn, and Elliot realized soon he wouldn't be able to continue to take his lessons after work. He had requested more free time, and Mitchell granted it. After all, not much was happening with the Saharan affair. Dr. Calvert had seemed to vanish into the same thin air as Dornblaser. Arrest warrants remained outstanding for them both. Mitchell seemed to be more relaxed about him, and though Elliot was careful to not be seen looking over his shoulder, it appeared he was not being followed or watched.

In late September, with the Potomac running low, Elliot began to meet Marks at daybreak for runs over Great Falls. Eric told him he'd never seen a student excel as Elliot had and that now was time for him to stop taking lessons and start paddling other rivers and with other people. Elliot thanked him and took his advice. He hooked up with some other paddlers and made a weekend trip to the Gauley River.

They drove late into the night Friday and stayed in a hotel an hour from the river. When they pulled into the parking lot of the Summersville Dam in the morning, it reminded Elliot more of a circus than anything else. There were hundreds of rafts, dozens of buses, and hundreds of kayakers. He soon discovered the Gauley was nothing like the benign Potomac. Huge undercut boulders and numerous rock sieves were threatening everywhere. It was a spooky feeling; real danger lurked at every bend, ready to snare the careless or unwary. He handled the whitewater but felt ill at ease paddling with the group. It seemed that it was every man for himself, and he was doing survival paddling. Other guys played and showed off while he settled in eddies. Upon their return to the parking lot in the afternoon after completing their run, they found it abuzz with the news that a kayaker in a later group had drowned in the first major rapid. He made the decision to retreat to the Potomac until the next spring and work on his technique.

On the work front, all investigative leads into the mysterious disappearance of Dornblaser and the whereabouts of Dr. Calvert had been exhausted. Though the case was far from "closed," Islamic affairs was breathing a quiet, collective sigh of relief that the news-hungry, short-attention spanned American populace seemed to lose interest in the bizarre scenario. To Elliot, however, it was far from over. He found himself dwelling on it constantly, trying to think up new angles.

The Langley headquarters of the C.I.A. houses one of the world's largest computer systems, with links into every nation's crime data banks. Fully aware that Mitchell would be watching his every move, Elliot charged ahead, checking every possibility in their seemingly dead-end search.

He started with Barkoui, more precisely, the fake Barkoui. It seemed to him that if someone had snuffed a renowned terrorist like Barkoui just to get closer to Calvert's project, that person had to have inside information about what Calvert and Dornblaser were really up to. The problem remained that the impostor had almost undoubtedly perished in the explosion. Starting with Barkoui's file in the agency's own records, he once again ran through it looking for clues. Barkoui's last confirmed appearance was actually in Algeria. It had been during a wave of killings linked to Islamic fundamentalists in April of '97, just before the Eid-el-Adha: the feast of sacrifice. Thinking that possibly Barkoui had met his killer/impostor there, Elliot hacked into the Algerian O.I.J. computer records of the event and called up photos taken during the riots. Calvert's security man had spoken freely of a troublemaking worker that was the suspected ringleader of the Bedouin attack on the French archeologists. He had been described by Khalem as tall and muscular, with a thin face and moustache and goatee. The key clue above these physical characteristics was that Dornblaser had apparently nick-named him Frank Zappa. As Elliot scrolled through the digital images, he laughed to himself that they almost all looked like Frank Zappa. And then he stopped. He enhanced a photo of a group of people fleeing government security forces. A man in the image caught his eye. The man was standing off to the side of the fleeing protesters, but he wasn't running. His gaze seemed to be fixed on something outside the frame of the photo. Probably no way of ever knowing what he was looking at, thought Elliot, but the man looked almost exactly like Frank Zappa and appeared to be taller than those fleeing in the foreground. Elliot had his terminal make an enhanced blow-up of the man in the picture and then entered it into a search program in Interpol's files. Twenty minutes later the computer came up with a match. The photo was of a Romanian fugitive named Constanti Braila who had been linked with executed president Nicolai Ceaucescu's secret service. He had disappeared after the revolution of '89. As

Elliot compared the two photos, little doubt remained that this was the man. Bringing up Braila's Interpol file, he found it odd that his religion was listed as Romanian Orthodox, not Islam. He had apparently come from a wealthy family in northern Romania.

Transylvania, thought Elliot. That's appropriate.

Ceaucescu's regime had done a good job of destroying records in its last days. No more information was on file. Looking into the Interpol picture, Elliot felt a shiver run down his spine. Evil seemed to ooze from every pore in the man's face. Elliot thought it odd that the date on the photo was '86 and, when compared to the '97 photo from Algeria, the man had not appeared to age. He began to imagine Braila stalking Barkoui in Algiers, murdering him, hiding his body and assuming his identity. But why? Had he already known about Calvert's project which would be bringing plutonium into Algeria?

Elliot put in a scrambled call to the company's covert headquarters in Bucharest and asked for any information on Braila. An hour later a classified cable came through. The Braila ancestral home outside of Cluj had been burned and bulldozed after the revolution. Braila's next of kin were all dead, the last a half-brother named Yuri Agafya who was reported as missing in '84. Missing? Undaunted with this latest dead-end, Elliot trudged ahead. He asked the Interpol data base to churn out a list of all persons reported missing in Europe in 1984. A half hour later he was scrolling down through a list of over five hundred names. Agafya name came up early in the list, with the A's. Keeping the list on screen, he turned to another terminal and requested Interpol to provide him with travel information of Agafya in '84, i.e., border crossings. He had traveled by train through Hungary, Austria, and Switzerland, before crossing into France. Turning to the previous monitor, he had the computer eliminate all missing people except those in France. The list now was down to 37 names.

Where am I going with this? Think, Elliot. Okay, I know what I'm thinking. His brother kills an Islamic terrorist and assumes his identity. A possible modus operandi for the family. But who would Agafya want to pretend to be? He slowly reviewed the list of French names. Twenty-two were women. They were out. He started to call up the files one by one of the 16 men. He stopped, more than a bit startled, with Jacques DuBois. Jacques DuBois had been killed, drowned, come up missing, body never recovered, on a kayak expedition in the Himalayas.

But there was a bizarre footnote. His mother, upon seeing some promotional photos of the expedition taken before the double drowning in which Jacques and expedition leader Mike Clark's bodies had both disappeared, swore that the man pictured was not her son. Elliot couldn't believe what he was reading. Turning to a third terminal, he requested information from the Nepalese Interpol sub-bureau on the investigation of the accident. It had fallen under the jurisdiction of the Nepalese Himalayan Safety and Rescue Administration, the governing board which regulated mountain climbs. The report was long and detailed. Elliot found himself drawn into it.

It was an accident which shouldn't have happened. All safety considerations had been provided for. According to accounts by surviving expedition members, the drownings occurred during the only time when DuBois and Clark were the only kayakers in the water. Elliot was fascinated but unsure of any link between what had happened and the fact that someone he supposed was possibly the murderer of an Islamic terrorist had had a half brother who was in France during the same year a French kayaker drowned in the Himalayas.

After finding the E-mail address with the agency Web Crawler, he turned to yet another terminal and tapped out a request for a picture of the expedition team from the British Kayak and Canoe Federation archives in Nottingham, England. During the seemingly endless wait, he accepted the fact that he was on a wild goose chase and was wasting his time and tax-payer money.

A digital reproduction of a photo appeared on the screen. A dozen men sat in the snow before a banner that read "Everest Base Camp." Several kayaks lay on the snow in front of them. Many had their faces partially covered with scarves or turned up collars, but there, in the center, next to a man wearing a ball cap with a Union Jack and the name Clark on his jacket, was a man whose embroidered jacket patch identified him as Jacques. The man was the spitting image of Constanti Braila. It could easily be his brother. Another Frank Zappa.

Elliot felt drained and invigorated at the same time. He was on to something, but he wasn't sure what. He was still looking for something which would tie it all together. He began to scroll through the various notes and documents that the Federation had archived after the failed expedition. There was a letter written by Mike Clark, diplomatically explaining to a young American kayaker that his place on the expedition was to be filled by a French kayaker named Jacques DuBois. The young American's name was Peter Simon Dornblaser.

Elliot printed everything out and, using a highlighter, mapped out his circuitous route taken through the computer investigation, briefly noted his conclusion in a highlighted circle at the bottom of the letter to Dornblaser and, since Mitchell wasn't in, laid it all on Mitchell's desk and left.

Walking through the massive foyer of the agency headquarters on his way out, he flashed at how the black and white floor always reminded him of a giant chessboard. The Calvert case was also like a game of chess, and it suddenly made a lot more sense. As he walked out through the doors, he knew that he was now a piece in the chess game, and no longer just a pawn.

~&~

With Fall rains, the Potomac rose and the play spot of choice became Rocky Island with its quick, glassy surf wave. Like most other boaters, Elliot would drive to Great Falls Park on the Virginia side and put in at the base of the falls. Rocky was a half mile downstream. At the end of the session, he, like everybody else, would carry up over the rock cliffs and then walk the trail back to the parking lot.

There were a dozen boats in the eddy, waiting in line for their turn to surf. When it came to Elliot's turn, he slid his Prijon Hurricane out of the eddy and charged hard across the eddy line to match the speed of the current which was dropping into the trough of the wave. Correcting his angle with strong sweep strokes, he hit the trough and started to rise on the face of the wave. He pounded out a few more strokes and had it. It was such a glorious feeling. Large volumes of water rushed under the boat as it skipped and glanced about on the wave. However, one of the problems with surfing at Rocky was that one had to be courteous to those behind in the lineup, so after a minute of surfing he carefully angled his boat so that it pointed directly upstream and slid straight down into the trough. The bow buried under the pressure of the current and stood the kayak straight up and flipped it over; a perfect ender. But when he rolled up, the spray deck was off and the boat filling fast with water. Elliot struggled with the current in the now laden kayak, but didn't get eddied out until after the next little drop, Wet Bottom Chute.

Damn.

Elliot dumped the water out of the boat and carried it up around the drop. He was ready to get back in when he noticed a solitary paddler, working his way up from downstream towards the drop. It was a guy with a bushy beard whom he'd seen many times but never taken much notice of. The paddler didn't get out to carry the drop, and instead charged up. He drew abreast of Elliot.

"Hey! How did you do that?"

"Practice, practice." He paddled past.

"No. Please wait. I'd like to paddle with you."

The paddler stopped and turned around.

"Why?"

"I want to learn how to do what you just did. Really. Please."

He gave Elliot a grin and acquiesced to the enthusiasm displayed by the total stranger.

Elliot hurried into his boat and extended his hand to the man now patiently awaiting him in the eddy.

"Elliot Carlson."

"Ben Robertson, glad to meet you."

"Ben, I really want to learn everything about kayaking, and, I've learned a lot, but I don't know much at all about going upstream."

Ben looked at his boat.

"Well, for starters, your boat isn't much good for it. A Hurricane is just too short."

Elliot looked at Ben's boat. It was a fiberglass model he didn't recognize.

"What are you in?"

"It's called a New Vision. It's about a foot longer than the Hurricane, has less rocker and more volume."

"I've got a Crossfire too."

"That's a lot better. Tell you what, you coming out tomorrow?"

"Sure, what time?"

"Noon, at Angler's Inn."

They met as planned and Ben put Elliot through the wringer with the small drops above Angler's Inn.

After two hours of practice there, Elliot asked if they shouldn't go up through the gorge.

"Tomorrow. You just keep practicing."

Once Elliot had mastered several of the moves up through the drops, Ben changed the routes and he found himself learning even more techniques in the same climbs. Elliot learned that for the straighter moves upstream there were four stages: acceleration, alignment, the launch, and a follow through of a sustained barrage of strokes. He watched Ben intently when he demonstrated each new trick.

The next day, with the Potomac still running at four feet, they paddled up through Mather Gorge all the way to the S-Turn. Elliot was ecstatic and Ben was impressed with him.

"Ben, that was amazing."

"You are a very fast learner."

"Let's do it again tomorrow."

Ben laughed. "Elliot, don't you ever have to go to work?"

"I work!"

"What do you do?"

"I'm in property management. And you?"

"I teach English, but I'm on sabbatical." Ben thought for a moment. "Elliot, if I ask you to do something, will you do it?"

"Well, I guess so. Sure."

"Tomorrow, come back and do it again, by yourself."

"Why by myself?"

"We'll talk about that after you do it. Okay?"

"Okay."

Elliot found himself as a kayaker that next day.

Concentrating. Moving up through the eddies. Conserving strength for the next hard climb. Monitoring subconsciously his breathing. Stroking efficiently. Thinking through each climb while moving toward it. Executing them and simultaneously analyzing how he'd done and clearing his mind for the next. The midstream current a constant fixture of his peripheral vision, the side cliffs always close beside him. Vertical jumps and moves where he had to time the swirling eddy water and move side to side to optimize his position. And always,

always moving upstream. It was like a trance, yet his concentration was peaked. And at the same time, he was able to think, no, not think, meditate, no, not meditate, transcend. Transcend where he was at the moment and at that moment in his life, and his career, and focus on what he needed to do.

And he was doing what he needed to do. And the other thing he needed to do was find Dr. Howard Steven Calvert, and a soothing feeling rose from within him that soon, he would manage that, too.

Ben was waiting for him in the Angler's parking lot.

"Not going out today?"

Ben was leaning against his Rodeo, still in street clothes and looking pensive. "No. I just wanted to see how it went, and talk to you about it."

"It was . . . It opened the door for me, Ben. Thanks."

"Elliot, let's go somewhere and talk."

"Okay."

"Have you been where the boaters go for a beer?"

Ben certainly meant Trav's, but why was he being elusive?

"Sure. I know the place."

"Go ahead and change and I'll see you there."

Elliot stood dripping in the parking lot watching Ben as he pulled up onto the road.

Trav's was a rambling old house off of MacArthur, converted into a bar. It was part blue collar, part biker, and part boater bar. It was a fun place, with a touch of lowlife charm. Although it was only three in the afternoon, the parking lot was full of pickups, cars with boats, and Harleys.

Ben was at a table towards the back with a bottle of Budweiser. Elliot bought a Heineken at the bar and walked back to join him. Ben stood before he reached the table.

"Let's go out on the back porch."

The afternoon was turning chilly, and there was no one else on the porch.

"So today 'opened the door for you,' Elliot?"

"You knew it would, didn't you?"

"I did. You truly want to learn everything about boating, don't you?"

Elliot didn't respond and instead found himself turning defensive with his newfound mentor.

"Why?" asked Ben, rather pointedly.

"It has become the most important thing in my life."

"But why?"

"I personally want it for one thing, and my other reason I'd rather not talk about."

"You don't really work in property management, do you Elliot?"

He looked at Ben. He hadn't seen him yet without a helmet or a ball cap, like he was wearing now. What did the hairline look like?

"I made a phone call two nights ago, Elliot."

Ben looked to be in his early forties. A touch of gray showed in the beard. The bushy beard.

"I thought I recognized your name. But you weren't looking for me. You were learning how to kayak. You know everything, don't you, Elliot?"

"Not nearly enough. I want to find him. I want to go with him. You hold the key, Dr. Calvert."

"Don't use my name please."

Two minutes ago, he was talking to a great boater named Ben. Now, with a seeming ease in place of the shock he should have felt, he was talking to Howard Calvert. It seemed natural, inevitable. But it also had the quality of dream.

"I want to do something important with my life."

Elliot felt the calculating stare sizing him up.

"You are not ready. Not even close to being ready."

Elliot couldn't reply. He knew that he was just learning the obvious things, and he didn't even know what the hidden, the unknown might require. Still here was his one chance: the one person who had helped Dornblaser prepare for whatever it was that had had to be done.

"Get me ready."

"I'm running out of time. I'll be going to prison over this you know."

"I know."

"I help you, and you help me, and you'll be going to prison with me."

"I'm willing to risk it."

Howard looked down at his feet and with a light chuckle shook his head in disbelief.

"You're out of the same mold as he is. You know that, Elliot?"

"I'll take that as a compliment."

Elliot raised his bottle, and Howard clinked his against it.

"What's he like? You know him the best."

"He's crazy, but he is a great guy. He's uneducated, but smart. I've never seen anybody who can survive in as many environments. When we roomed to-gether in Morgantown, Pete quit his raft guiding job and I would think, 'okay, now he won't have any income,' But every day he would fix a kayak for a little money, or help the neighbor shingle the roof of his garage, or work as a stage hand up at the university theater. I never saw anything like it. At the beginning of each day he wouldn't have any money but by the day's end, he'd have gas in the tank and food in his belly. And on whitewater and in the river environment in general, his instincts take over. There the guy is practically indestructible. He is very independent." Howard seemed to grow introspective. "We had a lot of great times together. It makes me sad to think I'll never see him again."

"But why can't he come back?"

"Do you know who Mihalis is?"

"Who, it is? I saw the videotape you made for Pete. Mihalis is the kayak you found in the desert. Isn't it? Why do you say who?"

"Because it is alive. Pete found it, in the bowl below my research site." Howard looked up in surprise. "You saw the tape?"

"Yes, I, saw it, but, I don't think that he saw it. I erased it." He was feeling off balance thinking of Mihalis as something more than just a kayak.

Howard turned serious.

"Why do you think that he didn't see it?"

"When I searched his room, the tape was still in an envelope that was sitting on top of the TV set." Elliot detected surprise and concern in Howard's reception of this latest revelation.

"Do you know what Mihalis wants him to do?"

"No..."

"Mihalis needs Pete to paddle it into a tower which has been built over the pit in the bowl, and destroy the tower."

"Wait. Back up a second. There is no 'tower' in the bowl. It's full of sand again. And why Pete?"

"It will be at a different time. Also, I don't think this is the first time this has happened. After all, Pete found Mihalis in the pit below where the tower was, and may be again someday. As far as 'why Pete?', Elliot this has been the hardest thing for me to accept in my life.

However, I have to face the truth. I am a scientist who has been confronted with the reality of a separate reality in which Pete is the latest vestige of 'the pilot soul' a built in control to the concept of Mihalis against the tower."

"Ben. You'd better explain all this a little more in depth for me. I don't understand. What is this tower for?" Elliot wanted to bolt. All this was too much. It was crazy. Still something held him. He knew something essential was being said.

"It is to divert water from entering the pit. It essentially changes the drainage patterns of the northern half of the African continent, and thus affects weather patterns worldwide."

"But now there is no water there, at all."

"Well, ten thousand years ago there was, but this really has nothing to do with that. I did some spectroanalysis on some rock samples from the Wadi. The porous sandstone showed traces of sodium chloride."

"Salt."

"Sea water. My theory is that every time the poles melt, sea water flows in from the Atlantic, south of the Atlas range. The pit was an underground drain which led to the Mediterranean."

"But who built the tower and the city upstream?"

"Mihalis communicates through visions. But is seems the devil built the tower. Or some evil force like the devil. I know very little about the city."

"The devil?"

In spite of trying to sound skeptical, Elliot felt a knot developing in his stomach. More pieces were falling into the puzzle. The chess game was making more sense, whether or not he liked the shape of it.

"The devil. Scrap your Christian mythology. This Devil is more fundamental, less symbolic. Less immoral. More evil. Less caring. Less personal. But he's in our dreams. What does the agency think about the devil?"

"Officially, neither God or the devil exist. We try to rationalize everything in more accessible and tangible terms. However, the agency catalogs and studies discrepancies that don't fit 'normal' parameters of reality. That's one of the reasons, of course, why you have disturbed the agency so much." Elliot laughed. "First you just took some weapons-grade plutonium to a hostile Arab country. That was average stuff. Then, you guys started disappearing and reappearing somewhere else. That really pissed off my boss."

Howard noticed a new concern cross Elliot's brow.

"Talking about the devil, when I was at the Dornblaser's home, there was apparently this old gold piece that had come up missing. The story was that some ancestor won it in a wager with the devil. Do you know something about that?"

"Pete used to say that his roots to whitewater started with that great, great, great grandfather or whatever exactly he was. Apparently, he was a young river pilot on the Falls of the Ohio. As the story goes, the devil, or just some bad guy, sought him out, paid him with a gold piece, and tried to drown him. Instead he drowned the devil and kept the money. He later moved back to West Virginia and started a shipping company on the Monongahela River."

"So what do you think about Mihalis' claim that the 'devil' built the tower?"

"We have a different point of reference. Modern religion and our concept of Satan and God are based largely on events that occurred a few thousand years ago. However, at that time, there was virtually no network of communication, no media. Biblical events were recorded by few individuals and were subject to distortion, ranging from innocent changes which normally occur when a story or event is told and retold, to blatant manipulation. So our present concepts of God and the Devil are leftovers of a darker, more primitive era."

"Makes sense."

"Mihalis is, it says, a creation of God. Mihalis is an amazing thing. It is solid crystal. Indestructible. Sentient. It comprehends instantly new media and languages. I have no reason to doubt that it was created by God. My only question is: Who is this, God? But it all fits together with the age-old theme of God versus the Devil. To me, if this 'devil' is anywhere near as powerful as this 'God' that created Mihalis, Pete is in a world of trouble. And you may be too."

"I said before, I'm willing to risk it. Now, I know more and know that there's lots I don't know. But I'm still willing."

⁂

And so his training began. Howard pushed and pushed. Elliot learned and achieved. They became very careful not to be seen together off the river. No phone calls. Separate vehicles on river trips throughout the winter. They were running Class V in extreme weather. Elliot practiced intricate maneuvers in Class IV, over and over until he had mastered each one. Howard recommended that he train in slalom gates, so he bought a used Predator and hung out at the feeder canal with the racers. Elliot felt his upper body becoming hard and strong. His reflexes had always been quick, but now his agility had increased to a new level. He found that he made decisions much faster.

When not teaching Elliot, Howard worked on his paper on Moving Water Analysis. When it was completed, he submitted it to the American Geophysical Institute, who had been expecting the long awaited treatise from the famous fugitive research scientist.

The work done on the project and the math backing it all up were impeccable and immediately acclaimed. The study was revolutionary -- a fundamental generalization that covered interaction of fluids so comprehensively that it could be applied anywhere.

Howard and Elliot shared what each knew. Between the two, all of the pieces were falling into place.

Howard was dreading the moment when his world would soon come tumbling down around him, but he wasn't sitting around waiting for it to happen. He transferred funds the government didn't know about into numbered accounts in Switzerland and Panama.

Then he did what he hated the most, he had Anders Lieb retain a lawyer for him.

CHAPTER 10 — JOURNEY

June 14, 923

The child was becoming a man. Simon was now sixteen. He was getting big and muscular. He had the beautiful features of his mother and the curly hair of his father. Simon was spontaneous, inventive, and bold. Although he wasn't precocious, he knew he was special, and it showed. He had grown up playing all the games of Shawnee boys. With no brothers or sisters but lots of cousins, he had visited the villages of his relatives and played vigorously. He had learned to track animals and shoot with bow and arrow. He traveled the woods freely with no sense of fear. But he was also a kayaker, and because of kayaking he was beginning to see less and less of his cousins. He kayaked everywhere with Pete, and for the last year, whenever they ran Class V rivers, Simon went first. He was fearless, as his father had been at that age. He had been kayaking seriously for four years, and had been playing around in kayaks before that from the age of six.

Pete had shared the secret of Simon's potential fate with Sana some years back. She had taken it much worse than Pete had feared and had fallen into a serious depression for weeks. He swore to himself once again that he would never allow Mihalis to take Simon. Never.

As for Pete, he had aged gracefully. He was now forty-eight, but in excellent shape. Clean living, hard work, and a low-fat diet agreed with him. He and his small family lived in peace in their world. He grew detached from the society he had left behind, and thought about his former friends less and less each year. He had adopted the Indian style of subsistence and rarely drew from his stores in the trailer. The land gave them everything they needed. However, he kept his armaments ready for their defense, should a problem arise.

Sana was happy, still beautiful, always busy. She took charge of all household chores. She directed the planting of corn and told the men when to hunt and fish. She knew where to find dozens of medicinal plants and how to administer them.

One thing that puzzled them both was that Sana had never borne more children. Most Shawnee families were large, but Pete and Sana had a single child.

Their world was not without dangers. Packs of hungry wolves sometimes lurked about for weeks in the dead of winter, and Pete or one of Sana's brothers would occasionally have to dispatch a marauding bear; three large bearskin rugs warmed the floor of the cabin.

They heard tales of raiding parties of Iroquois reaching as far south as Ohiopyle, but the Shawnee were fierce when need be and had driven them back to the north.

One thing that intrigued Pete was the legend of Tokebelloke. Pete had come to understand "Apu Tokebelloke" as a place where falling water spoke to the people, but according to Sana's aging father, the term meant a place where Tokebelloke could be heard in the falling waters. Tokebelloke was a hole through which water fell into another world. It was four days to the south and as near as Pete could tell, that might well put it on the Gauley. Pete had asked years before to be taken there, and the old man looked at him as if he were crazy. No one ever went there, he was told. All too often. Matchelomeneton, the devil, resided there. Over the years, Pete had never ventured further south than the Tygart, even though the Gauley had been one of his favorite rivers in his former life.

Simon had accompanied him to the Tygart the year before. They had attained the Cheat up to the junction of the Shavers and Dry Forks and then walked overland to the vicinity of the junction of the Tygart with the Middle Fork. They descended the Tygart until it joined the West Fork and continued downstream on the Monongahela. When they reached the mouth of Decker's Creek, Pete had explained to Simon that some day Morgantown would be located there.

"Someday I would like to see it here in this place." Simon spoke in cadenced Shawnee, a language with built-in terms of respect.

"No, my son. It is very ugly compared to this world we live in."

"But why, Father?"

"To build the city and provide for the lives of all the people, they will destroy the world as we know it. They will cut all the trees and rip open the land for coal to burn to make power for the houses. All the fish will die in the rivers."

Simon looked at him.

"Why would the people do that?"

"Slowly, as the world changed, fish weren't important to the people any more. The forests weren't important. It happened over time, so no one tried to stop it."

"You tried to stop it, didn't you, father?"

Pete thought back to his wild youth, A huge billboard had been erected on a forested hillside above Interstate 68. He and a pair of friends had toppled it one night with a chainsaw. They had burned a drill rig in a strip mine high in the Daugherty Creek drainage. Nothing had changed. The billboard had reappeared. The strip mine project grew, and acid drainage killed the native trout in Daugherty Creek.

"It couldn't be stopped, Simon. It started long before I was born."

Pete would never forget that moment. It was the first time his son had ever looked at him with anything less than total respect and admiration.

Thankfully, thought Pete, he will never have to see what will come to pass in West Virginia in the 20th Century.

Then something happened. It was mid June, and Pete and Simon were surfing the waves and holes at the bottom of Lower Decision. The rains had brought the river up and the surfing was great. The sun was shining and father and son were having a blast. Not a care in the world. Pete heard a whistle and there was Sana's little brother. Shenan stood on the bank with an old Indian. The man had a different look.

Pete and Simon paddled over to shore and got out of their kayaks.

In perfect Shawnee the stranger introduced himself.

"I am Petawa. I have come from the west to meet with you."

With this he held up a knife. With a shock, Pete recognized the Spyderco he had given to Hawapiti, seventeen years before. The old man studied Pete's face, reading everything that it revealed. Then he squatted and began to talk.

"This found its way to my hands. I am a trader and I have traveled widely. Never have I seen something as this. It is not from the world, and now that I have seen you, I am convinced that you are also not from the world. My business is not only trade. It is of tremendous interest to me to know everything of the world. I have come here to know the person who possesses such interesting things."

"Okay... We'll talk."

All four of them walked up the trail back to the cabin, Pete and Simon with their kayaks on their shoulders. Pete was impressed with the man's dress. White feathers held in a hammered gold plate hung down from his hair. A fine buckskin vest, dyed vermilion. An ornate chest plate of bone and bead. Breechcloth of a hide he guessed to be antelope. Beaded mocassins. However, what really caught Pete's eye were his leggings. They were of a black and yellow spotted cat -- undoubtedly Jaguar.

But how?

Petawa was sophisticated and cordial. Sana prepared a feast, and the entire clan sat around the huge table outside the cabin. Petawa entertained them with tales of his travels. He had indeed traveled widely. As near as Pete could tell, he was from the shores of Lake Superior. He traded throughout the Great Lakes and up the Missouri to the Rockies.

Later that evening, after all but Pete and Petawa had drifted off to sleep, the old man sat transfixed as Pete recounted the tale of his arrival and the future world from which he had come. He had given Petawa a tour of the cabin and the trailer, so the trader would have a basis for his story.

Pete then asked him about the leggings.

"They interest you, do they?"

"I must say they do."

"They reveal the true reason I am here. I have visited with the greatest society in the world. It lies far to the south, past where the Father of Rivers enters the sea. There are men there, very wise men. They have knowledge of another world, far across the sea, and have fear of that world. These people are where paths cross. One path is the path of truth and knowledge which leads to the creation of a world where all can live in harmony. The path which crosses it is one of jealousy and warfare where the world ends in disaster. You, could help rub out the bad path."

"But how?"

"By making those who have doubts see the truth of what awaits our world."

I should stay out of politics.

"Pete, I believe that this could be the most important thing that you could do in your life."

"What you cannot understand is that if I do something like that, it could change the course of the future."

"Would it be a bad change, or a good change?"

"I don't know. Also I must think of my family."

Petawa waved his arms.

"They will be well if you are here or if you are not here."

"I have to think about their security."

"Very well. But as you sleep, think as well about the world your son will bring his sons into."

The next morning, everyone sat down to discuss the possibility of Pete going with Petawa, and to his surprise, they were all in favor of the journey.

"I, too, will go, father," Simon said tentatively.

"No, Simon. You must stay here with the family."

"You are too young to go so far. I need you with me." Sana was not about to let Simon go with them. To her, Simon was everything. Like so many mothers, she had transferred much of her love for her husband to her special child. But she also felt that Pete was a special outside creation with a responsibility that went beyond their community. She was willing to see him go, even if she couldn't be certain of his return.

"I lend you my husband for the trip you propose. He came a long way to get here. He can go many moons with you and still return."

"It is a thing said and done then," said Petawa, "We will meet the second moon of the next spring where the waters of the Ohio meet the Mississippi. You should be able to return by the following harvest."

Pete spent the rest of the year dreading and anticipating the journey. What dangers and marvels awaited? He worried about Simon. The young man was growing restless and rebellious.

Simon enjoyed the friendship of other Indian boys. He was a leader on their hunting trips and in playing their wild games of tag. However, kayaking set him apart. Pete was pleased that Simon was coming into his own as a kayaker. His speed, strength, fluidity and instinct were constantly reaching new levels. The two boated throughout the winter and made a winter circuit down the Yough and Sandy and up the Cheat.

Spring arrived and Pete readied himself for his trip. He chose his lightest Augsburg. Sana packed a month's rations of deer jerky and blackberry pemmican into small dry bags. He took the volume M of the Encyclopedia Britannica and packed it tightly in plastic and its own drybag. For clothing he took only two pair of river shorts, a fleece vest, a paddle jacket, ball cap and sunglasses. Almost an afterthought, he went into the trailer and found something he hadn't even looked at in over a decade. He opened the dry box and there it was, The WD-40 soaked rags he'd wrapped it in had done their job. The nine-millimeter was rust free, and clean as a whistle. He tested the action. It felt good. He popped in a full clip and threw three more clips in a dry bag. He was, after all, heading into unknown territory. Pack's words came back to him; "It's your best friend in the jungle."

Spring rains began and continued for days. It seemed as if a huge front had moved in and settled over the region. The Cheat rose to the limit of its banks.

Pete had figured it would take two weeks to reach Cairo, Illinois, where he was to meet Petawa. The day arrived when he was to go. Sana was visibly upset.

"You don't want me to go, do you?"

"No. But it is best for everything if you go and do good."

"I will come back to you."

"I know. But I am worried anyway. It is such a long journey."

"Take care of Simon."

Sana gave him one of her looks.

"Of course I will take care of my son you crazy old man! Now go and come back a whole being."

They kissed long and deep.

Simon walked down to the river with his father.

"My son, you are becoming a man. You must do your part to watch over your mother and our home. No journeys for you until I return. Understand?"

Simon seemed to resent his father's instructions. Why should he have to be told to do what was obvious? But the responsibility placed on him left him trembling and proud.

"Yes, I understand. Father, I love you with all my spirit."

"I love you too, my son."

Pete pulled out into the water which swept down into the canyon. The only difficult whitewater of the entire journey awaited him. At that level, the rapids of the Cheat were Grand Canyon size, but because he was taking the most conservative of lines through the big whitewater, he experienced no difficulty. The river was running so fast that by noon he had flushed out of the Cheat into the swollen Monongahela. All streams coming in from the sides were just about at flood stage. He was surprised at the large standing waves in the Mon. The Mon river he had always known as a youth was a series of flat pools backed up by a series of locks and dams. Now it was a real, living river. It was flooding and Pete found himself racing downstream incredibly fast. The current was laden with logs and whole trees and every so often a tree would rebound upward off of the bottom as it rolled downstream, and present itself in Pete's path. One never knew when it would happen. Pete paddled, alert to hazards that might loom. As night fell, he decided to camp. He stopped on the west side of the river where a small creek entered. It's banks were covered with blooming Trillium and the sweet blossoms proved to be a rich intoxicant for a peaceful night's sleep.

At daybreak he ate some jerky and washed it down with the fresh water of the creek. Then he was off. So far he'd seen only a few small villages as he'd whisked by, but he was aware that he was leaving Shawnee territory. He was worried about passing Pittsburgh. The junction of the Monongahela and Allegheny rivers, where the Ohio was formed, was throughout history a hotly contested, strategic point and he had no idea what to expect there. He had no desire to stop, or be stopped. He strapped the pistol in its shoulder holster around his life jacket.

As he passed the mouth of the Youghiogheny, heavy rain fell.

Good. This should help me slip past.

A short while later, he saw in the distance the mighty current of the Allegheny entering from the right. He moved over towards the left side of the Mon and sat motionless in the kayak as he sailed towards the junction. Some Indians in dress he did not recognize were pulling long canoes higher up onto the bank on the Pittsburgh side and saw him. They pointed and shouted in a tongue other than Shawnee, but did nothing. The currents of the two rivers swirled together, and he was past.

Pete estimated the flow of the Ohio to be over 100,000 cubic feet per second. He was kayaking somewhere around fifty miles a day and had about four hundred fifty miles to go. He would easily make his appointment with Petawa. The Ohio was gorgeous. The itinerant sunlight often cast giant shadows from the bluffs and cliffs while unrestrained beams glared off of the ripples. Magnificent flocks of migratory birds winged their way northward, and some came to light in the canebrakes at the river's edge. Pete enjoyed the sights of the voyage with a sense of surreality. He was seeing what no white man would see for another six hundred years.

Several days down the Ohio, Pete began to watch for the falls. He had a feeling they would be washed out and they were. Immense swells were all that remained. He thought of how his whitewater ancestor would someday come to pilot the flatboats of the pioneers through the rapids.

The swells were large and smooth, their height hard to judge. Continuing through them, he felt as if he were entering into a trance. Suddenly, he was no longer seeing the waves. A drop of water was falling slowly. Then it stopped and slowly rose, only to stop and begin to fall once again. He snapped himself out of it and found himself once again staring at the enormous swells. The Vision. It had been so long since it had come to him. However, its meaning was more distant than ever. He tried not to think about it, and had an uneasy feeling that perhaps somehow Mihalis was lurking somewhere a bit closer in the dark corners of his past.

He now knew he was more than halfway. The next morning he passed the mouth of the Wabash. Pete overtook two Indians in a canoe, but they were friendly once they overcame the initial shock of seeing a strange man in a strange boat. He started to communicate with them in sign language and then was surprised to hear them speak between themselves in Shawnee. He asked and they told him that he was once again in Shawnee country. They told him he was two days from the Mississippi and that a large settlement was on the narrow point of land where the two rivers converged. He asked if they would like to accompany him, but they were not going that far. They said goodbye where a huge cave mouth gaped out at the Ohio. Pete recognized it as the future, infamous, Cave-In-Rock where numerous robberies and murders would take place as the Ohio would become a highway for the westward expansion of the pioneers.

The banks of the Ohio seemed to be unbroken curtains of great trees: cottonwoods, willows and sycamores. As he rushed downstream with the current, they became a hypnotic blur in the periphery. The light green leaves of spring painted the curtain more and more with each passing day. Two days before the second full moon of spring, he arrived at the junction of the two great rivers, the future site of Cairo, Illinois. He was met on the bank by a party of Indians who beckoned him to come up into the town. Two braves carried his kayak on their shoulders. It was the largest population center he had seen yet, a thousand or more Indians by Pete's guess. The village was bustling, yet as he was led inward, everyone stopped whatever they were doing to look at him. Petawa was seated with several chieftains beside a mound of earth and almost jumped to his feet when he saw him.

"Pete, how good I feel that you have arrived."

Pete grinned back at him, feeling reassured by Petawa's presence.

"I told you I'd be here."

He was introduced to the chiefs, and Petawa made a speech in a tongue he didn't understand, but it was obviously about him and the voyage they would undertake together. When he was through, he turned to Pete.

"Tomorrow we go, but tonight we shall powwow with these friends."

Petawa knew everybody who was anybody and was diplomatic as well as outgoing. That explained, in part, his success as a trader.

They ate and then sat for the evening by the mound. The men passed around a long clay pipe. They were smoking Kinikenek, presumably willow bark and tobacco, but Pete detected more than a trace of marijuana in the rough smoke. They slept in a tipi near the mound and in the morning made ready to take off downriver.

Pete, kayak on his shoulder, followed Petawa down to the water on the Mississippi side. Two great birchbark canoes were tied up to trees. Two young men in fine dress were loading the emptier of the two. Petawa introduced them to Pete as his sons, Tawanpi and Petawash. Although they both resembled the old trader in their ways, they were obviously from different mothers and probably different tribes. One started to pass large ceramic vessels to the other, who in turn lashed them to the thwarts of the canoe.

"Water" said Petawa. "On the Father of Rivers it is hard and dangerous to take fresh water."

"Dangerous?"

"Some of our brothers below are poorly behaved," said Petawa with a laugh. With this he handed two bows, one long, and a short one made of horn, along with two quivers of arrows to the youth doing the loading.

Petawa showed Pete a bale of pelts.

"The winter fur."

They were indeed thick, soft, and shiny pelts of mink, fisher, and beaver. "These will bring a fine trade where we go."

Petawa said something in a dialect he didn't understand to Tawanpi and soon the young man brought a tipi pole from the village and began to chop it into three sections.

"Pete, with these we will fix your boat to the canoe."

Pete got the idea and with braided hemp they lashed the poles to the kayak so that it made an outrigger on the canoe. Pete put his sprayskirt over the cockpit and tied the body opening shut, effectively converting the Augsburg into a pontoon.   Petawa seemed to be giving his boys a lot of instructions.

"Aren't they coming?"

"No, Pete. We go alone. They will wait for the high water to pass and will go into the Ohio country trading dyes, beads, and these. . ." With that, Petawa looked around first to make sure no one was watching and then pulled some small axe heads from a pack in the other canoe. Pete took one and examined it. It was forged iron.

"Where did these come from?"

"Ah, now you, are the curious one, eh?"

"I sure am. I didn't know they could be made by, by..."

"By people so primitive as we are? I assure you it is not done without difficulty." He held one up, "Very valuable," Petawa then looked about again and reached into the canoe they were taking south. Unstopping the mouth of one of the ceramic water vessels, he inserted a hand and withdrew an iron chisel. It was of much finer work than the axe heads.

"The temple builders where we go are crazy for these cutters of stone," he said with a wink and a grin. "The rings your Shawnee wear on their ears are made, too, by my people on the shores of Gichygoomie."

"Lake Superior," Pete said in English.

Petawa shrugged a 'yes, I guess so.'

When the packing was done they were ready to shove off. Petawa had hugged and kissed his sons and wished them well. A crowd had assembled to see them go. They paddled out into the current and slowly slipped past the point of land where the two great rivers met. The Mississippi was immensely wide but didn't flow in such a rush as the Ohio had.

Petawa started out in the bow and Pete in the stern. The paddles were finely made from a light wood and felt good in his hands. In places the river was deep and in others they took shortcuts across the broadly curving main current by cutting across sandbars. At times they had to get out of the canoe and drag it carefully over the shallows.

They stopped each day before nightfall. Petawa was worried about hitting a snag after dark and sinking his precious load.

They spent the first two nights on sandbars. The first had driftwood scattered about on it and Pete suggested they start a fire. Petawa quashed the idea, citing the danger of river pirates.

I guess river piracy needs only a river and humans to exist, thought Pete.

The third day out, some canoes shoved off from the east bank after they had passed and Petawa urged him to paddle harder. Pete dug in and their long canoe picked up speed. Petawa constantly looked over his shoulder to see if the canoes were gaining, which they weren't. Pete laughed at Petawa. Petawa laughed also, and soon their pursuers gave up the chase and pulled back to their shore.

"They had you pretty worried, didn't they?"

"And you? Nothing?"

"Not really. Our canoe is longer than theirs. That makes us faster, and we had a lead to begin with."

"Yes, and they were stupid. They started late. But believe me, we may not always have such fortune. They are Creeks, bad people."

Later that day, Pete saw just what he meant. They came around the tail end of an island and immediately two long canoes with three braves each, came charging out from the eddy behind the island, whooping with lust for battle. Pete and Petawa both bent to their paddles but the raiders were in a faster current, and Pete knew they would soon be in range. An arrow sliced through the air over their canoe, narrowly missing Petawa. The trader dropped his paddle into the canoe and knocked an arrow. Arrows now seemed to fill the air. Petawa's arrow missed its mark and the enemy boats drew closer. Pete turned to look while he continued to paddle. The center brave in each canoe was standing and loosing arrow after arrow.

"Take up the other bow Pete or we will lose."

Pete hesitated for a moment and dwelled on the thought of his life ending miserably with an arrow through the ribs. He thought of Sana and Simon. As in slow motion, an arrow came hissing past his ear and shook him from his malaise. The canoes were now only some thirty meters apart. Pete reached below his life jacket and ripped open the velcro flap of the holster. He pulled the pistol out and leveled it at the painted brave about to loose another arrow. The bullet caught him square in the chest and took him writhing over the side of the canoe.

The blast of the gun silenced the war whoops instantly. Before the Indians could react, Pete fired again and the other standing brave went flying through the air, blood spurting from his throat. Pete's ears were ringing. The Creeks sat transfixed as their canoes coasted towards them through the gun smoke that hung over the water. Pete turned to Petawa who was staring at him with disbelief.

"Petawa, let's go!"

They grabbed up their paddles and pulled away from their foes. A safe distance away, they stopped and looked back. The Creeks were paddling hard, back to the island, and the bodies of the braves Pete had shot were slowly sinking into the Mississippi.

"That was the most incredible thing I have seen in my life."

"Unfortunately, it is an all too common tool of death in the time I come from."

"It was ugly, but beautiful at the moment."

"It did slow them right down, didn't it?"

Petawa laughed uncomfortably.

"I had wondered what it was you carried in the pouch."

"It's only for emergencies!"

"That was an emergency."

They paddled on downriver and soon the site of the skirmish was a speck disappearing on the horizon behind them. Pete meditated as they paddled. Once again, he had killed. It had been in self defense, but was it necessary to have shot the second Creek? Maybe they would have fled after the first shot, but maybe not. Was he getting mean in his old age? Oh, fuck those guys anyway. They made their living killing and stealing on the river. They had received what they deserved. The river should be a place of peace where one doesn't worry about being attacked.

The rest of their trip was peaceful. The Mississippi was beautiful. Great flocks of Canada geese and ducks of all varieties were gathered on the banks readying to migrate northward. At one point, they were met with the bizarre sight of a buffalo herd pushing and shoving each other into the river like lemmings. They maneuvered close to one of the drowned bulls, and Petawa quickly removed the hump from his back with his Spyderco.

"Tonight we eat very well."

The meat was better than the best filet mignon. As they ate, Pete asked Petawa why he didn't fear starting a fire.

"We are now close to the mouth of the river. No Creeks here."

"And what do we do when we get to the sea?"

"We will be met there. They know we are coming and will send a great canoe to take us across the sea."

Eleven days after leaving "Cairo," they crossed through the delta. Petawa was concentrating hard to keep them always in the main flow of the river as its channels divided and intertwined. By nightfall, they had flushed out into the Gulf.

"What now?"

"We shall wait for darkness."

An hour later, Pete saw a light across the water.

"Petawa. Look over there."

"I believe it is Chaan. Let's go."

They paddled towards the light. As they drew closer, Pete saw a torch burning on the prow of a boat, an immense canoe painted with intricate figures. Seven men were aboard. They were dressed in cloth tunics, skirts, and headbands. Their facial features were broader and somehow different from all of the Indians he had seen. Pete and Petawa drew alongside the great canoe and Petawa called out a greeting. One of the crew called back and both broke into smiles.

"It is Chaan," said Petawa. "He was the chief of the last boat that met me here three years ago."

Chaan and the rest of the crew seemed friendly. Each greeted Pete with a gesture of his hand and spoke his name. He noticed that each had the telltale callous of a veteran paddler between thumb and forefinger.

They transferred the load from the canoe to the larger craft. The Augsburg was lashed to the poles holding the outrigger. Petawa's birchbark canoe was allowed to drift.

"You don't need it anymore?"

"It is not that I do not need it. It is that it has become of no use. I cannot return home by water. They will bring me back, but more to the west. Then I must walk."

"How long will it take you?"

"Not long. Two moons. I have friends who will help me."

The paddlers turned the great canoe about and started paddling into the night. While Chaan and Petawa talked, Pete examined the boat. It was a dugout, and as near as he could tell, was made from a single tree trunk. Pete was amazed because it was close to fifty feet long. It rose to high, tapered ends. The paddlers knelt on board seats notched into the sides of the canoe. The paddles were long and heavy. They were not grasped with the palm of the hand over the top end, but on the shaft, which extended on up into the air. Pete picked up a spare and started mimicking their strokes. The heavy top end helped to counterbalance the blade and long shaft. Largely due to its extreme length, the great canoe moved swiftly through the water. Pete fell into the rhythm of the paddling.

Petawa came to his side and told him that Chaan thought perhaps he was one of the paddler twins, gods in Maya legend.

"I have told him the truth of your arrival here in this time. He understands. To him, your coming is great prophecy, foretelling radical events." Petawa paused, gazing at the captain for a moment. "Chaan is one of the learned society. He can find his home across the sea using the stars and the sun. Not like a river, eh? Where one cannot become lost." Petawa admired and respected this skill. And he recognized that getting lost could easily delay a trip a full year because of the changing seasons. Navigators had status akin to medicine men.

"Their people, like ours to the north, awoke in centuries past to beliefs in Gods. What has passed with these people is that they came to understand much of the universe. They do wondrous things. They have a form of scribing where they can put words into paper or stone, and it can be understood by other learned people. They have a system for recording the passing of days and moons and years. They can build giant houses."

"Over many, many years, they grew from children to humans and no longer needed to call on the gods to tell them when to plant maize or how to cure sickness. The problem is that now only the kings of the Maya call forth the gods. They seek the power of the gods, and holding this power, they battle the other Maya kings for the land. They make slaves of the defeated and offer sacrifices to the gods." Petawa made a gesture, drawing a finger across his throat. "What is left, is a great nation of people dying for the greed of their kings. The learned ones are powerless to stop this. That is why I wanted to bring you here. That is why Chaan has come. We must be careful when we arrive. Keep this with you." Petawa tapped the pistol through Pete's life jacket.

The voyage took nine days. They paddled in shifts, day and night. The great canoe never stopped moving forward. They paddled, ate, slept, paddled. In one sense it was boring, but for Pete, it gave him time to think. He missed Sana and their home. He missed Simon. How sweet it would be to be surfing the waves on the Cheat with his boy. The boy. The boy was becoming a man. Soon he would want to pass into manhood by the rite of the Vision Quest. Pete was uncomfortable with the concept and was reluctant to have Simon go through it.

Simon would have to fast for several days. The hunger would bring on visions. Sana's brothers had done their quests with no problems. They were all healthy, happy and well adjusted. He was just being a worried father. Pete thought of his son as emotionally vulnerable and having a different psyche than Shawnee boys, but he also knew that he was as strong and fast as the strongest and fastest. As accurate with bow and arrow. Simon was as ready for a Vision Quest as any Shawnee boy had ever been.

Pete also wondered if he would ever make it back home. Getting here had been easy; it had all been downstream. Going home would be a lot harder. But he had a plan. His knowledge of geography would carry him through.

Throughout the voyage, a school of dolphins remained with them, leaping into the air beside and ahead of the canoe. They were like the second hands of a clock ticking away the yards and miles of the voyage. Pete fell into the daily cycle of the crew. Each man would paddle for three hours and rest for one. During his rest hour, he would eat, drink, and when needed, defecate. This was done in a clay pot towards the stern. Then the man would dump the contents overboard and wash the pot with seawater. At night, each man would sleep for about three hours, two men at a time.

Food consisted of fruits, oranges or lemons and many more that Pete didn't recognize, stored in capped clay vessels. Water was ladled from large vessels and had a strong lemon flavor. Petawa pointed out that the lemon helped to keep the water fresh during long trips.

At Petawa's urging, Pete spent time with Chaan learning Maya. Sometimes the men paddling would sing Mayan songs in time with the paddle strokes. Pete would join in and later Chaan would explain the words. One of the songs was of Hunahpu and Xbalanque, the Hero Twins who are forced to play ball with the devil for their lives. In the final game, the devil tears off Hunahpu's head and substitutes it for the ball, Xbalanque, however, is very cagey and throws a rabbit onto the court. The devil chases the bounding rabbit thinking it to be the ball, and this gives Xbalanque time to replace Hunahpu's head on his body.

Pete asked Petawa about the ball games.

"I have seen one. It was violent. The players are prisoners of battle. The losing team is killed in cruel ways."

Pete found himself dwelling on this for some time afterward.

What kind of world am I entering?

The next afternoon they sighted land. They continued to paddle toward it but it seemed distant and they didn't seem to be any closer after hours of paddling. Pete's shift ended at darkness and he ate some fruit and lay down to rest. He thought about how tired he was of the steady diet of fruit and fell asleep dreaming of delicious food heaped high on steaming platters. When he awoke around midnight, he noticed he no longer smelled sea water and instead his nostrils were filled with the aroma of dry land. He rose, and wiping the sleep from his eyes, saw that they were no longer at sea but had entered a system of canals. Pockets of dense jungle alternated with expansive fields. By dawn it seemed that they had made dozens of right and left turns in the canals and Pete gave up trying to keep track of where they had come from. With the arrival of daylight, he saw hundreds, and then thousands of cook fires smoking from thatched huts and houses that lined the canals. Other dugouts, much smaller than theirs, began plying the canals with them. Men and women worked the fields they passed. Rich smells wafted through the air. They docked their canoe at a low wharf near a settlement of three thatched houses.

"We will take some food here," said Chaan while rubbing his stomach and smiling. Pete stepped out of the canoe and his legs felt rubbery and weak from so much time at sea. Chaan was met at the entrance of a gated compound by an old, heavyset woman wearing a colorful dress and headband. Her name was Cozul. She leered at Pete with something more than curiosity. However, anticipation of a hearty meal outweighed any uneasiness about her stares.

It was the feast Pete had dreamed of. Cozul produced food of all types in great quantities. There was an array of fresh fruit, corn, beans, rice, tortillas, avocados, roasted wild boar and steamed fish. Earthen bowls of rich sauces were set around the table for all to spoon onto their plates. Pete stuffed himself and felt the urge to lie down and sleep but Chaan announced that it was time to go. They paddled throughout the day and into the night.

Finally, in the early morning hours of the following day, Pete saw that they were arriving at the outskirts of a city. Now the banks of the canals were walled with stone. Pyramids towered over the houses and buildings. Causeways passed over the canals and people bearing loads on their backs were filing into the city. With the center of the city on their left, they turned right into a smaller canal and then left into a stone docking area surrounded with stone warehouses. Ahead, the canal ended in an earthen slope. Two other huge dugouts the size of theirs had been pulled up the grade.

Chaan called out and two men opened wooden doors on one of the warehouses. Soon their canoe was unloaded and their things packed away in the warehouse. Pete unlashed the Augsburg and the crew dismantled the outrigger. The balsa wood float of the outrigger was waterlogged and would be discarded. Placing small log sections on the grade, they all pitched in and rolled the great canoe up out of the water and onto dry land. Chaan had a conference with the crew and then they all said goodbye to Pete and Petawa and headed for their homes. Chaan said something to Petawa and left.

"He was cautioning them not to tell anyone about you," said Petawa.

"But why?"

"Last year, the old king, Kakupacal, died. The woman where we took our meal yesterday told Chaan that the king's son is ready to undergo his ascension to power. His name is Bahlum Xoc, but he plans to call himself Six Serpent Bird after he accedes. It is a bad sign, a sign that he will make war."

"Why? What does Six Serpent Bird mean?"

"The serpent birds live at the top of the world tree and rule over everyone else in the tree. It means he wants to conquer the other three cities."

"Where are we Petawa?"

"This place is called Chichen Itza."

"I have heard of it. There are only three more cities?"

"There were fifteen before the wars started two hundred years ago. Now all but these lie desolate, being eaten by the jungle, their peoples dispersed. Pete, it is more dangerous for you now than I had thought. We must be very careful. We will go with Chaan before the sun comes."

Chaan came back into the warehouse and had brought some cloth tunics. "I have sent a runner to call a meeting of the learned society. We must go." He looked at Pete and said something about his clothes.

"Pete, we must wear clothes of the Maya, we will leave our things here."

"Okay, but I need to take something with me." He removed the encyclopedia volume from the dry bag. It was still well sealed in the plastic and appeared to have survived the journey. He took off the life jacket but kept his pistol in it's holster. He kept on his river shorts, but traded his worn mocassins for some woven sandals. The sandals were too short and too tight, but Petawa and Chaan were jabbering away in Maya about how Pete had to blend in as much as possible.

Something had to be done about his height. Petawa pantomimed how he should walk bent over as much as possible and Chaan had a brainstorm, He produced a large bundle of long sticks: firewood, for him to carry on his back.

Once changed, they made haste for the city. At the far side of the causeway, two spear-wielding, but half asleep guards hardly noticed them among the swell of people headed inward. The city was magnificent. Pete could see several pyramids jutting into the morning sky across an immense plaza. They entered a small plaza through an opening guarded by carved obelisks and moved quickly across the stone paving to a columned pavilion. Inside, a group of men and women were gathering and more were arriving. It seemed to be a formal gathering. With the first rays of the sun splashing across the floor, Chaan called the meeting to order.

"Most of you have met our friend from the North, Petawa, on his past visit here. We received his message fifteen diurnas ago that he would return, this time with an interesting visitor. I have returned this morning from across the sea with them and I would like to introduce to you this man, Pete, who comes to us with prophecy. This prophecy strengthens our fears of the fate which awaits our people as we enter this critical moment. Pete, I come to understand, is an uncommon, yet common man from the future. A future where our world is only a crumbling curiosity. Ruins consumed by the jungle, as are now so many of the finest cities of our civilization. We are at a threshold moment. We did not learn from the follies of the Chimu and Mochica far to our south, and as we fall, we see the barbaric Toltecs to the west ready to rise to the same folly."

"At this moment, we must make a stand and shun the practice of calling forth the gods for selfish gain and let them dwell in Xibalba. We must turn to the realities of our place in the world and nurture widespread respect and understanding of the natural ambience and balance of forest and water. We must end the reign of the kings and call back those scattered by the wars."

A murmur rippled through the crowd and turned into loud murmuring conversations among the audience. A man stood and called out to Chaan.

"You produce here a strange looking man with light hair and skin. Can he speak?"

"You must say something," said Petawa in Shawnee to Pete.

"I didn't really understand what Chaan was saying."

"Don't worry. Everyone here feels the same as does Chaan. Just say in your words what has brought you here, and I will put it into Maya."

Pete and Petawa stood and the crowd fell silent.

"My name is Peter Simon Dornblaser. My home for the last seventeen years has been far to the north."

Petawa began to translate into Maya.

"Though it was always my home, until seventeen years ago I lived there in a different time. A future time. I was brought to your time by an angel. In my future time, many of my people doubt the existence of God. I too was reluctant to believe in God. Many of us only believe in what we can see and hear, and touch.

But I was made to come to this time by the angel, a messenger of God. It was with some reluctance that I did. I believe also that the messenger wants to take my son from me. This is something that I will not allow. In this respect, I am rejecting my God." The audience was silent and listening intently as Petawa translated.

"Your society is something I knew very little about. The people in my time believe that you were civilized, which you are. But we also believe that you were very peaceful, which I now know is not true. I am not here to pass judgment or offer advice. I wish only to let you know that your time is ending, and the world as you know it will pass into the hands of societies yet to be created. Within a few centuries, Conquistadors will arrive from across the ocean and take control of all of your world and your peoples.

"To help you understand, I have brought this with me."

Petawa translated while Pete unwrapped the volume and opened it to the section on the Maya. He laid the book on a stone lintel and a crowd formed around it. The reactions were varied. All were impressed with the book itself. Pete could tell that many understood the article as an obituary to their culture. Some recognized the pyramids in the photographs. Some scribes were discussing the text itself. Petawa said they were talking about having Pete help them understand the alphabet used to write it.

The audience began to divide into groups and debated amongst themselves, this new confirmation of what many had felt.

ॐ

Bahlum Xoc sat slumped against the wall in the temple of the Jaguars. He felt weak, weaker than he had ever felt before. The six days of fasting had left him delirious. The priests who attended him came and went as if they were a mist before his eyes. They whispered to each other that he was now ready. The ball game would be staged that afternoon. How glorious to see blood flow. They had placed the stingray spine in his left hand. Long quetzal feathers were knotted to the top end of the spine, the bottom end so sharp. The object carried immense power. Was it not the same lancet that Kakupacal had used? Outside the temple the priests laid long scrolls of fig paper in the brazier. Yes, today. Nothing could stop him now. The Serpent would rise. All would know that it was he who would rule. He who would lead the armies to sack the other two cities. He who would drive the defeated back to Chichen. He would mutilate and bleed their kings and priests to death. Then he, as Six Serpent Bird, would rule the entire world. And of course, then there would be no one to stop him from granting a miserable death to the despised learned ones. How ill they had made him feel.

The priests floated back before his eyes and tied linens around his arms and ankles. They set his headdress and hung a necklace around his throat. He felt the necklace oozing on his chest. Reaching a weak right hand to his chest he felt the moisture. Raising his hand, he felt blood drip into his lap. The eyeballs of the necklace were fresh. It was a good sign.

∾∾

Throughout the morning and after lunch, Pete had answered questions about the encyclopedia. The questions had been thoughtful and he answered carefully. Two scribes were forming a glyph outline of what the Twentieth Century was like, and Pete did his best to fill in the massive void not covered by the volume M. There was a concurrence that Twentieth Century problems were rooted mainly in overpopulation, environmental destruction, and warfare: the same problems that confronted the Maya.   From the tops of the pyramids, came the sound of conch trumpets. They repeated a simple tune. How beautiful they sound, thought Pete.

Surprise and shock ran through the group. A clamor grew from the audience towards the rear and several hands pointed to a company of spear-wielding soldiers who were racing across the plaza towards them. Chaan said something hurriedly to Petawa.

"There will be a ball game," Petawa in turn said to Pete, shrugging a gesture toward the approaching soldiers, "and we are all invited. They have come to make sure we attend." The soldiers entered the pavilion and circled the group.

"Don't worry, they are merely sent to carry out the order. They don't know who we are or that we are out of place here."

Pete put a nervous hand on the Smith and Wesson.

The troops accompanied them across the broad plaza to the base of the largest pyramid. The sun hung low in the afternoon sky and the city's elite were arriving in droves for the game. The court was fronted by a beautiful temple and priests in elaborate dress. The court itself was about seventy five feet wide and a hundred twenty five feet long. The ends were open, but the sides were bordered with walls eight feet high. A stone ring with a small opening hung vertically from each wall. Soon a thousand or more people had taken seats on the slanting galleries on either side.

The learned society was seated near the edge of the court. Pete looked to the far side and saw a huge mural carved in relief in the stone wall and painted with brilliant colors.

"Can you understand the story it tells?" asked Chaan in Maya.

"No. None of it."

Chaan explained it to Petawa, and he translated for Pete.

"The figure in the center is the god of water."

Pete could barely discern it in the busy and complex carving.

"Mankind has perished from the earth four times, but the water god wants to bring new life forward. After an almost endless search, the water god finds a bone of man and grinds it into powder. Taking a spine, he stabs his penis and his blood drips into the powder. From this nourishment, mankind returns again to the world."

Pete felt uncomfortable and nervous. Petawa noticed.

"You have reason to feel so. We are about to see men die. At the end of the game, the king will be lifted to power. This I have never seen, but the Gods will be called forth."

Another trumpet blast came from the pyramid, and two teams of men, flanked by more spear-wielding soldiers, streamed in from the ends of the court. A man dressed in a feathered costume carried a ball the size of a basketball and rolled it onto the court between the two teams.

Instantly, the teams pounced on it and each other. A roar went up from the crowd. Pete assumed that the idea was to pass the ball through the hole in the stone, and he was right, but the use of hands was prohibited. It was going to be impossible to score; the hole looked to be the same size as the ball and the ball appeared to be very heavy.

The game was more like a gang fight. The players were beating and kicking each other and some were slow to rise from the ground. One player managed to get some good leverage on the ball with his foot and lofted it against the stone ring on the far side. The crowd roared especially loud. Another player was thrown against the wall and his head bounced off of it with a loud crack that could be heard from the galleries. He fell, blood oozing from his hair, and didn't get up.

The game raged for over an hour. The finale came when one team had only three players standing and the other team actually managed a goal with a well placed strong kick of the ball. The crowd rose to its feet and cheered. Pete also rose, but was appalled with the display of violence. A company of soldiers entered and led the winning team off the open end of the court. The other soldiers led the losers, who had to carry and drag half of their team, up to the top step of the temple. The losers were made to sit cross legged in a line facing the court What followed was more barbaric yet than had been the game. A naked man, adorned only in cloth strips tied around his arms and legs, emerged from the temple and stood behind the prisoners. He was big and muscular, but looked weak and dizzy.

"It is Bahlum Xoc," said Chaan in hushed words.

Xoc knelt behind the man on the end and reached with his right hand around the prisoner's jaw. Placing his thumb inside the man's mouth, he grasped the jaw, and with a tearing sound that could be heard from the galleries, wrenched the jaw from the prisoner's head and flung it down in front of him. Blood gushed from the opening that had been the prisoner's mouth, and his tongue darted about in spasms. Xoc, looking invigorated, rose and repeated this with the next of the losers. As he went down the line, he seemed to be gaining strength. His victims were losing consciousness. Once he had torn the jaw from the last, a priest emerged from the temple and handed him an ornate knife. He then went back down the line, cutting the fingertips off the prisoners as he went. This seemed to bring them back around, as they were now writhing in pain once again.

Pete was aghast. He felt bile rising in his esophagus. Cruelty so blatant couldn't be real. The perpetrator couldn't be human. Was he dreaming? Was this a horrible nightmare? Had he been chosen to witness this?

Xoc completed his task and walked down the steps through the blood that was now freely flowing. He squatted over the top of a large pot, and reaching behind his head, pulled a feathered object from his headband. It was long and sharp. As the blood of the dying continued to run down the steps toward him, he held his penis in his right hand and with his left stabbed the spine into it. Blood streamed from it and fell into the urn at his feet. Grimacing in pain, he shook the blood from his split member. Two priests walked down from the temple. One bore a lit torch and the other an extremely elaborate feathered backrack. The backrack was hung from Xoc's shoulders as he continued to bleed into the urn. This priest now went to the urn and began to pull a long, blood-drenched scroll of rough paper from it. Gathering it together, he laid it at Xoc's feet.

Pete looked around and all were transfixed by what was happening. They seemed to be anticipating some horrible event.

Now, the other priest lowered the torch to the paper and it burst into a bright flame which surged upward. The priest handed Xoc a carved stone scepter. In a flash of flame and smoke, a giant serpent appeared rearing upward from the fire. It opened it's mouth and belched forth a vision of a rapidly forming figure.

Pete felt as if he were hallucinating, but the vision was real.

The vision was an infant that quickly metamorphosed into an adult. But it wasn't human. It was, something that he had seen before, in his dream in the bedroom and at another time he couldn't place. It was the devil. And it was staring at him. The serpent casting the vision rose higher and painfully twisted down towards the gallery in which they sat. In several languages at once, the devil spoke:

"So I have found you! The crystal had obscured you well. But now you shall expire forever, as will your spore, and I will no longer suffer from your plague. The tower will never again know the pilot. I commend you to feel the sweet agony of death at the hand of my servant."

Xoc strode forth around the flame and down onto the court.

A commotion erupted behind Pete as a group of soldiers ran down the gallery and then yanked him up to his feet. Chaan and Petawa were knocked to the ground brusquely and he now saw only the men surrounding him, tearing at him. The tunic was ripped away and with it the shoulder holster. The next thing he knew he was being thrown through the air and landing with a painful crunch on the paving stones of the court. Struggling to get to his feet, he saw Xoc approaching. His upward look was met with a glancing blow of the stone scepter, and he went back down, pain erupting from the side of his head. Instinctively, he rolled away from Xoc and, gathering his wits, sprang to his feet. Xoc came at him and swung the scepter again. Pete raised his arm, protecting his head but subjecting his left elbow to a smashing blow. Once more he was knocked to the ground and rolled away. Xoc paused for a moment and looked up at the vision being exhaled by the serpent.

"You must pay for the sons I have lost. Water is not prescribed for your death in this place. Now your soul becomes mine. Kill him!"

There was a clattering of metal on the stones. The Smith and Wesson was spinning to a stop between them. Xoc was ready to deliver the coup de grace, but instead looked down at the strange object on the ground. Xoc reached down and picked it up. He was grasping the grip and the clip fell from the gun. In a flash, Pete leapt and caught the clip as it bounced off of Xoc's foot. Xoc dropped the gun to the ground and Pete grabbed it. Xoc grabbed Pete by the hair and hoisted him upward as Pete slammed the clip back into the gun. Xoc twisted Pete around by his hair and swung the club towards his face. The gun went off and Xoc shuddered with the impact of the bullet. He reached down and tore at the pain in his stomach. Looking Pete in the eye, he let out a scream and raised the club again. Pete ripped free of his grasp and took a step to the side. Pete raised the pistol and pulled the trigger. The bullet exploded Xoc's heart. He dropped to his knees and then fell flat on his face. The serpent slowly consumed the now screeching vision and shrank bank into the urn from which it had risen. The crowd broke it's silence with sudden wild yells which turned into cheers. Pete felt faint and started to pass out. He saw Chaan and Petawa standing over him and everything went black.

૏

Twenty-two days later he awoke. An old man was patting a poultice of mashed cecropia to the wound on his temple.

"Who are you?" he said in Mayan.

"I am called Bacab. Rest. You will be healthy soon."

Pete passed out again. Bacab sent for Chaan, and when Pete awoke later in the day, Chaan and Petawa were there.

"How do you feel, Pete?"

"I've been better," he said, managing a grin. "Did I kill that son of a bitch?"

In Maya, Chaan said: "Pete, you don't know what you have done."

Petawa filled him in. The killing of Xoc caused a revolt. His priests were thrown into the well of the sacrifices. Runners were sent to the other cities to tell them what had happened. Their rulers came to an accord to abdicate control to the learned society.

Chaan was beaming.

"It has ended. Many tomorrows lay ahead."

"I need to go home. I fear for the safety of my family. He saw me here. The Devil, Matchelomeneton, will seek them out."

"Cizin needs a servant to act here in the world. You repulsed him. He has been sent back to Xibalba."

"Chaan, once before he sent someone for me."

"And what did you do?"

"I killed him."

Chaan grinned at Petawa.

"This man you brought here cannot be be easily finished."

Petawa patted Pete on his right arm and smiled.

"No, he is very substantial."

"I have to go."

"And how will you go now, like this? You must rest for a diurna. Then we will go." It was true. He couldn't move his left elbow. He couldn't paddle a single stroke in the state he was in.

What had happened was real. But Pete couldn't shake free of its dream. It was a nightmare. The Devil had not been substantial, but he was more terrible than a substantial devil would be. Xoc, was physical and real and brutal. But he was allied to the nightmare in a paroxysm of horror. Surviving this horror would require healing time, too.

"Pete, Chaan has told me that the scribes would like for you to teach them the language of the book."

"That's okay with me, I'm not doing anything else I guess."

And so it went. Over the following days, the scribes would come to the house of Bacab, and Pete would do his best to teach them English. He started with the alphabet and the phonetics of the letters in their different uses. Doing so, Pete found himself becoming more fluid in Maya each day. Soon he was strong enough to get around and began to give his lessons in the observatory. The scribes had been simultaneously teaching others English and soon his audiences included mathematicians and agriculturists, engineers and administrators.

One day, Chaan brought two men to the observatory.

"They want to study your weapon."

"No. If your society is to endure, it must be done without such things."

"Pete, we worry that some day men will come across the sea, as the book clearly shows. They will have such weapons. We must be ready."

Pete thought for a moment.

"Maybe you need to go to them first...."

⇔•⇔

The Augsburg was lashed to the new outrigger. They came to where the canals met the sea and it was time to part company. It was an emotional moment for all three. Petawa and Chaan were heading for the coast of Texas where Petawa would begin his trek northward. Chaan presented Pete with a beautiful pair of jaguar mocassins. Petawa was taking packs laden with jade and colorful dyes. He would go as far as the junction of the Ohio and Mississippi and meet his sons there. They would travel northward to Chippewa country together before the winter snows.

"Someday I will come to Monongahela country to see how your Simon has grown into a man."

"Pete, will you come back here someday?"

"I don't know, Chaan. I don't think I could survive another visit like this one." They laughed and said goodbye.

Soon the dugout had vanished on the horizon. Pete eased into paddling. He was still sore and stiff from his beating at the hands of Xoc and worried that his left elbow would bother him for life.

He had a daring plan for his return: He would paddle along the north coast of the Yucatan peninsula and, where it turned south at its eastern tip, he would strike out for Cuba: 125 miles of open water. Chaan had warned him of strong currents and the possibility of hurricanes that proliferated during the wane of summer, but he had no more time to waste. He had committed the map in the Mexican section of the encyclopedia to memory. His course to the western tip of Cuba would be east by northeast, roughly a heading of eighty degrees. When he reached the cape four days later, he landed to take on water and to rest. He slept soundly that night and with the dawn set out. The sea was flat, and he felt he was making good time. The sun beat down without mercy and he was sweating profusely. He wondered if the three gallons in the jug between his knees would cover his needs until he reached Cuba and found water.

He paddled throughout the day and into the night. By dawn he was exhausted and was starting to see things and felt himself dozing off.

His experience with the Maya now seemed oddly far behind him, as if it were as unreal as the visions flashing before his eyes. The warmth of the sun brought him slowly back to the reality of his present situation. Pete knew he had to concentrate on his immediate goal -- landfall on the Cuban coast.

He drank with a reed straw inserted into the ceramic vessel, trying desperately to balance his need for liquids and the need that he ration what he had. Pete paddled throughout the day and into the night, constantly checking the compass on his watch. He was once again tiring and starting to see things. He knew he had to make a superhuman effort for another two days. It was a sickening thought, but there was no turning back now. He was driven also by the desire to be home, to see Sana and Simon again. By noon, a blessing came in the form of a bank of clouds which shielded him from the sun. New strength and energy came and left in cycles. The strokes became an endless repetition, broken only by rests taken to eat and drink. By dawn he was out of water.

The afternoon of the third day he spotted land, and although weak, he was elated. Towards dusk he landed on a beach. Walking on shaky legs, he found a coconut on the sand below the palms and with trembling hands opened it with his knife. Never had a drink of anything tasted so good. He had another, and another. He carried the kayak up to the palms and slept.

The next morning he woke feeling better. Taking a compass bearing, he calculated that he had landed on the north coast of Cape San Antonio. He rested for the day, and with the next dawn, set off along the north coast of Cuba. He decided to travel a mile offshore to avoid contact with natives as much as possible and only landed after dark each day. Chaan had told him the Caribs were unpredictable people and he had had enough fighting. Just in case, the nine millimeter had come out of the dry bag and was once again on the life jacket. Four easy days later along the coast, he came to another cape. What he remembered from the map he had studied was that this would someday be the site of Havana. Or would it? Somehow things had changed. Pete no longer felt that he was just a visitor of a past time. It was more as if the future time from which he had come would no longer exist.

He rested a day there in preparation for the next hard leg: crossing northward to the Florida keys. The next morning greeted him with stormy seas so he waited two more days to make the crossing. Finally, he awoke to perfect weather and he set out.

This time he thought: What the hell, Cubans do it in rowboats.

It went okay, though many times he wished he had a rowboat to stretch out in and take a nap. On the second morning he saw the keys ahead. Jumping dolphins accompanied him to shore.

Glancing at his watch, he noticed it was the Fourth of July.

Feeling giddy from lack of sleep, he took out the Smith and Wesson and fired some shots into the air.

I'm on my way home

Pete spent the next two months working his way up the Atlantic coast. It was boring, and he thought constantly of how sweet it would be to arrive. To be with his wife and son. Never again would he leave home.

The journey turned into long days spent paddling a mile offshore and returning to sleep on a beach after dark. Waking early and shoving off again. As such, he was seeing very little of the coast he was passing and less of its inhabitants. He became aware that he was passing to the outside of a chain of barrier islands. The paddling would be easier in the bays, but more dangerous and with more likelihood of becoming lost, so he continued in the open sea. At one point, he realized he was being stalked by a huge shark and drove it off by wounding it with a shot from the gun.

Pete kept checking his heading, and when the coast no longer ran north by northeast, but began to run north by northwest, he knew he had rounded Cape Hatteras. He now started to watch for the mouth of Chesapeake Bay. His plan was to ascend the Potomac to its source. When he found the bay he ended up making a few wrong turns. It had been rainless and dry, and the rivers bore little current to give clues to their size or origin.

Finally, he found the Potomac and paddled upstream past the site of the capital of a nation yet unborn and reached Little Falls. There seemed to be more of a concentration of Indians, and he became nervous. He yearned to be with his people, the Shawnee. At Great Falls, there would certainly be a village. He had to pass right by it.

Better to do it at night.

He slept in some rocks in the middle of the river and woke after dark. At midnight, with an overcast sky, he started to paddle upstream into Mather Gorge. It brought back memories from his youth, paddling at night up through Mather Gorge with his friends while doing acid. That had been fun and games. This was more serious. He reached the base of the falls an hour later, and, with the river low as it was, Pete decided to carry up over the island between the spout and the Maryland Falls. He had to make some tricky ferries and moves, but by three he was up and over the falls and heading upriver. At dawn, he pulled over to sleep in the rushes and woke after dark to head upriver again. He continued in this manner for two more days before resuming a daylight schedule. He figured he had another two weeks left of ascending the Potomac. He was almost home.

CHAPTER 11 — DESCENT INTO DARKNESS

He climbed once again the boulder above Big Nasty as he had so many other days, and looked downriver.

Nothing.

Where was the old man who had promised to return and had not?

He needed him. Everything was changing and he needed his wisdom. Feelings were awakening within him and he didn't know what was happening. It seemed he only fought with his mother and his uncles. No one understood him anymore. Would the old man understand him when he returned? Of course he would. They would go kayaking and talk and everything would be okay again. But what if he didn't come back? This thought flashed again and again in his brain. He climbed down off of the boulder and started to attain upriver.

I must become a man. I must make my vision quest now.

He had thought about it for months. He was the child of the river, the son of a kayaker. His vision quest would have to be what he had always known it would be. He would confront Tokebelloke.

Simon reached the pool by the cabin at dark but kept going. He was hungry but he would not eat. He could not. He must fast.

☙❧

Chicaq was in the rhododendron and watched Simon pass by, and he knew where Simon was going. He must respect the boy and not say anything to Sana or anyone else. The vision quest was the most personal thing a man would do in his life. Chicaq remembered his: He had fasted four days and then lowered himself into the rocky crevice on the rim of the canyon far downstream. He had prayed. He was alone, closed in by the stone. And yet he had not been alone; the spirits had swirled around him. The good and the bad. He had confronted them and confronted himself and had emerged refreshed and confident. He had emerged a man and this man had purpose.

He smiled as he watched Simon disappear into the darkness and then he returned to camp.

꙰

They swept into the village in broad daylight, whooping and yelling. The killing was indiscriminate, brutal, and complete. They were sixty four in number and the villagers less than forty. Thelaq had never seen such a murderous rampage. This Huron Yegua, who had led them here, was indeed possessed by the devil. Possessed to the level that evil must have run in his blood. Yes, it was true, his Iroquois were killers, but not like Yegua. He spurred on their killer instinct, their lust for blood. The last of the villagers circled together and begged for mercy, but Yegua himself strode into their midst and crushed their skulls with his war club. It had been obvious to Thelaq that Yegua was furious that he had once again not found the village of those he sought. He was killing out of sheer meanness, and he enjoyed it. He was tall and lean, face like a tomahawk, and a smile that was all teeth when he killed.

Once all were slain, Yegua walked about and examined each body, and gave each another blow the the skull. Then he walked down the bank and began to wade across the river with the Iroquois following him.

꙰

Kiri silently crept around the boulder. The buck was rubbing his antlers on the young oak, and was upwind. He moved into the open and pulled the arrow back against the bowstring. He raised it and was ready to let it go when suddenly, several does bounded down the hillside and, splashing across the creek, scrambled up the other side with the buck in pursuit. He could still slay the buck, but he didn't. Something had spooked the does, and he knew he hadn't. Kiri quietly climbed the bank and lay in the ferns. He heard them before he saw them. Rising behind a fallen hickory he could see them. They were many, they were Iroquois, and they were painted for war. He slithered on his stomach down to Roaring Creek and ran. Minutes later he reached the cabin.

"Sana! Chicaq! Shenan! Simon! Thepa! Hurry! Thepa, where is Simon? Hurry! We must go! Iroquois! Many Iroquois are coming now! Sana, where is Simon?"

They gathered in front of the cabin. Chicaq looked at Kiri and then at Sana.

"Simon has left for his vision quest. I saw him last night."

"Sana, we have to go. Now." With this Kiri entered the cabin and opened the closet. He took out the SKS and grabbed two of the little boxes of hard points that went inside. He had secretly watched Pete one time putting them into the gun, and knew how it worked. He ran back outside, almost knocking down Sana, who was running in through the door. Sana gathered some things in a pack and ran out.

"Let's go!"

They fled into the forest.

∾⁖

Pete ran the last of the rapids of the Top Yough. The river was very dry, but it was sweet to be going downriver once again and sweeter yet to think that tomorrow he would be home.

Home

He eddied out at Sang Run. He would spend the night with Hawapiti and his people. But no one came to greet him, and he heard no sounds from above. He saw no need for caution, however. These were his people, Shawnee people, and . . . They were all dead. Bodies were everywhere and their blood had turned black on their faces, clothes, and the ground. Pete found two small children with their heads smashed. He felt sick. He looked across the river and could see where the rushes had been trampled down. Whoever had done this was heading for his family.

Pete paddled across and hid the Augsburg and paddle under some leaves. He slipped the remaining two clips into the pocket on his life jacket, grabbed the dry bag, and took off at a run. He went as fast as he could through the night. He crested Laurel Hill and was at the headwaters of Roaring Creek by noon. He went sailing down the hillside to the north of the creek. Dozens of moccasined footprints appeared wherever the ground was muddy.

He was drawing close when he heard it. A long, drawn out, scream of pain and agony.

Pistol in hand, Pete ran from tree to tree. Between the river and the cabin, Shenan and Chicaq were strung up from tree branches. Shenan, the child he had brought back to life with CPR so many years ago, was dead. His stomach had been sliced open and his intestines lay coiled on the ground below him. Chicaq was being skinned alive. Three Iroquois were slowly pulling strips of skin from his chest and back. Twenty or more others sat or stood around watching and laughing.

Where was Simon? And Sana? And Kiri and Thepa?

Pete felt anger rise. His cheeks burned. But there were too many. He needed a plan. Quietly, he withdrew into the forest.

Once a safe distance away, he ran to the hillside to the east. Making his way   under the overhanging cliff, he stopped at a crack in the sandstone. Reaching a finger into the crack, he found the loop of wire and stuck his finger into it. He pulled on the wire and it came playing out of the crack. It went taut at his feet, and he leaned back and pulled. Slowly out of the sand rose the shotgun, wrapped in plastic. He brushed the sand away from the plastic and opened it up. It had been packed in four layers of plastic. It was dry. He unwrapped the oil-soaked rags and checked the action. Now he ran through the trees toward the backside of the cabin. Pete slipped up behind the cabin. One of the windows was open.

Shit!

There were Iroquois inside too. Another scream came from Chicaq. It was time to act. Pete ran around the front of the cabin and leapt through the door. Before the surprised Iroquois could react he slammed the door shut and threw the bolt. He aimed the shotgun at the brave closest to him and blew him in half. The three others came running across the cabin at him. The first had his head blown off and the second went down in a heap. The third knocked the shotgun from his hands and grabbed Pete in a headlock. Pete, though nearly fifty, had just paddled thousands of miles and was pure fiber and fury. With a twist of his hips, he threw the Iroquois into the wall and drove the wind from his chest. He let go of Pete's throat just enough for Pete to push him away. Pete drew the pistol and was ready to fire, but instead brought the butt of the gun down on his head, cracking his skull. Jerking in nervous spasms, the brave fell to the floor. Pete ran to the open window and bolted it shut. Now the Iroquois outside were trying to bash in the door and windows. Pete pulled the Claymore trigger down from the ceiling rafter and hit the trigger three times. The blast rocked all sides of the cabin. Afterward all that could be heard were the moans of those not killed outright. He reloaded the shotgun and stepped outside. Several Iroquois were wounded but not down. He killed them.

Pete now ran to Chicaq. The good uncle was dying. Hawapiti and his people, Shenan, the two dozen he had just killed, and now Chicaq. He had seen more death in the last twenty four hours than ever before.

He cut Chicaq loose and gently lowered him to the ground. Treating his wounds would be futile. He had been peeled like a banana from the neck down.

"Chicaq, Where are Sana and the others?"

The man could barely speak.

"Sana, Kiri and.. The.. Thepa have... have gone down... the river."

"And Simon? Chicaq, where is Simon?"

"Agh... Pete. Oh Pete. Simon has taken his... quest. Forgive me... I told... I told them where he went... Pete... the pain was very great... I told them."

"It's okay, they're all dead now."

"No. The others. Half of them...left in the night. I have betrayed Simon. Shenan..and... I came... back... to... see. They... cap... captured us."

"Chicaq, where did Simon go?"

Chicaq looked him in the eye.

"Tokebelloke."

Damn

"Pete. Bad Huron... Matc...Matchelomoneton....

Chicaq lapsed into unconsciousness. Then he was gone.

Pete buried the brothers together in the forest behind the cabin. With anger and dread choking him, he dragged the Iroquois by their hair, one by one to the riverbank and piled them atop a mass of driftwood. There were twenty-nine of them. The Claymores had ripped many limb from limb, and he gathered up the pieces. Pete opened the trailer and grabbed a five gallon can of gas. He splashed the pile with gas and threw the can onto the top of the corpses. It tipped over and the remaining gas bubbled out of the jug, seeping down through the pile.

Back at the cabin, he gathered the tomahawks, war clubs, and knives of the Iroquois and stuck them in a circle in the ground. In the middle of the circle he made an X in the sand and drew an arrow pointing south. He wrote PSD by the arrow. He went back into the cabin to get the SKS. It was gone.

Kiri.

Good.

He had intentionally showed Kiri how to operate the SKS. He had gone through all the phases of loading and firing with Kiri watching from the around the corner of the trailer. Just in case.

Pete dressed in a ragged pair of army fatigues and a black T shirt, and stuffed his ancient black polarfleece jacket into a buckskin pack with some pemmican. The Smith and Wesson hung in the shoulder holster. He took three boxes of shotgun shells from the trailer and locked it up behind him.

He would go by land. Simon would have been able to go no further than the forks by boat. Then he would have had to walk. The Iroquois had gone on foot and would be easily tracked. He also didn't want to take the chance that the Iroquois might return to the cabin. Any of them backtracking on the trail would be met with the twelve gauge and no mercy whatsoever.

He set fire to the pile of dead warriors and watched them burn for a moment before taking off.

They were easy to follow. He encountered various items pilfered from the cabin discarded along the way. A book here, a broken clay plate there.

Two days later he spotted six returning northward along a ridge top. He saw them before they saw him. Crouching in a notch in some weathered sandstone, he waited for them to pass by and then shouted out.

"Where are you assholes headed?"

They whirled in their tracks and went down with four pumps of the shotgun. Two were still alive, but could not get up. He stood over the more conscious of the two and in Shawnee asked:

"Where did you leave the others?"

The brave wouldn't speak. Pete debated torturing him and decided against it. I'll find them

Pete began to walk away.

"Yegua will eat the heart of your son. Your seed will disappear."

Pete continued south, the dying man's words reverberating in his head. Yegua must be the Huron. Sent by the devil. I should never have left home. Never gone with Petawa.

He broke into a run. The trail was fresher. Later in the day he broke into the clearing of another Shawnee village. Another massacre. Eight Iroquois were still there, laying about, taunting a young girl. They had tied her wrists with thongs to braches from two different trees. Try as she might, she could not bring her hands together to untie herself. Blood ran down her thighs from under her dress. Pete strode into the clearing and they lept to their feet. Being caught unawares, they were no match for the 12 guage. He freed her from her bonds as tears ran down her face.

"Have you seen a boy come through here?"

"Two nights ago, he had come. He was weak from the fast of the quest and had refused food. Yesterday these had come, led by a horrible warrior who too, had asked for the boy. They had killed all who did not escape to the forest, except for her.

"Can I help you?"

"No. I will go to the forest and hide until they come back through and leave. I know who you are. You are the white one from another time. If the boy is your son, you must hasten."

He took off at a run. With each step he took he felt more rage. He added up the body count. Forty-three. Judging by their tracks, there were still many more.

Towards darkness, he recognized the cone-shaped mountaintops of Gauley country ahead. The path was still obvious in the failing light and he forged ahead. Around ten o'clock he smelled venison roasting. He saw the small fire through the trees. Three Iroquois lay about. More might be nearby. Better not to make noise shooting. He could sneak by them easily.

But then they would still be alive, and they might pass by his cabin on their way home. The tortured figures of Shenan and Chicaq appeared in his head. He spent a long moment thinking of his next move, listening to the drone of cicadas and the murmurings of the gorged Iroquois.

He walked up to them, dry leaves rustling underfoot. One looked around just in time to have his head smashed by the butt of the shotgun. The other two leapt up and he knocked one down with a swing of the shotgun to his face. The one remaining grappled with him, trying to rip the gun out of his hands. Pete let it go and the brave stepped back and swung the stock at him. He lunged at the Indian and whipped his left arm up and around, trapping the brave's arm with his. Pete gave him a strong shock to the solar plexus followed with another to the bridge of the nose. He went down and Pete finished him off and then looked at the other, whom he had smashed with the barrel of the shotgun. He was slowly rising, but in great pain. One half of his face had been laid open in a huge flap of skin and muscle. Blood ran freely from it down his neck and chest. Pete raised the gun to strike him again when the brave collapsed and rolled to his side. The uninjured side of his face revealed his youth. He was no more than a year or two older than Simon. He was beautiful in his innocence. Life was draining onto the leaves. His life would end here. He would never return to his family.

Why had he come? Perhaps he had only been caught up in the romance of going on the warpath with the older braves. Would his mother cry and suffer when he did not return? Of course she would. What would become of his soul? How would Kijemoneto judge him?

Pete felt a deep stab of anxiety. How would Kijemoneto, judge him? He was killing indiscriminately. How had he come to this? The first men he had killed had been the Bedouins. They had been faceless forms, without personalities. With the exception of Barkoui. The faces of their deaths had been cloaked by their robes, turbans and dust. Now this youth lay dying at his feet, his anonymity dissolving by the second. Pete thought: I could finish him off, end his suffering. But he couldn't bring himself to do it. He turned and ran. In the seconds it took to pick up the trail of the Iroquois, the sentiments of guilt were left behind in the rustle of leaves.

Forty-six.

It was a murderous night. By dawn the count was fifty.

Pete paused for a moment in a grove of huge oak trees. No sound but the birds singing. He needed to gather his thoughts.

What is happening? Why am I encountering so many along the trail? Is it because the leader is in such a hurry that he is leaving them behind, and they are not motivated to follow? Does he know I'm coming? No. How could he?

And what has happened to me? I have become a killer like them. A blood-thirsty killer. No. They killed innocent people. I kill to stop them from killing more. To stop them from killing my son.

He took off again, hot on their trail. He was now descending into the valley of the Gauley River. Their tracks turned down into a creek and he followed. The water was still cloudy in the pools where they had stirred it up with their passing. The creek started its steep plunge for the Gauley. Soon its banks turned from boulders to solid sandstone, and the creek was cascading down over slides and falls. He was climbing down now, more than he was walking. Pete came to a fall in the creek where he had to lower himself about ten feet, clinging to a rhododendron branch that they had also obviously used, and then had to jump another eight feet from an overhang to the flat sandstone below.

To his shock, there under the overhang, were the Iroquois. He leveled the shotgun but did not shoot. There were too many, and, with another drop in the creek lying right behind him, the quarters were close and confined. They were staring him down, nervously handling their clubs and tomahawks. He counted. There were thirteen of them. The tension grew by the second, and the seconds passed slower and slower.

One of the Iroquois laid his war club on the rock, and raising his hands, stepped forward.

"I am called Thelaq. We know who you are. You are the one."

The man spoke Shawnee well.

"We have followed Yegua here. We have killed many Shawnee people. You can kill some of us, but we will kill you. And Yegua will kill your son. Then Yegua will live on."

The tension was almost unbearable, but Pete listened.

"Iroquois are proud people, fierce warriors. We raid to the south as we have for many generations. Yegua came from the north. He told us Kijemoneto called on him to rid the world of a white devil. He filled us with his rage, and in one night we all began to think like him. We killed all Shawnee we passed. Soon some of us knew that Yegua spoke like a serpent. But the rest of us: the more we killed, the more we wanted to believe Yegua. The more our souls needed to believe him. We have done wrong to the Shawnee people. Now we will go no further. We will go to our nation. Do you understand?"

"I understand. You must understand me. I must stop Yegua from murdering my son. But I cannot take the chance that you will kill more Shawnee as you go north."

"Did you not kill Iroquois as you came south?" Pete was aware of the dried blood on his pants.

"Yes. Many."

"You are not the devil. You are a man. You killed with reason. We have lost our reason to kill. We go home in peace. You can believe me and we go our paths."

"I have not decided yet."

Thelaq pointed downstream.

"You have no choice at this moment." The man was absolutely right, and all knew it.

Pete spun and jumped off of the ledge that had been behind him, and ran downstream in the creek bed. Stopping before rounding the following bend, he saw the Iroquois climbing back upstream.

Continuing down, Pete noticed how deep the mini-canyon of the stream had become. The only way out was back upstream, or to continue downstream. It was solid sandstone now. He was confronted with a cascade of slick rock. Descending would be tricky. The little water that did flow in the creek had left the rocks slick from one side to the other. The slide curved downward out of sight.

A voice called out. He looked up and across the creek where an old man in an aged bearskin robe sat under a sandstone ledge. On the ledge beside him were several ceramic pots, many of which were broken. It was the humble man's home.

"Why do you come?"

"I am searching for my son."

"Do you not know that no man comes to this place?"

"You are here."

"Yes. It is true. I have been here for what seems forever."

"And why did you come?"

"Tokebelloke called me here when I was young. No older than the boy you seek. I was afraid to continue past this place. Then I could not leave. I am trapped in time." The old one looked around, gazing at the same rock walls he'd gazed at a million times before. "My fate is to watch the entrance to Tokebelloke."

"My son was here?"

"Here, and then gone." The old man pointed below.

"And another man?"

"Not man, Matchelomoneton. He did not pass. I knew Kijemoneto would not let him pass. He will search another way. He is here for the wrong reason, as are you."

"Why did he not pass?"

"To pass," the old man pointed below, "one must have faith in the work done by the waters of ages past. This one knew very little of the water."

"I am going to go down."

"You are too late. Tokebelloke has called him and he will go."

"What is Tokebelloke?"

"It is an opening in the world to other times," the old man sighed. "You will see."

Pete looked down over the lip of the cascade. The rock was smooth. He sat down in the water and inched towards the edge. He started to slide and realized he was going. Instantly he was falling, and then sliding, and then rocketing downward. The slide kept curving and dropping and all he could do was go with it. At times he thumped and thudded off the rock but kept going down. At first he tried to slow himself. Then he looked for some way out, some way to escape. But finally he resigned himself to whatever happened and just slid. He went around curve after curve and down drop after drop and then it was over. He slid off of the edge, falling through air, and he landed in chest deep water in the pool below. He waded out of it and tried to drain the water out of the shotgun. He looked upward where the slide was like an immense curving staircase that twisted out of sight. Below, he could see the river. He came out on the bank and saw that he was upstream of Sweet's Falls.

But where is Tokebelloke?

It could be only one place: Iron Ring. Legend had it that Iron Ring had been dynamited by loggers in the 1800's. It had to be Iron Ring.

The Gauley was low. Only about one thousand c.f.s. Pete ran on the rocks, upstream. He came around the bend, and there it was. It was not, however, Iron Ring the rapids. It was a falls: a river wide shelf of sandstone. But the water didn't flow over the falls, It emerged boiling from underneath the shelf.

❧❦

Simon sat at the edge of the swirling water. How beautiful it was. He was transfixed by it. He had never seen anything like it. The river came from the left and poured up onto the sloping right shelf but couldn't jump its own falls. Instead it swirled around in the perfectly carved bowl in the rock and dropped inside. He thought he could hear voices in the water, voices in the bowl, voices from beyond the other side. They were beckoning. Now he lifted his eyes and the world was swirling, and he couldn't stop it. A tall warrior with a bright smile leered at him from the other side of the bowl. His father stepped to the edge of the swirl between them. The voices cried out to him. It is not your father. You are pure. Look at him. He is not pure, not your father. No, he is not my father. My father is pure. Test him, the voices cried out. Test yourself. Yes, this is my vision. Simon stood and dove into the swirling bowl. He looked up to see his father throw down the gun and reach out to him as he was carried around and around by the water. The other was running towards his father. Then the water took him down and he drifted into dreaming sleep.

❧❦

Pete had not heard the approaching Huron. Yegua grabbed him, and together they went off the lip of the dry falls and into the boil, emerging below. They grappled in the pulsing water and Yegua got his hands around Pete's throat. Pete was backpedaling along the bottom of the river wherever he could touch bottom, trying to keep the weight of the Huron from holding him under.

"You will die now by my hands!"

Yegua was choking him, crushing his windpipe. He realized that his backpedaling was keeping the Huron above the water, and breathing, so he let them sink down. He grabbed the knife from the Huron's belt and thrust it into his stomach. Yegua flinched with the pain, but maintained his grip, as the waters turned red around them. Pete held on to the knife and forced it upward, twisting it as he thrust. Finally the grip loosened and Pete pushed Yegua down. He felt his lungs burning but held on as the Huron weakened. Then he broke loose. With his throat feeling crushed, Pete swam into an eddy. Gasping for breath that wouldn't come, he waded up onto the gravel and collapsed.

CHAPTER 12 — TWO QUESTS

Mitchell had been bracketed for the second time in his life. The first time had been more literal. It was in a Huey over DaNang when red tracers from an antiaircraft battery had appeared on both sides of the chopper. Hand of God stuff that they had not been shot down. That had been war. This time, it was really pissing him off. He had been bracketed by his own people. CIA, NSA, Brookings Institute, and hell, even the goddamned US Navy. Some think tank guys had gotten hold of some stones from the city in the desert, a half burnt rubbing of some symbols from the murdered French dig team, and some highly detailed blow-ups of a photo from SSA of similar symbols on a kayak Dornblaser had pulled from the bowl downsteam of Calvert's project. They came up with the conclusion that they had pieces of a jigsaw puzzle of how to create energy. Now, nobody gave a crap about the plutonium, they wanted his fugitives for something else. The same guys came up with a "model" that indicated that Elliot Carlson was in direct communication with at least one of them: probably Calvert. Though he didn't want to believe it, if it was true, he would have Elliot drawn and quartered. Elliot was apparently clueless that the noose was already around his neck and that Mitchell was the one who was going to pull it tight.

-⁊∘᧩-

"Elliot, I want to give you something."

"What?"

Howard pointed to the New Vision on the roof racks of his Rodeo.

"That's one I haven't seen. How many of these do you have?"

"Three, at the moment. This one isn't the prettiest or the newest, but it's the toughest. I want you to take it when you go. This boat holds the key. In more ways than one."

Elliot broke his gaze locked on the kayak and looked at Howard, studying him. Something had happened. Or something was going to happen and Howard knew it.

"You're getting ready to be arrested, aren't you?"

"Yes, I guess I am. It's better to get all this behind me now." Howard started to untie the kayak. "You've come a long way Elliot. You're ready. I only wish that I had the guts to do what you're going to do."Elliot knew, at that moment, that Howard was forcing his hand.

"Okay Howard, let's have it. Why have you trained me to do something that you should be doing yourself?"

"Pete is my friend." He looked at Elliot. "But I'm afraid that I have betrayed him."

"But how?"

"Mihalis. I feel that I was too sold on Mihalis to see the real picture. I feel that Mihalis really doesn't give a damn about Pete, or what happens to Pete." Howard paused for a moment. "I could go. I could try to help. But. . . I don't have what it takes. You do. I can't snow you like I did Pete."

"I'm not going to tell you that I'm not 'afraid' also. I'll be taking a huge risk, just in going against the company, like I've already done. And Mihalis, if it doesn't care what happens to Pete, is going to care even less about me. But you're right, Howard. I'm the guy for the job. And I don't want you to feel guilty about me going instead of you. This is my choice." Besides, thought Elliot, it was going to be the most exciting adventure of his life, no matter how far it went. "And I think you should also understand that this is the kind of trip Pete would have chosen. Would he back off from a dangerous river just because his life was at stake? He wouldn't back off from this, either."

"I know you're right. Still, I talked him into it." Howard looked at his watch, with more than a hint of nervousness. "Elliot, please go, now."

They shook hands. Elliot climbed into his Pathfinder and started it up. "I'll see you here tomorrow."

"Just go. And thank you."

Elliot pulled out of the parking lot, with Howard still packing away his river gear. As Elliot rolled up onto the road, a line of Virginia State Police cars were roaring towards him. Elliot drove on and watched in the rearview mirror as they turned into the parking lot, lights flashing.

So it was over. Or just begun?

A lump rose in his throat. They must know about his connection with Howard. He couldn't take the chance that they did not.

Shit! The helmet!

He had no idea where it was. Howard had told him it was somewhere safe, and that he would find it when the time came.

But how?

Howard had told him it was best he didn't know. It was imperative that the time/space command technology didn't fall into agency hands, for obvious reasons. The cell phone beeped.

"Carlson here."

"Elliot, this is Southgate. Could you come right in? It's important."

"Yes sir. I'm on my way."

Southgate was Major Jones code name. Certainly, Jones had called, instead of Mitchell, because he would be able to read Mitchell's voice. The shit had hit the fan. His car surely had a transmitter on it somewhere. They were tracing him and would trace him all the way in. He would end up sweltering in a cell for the rest of his life.

Elliot pulled into the Difficult Run parking lot.

Think. Got to find the helmet.

Howard had never even told him where he lived. "It's better for you that you don't know," Howard had said.

Think, Elliot. Okay. Today Howard gives me his kayak. Today Howard gets busted. Rationalize. Howard gets busted by Virginia State Police, not U.S. Marshals. Howard turned himself in! State Cops would have no interest in me. I was just another kayaker. The agency scanned the bust and located me with the transmitter. They know. So Howard gave me the kayak, minutes before. . .

It came back to him. "This boat, holds the key, in more ways than one". Goddamit. I just wasted two minutes figuring this out! Howard had just come out and told him where the key was in the case of their conversation being monitored by long distance mic or similar technology.

Elliot climbed onto the roof of his Pathfinder. He looked into the cockpit opening of the boat. Nothing up front, Nothing in the back. Nothing. The inside of the boat had a few patches on the kevlar. Two were very well done, but the third, was sloppy and lumpy. Drips of resin had run off of it onto the laminate as it had dried. Not like Howard. Elliot picked at it with a fingernail and it lifted a bit. With more determination, it started to peel off, and Elliot could see that there was something underneath. He ripped the patch away, and a thin, plastic-wrapped package was exposed. It contained a security card and a Master Lock key. On the card, was written in red letters: Merryfield Security Storage. The key had a small tag of duct tape with 436 written on it.

Elliot jumped down off of the roof and into the Pathfinder. The Agency had certainly monitored the four and a half minute stop he had just made. He had to make it to the Beltway before they closed in on him. As soon as he turned off of Old Georgetown Pike onto the Beltway, they would know he wasn't coming in. He hit the Beltway and blended in with pre-rush-hour traffic. He was heading south, and in ten minutes was at the Gallows Road exit. In another three minutes he was slipping the security card into the box at the gate. A minute later he was parked in front of unit 436, untying the New Vision. He rolled up the door of the unit and there was a cardboard box, all by itself, in the center of the floor.

Elliot carried the kayak inside and set it down. He grabbed his river gear and paddle from the back of the Pathfinder. Reaching under the front seat, he withdrew his Walther and three clips. He ran back inside the unit and ripped off his clothes. He put on his paddling shorts, spraydeck, and life jacket. He threw his paddle jacket, T-shirt, pants, sneakers, and Patagonia pullover jacket into the back of the New Vision.

He turned to the box. The helmet was inside with a note lying on top. It read: "You know how to use this. I expect a full report when, and if, you can get it to me. Say hello to my old buddy. Good Luck. Your Friend," and signed, "Howard S. Calvert."

He slipped the note into the pocket of his life jacket and, putting on the helmet, climbed into the New Vision. Just then, he heard tires screeching and doors slamming.

READY
appeared on the screen.

With the paddle in his hands, he said: "Helmet, Mihalis track and transfer." The last thing Elliot saw was the Walther and the clips on the floor, just out of reach. The agents were running for the open storage unit door, guns drawn. A flash of light shot out into the alleyway and almost blinded the lead man, who fell down, more from surprise than anything else. The others whipped in front of the doorway, ready to fire. All they saw was a pistol on the floor near a cardboard box.

❧❦

He awoke with a bitter taste in his mouth. He was lying in water. He couldn't see. Slipping around a bit on the slimy rocks on which he lay, he tried to get a handhold. Raising himself up out of the water, he could begin to see light and then the blue of the sky and the green of the trees. Slowly the world came into focus.

Where am I?

He looked down at the water. It was gray and had flecks of debris tumbling in it. The rocks were reddish. The rocks by the water's edge were orange.

What has happened to the trees?

The trees were scrawny, with small leaves and wrinkled bark. The plants below them were unknown to him and ugly.

He was drawn downstream by an unknown urge. He started swimming in the pool, but the water disgusted him and burned at his eyes. He gave up and decided to walk on the shore.

At one point he decided to go up through the trees in search of easier walking. He came to where the bank was all little broken rocks that were mixed with a greasy black dust. Above the rocks sat a strange thing. It was a trail, but so very odd. Two brown strips of metal, shiny on top, ran as far as he could see in either direction. They sat on top of pieces of wood, wood that was hot and oily and ugly. It was hard to walk there. The little rocks ground into his feet. The wood was too close together to take a good step from one to the other, yet too far apart to walk stepping on every other piece. They were turning the soles of his feet black. The metal strips were too hot to walk on. Dead trees with short straight branches were tied together with black ropes and extended into the distance beside the trail.

After an hour of walking, he heard a sound coming from behind him. As it grew louder, he looked back and saw it. It was like some huge beast, and it was coming down the trail toward him. He jumped into the plants beside the trail and crouched down. The noise grew to an awful roar and sounded like the end of the world. He prepared himself to face death. He stood and confronted the approaching beast, trying not to show fear. The beast pounded past him and surged on, but was followed by an unbroken string of more beasts. They made their own noise. They looked a bit like the trailer, but were bigger and taller and were an ugly brown. They had writing on them. Letters and numbers and some words. It was English. Father had said everyone spoke English in his time, and here it was written on the beast. He stood hypnotized by the sight and sound of it passing. It kept coming and coming. He began to realize that it wasn't a beast after all. It obviously wasn't alive. It didn't even know he was there. There were things on each end of each beast and he began to make a plan.

I could jump and grab hold of it. It will take me where I'm going. But if I miss in my jump at it, I will be crushed underneath. I won't miss.

Simon ran alongside it until he had matched its speed. He didn't watch the beast, but the stones below his feet. Out of the corner of his eye, he could tell that he was running faster than the beast and soon caught up to the end of one of its trailers. He now looked right at it and jumped up, grabbing the bars, and swung himself up. He climbed to the top and saw that the trailer was full of black rocks. Coal.

He looked ahead, proud of himself and enjoying his ride. After some time had passed, the beast started to make a new noise and began to slow down.

Finally, it came to a stop. Looking forward, he saw a man. The man was some distance away and hadn't seen him. But he was walking back along the side of the beast towards him. The man was very strange. He was thick. Simon realized that the man was fat. But fat like he had never seen. He climbed to the other side of the beast and jumped down. A wide trail went down through some trees that almost looked normal, so he ran down it.

The trail led back down to the river. A man was sitting on the bank. He was drinking from a little cup with a hole in the top. Two other cups lay at his feet. They had writing on them. The man was small and his clothes were dirty and torn. He looked up at Simon and smiled. He was missing almost all of his teeth.

"Boy, where's the rest of yore clothes?" The man was speaking English.

"I lost my moccasins."

"Moccysins?" The man was shaking his head, almost laughing. "Where the heck you come from boy?"

"Tokebelloke."

"Where the heck is zat? Never heard of it."

Simon pointed upriver.

"What's yore name?"

"Simon. What are you called?"

"I'm Dickey. Tell you what," he said, slowly rising, "why don't we go up to the house. It's best Anna take a look at you."

He followed Dickey up the trail and they crawled under the beast. The thick man was gone. They walked down the trail on the other side to where it crossed a stream. They crossed and went up to a house. It wasn't like the cabin; it was ugly, It was leaning a little bit to one side, and had broken things thrown around on the ground everywhere.

"Anna, come here and look at this boy."

An old woman came out of the house. She was looking him up and down.

"Child, where in heaven's name did you come from?"

"Tokebelloke."

She looked puzzled.

"I never heard of it neither. He said it's up the river."

He had the face of a boy, she thought, but he is strong as an ox. And them strange shorts, don't hide nothin' hardly.

"Where's yore folks boy?"

"Sez his name's Simon."

"Simon, where's yore ma and pa?"

Simon was confused.

"Yore mother and yore father," said Dickey, trying his best to help.

"My mother is to the north. My father went away and never came back."
Only then did Simon recall seeing his father at Tokebelloke.

"Ain't that a shame Dickey? A man leavin' a fine boy like this."

"My father is Pete Dornblaser." Simon found himself blurting out.

"There was a guy named Dornblaser about thirdy fordy years ago blew hisself up with a bunch of Ayrabs."

"Dickey, I think you best take him over to Joanie. She'll know what best to do with him. Best get him cleaned up a bit first," she said pointing at an old oil drum that served as a rain barrel by the shack. Simon upon seeing the water in the barrel cupped his hands in it to scoop up a drink.

"No, no, no!" Dickey exclaimed. "That ain't for drinkin' boy, just clean up a bit with it." Simon was dying of thirst but took heed and splashed the water over himself to cleanse off the sweat and the grime from the river.

Dickey led Simon down the dirt road by the tracks. All he could think about was how different the boy was. He obviously wasn't retarded, just different.

All Simon could think about was how thirsty he was. How odd that there was no drinkable water anywhere. The river was grey and poisonous, the creek orange, the puddles brackish and black.

They climbed the sloping driveway to Joanie Keener's house. Dickey knocked on the door.

Simon was feeling weird. This house was big, but still ugly. Stupid colored ducks and geese stood lifeless in the grass. A very strange thing was behind the house. It had wheels like the trailer, but was much smaller. They met an old woman. She had a kind look, but seemed to greet Dickey with a guarded familiarity.

"Dickey, you have been drinking, haven't you? Oh my, what have we here?"

Joanie looked uncomfortable. My Lord, what have you brought me today? She thought she had seen everything in her seventy years.

"My name is Simon."

"Simon. Simon what? What is your last name?"

"Dornblaser." Simon thought about how when his vision ended, a new name would come to him and he would no longer be Simon.

"Well Simon, I am Joanie Keener. Where have you come from?"

"I found him down by the river."

She foiled his interruption; "I imagine you were drinking beer down there."

"No ma'am."

He was drinking something, thought Simon.

"I came from Tokebelloke," said Simon quickly remembering that this had been met with strange responses and blank stares twice already. How can these people not know of Tokebelloke?

"But just how did you get here?"

Though he wasn't exactly sure himself, he explained how he had swum down through Tokebelloke and woke up in the river and everything was nasty and ugly. "I am on my vision quest."

"You are on what?"

"My quest. I must become a man."

Joanie was getting more and more uncomfortable. "Where are your parents?"

"My father left and my mother is back at the cabin."

Typical man, Joanie thought. "And what is that you are wearing?" referring to his loincloth. "I don't think your mother would approve of that."

"She made it for me."

"Don't he remind you of them river rats that used to ride them boats down the river?"

Joanie thought back. He did seem to remind her of the river guides she had seen, back when there was still rafting on the Gauley. Before the transition.

"I too, kayak the rivers," he said somewhat proudly. He thought about what Dickey had said. I must be after my father's time. People still went down the rivers when my father had left his world in 1998. He had gone backwards in time to 906. Now it was 922. Where was he now?

"Simon where does your mother live?"

"Cheat River."

"Does she know you are here?"

"No, I left without telling her."

"Do you want to go home?"

Simon looked around nervously. He was ready for the vision to end. Everything here was horrible, except for Joanie. She was very nice and kind.

"Do you have water?"

"Oh dear me, yes of course. You must be thirsty."

Joanie went inside and came out with a glass of water from the refrigerator. Simon marveled at the glass. He could see the water inside. He held it up, looking at it.

"It's good bottled water. Don't worry."

He drank deeply from the glass. It was cold and good. He drank it all and then held up the glass, looking at it. Then he looked again at the windows on the house, on the beast with wheels. What was this magic, that could be seen through so? Simon turned the glass in his hands, looking at it. Joanie was becoming worried. The boy wasn't retarded, like so many from the contamination. He seemed so good, but now was acting quite strange. He held the glass up between them.

"What is this?"

"It's a glass."

"I have never seen it."

"Don't you know it's bad to lie boy?" quizzed Dickey sharply.

"I do not lie."

Joanie intervened. "Simon, it's okay, I believe you."

"Have you heard of Mihalis? It is a kayak made of crystal that you can see through, just like this."

"This isn't crystal though Simon, it is just a glass. I have some crystal, would you like to see it?"

"Yes please."

"Come into the house. I'll show you."

He followed her in while Dickey waited outside. The house was full of things, but everything was neat and clean and in order. The house was very different than the cabin and it reminded him of home. His mother always kept everything in order. Sana was always asking his father if he couldn't put this or that out in the trailer. And father had always listened, and dutifully taken this or that out to the trailer.

All of Joanie's things were so colorful. Little figures of animals and children jammed in little shelves everywhere. Hanging from a window shade was a cut crystal disc. Light splayed from it, revealing the color spectrum. Simon was drawn to it.

"That is crystal Simon. Would you like it?"

"Yes, it is beautiful."

"I will give it to you, if you will do something for me."

"What do you want me to do?"

"I'm going to give you some clothes to wear."

"He was transfixed with the crystal. Joanie went into another room and came out with some clothes.

"These were my brother's."

"Where is your family?"

"God bless them. They are all gone. I'm the only one left."

"What about your children?"

"I never married. The church is my family. We will go there in a bit to ask a blessing for your trip home. Now go to the bedroom there and put these on, okay?"

It took him a while to figure out how to put on the pants, but he did. They were of a thick brown material and made him feel hot. The shirt was white and had a yellow face with a smile. It said: HAVE A NICE DAY. He needed her help with the socks and boots.

"That's better," she said with a smile. "Do you know what it says on the shirt?"

"It says 'have a nice day.' Joanie, I do know how to read. My parents taught me that."

"Simon, what did you do with your, shorts?"

"They are underneath," he said, pointing to the pants.

Joanie looked at him as he spun the crystal disc on its string in front of him, watching it in the light.

"What is your mother like?"

"I love her. She is beautiful, and she loves me. She has long black hair, not curly like mine. She is at the cabin, with my uncles."

"So you live in a cabin?" That could explain his backwardness thought Joanie.

"My father built it."

"Is it right by a road?"

"A road?"

"Roads, highways, like the road in front of the house here."

"Oh no, no roads, only forest and trails."

"And how did you get all the way down south here? In a car?"

"A car?"

"Yes, a car like mine," she said pointing to the beast outside the window.

"No Joanie, I came walking for four days. Then I fell into Tokebelloke and when I woke up, the world was ugly and I rode the big black beast to where I met Dickey."

None of it made any sense. "Simon, I want to show you something." She took her calendar from the grocery store down off of the nail that held it to the end of the shelves by the sink. "This is a calendar. This is how we keep track of days and weeks and months."

Simon realized that his father was always making calendars with the stub of a pencil or an ink pen saying how they had to keep track of the passing of time. "Yes Joanie, I know what it is."

"This is 2038 Simon."

He looked worried. "Simon, what year are you from?"

"922."

They made the short drive down the river road to the Swiss Methodist Church. Joanie said it was best that they seek the blessing of the lord for the long drive they would now make to take Simon home. As they walked inside, Simon saw row after row of long benches made of wood. He ran his hand across the top of the first one.

"Simon, that reminds me that we had these pews made with money we made selling hot dogs to the rafters and kayakers way back when." Simon looked up and was startled at the sight of a figure of a man in pain, nailed to wood, hanging in the back of the church.

"That is Jesus Christ. Do you know who he is?"

"My father says his name a lot, usually when something breaks." He noticed that Jesus was wearing shorts no bigger than his loincloth.

Joanie sat in a pew and folded her hands on the pew in front of her. "Lord, please watch over this young man and help him return to his family. He is a good boy and means no one any harm. Amen."

They were driving north towards the gate that led on to what had been I-79. When the car in front of them went through the barrier snapped up into place again. The soldiers in the armored vehicle looked hot, sweaty, and bored. A man in a black uniform stepped up and passed a black baton across the driver side of the windshield. "Never had this thing on the National before have you ma'am?"

"No sir."

"You Joan Ellen Keener?"

"Yes sir."

"Let me see your license please. Who is the boy?"

"He is my nephew, Simon Keener."

Joanie cursed herself inside for lying.

"Okay I need his too."

"Here's mine, Simon doesn't have one. He's retarded."

"Oh. Sorry ma'am, some of the M.C.'s don't look it."

"M. C.'s?"

"Mentally challenged Ms. Keener. That's what we're supposed to say. National policy. Destination?"

"Albright."

"Okay but listen, you will have to get off at exit 148. N68 is now a security zone so you have to go in through Kingwood. Ms. Keener, I'm going to warn you now that you may have a problem with the boy not having ID with the officer at the other end." He tapped his clipboard. "They already know you're coming. Have a nice trip and keep it under a hundred."

"Look Joanie, trees!"

Indeed there were. Behind the concertina-topped cyclone fence was a stand of young pines, several acres worth.

"The National planted them. Really, they were planted by retarded people, that work for the National."

To Simon, they were flying as they drove north on N79. She was surprised that he wasn't afraid to ride in the car. For him, it was an exciting new experience. He had been full of questions: Where are the mountains? They were stripped away to get the coal. Why? To make power. For what? The national grid. Where are all the trees?

They were cut down to make paper and lumber. Where did all the people come from? Other people. How many are there? In West Virginia, ten million, and in the National Federation of American States six hundred million. Joanie could tell he did not understand how many a million was.

Joanie was just about the slowest driver on the highway and Simon looked at the people in the other cars when they passed by. "Joanie, I don't see any Shawnee people."

She was about to say that there hadn't been any Indians for hundreds of years but caught herself. The truth would probably really upset the boy. Fortunately it was he who changed the subject.

"There are many retarded people, aren't there Joanie? Why?"

"The National says it's because of the contamination."

It was widely suspected that it was because of something in the food. Almost everybody had to buy their food at the National. One of every three or four babies had been born retarded and sterile for almost twenty years now.

The transition had been a terrible thing.

They passed by the trees, and the scenery returned to the monotony of the barely reclaimed strip mines. Each had a sparse covering of grass. Orange run-off, trickled through courses of broken rock.

"Simon, you know your mother is not going to be there. Don't you?"

"Yes. Now I know. Joanie, I thought that this was my vision, but it is real. Isn't it?" Joanie had brought him to the Cheat because that was where he said his home was. Now he knew that if his home was here a thousand years ago, it certainly wasn't here now.

"It is real. I wish it wasn't, but it is. It's a shame you couldn't have seen all of this before it was ruined."

"Joanie, I did see it."

"I guess you did, didn't you?"

They came to the split in N79 and N68. A long line of vehicles was pulled over in the right lanes, waiting to pass through the gate. It was faster to leave the National than to enter it, and in twenty minutes they came to the gate. The officer passed the wand over the windshield.

"Joan Ellen Keener?"

The man was mean looking and red in the face.

"This the unregistered retard?"

"Excuse me sir but you don't have reason to talk that way about my Simon"

"Look lady, I don't know why you breeders don't stay in your holes. Swiss," he said looking at his clipboard, "never even heard of it. What do you think you're doing coming out on the National with an unregistered?"

"You look here sonny. I remember when anybody could go anywhere they wanted. My credits still pay your credits and I do not appreciate your attitude whatsoever. Now you let me through this gate this instant, or when I get home, I'll be more than glad to tap out a complaint, officer......," Joanie strained to look at his badge, "NS87264. I think I'll write that down right now. Simon please get me a pen out of the glove box."

He knew what a pen was but not a glove box and he started to feel around on the dash in the direction that Joanie was looking. What a complete and total retard thought the officer as he watched Simon. "Okay, get out of here lady and get him registered soon or Energy just might take him off your hands."

That way, he just might be good for something, the officer thought as they drove off through the gate.

Simon looked at Joanie and smiled. "I guess you told him."

Joanie laughed, but inside she was worried. Why has Simon come here at this time? Why couldn't he have come when things were still okay? Lord, what are you putting this boy through?

Soon she was able to relax somewhat. The drive was pleasant. The people were kind when she had to stop and ask directions, and there was less National presence. Armored vehicles, with soldiers mounted on top, patrolled the roads, but didn't stop the cars and trucks.

"Simon, take this and put it in your pocket." It was a card, shiny and hard. NATIONAL DEBIT was written on it. "This is money Simon. When you want to buy your food, you just go to the national, pick out your food and give them the card. My name will come up on their screen and you tell them that I'm your aunt, and remember, always say you're retarded if anybody asks you any questions. She turned to him. "The National is a monster. You have to be very careful. Always be good. I don't want anything bad to happen to you."

"I am always good."

Joanie looked at him. She already loved him like a son.

They arrived at Kingwood. Joanie pulled into a National Fuel and asked for directions to Albright.

"Can't drive there Ma'am. That's Energy. It's restricted."

In one sense, Kingwood had suffered in the transition as it had become a de facto, end-of-the-road community. But it was now the southern entrance to one of the Energy zones, and that meant commerce.

"My nephew wants to see the river."

"Why would he want to see the river? There's nothing there."

"His parents lived down there, before the transition."

That wasn't a lie, Joanie thought proudly.

"You can take the Energy bus or walk. Is the boy registered?"

"No."

"I thought not. The way he's dressed and all."

"Yes, he's retarded."

"If he's not registered you have to walk."

"How far is it?"

"About three miles from the gate."

"Simon, I can't walk three miles."

The man left to attend a customer.

"Joanie, I think maybe you should go home. I'll be okay."

"Oh Simon, I don't know. Why don't you come back with me?"

"I am here for some reason Joanie. I can feel it inside me. It is something I have to do. You've been kind. I'll always have good thoughts of you."

Joanie was crying when she left him at the gate. He's a good boy, she thought. He'll be all right. As she drove off, she knew she was lying again, this time to herself.

Simon walked down the road. It was still hot, although almost five in the afternoon. It felt weird walking in boots. The pants felt like the buckskin he wore in winter.

A horn blew behind him, and a truck rolled past as he jumped out of the way. The road now curved downward, and he could see the river. Below him, next to the river, were the ruins of a large complex. On the other side of the river, and slightly downstream, was a huge, smoke-belching building. By the river's edge was a tall, cone-shaped tower. Steam was coming out of the top. Shiny cables, suspended from silver towers connected everything. Immense piles of coal lined the river. Coal was pouring out of a long thing, with a roof on it, that stretched downstream out of sight. He could see hundreds of workers, with yellow helmets, throughout the complex.

The river was orange and ugly. Plants weren't growing down by the water. Trees were almost nonexistent.

The nearer he got, the larger the plant loomed overhead. It emitted a steady, loud, humming sound. Steaming water poured into the river from big pipes at the base of the cone shaped tower.

Simon walked across the bridge that spanned the river at the downstream end of the complex.

This is a mistake, he thought, while nervously twiddling the crystal disc that now hung around his neck on a string. This can't be my home.

He walked past the guarded gate of the power station. No one seemed to pay any attention to him. The road continued downstream, along the river. On the other side of the road, was the long skinny thing from which came the coal. At one point, the road, started to veer away from the river. Here a stream flowed under the road. He stood on the bridge and looked around. Downstream, the river flowed between two hills with flattened tops. In the distance, on the right hill, he could see the top of a great beast, slowly moving back and forth. The long skinny thing, with the roof on top, ran down the hill and angled off to the right before straightening out to run towards where he was. There was a flat area stretching out towards the river. He walked down onto it, drawn to it. A wind whipped upstream and swirled the black dust around. The filthy water of the river tumbled over riffles downstream. Straining, he could make out the first surfing ledge of Decision Rapids.

"Kijemoneto, please wake me from this vision."

Nothing happened. Kijemoneto had abandoned him, as it had abandoned the land.

Simon tried to feel the presence of his mother. He couldn't feel anything. She would have been dead now over a thousand years, but still, he should feel something.

It is because this was not her destiny, nor the destiny of my people. I will return to my time, somehow, and make sure that this can never happen.

This can never happen.

Simon walked down to the river. He sat until the sun set between the hills. What will I do? I must wait for a sign.

It came. In the waning light, he saw paddle blades slashing their way upstream. The kayaker finally came to shore four hundred yards downstream. He climbed out of the boat and carried it up to a small house located near the coal conveyer.

Simon walked to the house. It was ramshackle. The ground was covered with the same black dust. He knocked on the door. A voice came from inside.

"Who is it?"

"Simon Dornblaser."

"Who?"

"Simon Dornblaser."

"This some kind of joke?"

"No."

The door opened. A young man only a few years older than Simon, with long blond hair, beckoned him inside. The other closed the door and suddenly grabbed Simon by his shirt, threw him to the floor, and jumped on top of him. The man was strong, but in a flash, Simon turned the tables and had him pinned solidly to the floor.

"What the fuck do you want?" said the man, gasping for breath.

Simon let him go and stood up. The other rolled over on his back and looked up at him. Then he stared at the wall behind Simon. Simon looked at the wall. It was a picture of his father. It was his father, but it wasn't. It said: WANTED Peter Simon Dornblaser Espionage, Interstate Flight to Avoid Prosecution. Possession of Explosive Devices and Material. Customs Violations.

Below, it read: Computer Enhancement of Earlier Photo

"Goddamn. You are who you say, aren't you."

"Yes."

"My name's Barton, Barton Core. Glad to meet you."

Barton extended his hand, and Simon helped him up off of the floor.

The walls of Barton's house were covered with old pictures and posters of kayaking and rafting.

"You are the kayaker I saw leave the river."

"Yes. I kayak. Do You?"

"Yes. Almost every day."

"Where?"

"Here."

"Bullshit. I'm the only kayaker here."

"Maybe you are now."

"Where the hell did you come from?"

"Swiss."

"On the Gauley?"

"Yes. You have been there?"

"No, but I've read about it."

"Then you have heard of Tokebelloke."

"Of what?"

Then it came to him.

Barton went to a corner of the room and pulled a stained and ragged book from a crate on the floor. There was a black and white picture of a kayaker on a river on the cover. Barton had found the book, along with the pictures and posters, in an old house scheduled to be bulldozed for the coal conveyer. That had been ten years ago.

The old man who had owned the house had been a local kayak guru. He had resisted all the changes brought on by the transition as much as he could, but the continual environmental degradation of the river had been too much for him. The old man had packed his household possessions and a dozen kayaks in a big moving van and left for good. Barton had begun to poke around in his house and found four kayaks of different designs in the basement. There was also an assortment of old gear and paddles and tons of memorabilia and other junk.

He thought back to that time in his childhood.

Barton's father had been killed in a mine accident when he was eight, and his mother had descended into alcoholism. She had remarried to a coal truck driver with a mean streak. He had beaten Barton, and his mother. His stepfather's house had been in the path of the coal conveyor project, and had to be demolished. When they moved, Barton already had a plan to run away. He had looted the kayaks and other things and hid them underneath the abandoned house that was now his home. When he was thirteen, he ran away from his stepfather's trailer in the Energy settlement up Muddy Creek. They had tried taking him back home twice and gave up when he continued to run off. His mother supported him with credits for food at the Energy settlement National. No one cared that he lived in the little house by the noisy conveyer. He had taught himself how to kayak. It was his life.

"In the Gauley chapter of this guidebook it mentions this 'Tokebelloke'." Barton had read the book so many times, he almost knew it by heart. How he wished he had been born at an earlier time when other kayakers roamed West Virginia, running all the rivers before they had been destroyed. Before the transition.

"It says here that the 'Indians called the Gauley, Tokebelloke, which means: Golley! That's falling water!' That's all it says."

"I need to go back there. I must fall into Tokebelloke, and return to my own time."

"Easy, dude. Don't be so intense."

Barton sat staring at Simon for a moment.

"Man, I don't get it. What is your story anyway?"

Simon told him, at length, and when he was through, Barton let out a long whistle.

"That is some heavy shit. I got some bad news for you, though. I don't think that hole you fell through exists anymore. I think the guidebook would have mentioned it. 'Don't run the center chute in Tokebelloke rapid, as it drops into a time warp from which there is no return.' No, it doesn't say anything like that."

Barton thought for a moment.

"It could have been at Iron Ring."

"What is Iron Ring?"

"It's a rapid on the Gauley. It says here in the guidebook that it was dynamited by loggers to break up logjams. That was before people started to run the river. So Solly, Simon. Don't think you're going home. Not that way, anyway."

"I cannot live here, in this time. The world is ugly and dead." Thinking for a second, he turned to Barton. "Does no one try to stop them from killing the land and the water?"

"Oh yeah. There's crazies out there. Best to stay way away from them."

"Why?"

"Because, the National catches you even thinking out loud about something like that, and you could become rom."

"What is rom?"

"Rom means recycled organic material. It means you get your dead ass dumped in some strip mine by the Nationals."

"But what do the people do, the ones that try to stop the destruction?"

"Simon, face it, it's already destroyed. All those guys want is revenge. Here you just live your life and don't deal with anybody you don't have to, and everything is okay."

Simon looked depressed. Barton decided to try to cheer him up.

"Tell you what Simon, tomorrow we'll go down the river and have a great time. Whaddaya say?"

"Sounds good to me."

Barton gave him an old sleeping bag to stretch out on the couch, and they slept.

Simon dreamed. But his dreams were nightmares of falling and a blighted world.

҈

The second shift at the power station had just ended, and the tired and weary formed in a line to get on the buses to go home. The third bus had loaded with workers headed for the Muddy Creek settlement and rolled out through the gate. A few of the men and women were lively and talkative, but most were already dozing off in their seats. The bus was trundling along past the conveyor when they saw it. Over towards the river, a bright flash, and then a dying glow, then darkness again. The conversations stopped. No one spoke again until they had left the bus at the settlement. They fanned out in small groups walking towards their trailers. Some were explaining to those who had been sleeping. Some, who had been awake, were comparing what each thought they had seen. Nobody even considered going to the NSA office with a report of the incident.

҈

He forced himself to wake, to shrug off the dizziness and nausea, to make his eyes function. He could hear voices close by. They were speaking English, one voice giving orders, a yelp of pain. The world was quickly coming into focus. He was in a weed choked depression, it was a drainage ditch. He slipped off the helmet and quietly climbed out of the kayak.

"Lieutenant, they want a confirmation from you ASAP!"

"What is there to confirm, Goddamit? We've got two men down. Give me that thing....NSB26, this is NSB26 mobile LYRZ12. Do you copy?"

"Go ahead, 12." The radio noise echoed about the area.

"This is Walters. We've got two men down, I repeat, two men down. Need assistance. We are two klicks north of the Power Station. Do you copy?" "Assistance will arrive in five minutes, 12. Are you under attack? Repeat, are you under attack?"

"No, we stopped to investigate something and....."

"Twelve, you have a code 9 transfer, you are not permitted to stop in any sector before destination. Await instruction."

Elliot had quietly changed into his street clothes and slid the boat and gear deep into the tangled undergrowth. Although his head was pounding, he crawled up to take a look through the weeds.

Where in the hell am I?

Two soldiers, dressed in black uniforms, were crouched over two others, who lay motionless on the ground. A military truck, tarped on the back, was parked behind them. Elliot didn't recognize the make or model of the truck. It looked like a Humvie, but sleeker. They were in a flat, open area, ringed with flat hills devoid of vegetation other than a smattering of grass and scrubby trees. A conveyor ran along the far side of a road. Then he saw it, sticking out of the back of the tarp. It could only be one thing. It's brilliance and clarity practically resonated in the midday sun. It was Mihalis.

Elliot was starting to put two and two together. He was in a different time. It had to be the future. He already didn't like the look of it. The soldiers had seen Mihalis from the road and, when they investigated, had decided to load it into the truck. Mihalis had let two of them have it. Some kind of shock probably. The officer was in trouble. He wasn't sure what a Code 9 transfer meant, but he had an idea. Now a yellow truck with Energy written across the side had stopped along the road. Two men with overalls and yellow helmets got out and came running over. The driver remained behind the wheel. The officer waved on the two approaching workers.

This guy is a real loser, thought Elliot, as he watched the yellow truck start to pull away. The workers suddenly pulled pistols on the surprised soldiers and fired. No sound. Silencers. The workers stripped the shirts off of the two soldiers who had been unconscious, and then shot them also. Grabbing up two helmets, they jumped into the vehicle and drove off. It had taken less than a minute.

Out of the frying pan and into the fire. I've got to get out of here fast.

Elliot looked around, and was fairly confident he had been the only witness to the incident. If the voice on the radio was correct, he had three minutes before more soldiers arrived. Not enough time to get to the river and escape in the kayak. He suddenly realized he was in what had been the campground.

My God. What has happened to the world?

Climbing up out of the ditch, he straightened the weeds he'd bent over. There was nowhere to hide. He had to protect the integrity of the helmet's hiding place by leaving. He started running north towards the road and the conveyor. He ran from support column to support column under the conveyor and stopped at each to listen for approaching vehicles. There was a small house nearby, below him. No, too dangerous there. That would be the first place they would look. Noises. Two more military vehicles, the first with heavily armed soldiers clinging to the top. They passed without seeing him.

Elliot's mind raced. This was a local patrol. Whatever a Code 9 transfer was, probably weaponry of some kind, it would be important enough to bring in more, and more heavily armed, units. The operation to steal the truck had been opportunistic, yet slick and organized. It had been some type of inside job, judging by the stupid trust the officer had put in the workers.

The country must now be controlled by some authoritarian government.

He felt a flush of complicity. Had he not devoted his energies to just such an agency? He thought of Ebeneezer Scrooge reviewing previous mistakes before the tribunal of the ghosts of Christmases past.

No time for this. I need to find some cover and buy some time.

He hoped that the soldiers would concentrate on locating the stolen vehicle. There were some clumps of trees by Muddy Creek down below. He ran down across the road and over the slaggy stones to the place he would hide.

I need to think. Make a plan.

৵৽৹ঌ

They hit the water before dawn. Barton preferred it that way. Simon knew enough by now that he did not have to ask why. Each was surprised at how good the other was. Barton was fearless and led Simon down through a series of tough moves in the jagged rocks. The river was different from the river Simon knew. Millions of cubic yards of blasting debris had tumbled into the river from the mines above. In some places, the sliding rock dammed the river's flow and created violent rapids. But several of the old rapids had remained intact. In these, thought Simon, the song of the water remained the same. The hills were barren, the rocks orange, and the water gray, but the currents were still alive and still whispered their riddles to him. By noon, they arrived at Jenkinsburg, the junction of the Cheat and the Big Sandy. The rusting girders of an old bridge reached up out of the water.

"The Nationals blew it up. It was so old that only light vehicles could cross. The National doesn't have light vehicles."

"I understand."

The Big Sandy flowed with water equally gray, it's rocks equally orange, it's canyon walls equally barren.

"It's like this everywhere they re-mined the coal."

Barton knew that the coal-hungry power station was being fed now by the next stage in the removal of the mountain to the north of the canyon. A huge dragline, this one even bigger than the last, was stripping away another hundred vertical feet of blasted rock and earth to get at yet another seam of coal. Much of this overburden was being shoved over the side of the canyon rim, and some of it slid all the way to the river or to the Sandy. What would remain above was another version of what already existed, a vast barren plain. Barton knew that the plan was to turn it into an extension of the NSA air base of the Bruceton Security Zone.

Originally, the BSZ had been designed as a hub airport for domestic flights. After the transition, it had been immediately converted. It was ideally located -- far from any urban center and, thus, not vulnerable to attack by insurgents. The zone housed one of the many regional food processing centers. Food came from the west somewhere and was warehoused in the zone. From there it was "processed," and metered out to the population centers in the East. Along with everybody else, Barton knew that the processing was where the food was poisoned and that those who ate it ran the risk of bearing retarded children. The retarded were only suited for mindless, manual labor. That was what the National wanted: a subdued population. It was estimated that within a few more generations, half of the people in the Federation would be retarded and sterile. Few would bear children; those who did would continue to bring more retarded into the world. Though the overall population would decrease, the percentage of retarded would continue to rise. Where it all was leading was a matter of continuous, cloistered, debate.

I don't care. I'll never have any children anyway. I'm just going to enjoy myself and the summer weather. What is today? The second? No, it's the third.

The third of July.

Simon was depressed. As they had paddled down the Cheat, he had hoped in vain at each bend in the river, that upon rounding it, he would be greeted by the sight of the world as he had known it.

"Barton is there nowhere alive?"

Barton looked furtively about, as if someone might be listening. "Come with me."

They paddled down past the junction another half mile to the mouth of Bull Run, a steep tributary creek. Simon knew it well. He had hiked up it numerous times. That was then. Now it shared the homogenized desolate look of the rest of the world..

"We have to hide the kayaks and walk. Okay?"

Simon was anxious to see what Barton had been nervous to even talk about. "Let's go."

Barton led him upstream. After several minutes of hiking through the barren ground lining the creek, they began climbing over steep rapids and falls. The walls of the small canyon closed in, and they clambered up a curve in the streambed. A cool breeze passed over them, coming from upstream. Simon could smell something. It was the smell of life.

"Look, Simon, trees."

It was true, there was a pocket of forest, untouched in the destruction that ringed it. It straddled the creek and ran upstream around the next bend.

"This is the most beautiful place I have ever seen," said Barton.

It is beautiful, thought Simon, but how sad that it is all that remains. He was overwhelmed by the paradox. Somehow I must avenge the world, and keep them from taking this too.

He halted on the thought and remembered what his grandfather had once said to him. "Take the past into the present and live with it." He had not really understood it at the time, but now he did.

I'm sorry, old one, I believe not even you could accept what has been done. They walked up the creek through the forest around the next turn in the small canyon.

"Simon, this is where it ends."

"What is that?" A junkyard lay at the upstream end of the forest.

"Those are old cars that have been pushed off the road from up above."

They walked up to the pile of twisted metal, rusting away in a heap. There were scores of cars and pickups.

"Barton, look!"

There, shimmering in the sun, was Mihalis. It had come to rest on top of an old car and it's perfection clashed with the condition of the discarded vehicles surrounding it.

Barton climbed over the junked cars to it and reached out to touch it. Mihalis let out a jolt that shocked his fingertips.

"Motherfucker! Did you see that?"

Simon had seen it, yet the crystal seemed to beckon him forward. Confidently, he ran his hand along it. He rapped it with his knuckles and a chime-like tone came from it.

"Barton. This is it!"

Barton felt uneasy.

First Simon, now this.

Simon was captivated by Mihalis. Barton started to look around.

"Simon, look. Up there," he said in a hushed voice.

A National truck hung suspended upside down in some trees above them on the embankment. Gas was still dripping from it.

"Dude, this is some bad Juju. We gotta get out of here."

"I'm going to take it with me."

Barton was starting to feel as if he were in a bad dream.

When they reached the river, they hid the kayak Simon had been using by burying it in the sand below an overhang. Then they got in the kayaks and started to work their way upstream.

৵৵৵

He stepped out into the open with his hands clasped over his head and knelt down on the slag.

Running upstream, he had eluded one patrol as long as he could, but another was working its way down to meet it. He could hear them approaching. He was trapped. If he went up the bank, he would be seen and shot. Better to try to surrender. He was unarmed. He was vastly outnumbered. Worst of all, he was ignorant as to what was going on. That was what Elliot hated the most.

He was surrounded quickly by boots pounding across the slag. Gun barrels pointing at him. An officer strode to him from behind and pushed him to the ground, then pressed his head to the slag with his boot. The officer ripped the back pocket off of his jeans in freeing his wallet.

"Where's your registration?"

"That's all I ha..."

His face was ground deeper into the slag.

"Rings!"

"Yes sir."

"You recognize this man?"

The officer grabbed his hair and pulled his head up off the ground.

"No sir. I. . . don't think he's from the settlement."

"What is your explanation of this ridiculous crap in your billfold?"

"I can explain everything," Elliot said trying to buy time.

"Sergeant, bind him."

Elliot felt a strip of plastic clip around his wrists which had been wrenched behind him.

"Take him up to recycling. Hold him until I radio up there."

"Yes sir."

Elliot was yanked to his feet. With a gun barrel jammed into his back, he followed the line of soldiers climbing up the bank. He noticed the soldiers weren't very professional or well disciplined. Many seemed downright stupid. However, the officers, were Nazi-like.

When they reached the road, four tarped trucks rolled up, and he was shoved into the back of one of them. The sergeant clipped him to the seat against the cab with another strip of plastic, this time around his throat. The sergeant jumped out and four soldiers climbed in. The other trucks, loaded with the two patrols, circled around and headed back towards Albright. The truck he was in headed up Rt. 26, going north, and then turned west onto a rough road. The truck bounced along, and Elliot thought he would break his neck if he slipped off his seat. Elliot studied everything: where they were going, the guarded gates they passed through, the faces of the soldiers, their guns....

❧❦

"NSB26, this is NSB26 mobile EDRT04, come back."

"Go ahead 4."

"Cogar here. Need a check on a detained suspect."

"Registration number?"

"No registration."

"How do we check, Captain Cogar?"

"Suspect has an old operator's license. State of Virginia, Carlson, James Elliot. D.O.B., 3/16/66. Social Security Number 234-12-6547."

"What was the geezer detained for?"

"He's not a 'geezer,' he's early thirties."

"Okay, processing."

A moment later, the reply came back.

"Cogar, this is 26. Does he match the photo?"

"Yes, 26."

"Scan it to me now."

The captain passed the license through the slot in the radio.

"Four, it matches. This Carlson is a level 10 enemy of the Federation."

❧❧

The truck rolled to a stop in a compound composed of four trailers within a concertina-lined fence. Elliot heard another shot and saw where it came from. An officer was executing a line of bound men and women. They were kneeling, facing an excavated trench. Three of the soldiers jumped out of the truck and disappeared from his view. The other cut the strip holding his neck to the seat and clipped the knife to his belt. Roughly grabbing Elliot by his shirt, he yanked him to his feet. The soldier jammed the gun barrel into his ribs, and Elliot slowly made his way toward the back of the truck.

This is it. Now or never.

Elliot stepped up to the edge, still no one in view. The soldier was right behind him, he could see the gun barrel at his side out of the corner of his right eye. Elliot crouched as if he were going to jump down but instead threw himself up and backward with all his might. He snapped his head backward at the same time and, with more than a little satisfaction, felt his skull smash the soldier's nose through his face and into his brain. The man crumpled to the floor. Elliot stepped over him and rolled onto his back, and, as he did, slipped his bent legs through his bound hands. This was something that he had practiced before. Now his hands were in front of him. He knelt by the quivering soldier and quickly removed the knife from his belt. As he cut the strip binding his hands, another soldier appeared at the back of the truck, raising his weapon. The soldier tried to shout a warning but found his wind cut off. As he fell, he grabbed at the knife sticking from his throat. Elliot, reflexes tightened, awareness peaking and adrenaline flowing, and now, with the guard's gun in his hands, launched himself from the back of the truck as the first of the bullets tore through the tarp. He hit the ground and rolled. He came up on one knee and took out the other two soldiers with a ripping blast from the automatic weapon. He ran behind the closest trailer as a spray of bullets erupted on the ground behind him. He counted to two and then, sticking only the weapon around the corner, let loose with another spray of bullets. He heard men screaming in pain and knew he'd hit at least two. Elliot ran the length of the trailer and came around the far side. The executioner and another soldier were crouched, weapons trained in the wrong direction. One burst took them both. Two more soldiers were at the gate of the compound. One raised his gun to fire while the other shouted into a radio. With two quick shots, they were dead on the ground.

It was all over. Four men and two women huddled in the trench that held half a dozen freshly executed civilians.

"Who are you?"

"I'm Elliot, come on," he extended his hand and started to help them up out of the trench. "There's not much time."

Elliot had cut two of them loose when the radio in the truck crackled.

"OMRT07, this is EDRTO4, come in."

Elliot ran to the truck and started the engine.

"Go ahead 4"

"Seven, what's your 20,?"

He recognized the captain's voice.

"Just arriving, sir. Over"

"What's the problem out there? Over."

"No problem here. Over."

"Seven, hold the prisoner, do not recycle. Repeat, do not recycle. Do you copy?"

"Yes sir. Over"

"1 will arrive in two minutes, 4 out."

Elliot shouted to the prisoners.

"Let's go, no time!"

One of the women ran up to him.

"Wait. There's something we can do."

They were all loose now and one of them had taken a ring of keys from the executioner's belt. He ran into one of the trailers, and, after what seemed a short eternity, emerged with two grenades. He and another man went for the gate of the compound, untwisting the tops of the grenades as they ran. When they reached the gate, they looked like they were sprinkling the contents onto the road.

As they ran back, the others were putting on helmets and dragging the dead soldiers to the trench and dumping them in. They now heard the rumble of the approaching trucks and gathered behind the trailer, each now with a weapon in hand.

The trucks came rolling in through the gate, and, one after another, went sailing through the air in fiery arcs and landed in burning heaps.

"What kind of explosive was that?" Elliot had never seen such concentrated power.

"Thermex," said one of the men.

"Look, mister, thanks a hell of a lot for saving us. We got to go. You want to come with us?"

"No. There is something I have to do, but can I have that machine pistol?"

"Take it, and God bless you."

They mounted in the truck and started to pull away.

"Happy Independence Day!" yelled one of the women.

Independence Day?

"Hey! What year is it?"

They looked at each other strangely as the truck drove off, and one yelled: "38!"

⁎⁎

They were being watched from above.

They had made it as far as Coliseum rapid and decided to camp for the night. A big can of beans was simmering in the coals of a small fire, and they were sharing water from a plastic bottle. Simon was content with his new toy. It had paddled like a dream.

So magical, he thought. Certainly it was the one and the same that his father had told him about. He chilled as he realized that his father's memory was fading. Leaving him. His mother's, too, and that of the world he'd left behind. He would trade this kayak in a second to be back there with them. Simon turned his back on Mihalis and walked up over the rocks toward the fire. That was when he saw them.

A slide of small stones had preceded them as they came down over the hill. There were five of them, all wearing bandanas around their mouths and noses. They had guns.

"Stay where you are and don't move."

They came down into the little camp.

"Simon, just stay still."

"That's good advice for your friend, Core. Where'd you find him?"

"He's from out of town."

"I'll say. What is he, Mexican?" The other men laughed.

"Look. What do you guys want?"

"Want you to do something, Barton."

"And what might that be?"

"Tomorrow is the big day, and we want you to be part of the celebration."

"Come on, dude. I don't want any trouble with the Nation..."

"You don't have a fucking choice! Do you understand?" Simon could feel the man's intensity. "It all happens, tomorrow before dawn. You don't do what we say, and we'll remember afterward."

Simon was burning to know what the man was talking about.

"By the way, Barton, don't think you can go home right now. We capped some Nationals half a klick from your house today."

They laughed.

"Okay, what do you want me to do?"

The leader looked at him suspiciously.

"What you're going to do, Core, is take out the dragline on the north rim."
Barton laughed. "And how am I going to do that?"

"With this." One of the other men took off a small backpack he had been
wearing and handed it to the masked leader. He opened it up only enough to
reveal a small gray box with a red bulb and a switch. Wires ran from it and
disappeared into the depths of the pack. "Two kilos of Thermex. Get inside the
dragline and stuff it into any tight space. Flip the switch and get the fuck out.
You have one minute."

"One minute! You guys are crazy. You know that?"

"Yeah, we know. But you don't do this and you are rom. Got it, Core?"

"But why me?" Barton said plaintively.

"Because you can get to it from the Sandy, from your Goddamn little good-
for-nothing boat!" he said, stepping forward.

Barton raised his hands. Simon readied himself to defend him. Barton
sensed it and knew he had no choice but to acquiesce, or he and Simon would
end up dead. "Okay, okay. I'll do it. . . . If I can."

"What do you mean, 'if you can'?"

"It's a long way, and it's almost dark, and..."

"Look, you little son of a whore, we know how fast you can go."

He pointed to Mihalis lying on the shore. "I see you already made it to the
junk pile and back with that Goddamn bulletproof piece of shit."

They started to leave. "Before dawn, Core!" The man passed a finger across
his throat.

∾∾

Elliot had run from the compound, crossing the plain to the conveyor in
the distance. He knew it would provide the necessary cover and take him back
to the helmet and the kayak. Once the rebels' escape was discovered, the soldiers
would go after the missing truck, not him.

These people aren't trackers.

In an hour, he had reached the point where the conveyor began to drop
over the hill. Down on the flat by the river, he could see a patrol at the site of
the attack, perilously close to where his boat was hidden. The soldiers, however,
were just standing around. He waited and watched. Above him the conveyor
rumbled continuously, moving coal downhill.

Nightfall. The soldiers mounted in their truck and rolled north on 26. Elliot cautiously moved downhill under the conveyor. At one point, he almost ran into two guards lounging by the stanchion, but as he crouched down behind a bush, the two strolled off. He ran to the ditch and jumped down. The kayak was still there. He dragged it out. Once he was at the river's edge, he changed into river gear and stuffed his clothes into the back of the New Vision. As he paddled out into the current, he saw the lights of approaching trucks.

He had escaped death. Training and conditioning had helped him. And he had been lucky. He had escaped, and now could continue in his quest for Dornblaser.

It had been like some kind of surreal exercise. A test.

∾∽

"What are we going to do?" Simon asked when the men were out of sight.

"I'll tell you what we're gonna do. We're gonna eat these beans, leave this fucking bomb right here, and go home like nothing ever happened."

"Why? Why not do what they said?"

"Simon those guys are whackos, that's why. What if there is no plan for 'the big day'? What if it's just us? We could get killed and they would just laugh."

"The National is bad. The mining is killing everything. We have the bomb. Why don't we do it, even if it only saves that little forest?"

"Look, you dumb Indian. Who do you think you're talking to? You see a bunch of other kayakers out here? Hell no! I spent my life not listening to what other people say. I've got it good here. I'm not going to kiss it all goodbye for them, or for you."

Simon was angry, and Barton could tell.

"Simon, don't you understand? It can't be stopped."

They ate the beans in silence. Simon felt as if he shouldn't eat. One wasn't supposed to eat until the vision quest ended. This wasn't a vision anymore though. Was it? Was it real? Finding Mihalis seemed to be a successful end to a his Vision Quest. But success should lead him back to his village, his people's way of life. Not this, a dead and violent world.

When they finished, Barton rose.

"Let's get out of here, dude. We'll be safer further upriver."

"Okay."

So they left the backpack there on the rocks and started to slowly attain upriver through the darkness. Barton led the way and the going was slow. They didn't talk.

Simon thought about his vision quest. If this was his vision, then he must be true to it. He couldn't take Barton's easy way out. As Barton made his first charge at the bottom of high falls rapid, Simon peeled out and floated back down to the pack.

⤳⤶

Simon turned up into the Big Sandy around ten-thirty. He had decided that he would head upriver, carrying Mihalis wherever necessary, for three hours or so. Then he would climb up over the canyon wall and find the great beast that tore at the land.

The backpack was in the stern of Mihalis.

what spirit the child has

⤳⤶

Two ships passing in the night.

The shock was mutual. Elliot couldn't believe his eyes, and neither could Barton. They were slowly approaching each other across Cornwall pool.

This must be Dornblaser, Elliot thought at first.

It can't be Dornblaser; he's too thin.

In the darkness, Barton couldn't make out much. Then he saw the odd profile of the helmet, and the grip of the pistol sticking out from under the life jacket.

They drew together, and stopped paddling, each examining the other. Elliot broke the ice.

"Who are you?"

Who the fuck are you?

"I'm, Barton Core. Who are you?"

"My name is Elliot Carlson, I'm looking for Pete Dornblaser."

"You're too late, he's...Wait a second, you're looking for Pete Dornblaser? Not Simon?"

Simon?

Then he understood.

"Pete's not here. Is he?"

"I . . . don't know, but I don't think so."

"Look, Barton, I need somebody to tell me what's going on around here."

Barton looked him up and down and further checked out the helmet.

"Let me guess. You're from a different time too. Aren't you?"

"Yes. I'm from 1999. Please fill me in on what's happened to the country and the world."

They drifted in the current of the pool and Barton told him.

"So where is Simon?"

"Dude, you don't want to know."

"Yes I do. It's of critical importance to me. I guess that's why I'm here."

"Oh man. . . Look, he's got a bomb and he's going to try to blow up the dragline on the north rim.

Holy Shit.

"How can I catch up with him?"

"Go to the mouth of the Sandy and then start carrying upstream."

"How much of a head start does he have?"

"About an hour, maybe more."

"Come with me."

"No. I've had enough. I'm going home."

"Where's home? So I can find you later if I need to."

"I live in an old shack by the coal conveyor at the put-in"

"I just killed four soldiers, right there, about an hour ago..."

Barton stared at him and thought: why do all these people want to fuck up my life? "Okay, I'm in. Let's go."

∾∾

Simon stuffed his gear in Mihalis and left the kayak on the rocky shore. He began climbing upward. He went barefoot and wore only his loincloth and the backpack.

He was shocked at the destruction on the Sandy. He couldn't recognize any of the rapids. Everywhere, there were huge slides of blasted rock and earth, shoved down into the canyon from above.

Certainly they wouldn't have dared to desecrate Apu Tokebelloke. That would have been a clear crime against Kijemoneto. Unthinkable.

He reached the top. In the distance, he could see bright lights. It was the great beast, and it was in the act of destroying the land. A flat plain stretched between it and him. In spite of the distance it looked immense. He took off at a trot, observing and planning as he went.

The crane was in a hole that it had dug, and it was slowly but surely enlarging the hole. The lights swung with its great arm and lit the surrounding ground for hundreds of yards. As he began to draw near, Simon swung off to the north to stay out of the sweep of the lights. Now he was only four hundred yards away. He lay on his stomach and looked at the beast, studying it.

It was taking huge chunks of rock and earth with every sweep, drop, and pull of its arm. The scoop was big enough, thought Simon, to swallow up ten cabins in one bite.

Near where the arm left the giant housing of the beast, there was a window. Inside the window was a dim light. A man sat inside, pulling levers.

Simon was surprised at his own stupidity. Of course, there would have to be a person to run the beast. How to kill it without killing the man? He couldn't bring himself to do it. He had never killed a man. It was only right to kill if one killed on his own lands, repulsing an invading warrior who threatened his life or the lives of family. He was on his lands, but was the man threatening his life? No. Somehow, he would have to get the man outside the crane, then destroy it with the bomb.

Simon ran to the edge of the pit and crouched down. The hum of the beast's engines reverberated from inside it. The arm and bucket made loud clanking and pounding noises. The pit was much deeper than he had thought. Much too deep to jump down into. To his left, he could see the sloping path the beast had made down into the pit. The area was lit by smaller lights, but there were no windows and nobody in sight. Simon ran to the opening and headed down the slope towards the crane. Its grand size dwarfed him and he began to have doubts that the small bomb could damage it.

The beast stood on two pairs of thick legs, which in turn stood on two long, thick plates of metal that ran between the legs. He could see now how the beast could walk. It would lift one set of the legs and still be supported by the others. At each end of the plates were massive offset extensions that helped the beast to balance while it took a step. He could see its tracks underneath it and behind it. Simon walked underneath the beast to where one of the legs went up inside it. The leg had ladder rungs. He climbed up and stepped on to a ledge that ran around the opening for the legs. There was a doorway leading inside, and a stairway leading up to another level. As he climbed the steps, the sound grew to a thunderous roar. There were spinning belts and pulleys and smaller noises coming from every direction. A railed walkway led to another doorway and past it another stairway going up. At the top, a narrow hallway led to a closed door. Carefully, he opened the door.

In the control room of the power station, dozens of video monitors were being ignored by a sleepy crew of six men and women. One of the screens showed the operator's booth in the dragline on the North Rim, some ten miles away. The man operating the dragline was fiftyish and scrawny. At night, he worked alone, an eight hour shift that started at 10 p.m. and ended at six in the morning. Dozens of massive earth movers buzzed around the dragline when it was time to move coal to the conveyor. But at the moment, the dragline was removing overburden.

The man running the dragline wasn't in his seat, he wasn't in the booth. He was out in the darkness, a hundred yards from the pit. He was on his stomach, arms and legs tied behind his back with a section of thin electric cable.

Simon ran back to the dragline and climbed up inside. On the engine room level, he found what he'd been looking for -- the massive gears that made the legs move.

––

"Hardessy, look."

The operator wasn't in his seat in the dragline.

"How long's he been gone?"

"I don't know, he's probably taking a piss."

"He didn't call in. You know he's got to call in before he gets up for any reason."

"I know, but he's just taking a piss. Get off my back."

The screen went to snow.

––

Simon had never witnessed an explosion. One second he was running into the darkness, the next he was surrounded with light and lifted off of his feet by the blast. He was thrown through the air and landed hard on the broken soil. Pieces of metal rained from the sky and clattered to the ground all around him. Ears ringing, he turned and looked at the flaming mass that seconds before had been a fifty million dollar dragline. Gaining his bearings, he got to his feet and started to run back towards the Sandy. In the distance behind him, lights from approaching trucks stabbed at the darkness.

Simon saw the two trucks roaring off to his left as he ran.

He was afraid, but he wasn't. He was tired, but he wasn't. He was high on what he'd done, but he wasn't. He wasn't anything. What did it all mean? Barton was right. It was only revenge. It didn't change anything. They would build another beast.

Kijemoneto, why have you brought me here? What am I? Is this just a vision, or is it real? Now there is nowhere to go. Nowhere safe. It does not matter.

I do not want to live. I want the vision to end.

Now the truck lights had split, and one was racing back towards him in the darkness. To the east, a faint lightening of the sky foretold the coming of day. Simon paused for a second, looking.

Suddenly, another light erupted to the southeast, a huge flare shooting into the sky.

It was the power station. The Big Day had begun.

Simon stared, transfixed with the sight. The dragline was still aflame, and now much further into the distance behind it was this newer, and much larger, display of fire. He tore himself away from the spectacular view. The truck was continuing towards him. He was now at the rim of the Sandy gorge. But he was lost. This wasn't where he had climbed up. Looking around, he realized that the truck, was coming from where he'd climbed up. He started to run down into the gorge. He would have to make his way downstream to where he'd left Mihalis when he got to the bottom. He stopped and looked down, straining his eyes to see in the darkness. He felt something. Now a searchlight strobed through the night, sweeping down to the river below. There, half covered with black slag, were the tops of the huge boulders of Apu Tokebelloke, Big Splat. The river was diverted to the right of the slag demi-dam. The waters no longer spoke to him, nor would they to anyone. The great speaker had been silenced. There was no hope left. Simon sank to his knees in the slag, and started to slowly slide down hill. He didn't care. He fell to his side and began to cry.

The searchlight found him, and then the bullets began to strike the slag around him. One tore into his arm, almost ripping it from his body. He didn't feel the pain. He was no longer there. He was somewhere else, where the world was still alive. He was playing in the river with his father, surfing the waves, screaming with joy. Flipping over and taking a drink of water before rolling up. The water quenching his thirst. The water giving life. The water being life itself.

Elliot ran up behind the truck and started firing. All six of the soldiers had been shooting at Simon and had their backs to him. Gripping the machine pistol tightly with both hands, he swept back and forth until the clip was spent. They all died quickly.

He looked back and saw the other truck's lights now turn in the distance. No time wasted, he bounded down the slag to Simon. He was unconscious and bleeding. He would at best, lose the arm, but would probably die. The boy looked so young and helpless. He took his river belt and made a tourniquet to staunch the flow of blood.

Damn it all to Hell!

He threw Simon over his shoulder and began angling slowly across and down the embankment. Simon's arm dangled uselessly in front of him. He didn't think he could make it to the river.

Got to make it. It's his only hope. Got to keep going. When he reached the river, Barton was there guarding the kayaks. Barton was terrified. "Is he dead?"

"I don't think so."

Then they heard it; the unmistakable 'whump whump whump' of an approaching helicopter.

The helicopter was coming downstream through the canyon, flying low, probing the darkness with a searchlight. The light swept over them, their kayaks were on either side of Mihalis and they were both seated, holding on to their paddles and reaching across to hold Simon's near lifeless form erect in Mihalis. The guns of the helicopter opened up on them and Elliot felt himself exploding into a billion pieces, immersed in a great bathing flash of white light.

The pilot of the helicopter was blinded by the flash and felt the engines go dead, and he fell. The helicopter dropped like a rock into the river and yet another explosion shook the early morning sky.

☙❧

The sun blazed in his eyes. The searing pain he had felt in his back had quickly and mysteriously vanished. He realized that he had been feeling through the material of his pants for something in his pocket. Why? There was nothing in his pockets. The sun became a drop of water, falling away from him. He awoke from the dream and slowly remembered where he was and what had happened.

"Simon!"

He stood on the lip of the dry falls and threw another log into the swirling waters. It was sloshed around and around and finally sucked downwards into the vortex. When it disappeared, he turned around and watched the boiling water emerge from below the ledge. This log, like all the others, did not reappear. Once again he debated throwing himself into the swirl. He had no idea how long he had been unconscious. One day? Two? Possibly three? What if he went in and came out somewhere else other than where his son had ended up? It was too big a chance to take. There was another way.

Got to go home.

Pete stumbled and clawed his way through the rhododendron thickets and up and down over boulders until he reached the junction of the Gauley and the Meadow River. There he turned uphill and hiked up out of the canyon. The birds sang and the squirrels hurried about hoarding nuts for the winter, all acting as if he weren't there. He, too, felt as if he were not there, as if it were all a bad dream. What would await him when he reached his home? More sadness? He knelt to drink from a stream. The reflection in the water was that of a man much older than himself. Gaunt, dirty, shaggy. Eyes hollow and without hope, filled only with rage and desperation.

Fall was coming on fast. He headed northward and the weather turned stormy. Rain fell nonstop for days. River and stream crossings became more and more difficult. Lightning fell all around him, thunder pounding in his head. He spent a sleepless night huddled against a sycamore, rose and stumbled onward, half hallucinating. Iroquois ran from tree to tree. Bahlum Xoc stepped naked and bleeding into his path and disappeared. Invisible hands clutched at his throat trying to choke the wind out of him.

He stopped and tried to forage for some berries and nuts. Though he was weak with hunger, he had no appetite. He could hardly eat. A high ridge lay in his northward path. Pete drew upon his reserves of strength and will to climb it. At the top, he felt dizzy and collapsed to his hands and knees. The world was spinning. He found himself thinking back to something that Howard had once said:

"All accidents, on the river and off, can be traced backwards by the participant, to a single incident, the source of the accident. It always begins with something that diverts the participant from the preconceived course."

What had brought him to this point, where he lay on a ridge top, at death's door? Was it the injury of the student that closed his paddling school? No. He would have taken the time off to accompany Howard to Africa anyway. It was, as it had always been, his discovery of Mihalis. He felt at this moment, even more than before, that Mihalis was malevolent and selfish.

The dizziness vanished. The world became clear and in focus once again. He rose to his feet and looked out over the valleys that stretched out below him. Treetops splashed with fall colors waved gently in the wind. The world was alive, breathing. He was alive. He knew that Simon was alive.

"Mihalis, I will destroy you!"

CHAPTER 13 — THE CITY

Salt water.

He gagged. His eyes burned with it, although he could not see. His paddle wasn't in his hands, and he was upside down. The spraydeck was off and the boat was full of water.

"Never bail out. It's always better to roll." Howard's words came to him and he waved his arm again and again. Sweeping motions. Slowly, the kayak rolled up. and then the stern started to sink down, the water rushing to the back.

It was dark. His vision was returning to him, but it was still dark. He realized it was night. A grayness on the horizon prefaced the coming dawn. Eyes now focusing. His paddle floated nearby but out of reach.

A call for help, hacking and coughing, spitting out salt water. It was Barton. Another voice, trying to calm him, a voice unknown to him. A young voice.

"Barton relax. It is okay, we are not in current."

"Simon! You're alive!"

"I believe so...."

"But your arm?"

"Who put this strap on me?"

Elliot, tired of fighting with the half sunken boat, slid out. He held the grab loop and collecting his paddle, swam toward the voice.

"I did. I am Elliot."

"Where did you come from?"

"Where the hell are we?" Barton's impatience and stress was peaking.

Elliot interjected. "Let's help each other get these boats drained out and collect the gear. Then we'll talk. I have a feeling I know where we are."

"I'm not sure I want to know."

Elliot looked at Simon's arm. It was like nothing ever happened. He glanced at Mihalis and suddenly felt that it was looking back at him. A shiver ran through him. He looked at Mihalis and said, "Howard sends his greetings."

i know who you are
you can not keep anything secret from me

"Then you know I'm here to watch over Simon and see what happens."

very well

"Who the fuck is Howard, and what are you doing? Are you talking to the kayak?

"Howard was a friend of my father. Are you my father's friend, also?" Simon was groggy with disbelief. It seemed that his vision quest had carried him beyond any believable boundaries.

"No, Simon. I never really met him. I would have liked to. Mihalis helped Howard to build my helmet. The helmet unit is what took me to your time. And Barton, yes, I was talking to the kayak. Just as I had expected, it can talk right into your brain and it can also access your thoughts."

Barton made no attempt at hiding this thought: I'm starting to feel really sorry that I met any of you.

Soon they had the boats bailed out and the straying paddles gathered up.

Simon began to remember blowing up the dragline.

Kijemoneto, where is my vision going to take me now?

"If I am correct, we are in the Atlantic Ocean off of the west coast of Africa. We are at the 'mouth' of the ocean, where it empties into a great river."

"Whoa dude. Don't you have that backwards. Oceans don't dump into rivers...

"No Barton they don't, not in our time, but we are no longer in our time."

Simon remained silent, absorbing the conversation.

"Thousands and thousands of years into the past, or the future. I'm not sure, but it doesn't really matter."

"But why? What is going to happen now?"

"You could ask our 'friend,'" he said pointing to Mihalis, but it probably wouldn't tell you, so I will. It seems that Mihalis is playing a game, a big game. Downstream, inland, there is a tower, a tower that can only be destroyed from the water. With the tower in place, water flows errantly out over this half of the continent. With the tower gone, water drains to where it needs to go to restore a proper environmental balance.

So, thought Simon, all the words when they thought he was too young to understand, all the whisperings later, all the times his mother had tried to hide tears that couldn't be explained, all the darkness in his father when there should have been light.

He looked down at the kayak in which he sat. So this is the purpose of my life, the culmination of my vision, the destination of my quest.

how well the son has prepared

Elliot looked at Simon and Mihalis and began mentally hiding his thoughts from the crystal. There was plenty to concentrate on now.

"Before the tower, there is a city, and before the city, a canyon. We must be ready."

Barton asked him if the helmet could take him home.

"I don't think so. It is only programmed to send someone to where Mihalis is. Do you really want to go back there anyway?"

"No I guess not. I'm here so that's that." Barton however, felt lost. He had loved his life there on the banks of the Cheat. No matter all that was going on around him, it was a life that he had created for himself, felt comfortable with, and enjoyed.

The sun rose over the horizon. Elliot watched its position as it began its arc, checking it against the compass on his watchband.

"Did you feel that?"

"Yes, it was the pull of a current."

Simon was right, thought Elliot, the block of water that surrounded them had shifted slightly.

"Let's go," Elliot said, pointing toward the sunrise.

They started paddling. In half an hour, they could feel the current. In an hour, they could feel it surge. A little later, they were racing forward with it. Ahead, in the distance, a small rock was exposed above the surface. Instinctively, they headed toward it and eddied out behind it.

Basaltic schist, thought Elliot. "Okay, listen up. Soon this is going to get very intense. Simon, I am going to follow you and stay with you at all costs. Barton, you follow me."

"Why do I go last?"

"Mihalis is the fastest boat, and you are in the slowest. That way we will have less chance of getting in each other's way."

Simon led the way. The current was still picking up speed. Long, low ridges of stone, lying parallel to the flow, had begun to appear just above or below the surface, dividing the flow and threatening to separate them if Elliot strayed too far from Simon's route. Now, in addition to the barriers, the salt water began to slide over ledges in the bedrock, creating holes and waves. Simon turned these into an opportunity for some light-hearted play with the others soon joining him. He had to admit that it took a bit of the edge off of what was happening. But the drops increased in severity and height. The waves and holes became bigger and meaner, and now water was reentering the channel they were in from both sides. The volume of water tripled and now the holes were wide and offset. Difficult, but imperative, to avoid. On the positive side, thought Elliot, the water had perfect definition, the only turbulence being the backwash of the hydraulics. They were paddling well. Elliot and Barton both noticed how crisp and swift Mihalis was in the water, the absolute perfection of the unscratched hull aiding its ability to accelerate.

Now the river became even trickier and avoiding the holes turned into a game of chess. They found themselves having to surf waves from one side of the channel to the other, just upstream of killer recycling holes. They followed Simon through the series of surfs and ferries, each feeling that sooner or later somebody was going to miss a move and end up in one of the giant holes.

It happened. Elliot surfed too close to Simon on one of the waves and had to back off a little bit. He stalled on the wave and, caught off balance, flipped over. When he rolled, he had washed off of the wave and was dropping down into the trough of a wide, violent hydraulic. He sank in deep and came up surfing sideways. Elliot tried repeatedly to surf out of the end of hole he was facing, but each time its feeding curler denied him exit and he slid back in. Finally, he back-endered out of the hole and rolled up. Now he was on his own. Though at times he glimpsed Simon and Barton continuing the harried descent, he could not rush to catch up. He had to continue playing by the rules that the river set for them.

Slowly and carefully they weaved their way downstream. Simon looking for an an eddy so he could wait for Elliot, and Elliot wishing he could catch up.

Elliot dropped further and further back. Soon they were out of sight of each other, and he was left alone in the deadly game. Every once in a while he would see a shore eddy as he was rushed past it by the unrelenting current. After twenty minutes of being alone, he caught up with Simon and Barton who were both tumbling out of control in violent holes. Unable to stop, he paddled past. Unable to see back upstream, he had no idea how they were faring.

Now the river began to divide into narrower channels once again. The rock ledges separating the chutes were high and vertical. Elliot found himself shot into one of the channels and after several hundred yards, the rapids eased enough for him to eddy out.

What to do now? Chances were slim that Simon or Barton would end up in the same channel that he was in.

Damnation!

He continued a little further downstream and encountered an eddy from which he could climb up the separating cliff to it's top. From there he looked around. Upstream he could see the main channel dropping down over the hundreds of ledges he'd paddled through. The tops of the separating walls resembled an immense labyrinth. They extended downstream into the distance. Then he saw Simon climb to the top of one of the other walls, hundreds of yards to river left. Barton appeared a while later, much further yet off to the left. Although they couldn't hear each other, they agreed with hand signals to continue downriver in their respective chutes. In an afterthought, Elliot pointed at his watch and held up one finger, trying to say that in one hour they would repeat the process of climbing up to see where each other were. Barton mimed agreement. Simon didn't have a watch, but would try to estimate the passing of time.

Each spent the hour descending through tricky, narrow rapids in their chutes. There were no boulders, only the walls of the channels forcing maneuvers around hydraulics in the bedrock. Elliot was captivated by the perfection and beauty of the sandstone making up the cliffs. When the hour passed, he was disheartened to see that they were separated even more. Now, even communication with hand signals had become difficult. Added to this was hunger, and more, thirst. Elliot found himself weakening. It was now afternoon. When had he last eaten? Two days ago, before he'd met Howard at the river. Barton had given him water last night. He'd make it.

I have to make it.

He had an idea.

It must rain here.

He pulled his boat up into a crevice in the cliff and climbed up. Once at the top, he walked along the ridge until he found what he was looking for; a pothole full of rainwater. Brushing away mosquito larvae, he drank from cupped hands until his thirst was quenched. Looking downstream, he noticed that the plane created by the tops of the dividing walls was tilting downward at a sharper angle. The passage there would necessarily be more intense. As he readied himself in the eddy, he lowered the visor of the helmet.

READY
"Helmet, river screen on."
RIVER SCREEN ON

The visor came alive with a vibrant overlay of the river and a flood of data around the perimeter.

It took him a while to adjust to using the screen but quickly he adapted and found that the recommended routes were selected much more quickly by the computer than by his brain. He began to follow the route provided, explicitly and exclusively. Elliot found himself truly appreciating it's aid, as the tightly twisting and curving canyon was dropping steeply through raging class IV and V rapids. He was paddling hard, bracing, flipping and rolling. He was thrown hard into the walls and riding the pillows through the turns, having only enough time to ready himself for the next opposing turn. Eddies flashed by in the periphery, never enough time to grab one to rest.

Suddenly the channel straightened and began a headlong rush downward. Ahead was a turn in the canyon. My Lord, thought Elliot, it's going to be impossibly tight. Shit, which way does the river go? Then he saw that the rock in the wall ahead was different in color and texture. It wasn't sandstone. It was huge rectangular blocks, laid in courses, and the river didn't turn. The flow went straight into it, and down.

60 SECONDS TO OVERRIDE
NAVIGATION QUESTIONABLE

❧

Simon was charging ahead, down the steep ramp, and noticed the wall ahead too late to do anything about it. The water boiled and frothed around him. For a second he surfed the pillow against the wall and then was flipped and tumbled back into the onrushing water coming from upstream. He was taken deep. It was dark all around him. Mihalis was clanging off of the walls and the ceiling of a tunnel. He held his breath as long as he could...

All Barton could think about was his bad luck.

If I had been born in either one of their times, would I have left home, travelled through time and space looking for trouble like this salt water toilet? Fuck no!!

The water drove his boat vertically against the wall and the pressure smashed the deck almost to the hull, blowing off his sprayskirt in the process. The kayak instantly filled with water and sank.

I, am, so, royally, screwed.

❧❦

Everyone faces moments of true desperation in their lives. Moments when all hope is lost, as if blown away by an evil wind.

He waded around in the ashes of the cabin, soot on his cheeks where he'd tried to wipe away the tears. It was impossible to tell if the bones were those of Sana, Kiri, and Thepa. To hope that they weren't was not bringing him any comfort.

Pete had blamed himself over and over. He should have killed all the Iroquois there under the overhang, or died trying. Kiri should have been able to defend the family with the SKS. Was he caught sleeping or unawares? Not like him, he thought. He tried to imagine what the rush on the cabin had been like, their last moments.

Stop It! Got to concentrate. Got to center.

He retrieved the padlock key from it's secret hiding place in the stones behind the cabin and strode to the trailer. It was badly burned on the outside. The bastards had torched the firewood stored underneath, but hadn't been able to get inside. Some of the plastic kayaks had been melted by the heat, but most items were intact.

He pulled his best Augsburg I off of the racks. It was a vacuum bagged, epoxy-Sglass kayak built by Jackson Wright way back in the mid-seventies. It was an ugly off-green color and a bit heavy. But it was as tough as the rocks, off of which, Pete had bounced it countless times in years past. It would make it. He selected one of his finest New World paddles, and, on a whim, a bright white life jacket he hadn't used since he'd been sent back in time. He popped a fresh clip into the Smith and Wesson and threw two more, along with some jerky and pemmican, into a small dry bag. He slipped on a pair of river shorts and the jaguar moccasins the Mayas had given him as a going away present and then dug into the back of the trailer for the box. He opened it carefully and lifted out the helmet. It still shone like the day it was made.

Pete assembled the gear outside the trailer and then locked it back up and hid the key. He knew the chances of being able to return were slim to none, but he didn't want anybody in the trailer, ever. What would become of it? Would it be found by white settlers in another eight hundred years? Or be carried off by some future flood to be smashed on the rocks in the canyon below? Or would it disappear once he left this time? Who the hell knows?

Pete put on his spraydeck and strapped on the pistol in it's shoulder holster. He slipped the life jacket over it. He looked at the helmet. Would it work after eighteen years in the box?

Pete sat in the kayak and held the paddle in his hands. He took a last look around at the majestic forest that had been his home. He thought of the magic times he had spent there, living free, in love with his wife, raising their son. It was all gone for him now. There was nothing left but a hollow ache. And an urge for . . .

He slowly slid the helmet down over his head.

READY

Howard knows his shit.

"Helmet, Mihalis track and transfer."

The forest dissolved in front of him and he was melting through space. Disjointed fragments, atoms spinning, blackness, then gagging, coughing, choking on salt water. He swam to the surface. The Augsburg was floating half full of water. The water was placid. It rolled in gentle swells. He felt dizzy and nauseous. He held on to the kayak and waited for dizziness to pass. His paddle floated nearby. He felt better and swam over to it and brought it back to the kayak. Treading water, Pete tilted the kayak up on edge and scooped most of the water out with his free hand. He mounted from the stern and slid into the cockpit. It took another ten minutes to scoop out the rest of the water with his hands and by then he felt normal, his headache gone.

So this is the way it's going to go, eh, Mihalis?

Something deep inside him began to awaken. Somehow, he knew where he was. Somehow, he was no longer Pete Dornblaser.

But I am. You've changed the rules of the game. So, no more rules....

❧

The third unconscious body had been pulled away from the recycling boil at the base of the wall. Mike Clark had retrieved them. Retrieved them by kayaking into the boil himself and clipping a line to their life jackets and tow-ing them out with paddle power. It had taken superhuman effort. But Mike Clark was no longer human. He was a shell without a soul. He dragged this last one to the barge that awaited a safe distance away in the foaming moat that ringed the city. The barge handlers stared blankly at the dark young man as they pulled him onto the decking and laid him out alongside the others. Salt water seeped from their mouths and the older one started to retch and convulse. The handlers rowed the barge towards an opening in the city wall. Clark turned to the work of retrieving the three kayaks from the boil. Clinging grimly to a dim spark that remained in his brain, he smiled, thinking that this time three kayak-ers had arrived simultaneously. Before, it had been one by one, almost always dead. To top it all, one of them had arrived in the crystal. The Holder would be angered. He was always angered with the arrival of the crystal.

જ્જી

The barge handlers waited passively at the wide opening. Elliot was regain-ing consciousness. He was lying on his back, looking up at the midday sun. It glared through the tinted visor of the helmet. He rolled onto his side and looked at Simon who lay beside him. The boy's eyes were closed, but he was breathing. Elliot looked up and saw that the barge handlers were American-looking men dressed in tattered and stained cotton shirts and gray tattered pants cut off at the knees. Both wore rough leather boots, equally ancient. They had a glazed look on their faces. They reminded him of figures in a wax museum. Then he noticed a large man with an escort of oriental guards rushing towards them. The man in the lead was dressed in dark blue silk robes that flowed to the floor. The guards were dressed more modestly -- rough robes under woven bamboo armor, swords in lacquered scabbards at their sides. The man had jet black hair and a long nose that ended in a nefarious smile. He knew that smile. It was the same smile worn by Braila and Agafya. The man said something to the guards in a Chinese dialect and six of them stepped onto the barge. Two each, they grabbed them by their arms and lifted them to their feet. Elliot feigned unconsciousness. Simon didn't have to. Barton should have. "Let go of me you fucks!" This was met with a hard jab with the palm of the hand, right to Barton's left temple and he was once again unconscious.

Again the man spoke to the guards in Chinese. He was looking them over carefully as the guards carried them off. Once a safe distance away, Elliot stole a quick glance back and saw that the man had remained at the opening with a pair of guards, and was staring out at the moat. Then, out in the water, Elliot glimpsed a kayaker pass by the opening, with Mihalis towed behind.

He began to watch where they were being taken. They were in a long, cavernous hallway built of gray stone, very finely cut, and laid in straight courses. On both sides of the walkway there were channels brimming with water, rushing in the same direction they were walking. Every fifty yards or so, water fell in slender streams from round holes in the ceiling and landed in the channels. He searched his memory and drew a blank. This area hadn't appeared in the sonar photos; they must be at a lower level. After several hundred meters, the hallway was interrupted by a stairway rising upwards. They were taken up the stairs, and another hallway, it's ceiling slightly lower, ran at right angles to the one below.

Elliot noticed that the guards didn't speak among themselves or even acknowledge their presence. Like zombies, thought Elliot.

He realized one reason why the hallways seemed so big. They were the only ones there. Arched openings on the left and right led into large empty galleries, no sign of occupants or life. In the top of each arch there was a piece of crystal embedded in the keystone. At the end of the hall was a spiral staircase made of stone, going up and down. In the center of the staircase was a thick round column of laid stone. Elliot noticed more crystal laid into the stones. As they started to ascend, Elliot could see the length of the hall they had been carried down, and at it's far end lay an identical spiral staircase. They went up and up. At the top of the staircase was a circular hallway surrounding it. Arched openings radiated out from the hallway. More crystal.

The guards took them through one of the archways into a smaller hall. The hall soon emptied into a beautiful garden with a large stone-roofed pavilion in it's center. In the middle was a huge round bed covered with brightly colored silk sheets and cushions. They were deposited on the soft bedding. Without so much as a look back, the guards marched off.

When they had gone, Elliot rose and checked on Simon. He pinched the back side of Simon's left calf and the boy flinched with pain. His eyes began to open and he looked up at Elliot.

"Are you okay?"

"Yes. I think I am. Where are we?"

"We're in the city. We almost drowned passing under the wall, but we're here, and alive."

"Barton too?"

"Yes, he's right here. He is passed out now, but he was conscious before we were brought up here."

Simon started to trail off again. Let him sleep, thought Elliot. He hadn't slept in two days. His pituitary gland was probably pumping melatonin into his system.

He took off the helmet and began to set it down on the bed. Thinking better of it, he clipped it to his river belt.

I'd best keep this with me at all times.

He walked out into the lush garden. He couldn't recognize the plants and trees, but many were bearing fruits. He began to nibble on something resembling a bright red pear. It was delicious and he ate three.

He strayed through the garden to the circular wall that ran around it. They were several levels above the courtyards. Checking the compass on his watchband, he saw that they were at the northern end of the city. Elliot now began to orient his present position to what he remembered from the satellite photos. Each of the spiral staircases rose to a height greater than the rest of the city. The garden he was in was similar to the other eight that radiated out from the hall surrounding the stairwell. Off in the distance, he could see another asterisk shaped garden complex, radiating out from the other spiral staircase. Above where the staircase would be, water fountained upwards into the sky in a thick column. He looked back to where their hallway had emerged into the garden and saw an identical fountain above the staircase they had ascended. He walked back past the pavilion, where Simon still slept, and looked out over the wall at the other side of the garden. From there, he could see down to the moat that circled the city. Beyond, he could see withered trees and clumps of grass in the sand.

The water circled the city slowly but steadily. He assumed that it was flowing toward some exit port at the downstream end. It struck him that the water was probably sweeping around the far side of the city in the moat at a similar speed.

Small, shallow pools of water dotted the city and he concluded that the stone rooftops were also a series of reservoirs. Some were fed by water falling from carved stone spouts, draining water from higher rooftops. Others had water bubbling up into them from hidden sources.

Elliot now followed along the garden wall back towards the hallway opening and noticed that water fell in delicate streams from the hallway roof into small pools, in recesses on either side of the doorway. He dipped a hand into the clear water and lifted it to his lips. It was fresh and cool, and he drank.

ॐ

The tall man in the blue robes strode down the hallway, guards in tow, to the spiral staircase. Upward, the staircase would lead to where Elliot was drinking water. Instead, he went down. At the bottom of the staircase, another hallway stretched into the darkness. The guards halted and the man continued alone. As he walked into the darkness, he felt the temperature in the hallway rise, and he stopped.

"Father, I am here."

"Tell me, Rekh, what has come to pass?"

"Three men, in three kayaks, have passed under the wall. One of the kayaks was the crystal."

"So, the Pilot has arrived. Bring him to me."

"Father, they arrived almost at once, all floating unconsciously in the boil and I am not..."

"You are not sure which came in the crystal."

"No Father, I know it is most unfortunate."

"Unfortunate? The tower is in danger."

"Yes. I understand, but I feel that it can be easily discovered which, is the One."

"You, examined them?"

"Of course Father."

"And it was not clear to you which was the Pilot?"

"One showed much spirit."

"Tell me about him."

"He is young though one is even younger. He has light hair and is quite strong. He is poorly mannered."

Rekh felt himself beginning to sweat in the dankness of the hallway.

"One was barely breathing."

"Tell me about him."

"He is young, with a dark skin. He is strong."

"And the other?"

"The older, however, was very well equipped."

"The older came to protect the Pilot. If the Pilot was the older, he would have come alone."

"But what if that were a trick of his, to deceive us?"

Mize pondered his son's statement.

What a pity that he was powerless against the crystal. All could be killed, but that would solve nothing. The Pilot would be reborn and would return in a different form. How many sons had he lost tracking the present form of the Pilot through time? Four. It was a high cost to pay. Too high.

The crystal had succeeded in confusing him. If he could only achieve a clearer sense of the passing of time on the plane of the Pilot. To end the nightmare, and render powerless the crystal forever, the Pilot had to be killed by drowning. Drown the undrownable.

The moment was critical. The tower was vulnerable, but the Pilot was in his grasp.

Once again, the salt was poisoning the land. When completed, the rains would no longer fall. The sun would serve only to bake the life out of the earth. Then his eternal reign would be secured.

Yes, the Pilot was in his grasp.

"Rekh, I trust that you will do your best to determine who is who."

"Yes, Father."

He turned to go, anxious to leave.

"I have not dismissed you."

"Pardon me, Father. There is something more?"

"You have been preparing yourself?"

"I paddle two circuits of the city daily, Father. I feel very strong."

"I hope it is not necessary for you to go."

Rekh choked on the thought. There would be no returning once he passed through the exit portal. An even worse fate, however, would be to fail his father, and allow the Pilot to slip past.

Mize felt the thoughts of his son.

"Go now."

"Yes, Father."

Once he had left, Mize engaged himself in deep thought, contemplating his next moves and those of the enemy. He had just begun to attain the inner balance he sought when he felt the slow rumbling.

❧•❧

Elliot was creeping down the hallway at the top of the spiral staircase. He had a hand on the wall and felt it more than he heard it. There was a slight vibration. He put his ear to the floor. The rumbling turned into a vibration and then a hum. Something was moving within the city. Something big. But where?

The humming brought no clue. Think. To set the entire city reverberating, it would have to come from down low, in the center. Then he remembered the metal cylinder.

He ran silently down the spiral staircase until he came to the level of the hall they had been carried through. There was no one in sight. He took off at a run down the hallway. He looked back just in time to see the man in the blue robes ascending the staircase from below. He ducked through one of the arched doorways and ran across the open gallery to the far side. He slowed to a walk and crossed through it to where he was stopped by a channel of rushing water. The vibration was now much more noticeable. It seemed to be coming from behind the wall to the right, but there was no doorway. The channel of water flowed under the wall with no clearance. But a translucent glow shone through the rushing water, contrasting with the dark gloom of the gallery. Elliot was afraid to try flushing through. What if it shot him out into the river?

He dipped a hand into the water and brought it to his lips. The water was fresh. He unclipped the helmet from his belt and slid it on, just in case. He lowered the visor.

READY

He threw himself into the flume and was shot under the wall. When he surfaced, he was on the other side and was rushing towards a metal grate. He tried to grab hold of the side of the channel, but there was nothing but smooth stone and he was carried into the grate. Though the force of the water held him against it, he was able to inch his way up the grate. Finally, he stepped out onto the walkway beside it.

He had found the source of the noise. He was now in an immense round chamber, over fifty yards in diameter. The walls rose high above him, but there was no ceiling. He could see the late afternoon sky. Channels of water, like the one he had washed in on, entered at even intervals and flowed around the perimeter. Each hit a grate like the one he had climbed, and then fell downward through drains to some other level.

Dominating the chamber was the metal cylinder, and it was spinning. It was the source of the noise. Steam rose from the space between the walkway and the cylinder.

Elliot removed the helmet and clipped it to his river belt. Then he walked around the cylinder on the stone walkway. He was amazed at its grand proportion. On the far side was an arched doorway leading into another hallway. But more interesting was a delicate catwalk leading out over the middle of the cylinder. At the end of the catwalk, a ladder dropped down into the opening in the center. Cautiously, he walked out onto the catwalk and looked down. The colossal grayish cylinder was spinning rapidly, the screeching roar deafening. The ladder dropped from the end of the catwalk to a platform suspended halfway up from the base.

Elliot forced himself to think. What in hell is this? What powers the spinning motion? Then it came to him. The spinning was generated by water power.

The water flowing through the moat must be channeled under the city and into the fins on the outside of the cylinder. Somehow, it achieved immense energy. Then the final piece came into the puzzle.

My God, it's a time machine.

Relativity experts after Einstein had theorized that a spinning metal cylinder of sufficient mass could distort the flow of time, relative to the perspective of the participant within the cylinder. Due to the practical restrictions of experimentation, no results of dramatic proportion had ever been achieved.

This cylinder, thought Elliot, must have sufficient mass. He stared down at the platform and thought he was experiencing an optical illusion. The spinning motion of the gray metal was drawing his line of sight with it, making it difficult to focus on the platform. In addition, for some reason, he was seeing red. He moved his eyes away from the platform and the red no longer appeared. He looked back down at the platform and the redness showed again, now brighter. The spinning of the cylinder was making him dizzy and he grasped the railing of the catwalk with both hands. Slowly, the red image came into focus. It was a person, dressed in bright red. He shut his eyes, not believing, then opened them again. It was a bald man clothed in a red mantle. Around his neck hung a shining crystal disk. He brushed a hand across it and the intonation of the cylinder changed slightly. The cylinder began to slow down and the man climbed the ladder with an agility that surprised Elliot.

He took a few steps back on the catwalk to make room for him. The man stepped onto the catwalk and looked at Elliot. His face was large and round, eyes kind and illuminated.

"My son, welcome to Bwuy."

❧☙

Simon woke to the Barton shaking.

"Dude, Elliot is gone."

He rose slowly and looked around. The sun was setting and a gentle breeze blew through the pavillion. "We will look for him."

"No, I don't want to go anywhere. This place gives me the creeps."

"But it is beautiful here." Simon removed his helmet and set it on the bed. "Are you a hungry as I am?"

"Yeah, but where are we going to find something to eat?"

"We are surrounded with food. Look."

"How do you know it's safe to eat?"

"Can it be any worse than the beans?"

"Alright, you try first. And if it's okay, I'll eat too."

They wandered through the garden, foraging as they went. Simon sampled a variety of fruits and Barton followed his lead. A full moon was rising and began to light the city anew with its glow. Now, curiosity overtook hunger and they began to look around the city from the confines of the garden wall. Below them, and across the courtyard, was a girl, half walking, half dancing away from them. Her dress streamed and flowed with her movements. She disappeared through a doorway on the far side of the courtyard.

"Let's go find her bro."

"I thought you didn't want to go anywhere."

"Well, I feel better now that we ate, you know. I'm charged up."

"I think that if we go somewhere, it should be to find Elliot."

An uncontrollable urge was waking within Barton. "Okay, let's go."

Barton removed his helmet and put it on the bed. Simon put his on.

"Barton, perhaps we should keep our river gear with us, in case we have to leave.."

"Leave? We don't even know where the boats are. Besides, it's night. I'm not going anywhere at night." And if you want to walk around with you boating gear on like a total geek, go ahead.

They made their way down the spiral staircase. Where it emptied into the main hallway Barton stopped and turned to Simon. "You go that way and I'll go this way. The moonlight was lighting the far side of a gallery through an archway leading to the courtyard. Simon looked at him. He could tell what Barton was up to. "Okay. If I find Elliot, we will meet you back up in the garden."

"Got it." Barton took off at a trot through the gallery and Simon started down the long, dark, hallway.

Barton crossed the courtyard and went through the doorway where the girl had disappeared. The moonlight shone at the far end of the gallery within and he crossed quickly to the other side. He stopped at the archway and looked out. It was another courtyard, dominated by a large fountain in its center. The girl was seated with her back to him, facing the fountain. He crept silently across the paving stones. She was staring into the water, a small pile of pebbles by her side on the fountain wall. She didn't hear his approach over the splash of the water. He stopped behind her, contemplating his next move. She reached down into the pool and retrieved another pebble from the water. Her skin looked like velvet in the moonlight, and her diaphanous dress did little to hide the curves of her body. She turned to place the pebbles with the others and she saw him. For a moment, she was startled and rose a hand in front of her face. Her eyes poured over him with fear, and with wonder.

"What are yo doing?"

"I am collecting pretty little stones." She looked around as if, possibly, she had been caught in the midst of some wrongdoing.

"It's okay that I take them. Who are you?"

"I, am.. Barton. Who are you?"

Looking down at the paving stones she replied, "I am Poulee."

"You speak English."

"What is English?"

"The language we are speaking in."

"It is the language I know. The only language."

"You live here, in this city?"

"There is nowhere else."

"How old are you?" Barton was guessing seventeen or eighteen. Her body was ripe with post-pubescent voluptuousness. Her face was an exotic mix of features he had never seen before. She wore her hair in dozens of tight braids.

"I do not know. How old are you?"

"I am twenty two."

"You seem very young to me."

"Where is your family?"

"I am alone. I have no family."

No family, that's good.

"How do you live?"

She laughed winsomely. "I eat fruit in the gardens. I sleep where I like. I am happy." Her eyes crossed a bit and her brows arched. "Where have you come from?"

"It wasn't easy. We were almost killed."

"You came with others?"

He was enchanted with the surprise in her inquisition.

"Yes, I brought two others with me."

"So you, are the leader?"

"Yeah."

"But why have you come?"

"To destroy the tower."

"The tower?"

"You've never heard of the Tower?"

She looked at her feet, as if sad to disappoint him. "No, I'm sorry. I only know of what is here." Her eyes brightened. "But tell me."

"Well, the tower is a threat to the world. It has to be destroyed. It can only be destroyed from the river."

She shifted on the wall and her breasts heaved against the cloth of her dress. He felt himself becoming aroused. Ready for her. She was falling for his story. She looked at him with more awe as he went on.

"I was chosen to destroy the tower. I have been preparing all my life for this."

"Chosen? By who?"

"By god. My father was a great kayaker. He was sent a crystal kayak. In the kayak, I will destroy the tower."

Her eyes now seemed to genuinely show her amazement. She was enthralled with him. It was time to make his move. "I really like you Poulee."

"Why do you say that?"

He leaned forward and kissed her lips. She didn't return the kiss, but did not pull away. He kissed her again and this time felt her willingness. He kissed her deeply, and groped at her breasts and thighs. She moaned with abandon, and he worked a hand under her dress. Her eyes closed, she conceded to his advances. She was helpless to him and he laid her back on the fountain wall. He had never seen a girl more beautiful than she. He stepped out of his shorts and leaned over her.

"No Barton. Please, no......"

He paid no heed.

ঔৎৣ৶

"Who are you?" He had to shout to be heard.

"Ah. Much more important is who you are. I see a repentant man, very wise for his years. And inquisitive too, aren't we? I see you entered under the wall."

His long, slender fingers pointed to the water dripping from Elliot's spraydeck onto the catwalk.

As the cylinder spun to a stop, the screeching was becoming unbearable.

"Come with me, son. We will converse as we walk." Elliot led the way off the narrow catwalk to the doorway.

"You are impressed with my machine? What is your name?"

"It's amazing to say the least. I am Elliot Carlson."

"I am Zul."

"You are God, aren't you?"

"It is a long story, but, yes, to you I am 'God.'"

"Tell me please. I want to know."

Zul stopped walking and looked at Elliot. His eyes sparkled, even in the gloom of the hallway. His round face was glazed and animated. He slowly reached out and touched Elliot. Elliot felt an intrusion in his mind, as if someone had found and read a young girl's diary, discovering all of her secret thoughts, memories and feelings. The intrusion withdrew.

"Now I understand you better. I think that you have now realized your quest. You are the seeker of knowledge. The retainer of knowledge. Your methods at one time were questionable, but you have a good heart. You have reached out sufficiently to arrive here. I will not disappoint you. You merit an explanation."

They continued to walk, and the hallway emptied into an expansive gallery with soaring arches.

"So what do you think of my city?"

"It is truly magnificent." And it really was. It was perfect in proportion and construction. It had a forlorn grace unequaled in anything he'd ever seen in his world travels.

"It is not always lonely here. I live here in another time. A time full of laughter and life."

"Who built it?"

"That is going to be hard for you to understand."

Their voices echoed in the expansive gallery as they made their way across it."I was the architect. Everything you see, however, is not from this Earth. It was, shall I say, transported here?"

"But how?"

"The application of thought. I know this is a difficult concept for you. More important though, is the site of the city. On this planet, which is quite old, mind you, there are special places. Magical places. These places did not always exist but evolved over time. Bwuy is one of these places. The water you drank in the garden, that is now part of you as you are part of it, is water from the head of Bwuy. Bwuy means 'the light within.' Another of these special places is downstream from here. It is where the father of the boy you have come to protect found my mischievous angel, Mihalis."

Zul shook his head sadly.

"You know something of what Mihalis told another. This other is very keen indeed." Zul looked down at the helmet hanging from Elliot's river belt.

"Thought. Thinking is everything. It can be a world unto itself." Zul stopped and Elliot looked at him. "Something that we have in common, Elliot, is that the only thing over which we might have absolute control is our thoughts."

Zul seemed sad for a moment.

"As I said, I built this city with the application of thought. It was easy, compared to creating you, my children. That was difficult. It was a long, very long, process. Perhaps you might be able to imagine what it has been like for me to work so hard for something and see the end result not be what I had intended it to be."

"What happened?"

Zul sighed and looked into Elliot's eyes. "I had started alone, realizing my dream of setting human societies on the Earth. I had begun the work long before, using Bwuy as my base, and traveling backwards in time to place simple forms of life into motion. Then I made periodic voyages to tend the flocks, so to speak." Zul smiled. "Please excuse the metaphor."

They paused in the center of the gallery.

"There were problems of course. Some were solved, and some were not. But there was an element missing. At that time, a being arrived from a different world. This being, Mize, came as a bankrupt refugee and petitioned my support. He had ideas, beautiful ideas, that, at that time, I felt were ideal. I felt they would fill in the missing pieces. Instead, they became the very seeds of all evil. What he did was to convince me to add an element of pleasure to the act of reproduction. It seemed so wonderful at the time, but long before this element had reached the human level in evolution, I began to have serious doubts. However," Zul said with a sigh, "it was now too late. The pleasure principle had been deeply implanted in all earth life. There was to be no turning back. Things began to go awry."

Zul paused momentarily, as if pondering how much he should divulge. "In the beginning, there were two versions of people. Both were beautiful and dear to me. Mize saw to it that there were conflicts. A polarization where there should have been harmony. The final result was that one species ceased to exist. I cannot express the sadness that lives within me for this."

"Is Mize the devil?"

"That is one of his names. Yes. Think of all that is bad in humans. Jealousy, violence, rape, rage, aggression, infidelity, envy, hate. Things such as these were not in the original plan." Zul laughed. "But then, things never do go exactly as one plans, do they?"

They began to walk again, heading towards an archway on the far side of the gallery. A bluish light was emanating from it. Elliot wondered whether Zul was real, whether he was from this planet.

"I am not real, Elliot. Not to you. Not to this place and time. There are levels you cannot understand. So try to understand what you can. Mize was not satisfied with his success in meddling with you, my children. He has designs on the planet as well. Designs that could destroy the true god of this world."

"You mean, yourself?"

"No, Elliot. He is powerless against me. Your journey here was long and complex. It provided you with the answer every step of the way. You were merely remiss in not asking yourself the right question."

They were nearing the doorway. The light coming through the doorway now appeared like the reflection off of a swimming pool.

"Don't feel deficient, very few realize that their true god is within themselves, and all around them, throughout their entire lives."

They walked through the archway. Hovering in the air in the high-domed gallery was a giant sphere of water. Suspended in the sphere was Mihalis. On the floor below the sphere was a round pool of water held in place by carved stone blocks, Water dripped from the bottom of the sphere into the pool and also jumped up into the sphere from the pool. Elliot could sense a powerful field of energy dominating the room.

"Do you now understand?"

"Yes. It is the water."

"The water is everywhere. Even where it is almost immeasurable, it exists. It makes up the oceans, the lakes, the rivers, the clouds. It is in every living thing. Everyone knows this. But what they don't know, and refuse to feel, is that it is also alive. Sentient. Its awareness is on an entirely different level, vastly elevated. Its intellect is the same in a single molecule as it is in the greatest ocean

"Without it, the Earth would be like so many other lifeless balls floating in space. It is the heartbeat and the breath of the world. It moves in slow and deliberate paths. When it decides that some force threatens, it moves ponderously to shrug it from existence."

"As Mize threatens it now?"

"Mize, with his tower. He toys with a balance that is delicate and crucial to life on Earth."

"What is the sphere doing to Mihalis?"

"Confabulating. They are deliberating the run at the tower. Mihalis cannot leave the sphere until this is complete."

"What is being discussed? The water will help Mihalis on the way to the tower?"

"No. The water does not apply itself in that manner. No. What is passing is more of a debriefing, what you would term 'a review.'"

"I have come because Mihalis arrived. I have to scrutinize Mihalis as much as it's independence allows. I created Mihalis to deal with the menace of the tower. However, Mihalis cannot act alone against it. Mihalis needs a pilot. A willing pilot. I allotted one soul for this work. The tower has been built three times and destroyed twice, both by the same pilot soul. The pilot's recompense for his sacrifice at the tower is to be reborn. The rebirth, however, can only result in another sacrifice. Mize has become much more proficient in his methodology to detect and to ultimately destroy the pilot soul. Mihalis is running a deadly game with your young friend. His soul is not protected. But Mihalis feels that he can be slipped past the guards, where his father is too rebellious to be slipped through. I cannot stay the father's hand. What the father has done, willfully or not, must be paid for by the child."

"If you cannot stop it, what will you do?"

"Mize has a son here. He is obtuse and self-consumed, but dangerous. He is Mize's vehicle. Mize cannot rebuild the tower without such an implement as he. I feel that this moment may be used to rid the city of him. When Mihalis leaves, so must he, in pursuit.

"How did you know Mihalis was here?"

"The crystals in the walls reveal events. You know that time is linear, in respect to each observant. When Mihalis passes into this city, I know." Zul tapped the crystal disc hanging on his chest.

"What will you do now?"

"I have much to do, but the night is long. I would be pleased if you would accompany me."

Poulee ran into the darkness. She coursed through the long inky corridors until she reached the spiral staircase on the south end of the city. She stole up the staircase and ran into one of the gardens at the top. Once there, she paused to catch her breath. She closed her eyes, and when she opened them, a cloud had crossed in front of the moon. When it passed, the light blushed into the garden and she made her way to the pavilion. Rekh stepped from behind a column and slowly walked to her. She loosed the ties of his robe and ran her tongue from his navel to his as high on his chest as she could reach.

"I know which is the pilot."

"Tell me."

"Not so fast," she said, roughly pushing him onto his back on the bed. "First, you must pay."

Poulee climbed on top of him and locked him in her embrace.

"For once, your father will be glad I am here."

Elliot and Zul descended the steps until they came to a pitch-black hallway. Elliot felt the hair on his arms stiffen and rise.

"There is a polarity between myself and the holder of souls. It is best for you not to be between us."

Elliot stepped behind Zul and the pull diminish.

A dusky form began to melt out of the darkness.

"Mize, it is such a pleasure to be so near you once again."

"I dreaded your sarcasm from the first grinding revolution of the cylinder."

"And where is your houseboy, Rekh? I expected to be met by him."

"You are bold to have brought this man with you. Is he the Pilot Soul?"

"Ah, don't you know?"

"Your crystal bastard pretends a great game with them. I could kill them both."

"You can do nothing. That remains for your inept spore. If all goes well, I will not have to pay another visit to your dark time in my city."

"That is yet to be determined, Zul. May you pass a bad night."

The form melted into the darkness and was gone.

Elliot felt something brush past his feet. Zul bent down and scooped a cat from the floor.

"Don't you like cats?"

"Not really."

"They are my windows to your souls."

He stroked it, and it began to purr.

"Come with me Elliot, and we shall see what my little spy knows."

Barton returned to the garden and found neither Simon or Elliot. His high was becoming dulled with a newer sensation: paranoia. Doing her had been fun. And easy. And he was too dumb to realize it had been too easy. He stretched out on the bed and thought he would get some sleep. Sleep did not come. He was wide awake. And nervous. And afraid. He rose. He wandered through the garden, peering over the walls. Nothing. Nobody.

Barton went back down the spiral staircase to the long hall. The moonlight still beamed into the gallery through the archway. Criminals always return to the scene of the crime. No, don't want to go back out there. He eased his way down the hallway towards where he had last seen Simon.

Shit, where did he go?

He reached the mid-point of the hallway where the grand flight of steps descended to the hall below. It was dark. Guiding himself with a hand on the stone railing, at the bottom of the staircase he took an extra step down and almost fell on his face. There was the sound of water whooshing by on both sides.

This is fucking crazy. Better go back to the garden and wait.

He turned around to go back, but there was someone there. Someone in his path. Someone tall. Hands around his throat. Driving him to his knees. Dragging him along. Water. Salt water. The grip loosening on his throat. Nothing to breathe. Only water. A hand grabbing him by his hair. A knee in his back. Unable to move. Unable to breathe. Taking a deep breath, of water. Blackness within blackness, then nothing.

"Mize will try to discover the Pilot with a trick. What he does not realize is that the Pilot is not here. Mihalis has deceived him well."

"Zul, what will happen to Simon?"

"What impresses me about you, Elliot, is that you did not ask me what would happen to you."

They were walking rapidly through a series of courtyards in the moonlight. Before them, rose one of the taller towers of the city. One section of its parapet drew a jagged silhouette in the night sky.

"Vandalism." Zul pointed where the blocks were missing in the wall. Elliot suddenly recognized the French dig and the place where they had removed stones. How could that be? Was he here after the present?

"Zul, what has happened to the world?"

"Since your time? Much has come to pass. I must be careful to not tell you anything. Time is fragile. One must treat it as such, or face being forever separated from your frame of existence. Once you start down a different path, your world is lost to you." Zul paused and looked at him. "Mihalis has taken a huge risk in sending the one backwards in time to shelter the son."

"Father, are you here?"

'Yes."

"Father, the pilot is dead. I have killed him."

"How, did you kill him?"

"By drowning, Father."

"Which one?"

"The young man, with light hair."

"Tell me Rekh, how did you know that he, was the pilot?"

"He told Poulee things."

"And you trusted her. Rekh, there is an object on the floor by your feet. Pick it up."

Rekh felt around in the darkness and touched something metal on the floor. He lifted it into the pale light that struggled to penetrate the hallway. It was round, and heavy for its size.

"Go now. Confront the other two with it. Their faces will tell the truth."

"Yes Father."

"You must also ready yourself to go in the event that you fail."

"I understand."

❧❦

Simon had explored at least half of the city, moving stealthily through the shadows, climbing stairways to upper levels, and descending other stairways to the larger chambers below. It was a new experience for him. Until now, the biggest structure he had ever been in had been the dragline. This was a castle. The bedtime tales of his father came to life. There were narrow passageways leading into the grandest of galleries. Water coursing everywhere through open aqueducts.

But no sign of Elliot. Soon the dawn would come. He needed to find Mihalis and his paddle. Though he felt small in the immensity of the city, he knew that he had an important purpose. A mission. He had a feeling of urgency, and he knew that downstream lay another raw stretch of river waiting to challenge him. It would try to trick him. Try to make him swim. Try to kill him. Try to prevent him from reaching the tower. What would his father do? He would do the same that Simon was going to do. Destroy it. Destroy it with Mihalis. Ram into it with Mihalis. Unleash the power that resided within the crystal. Would the tower then fall and crush him? That didn't matter. What mattered was that he would have fulfilled a destiny created for him. His destiny. He needed to bend to his task and concentrate.

❧❦

Zul and Elliot stood on top of a tower which overlooked the moat. Below them, on the perimeter wall of the city, stood dozens of the Chinese guards. The kayaker that had pulled the two of them from the boil, slowly paddled back and forth in the moat. The barge was held more or less in the same position by slow sweeps of the handler's long oars.

"Who are these people?"

"Lost souls. I can do nothing for them."

"Why not?"

"Because they are in what you would call 'Hell.'"

"This city is Hell?"

"Heaven and Hell are not places. They are times."

Elliot absorbed the suggestion in silence.

"And the kayaker, he just paddles endlessly in the moat?"

"Endlessly. Waiting for the rare entrance of someone like yourself."

"Who are the men on the barge?"

"Mize has gone to extremes to eliminate the pilot soul. The men are ancestors of the One. Another son of Mize drowned them in an attempt to change history. But one of them had already sired a child. That son of Mize died later, attempting to drown the boy. But I believe you already had some knowledge of these things."

"Yes. I did, but only now are the pieces falling in place. And the guards?"

"They are what remain of a force that policed the crew that built the tower this third time. There was a city on an island in the Yangtze valley. During a flood, Mize tricked them into not leaving. They were drowned. Their souls were lost to him. He took them forward in time to before the last ice age, and put them to work rebuilding the tower."

"An ice age has passed since my time?"

"Yes."

"What year is this?"

"It can't hurt to tell you. In your years, this is approximately 43,000 A.D."

"I know you don't want to tell me details of what has happened over this period of time, but may I ask you a question about the past?"

Zul looked into his eyes.

"I know what you seek. Yes, Jesus Christ was my son, in the respect that I personally touched his soul. There was a period when I felt it necessary to place prophets on earth to help guide my children in paths that led away from Mize. His evil blood is so thoroughly intermingled within humankind, that the sentiments of the prophet sons are twisted and manipulated to the point of being lost. Most cannot comprehend their true meaning."

"Did he return after my time?"

"Please refrain from asking such dangerous questions."

"I'm sorry. It's in my nature to be inquisitive. I have a desire to know everything."

"You need to learn to be content with that which you possess. You know more now than anyone has ever known. I convey these things to you because you know the duty of holding knowledge."

Zul stroked the purring cat in his arms.

"Let us now go and see how your young charge fares."

⳹⳽⳾

Simon sensed danger. He crept back down the spiral staircase and carefully went into the courtyard in search of Elliot. He passed through the archway and saw a girl dancing on the paving stones by a fountain. He walked across the courtyard to her. She was looking at him as she twirled and capered.

"Where is Barton?"

"Do you think I'm pretty?"

"I am only concerned with my friend. Where did he go."

"I wouldn't give him what he wanted, so he left."

She frolicked further out into the courtyard to where a channel of water was rushing across it. He slowly followed.

"Are you a child of the water?"

"Why do you ask me?"

"I am searching for the Pilot."

"I am searching for my friend. I must go."

"Wait. I want to show you something."

She held out her hand and slowly opened it. She held a golden coin.

"Do you not recognize it?"

"No . . ."

A deep voice bellowed from behind him.

"You will drown anyway!"

Simon spun around just as Rekh landed on top of him. He was thrown onto his back with Rekh trying to pin him down, grasping for his throat. Simon swiftly brought a knee up into Rekh's groin, and the man howled with pain and rage. Simon punched hard up into his chin, and Rekh fell on top of him, momentarily stunned. He pulled Rekh off of him, ripping his robes in the process. Rekh recovered enough to grab an ankle as Simon jumped to his feet. Falling to his hands, he kicked Rekh hard in the eye with the heel of his free foot. Screaming, the larger man released him. He jumped up again and turned to run, but the girl was there, a knife in her hands. She slashed at him and he dodged back towards Rekh. Simon ducked as Rekh struck out and the girl again slashed. Rekh howled in pain again, and Simon leapt to his feet. The knife was embedded in Rekh's palm. Rekh wrung his hand in the air, dark blood spurting from the wound. Poulee fled from his side, in fear of his rage. Rekh tore the knife from his hand and looked up just in time to see Simon dive into the aqueduct. The rushing water carried him quickly to the edge of the courtyard where the aqueduct disappeared under the wall. Simon surfaced momentarily and saw Rekh dive in after him. He held his breath and went under the wall. Several seconds later, he surfaced again and saw that the channel of water was racing between two high walls. Ahead, it disappeared under another wall. Just before the wall, a huge chain hung down from above, ending just above the surface of the water. Simon grabbed hold of the bottom link as he was sweeping past. Though the current tried to tear him away, he was able to climb hand over hand up the chain and out of the water. Rekh surfaced and was rushing towards him. He climbed higher and kicked at one of the side walls and began to swing on the end of the chain. Rekh made a stab at grabbing the chain, but Simon swung it out of his reach and Rekh was swept under the wall.

Simon slowly spun with the chain and looked upward. There was light coming from an opening high above him.

❦

Not finding Simon in the garden, Zul and Elliot descended the spiral staircase to the hallway. The girl came running through the archway, and froze in front of them.

"My child, what is your name?"

"I am Poulee. Who are you?"

"My name is Zul."

She tried to hide her fear.

"And you?" looking at Elliot, "You would be the Pilot."

Elliot studied her face.

She opened her hand, revealing the gold disc.

"Is this yours?" she asked, handing it to him.

He took it and looked at it. It was a U.S. twenty dollar gold piece from 1788. It was the surely the gold coin taken from the Dornblaser home. "It's not mine," he said, but years of practicing and employing his most poker of faces failed him at the moment. She saw the recognition in his face. Their eyes met and, leaving the coin in his hand, she ran down the hall into the darkness.

"Zul, she is allied with Mize. That coin was taken from the home of the Dornblasers. Zul was troubled by her unexpected appearance. If he was not mistaken he was familiar with her troubled soul. "I saw what happened. Our encounter must unfortunately conclude sooner than I had envisioned. Something is happening. Go to the west gate. Your kayak and paddle are there. I must go to Mihalis and take it there. If you see your young friend, take him with you."

"And Barton, the other?"

"The eyes of the young woman bore bad tidings for him. We must ensure the safety of Simon

'What can I do to protect him?"

"I believe that, though inadvertently, you have done much to distract attention from him."

"That is for the best."

"You would have me think that you say that only for the survival of the boy. What you really feel is that you are more capable of defending yourself against Rekh. Elliot, I must warn you that your time as you know it is reaching its end. Let me pose a question if I may."

"Of course."

"You have sought knowledge and knowledge you have found. If you survive, what will you do with it?"

"This, all of this, has humbled me. I guess that I will just try to live my life as intelligently as I can, for the betterment of myself and those around me."

Zul put a hand on his shoulder. "Yes, I believe you will. Now, we must act."

Without saying anything more, Zul started off through the archway from which Poulee had emerged. Elliot slipped the coin into his life jacket pocket and headed for the stairway.

60 SECONDS TO OVERRIDE
NAVIGATION QUESTIONABLE

He found himself ripping the spraydeck from the cockpit rim and ejecting from the Augsburg as he flipped. Then he was swimming forward, paddle in one hand, until he could seize the bow grab loop with his free hand. He was flowing to the wall which rose ominously in front of him. The Augsburg filled with water, and was sinking fast. He hit the boiling hole at the wall. It buffeted him hard for a moment and then the water took him down like a shot into blackness. Pete counted off the seconds. 38, 39, 40, 41. . . . A turbulent buffeting, a sudden diminishment of the force of the water. The urge to rise to the surface. No. He pulled the Augsburg down, and hoped he was swimming in the right direction. 49, 50, time to go up. 54, 55, 56, 57, the surface. Air scorched into his burning lungs.

OVERRIDE CANCELED

He had surfaced just on the outflow side of the boil, some ten meters from the wall. The city lay across the turbid moat. It all seemed familiar. The moon hung low over the city and lit the moat with it's pale light. A kayaker was approaching. Pete was still trying to catch his breath, the Augsburg was full of water, there would be no running from him. As he reached for the Smith and Wesson, he noticed something in the moonlight. The kayaker's tattered life jacket was adorned with a threadbare Union Jack. Something clicked in his memory.

"Mike. Is it you?"

It had been an eternity since Mike had heard his name. He recalled times long past and almost forgotten. Rich moments on the globe's greatest whitewater. The toast of the kayaking world. All stolen from him.

"Yes. I am Mike Clark. Who are you?"

"It's me, Pete Dornblaser."

"Pete? But you are older. Much older."

"I was only nineteen when you disappeared. That was thirty years ago."

Clark had pulled up beside him in the water. He appeared to have weathered, instead of aged.

"Mike, what happened to you?"

"Do you remember when I wrote that Jacques DuBois, was taking your spot on the Nepal expedition?"

Pete did remember. He had cried. How much he had wanted to be on that expedition with Mike Clark.

"That son of the devil drowned me. When I woke, I was here. His bleeding twin brother runs this place."

"How long have you been here?"

"Thousands of years. Thousands of years facing that wall, riding the boil. Waiting for things to surface."

"When was the last time something surfaced?"

"Pete, he, Rekh's his name, always ordered me to be on watch for a crystal kayak. Yesterday afternoon, the crystal came through, with another kayak. It was a design called New Vision. Three men. One in his thirties, one early twenties, one very young."

"The young one has dark skin?"

"Yes, he does."

"Where are they?"

"They were taken into the city."

"The young one is my son. There is an exit port for the water on the other side, isn't there?"

"Yes. The western gate."

"The crystal is going to take my son for a run at the tower. I've got to stop it."

"Grab hold. I'll tow you to the entryway."

Once there, Pete climbed out of the water and then pulled the Augsburg up to empty it.

"I can tow your boat to the western gate. You can go in and look for your lad."

"But what will happen to you if you are caught?"

"Pete, I'm dead, in this world anyway. I don't care what happens."

Pete pulled the pistol out of its holster and checked the action.

"Thanks Mike."

He called out as Pete began to rush inside.

"If you see that tall bastard Rekh, kill 'im for me."

&⸎&

Simon climbed to the top of the chain and stepped onto a stone lintel protruding from a narrow passageway. A strange light glowed from within. Curiously, he eased his way through the shadows toward the light. At the end of the passageway, he stared out into the gallery. Mihalis was being slowly tumbled within a giant ball of water, floating in the air. He walked toward it. The water calmed in the sphere, and Mihalis stalled in an attitude with its bow pointing at Simon. He walked to the edge of the pool, and gazed up into the sphere. He reached up into the water with his hands. It slowly began to drip down his arms. When he removed his hands, the bottom of the sphere started to droop down into the pool and drain away. Soon it was gone, and Mihalis lay floating in the pool.

Simon spun around and was face to face with Zul. Their eyes met.

"You are Kijemoneto."

"Yes, I am. Who are you, child?"

"My name is Simon."

"And who is your father?"

"My father is Pete Dornblaser."

"And where is he?"

"I do not know."

"Why have you come?"

"I have come to destroy the tower."

The boy showed no fear. Zul was impressed with him.

"You do not have to go. Destroying the tower is not your destiny. It is that of your father."

Zul put a hand on his shoulder.

"Did your father want you to destroy the tower for him?"

"No."

"Then why do you feel you must do it?"

"The tower is bad, is it not? It must be destroyed. I can reach it."

"And if you die?"

"My death means nothing."

"Would it mean nothing to your mother or your father?"

"To them? It would mean . . ."

"Then how can you think of sacrificing yourself if they would be sad?"

Simon thought for a moment.

"I have seen what awaits my land and people. I did what I could to stop the destruction. When my father left, it was to help a nation of people. He knows that there are more important things than oneself."

Zul felt a warmth radiate.

He looked at Simon.

"What hangs from the string around your neck?"

Simon pulled the crystal disc out from behind his life jacket.

"Joanie, my friend, gave it to me."

Zul reached out and touched it.

"Keep it with you, Simon. Now, you must go. Elliot waits for you at the western gate."

The enraged face of Rekh flashed in Simon's brain.

"Yes, you have encountered this man. He will try to stop you again, but you must concentrate on what you need to do."

"I am ready."

"Simon, I will take Mihalis to the gate. I believe that I can fool this bad man, one more time before you leave. You will go a different way."

"Where do I go?"

Zul lifted Mihalis out of the pool.

"Swim down deep into the pool, the water will take you to the gate."

"I am glad I have met you, Kijemoneto."

"I will be with you."

⧼

Pete padded softly down the long hallway, the squishing of the soaked Jaguar moccasins was muffled by the water rushing past on both sides. He knew where he had to go. First the western gate, and then carefully work his way back through. Ahead, partially blocking the hallway, was the grand stairway going up. He somehow remembered it. It had haunted him, from the depths of a lifetime of mysterious dreams. It represented danger, and temptation. A file of soldiers, swords drawn, was running down it toward him.

⧼

Simon dove into the pool and swam down. It was deep. He couldn't see the bottom, only darkness. Suddenly, he was falling, and he landed with a splash in a chamber below. When he surfaced and looked up, he could see the pool above him in a hole in the ceiling, like a rippling mirror. There were ten stone gates at water level in the chamber he was swimming in now. One began to open, and he was slowly sucked towards it by the flowing water.

⧼

Elliot reached the western gate. It was a wide, arched opening in the city wall. The channels of water had been augmented by flows from dozens of other channels of fresh and salt water.

Facing outward, his kayak and paddle sat on a flat stone platform across the right channel. The platform was about four meters higher than the water in the moat. At its top, a delicate stone bridge ran across, above the flowing channels. Elliot crossed the bridge to his kayak.

The current in the moat came sweeping around the city from both sides.

Across the moat, an arched portal spanned the exiting water. The horizon line indicated a steep drop or falls. Elliot wondered what kind of turbulence lay below?

The helmet.

He unclipped it, and slid it on.

READY

"Helmet, river screen on."

ঌৎঌ

Zul carried Mihalis down a long walkway.

"I am displeased with your actions."

you created me to perform a certain function
i believe i am conforming to my duty

"You know it was incorrect to involve the boy and the others. One is almost certainly dead at the hands of Rekh."

the tower must be destroyed
the boy is willing and thoroughly prepared
the man has dedicated himself to protecting the boy
and the other, well, frankly he was not worthy.

Zul continued walking, thinking how out of control Mihalis had become.

just remember master i am what you created
nothing more and nothing less

Rekh appeared through an archway. His fine silk robes were torn and dripping wet. His left eye was swollen almost shut and his right hand wrapped in a bloody bandage. He raged. "Where are you going with Mihalis?!"

"You look dapper, Rekh. Have a rough night?"

Zul continued walking, and Rekh kept pace on the far side.

"Damn you. You are heading for the western gate!"

"Yes, and I believe I will arrive much more rapidly than you."

He pointed ahead to where Rekh's walkway ended against a wall.

Zul knew it would take Rekh at least two minutes longer to arrive at the gate. He kept walking, and Rekh disappeared through an archway.

෨෧

The Chinese guards spread out across the hallway in an impenetrable pha-
lanx. There were more than twenty of them and he had only twelve rounds. He
felt sick, as he thought about the other clips in the dry bag, now being towed
around the city in the Augsburg. From the looks of them, he wasn't sure if bullets would have much effect anyway. They appeared to not be living beings.

There was no time for delay, but the guards were slowly advancing. He
looked at the channels of water. They could carry him past.

"Who are you?"

Pete looked up to see a young woman walking down the stairway.

He said nothing.

"I said, who are you?"

The drip was freezing in mid-air.

She glided down the stairs and, as if on ball bearings, slipped between the
guards. He felt a wave of confusion. Memories. Were they sweet or painful? He
tried to remember. What is happening to me?

Water dripping into a puddle. A dark room.

Now blazing sun. Making mad love on burning hot rock shelf. His sword
carelessly cast down beside them. Sweat running down him onto her. Their
black skins contrasting with the white stone.

She stood before him in the hallway. "You cannot have forgotten me." She
untied the strings of her dress, and it fell off of her body to the paving stones.

Mihalis lay at the water's edge. The sun beaming brilliantly through it. "You
are my lord, my king, I love you." Thrusting hard into her. One of her hands
no longer ripping into his back. A blaze of pain as the steel entered his flesh.

She stood before him, her soft body beckoning. Skin pale, as the dawn light
mellowed into the hallway. Her hand slowly reaching for the gun.

෨෧

Zul appeared with Mihalis through the portal on the opposite side of the
rushing channels. He laid Mihalis on the platform.

Simon rushed out of the hallway and stood looking back and forth at Elliot
and Zul.

"Simon, hurry, across the bridge."

Simon swiftly climbed the steps and crossed over to Zul.

"Now both of you, get into your boats and ready yourselves."

Zul climbed the steps, and crossed the bridge to the center column.

Once they both had their spraydecks on, Elliot realized what Zul was doing. Rekh came charging around the southern side of the city in the moat. He was in a large blue kayak. It was high volume and long; it would be very fast. From where he was below them, Rekh could see Simon and Elliot sitting. He knew they were in kayaks, but he couldn't see the boats. He didn't know who was in Mihalis. He caught the eddy below Elliot and then ferried hard across the rushing channels to the eddy below Simon.

"You don't want to leave, do you Rekh?"

Rekh stared icily at him and gritted his teeth.

"Which is the One? Make the wrong choice, and you have to go, don't you Rekh?"

"You underestimate my speed."

"No. I don't think so. You can kill only one. Which is he?"

Rekh knew. It was Elliot, the older. He had failed his father's test of the coin. Rekh would not have to leave.

☙◦❧

Her hand was slowly slipping around the pistol.

He had come so far. There had been no rest. He was weary and weak. Weakening more and more. No more fighting and killing. He could give in to her.

The drop of water falling. Ever so slowly. Now splashing into a puddle in a dark room. Looking down at the dripping water. The water dripping from his chest. From the jeweled finger guard of the knife in his chest. Laughter. Coming from behind him. Her laughter and another's, mixing. The dripping water was now turning red.

He ripped the gun away from her and took a step back. He leveled it at her forehead and fired. As she dropped, the guards bolted forward, swords raised. He took a second to jam the gun into the shoulder holster and then threw himself into the channel. He swam as deep as he could and heard the blades slicing into the water above him.

☙◦❧

Rekh ferried back and forth, muscles rippling on his arms and shoulders. Zul held up the crystal disc.

"Make your choice Rekh."

Rekh ferried to the eddy below Simon.

Always so pathetically readable, thought Zul. It will be such a pleasure to be rid of you forever.

Zul rubbed the disc and Elliot heard a roar of water coming from the portal behind him. He looked back and water shot from the portal.

Rekh blasted out of the eddy and ferried across to Elliot's side of the channels. The water from the portals shoved Elliot and Simon off of the platforms and cascading down into the moat. Elliot and Simon were both flipping as they fell. The cascading water flipped Rekh too, but as he was tipping over, he grabbed Elliot by the helmet.

60 SECONDS TO OVERRIDE

Elliot felt narrow plates slip out of the bottom of the helmet and lock under his jaw. Rekh knew he could hold his breath longer than Elliot could. Elliot struggled against the grip on the helmet but couldn't break free. Simon rolled up and saw what was happening.

"Simon, go!" shouted Zul.

47 SECONDS TO OVERRIDE

"But I cannot leave him. I must help him."

"Simon, trust me, he will not die. You must go."

Simon looked again at the struggling men and boats, swirling in the moat. I trust you.

Simon took an anxious look at Elliot in the grasp of Rekh.

Goodbye, my friend.

He turned Mihalis in the moat and started paddling hard for the exit portal.

Rekh maintained his iron grip on the helmet. Through his closed eyes, he imagined the strength and life draining away from the One. Once he was dead, he would allow the crystal and the corpse to wash useless and spent through the portal into the chasm below. How beautiful it would be. His father would be pleased.

The man had slowed in his struggles. Rekh also felt weak. He needed air. Then, to his surprise, he felt the helmet in his hands grow hot, then cold. The hot and cold pulses came faster and more intensely. He opened his eyes and saw the words NEW VISION written in metal flake across the stern deck of the man's kayak.

No!

Rekh released his grip on the helmet and rolled up. The kayak was not Mihalis. A flash of light stunned him, and when he regained his sight, he was alone in the moat. A shout came from above.

"You lose, Rekh!"

"Damn you, Zul!"

Rekh turned towards the portal as Simon was nearing the brink.

Pete rushed out of the hallway and slid to a stop. Zul looked down at him, astonished.

"Oh my."

"Simon, stop!"

Simon plunged through the portal and down the steep slide below it. The waters converged in a massive rooster tail and he nailed it perfectly, riding high into the air. Pete saw him bob up, and then he was gone. Rekh was drawing close to the brink.

Zul descended the steps from the column and stood at Pete's side. He put a hand on his shoulder. Pete turned and looked into his eyes. He was going to say something and found himself instead dropping to one knee.

"You have returned."

"My son. I came for him."

"Your love for him is great."

Pete looked up at Zul.

"Help me. He is my only child."

Mike Clark pulled up to the north platform, the Augsburg in tow.

"Go."

They crossed the bridge to the north platform.

"Give me your belt, I'll lower you."

Pete took his river belt and handed it to Zul.

Zul put his hand on Pete's shoulder once again.

"Nameloc, you have endured lifetimes over and again, each ending in death at the tower or the hands of the horrid. This however, with the boy, shall be the last. I release your soul from this amaranthine servitude."

Pete felt his head spin and then suddenly clear. He was no longer the Pilot, the servant. How many times had he stood here before? At the exit of a ruined city? Sometimes Zul had been there with him and sometimes not. But the brackish sea breeze was the same. What was different was that this time, he stood face to face with another man. Just a man. This time he was not there to destroy the tower, he was there to save his son. Zul saw all of this in Pete's eyes and understood.

"Thank you Nameloc. I do apologize for all of this. All of it. There will have to be another way."

"I have to go, now."

"Hurry! Lower yourself, I will hold the belt."

Zul leaned back to support Pete's weight on the strap and Pete climbed hand over hand down it to where Mike steadied the Augsburg against the wall.

Pete secured the spraydeck to the cockpit rim and looked at Clark. "Thanks Mike. I hope... I hope things change for you."

He pushed away from the wall and stared up at Zul.

"I killed a woman in the grand hallway."

"She was not innocent. Go. Your quarry lies below."

Without another look back, Pete lowered the visor of his helmet and headed for the portal.

CHAPTER 14 — THE DUEL

The breaker of the tower shall be crushed,
Cast down 'midst shattered stones,
Forsaken by all-seeing God,
To mourn his death with moans.

–Old Russian Proverb--Alexander Solzhenitsyn

The entire flow of the river was channeled between vertical cliffs. Two meter waves sloshed between the walls. There were few holes and no boulders. The water was deep enough so that there weren't any ledge hydraulics.

Simon was troubled with the scene he'd left behind, the uncertainty that lay ahead, and the knowledge that a killer was on his tail. But he still loved to play the waves of the big river.

At times, Rekh could glimpse Simon ahead of him, but he wasn't gaining. Rekh was much stronger than Simon and his kayak faster than Mihalis. Simon, however, was a much better paddler and was handling the water better. As Simon crested a wave, he would read the next and plant a stroke in the trough on the side the wave was coming from. In this manner, he synergized with the wave and, using little energy, was able to shoot from wave top to wave top. Rekh was bracing and wasn't focusing on the whitewater. He was boiling with anger and hate over having to leave the city. Nothing good awaited him below, and he knew it.

Pete was minutes behind, and unable to see either of them, but he was paddling like Simon – smoothly, efficiently. He was also reliving his actions. Why had he killed the girl? Because of the dreams? What if it wasn't her?

He remembered when he was young. Another youth had stolen two of his kayaks from the porch. He confronted the youth, but the youth had denied it. There had been no proof, no witnesses. So he had taken no action. He had wanted to beat him to the ground, but he hadn't. The reason: he had been raised to respect others. Making a judgment that might be wrong, and punishing another who, possibly, was not guilty, would be immoral.

That was then. So much had passed. Now he was judge, jury, executioner.

What if the girl had not been the one who had killed him twice before?

A huge wave slapped him in the face.

Wake up, Petey. He concentrated on the rapids and started to paddle harder.

കeditം

The whitewater had huge, clean waves. Simon began to enjoy riding them. Then he made a mistake. The canyon widened a bit, and the current piled into an area of lesser gradient, creating a perfect wave train with long eddies on each side. He paddled into one of the eddies and then surfed out onto a wave. It was big, glassy, and fast. He was carving the wave face to ribbons. He recalled days on the Cheat with his father. He sliced back and forth and then rose high on the crest. He felt that if he surfed the wave long enough, his father would magically appear. No. His father was gone. He would never reappear. Time to go.

Aligned perfectly, he dropped into the trough and piked off a sky-high ender. He rolled up and eddied out again. Looking upstream, he couldn't see Rekh. The eddy current slowly carried him upstream beside the side cliff. He looked out at the beautiful waves.

Worry for his father made him feel how rich it was to be alive. To experience such wondrous things as surfing the waves.

He glanced back upstream. Rekh was coming fast.

Simon peeled out of the eddy and started racing downstream once again.

the pilot would not have committed such an error

കeditം

They had been racing downstream for hours. It was now close to noon. All three were tiring, but none slackened the pace. Neither had the river. Monstrous holes began to force them to weave through the rapids.

Pete hammered hard strokes through the waves. He cleared his mind of each obstacle the instant he was past it and concentrated on the fastest line through the next. Now he could see Rekh ahead of him. Rekh was making mistakes. Off line at times, he would surge powerfully ahead again when he recovered. Then Pete saw one reason why Rekh was erring. He glimpsed Simon ahead of Rekh. Rekh was so preoccupied with catching Simon that he was making mistakes and losing ground with each correction.

Pete put his head down. Soon he felt that he had to be gaining on Rekh.

Suddenly, he had an overwhelming sense of deja vu. He had seen this part of the river before. The waves and holes looked familiar. Then he realized that he had seen it before on Howard's computer monitor. They were in the grid! All hell was about to break loose downstream.

Holy Shit!

He looked up. Less than a hundred meters separated him from his son. Rekh was between them. They were now leaving the grid and the horizon line warned of the imminence of the steeper section which lay below. He saw Simon paddle hard off to the left. Rekh followed suit, but too late, and smashed into the shoulder of a huge hole. He cleared it with a deep, strong stroke. The helmet was keeping Pete one jump ahead and warned of the hole at the same moment Rekh was hitting it.

The next huge ledge hole dictated a far right side run, and Simon was scrambling hard for it. This time, Rekh reacted with sufficient speed to follow him and actually gain some ground. Pete was already far right and was almost on Rekh's tail.

The third hole, and the meanest yet, offered no tongue around it. After a dangerous hesitation, Simon paddled hard down the drop and used a trick his father had taught him. In the last second before hitting the foam, he sought the creasing water in the drop, planted his paddle hard on top of it and actually started to roll over onto the side of the power stroke, In this manner, his weight was largely on the paddle blade, Mihalis was left light enough to rise high in the foam and slide out through the hole.

Rekh punched into the hole for all he was worth. He was just cresting through as Pete slammed in using the same tack as Simon.

❧❦

For Rekh, the rapids brought no fright, no thrill. He raged. He could taste how sweet it would be to grab the young one by the throat and drag him under. His life was coming to an end because of the boy. The boy had to die. Had to feel his rage. Had to know he was paying for having destroyed Rekh's easy existence in Bwuy. The boy was only a few meters ahead. He reached within himself for more strength. They were passing to the left of a huge sandstone boulder. He was drawing near.

Close enough to knock him silly, thought Rekh.

Rekh choked up on his paddle shaft and began to swing when out of the corner of his eye, he saw another kayaker whipping across the eddy toward him.

Pete speared the bow of the Augsburg into the side of Rekh's boat, knocking him off balance as he swung at Simon. The blow passing over his head, Simon surged ahead. Rekh and Pete were left staring at each other in the turbulence.

Rekh was shocked. Who was this? Another strange helmet. It could only be the true pilot. The crystal had stymied him with another surprise.

Pete stared into Rekh's face. He had seen it before. In the truck with the murderer of Salil. The Huron leaping on him at Tokebelloke.

Together, they hit a huge pillow of water as Simon cleared out downstream. They tumbled in the foam. Rekh grasped at him but missed. Pete rolled just in time to respond to the next pillow. He was bracing into it as Rekh swept in upside down against him. They washed through as Rekh rolled. They were now side by side. Pete knew they were heading for the dividing pillar. To the right was the tunnel. To the left, was the channel that ended in the undercut strainer. The helmet dictated a right side run.

Simon had already passed. Pete played chicken with Rekh. They were rushing toward the pillar and Rekh had no idea where to go. Pete knew but made no move. Rekh made his decision and charged left. Pete paddled high up onto the right side pillow and rolled over just before the tunnel. As he was carried through, he fought with his memory for a hold on that day so long ago when he had hiked the Wadi with Salil. Two more severe challenges lay ahead, before the bowl. Before the tower. Before he would lose his son forever.

He rolled up as he shot free of the tunnel. To his left he heard the horrible sound of breaking and ripping fiberglass. Rekh's boat was being torn to bits in the knife-like pillars of sandstone in the undercut. As he stared at it, Rekh surfaced beside him and grabbed his left paddle blade.

His face was beet-red, his eyes ablaze with hate.

"At least you will pay with your life for this!"

Rekh tried to rip the paddle from his hands. The current was taking them towards the pourover ledge on the inside of the next turn. Pete yanked to break Rekh's grip on the paddle. Together, they dropped off the edge and slammed into the hole below the pourover. The Augsburg was back-endered and they were spun hard in the swirling water. Pete held his breath and firmly grasped the paddle shaft, trying to prevent Rekh from ripping it away from him. The odd shape of their assembly carried them to the side of the pourover and freed them into the current. They shot across to the pillars buttressing the outside of the turn. Rekh was taken into the cliff and, as he passed behind the first pillar, the blade of the paddle snapped away from the shaft. Pete, still upside-down, sensed the break and rolled up with the other blade.

Rekh passed behind the pillars and grabbed the bow of the Augsburg with both hands. The river carried them to the next horizon line. Pete knew he could run the falls that awaited them anywhere but where they were in the middle. Rekh was trying to climb up on the bow. Trying to flip him. The bow was sinking under his weight. They dropped over the first ledge of the falls and into the seething hole below. With Rekh's weight added to the bow, the Augsburg sank deep and landed in the pot hole. Part of the current wanted to take the Augsburg down through, but the water coming from above bent Pete double in the kayak. Pete felt Rekh release, and the Augsburg bobbed up in the foam and was carried over the second ledge. Now, almost out of breath, he felt himself being tumbled continuously in the foam He felt something in the water and knew it was Rekh. Suddenly, he was out of the grip of the recycled water and was rolling up. Rekh was there, swimming toward him. He stroked hard with the remaining blade, but it was too late. Rekh was on him again. Pete swiped at him with the jagged end of the paddle shaft, but Rekh grabbed hold. The current carried them to the divisions in the channel. Pete looked up. The tower. It loomed high above. It's brown stone streaked with black. Simon was nowhere in sight. He knew there were no more eddies. He had lost.

Rekh had the broken shaft in both hands. The river took them against one of the splits. Pete leaned downstream as Rekh's back plastered against the rock and he drove the shaft of the broken paddle through his chest. Blood poured from Rekh's mouth, and his eyes rolled back in his head. Pete tried to pull the paddle free but the water took it, flipping him over in the process. He hand-rolled up and stared as the water rushed him towards the lip of the bowl.

⊱⊰

Simon focused on the river. He launched off of the lip and tried not to look down. Almost the entire circumference of the bowl was one unbroken curtain of falling water. He was falling. Falling water all around him. A deep, soft landing in the foam. Paddling hard through the boil. The water, confused over the presence of the tower, surging around in the bowl like a staggering drunk. Simon rode the surge closer and closer to the tower. The tower loomed. He couldn't see the top. It dominated the bowl. The water slapped into it in waves without rhythm or cadence.

He could see that the waves had eroded deep into the stone base. It would be weakened. Vulnerable. He caught a surging wave and rode it toward the stone. The bow of Mihalis rammed into a notch in the base, and he felt a hammering burst of energy pour forth from the crystal into the tower.

Cracks radiated from the point of impact like a giant web. He was carried back from the tower by the retreating wave as another surge smacked into the impact zone. It broke through the fractured stone, and the tower began to implode under it's force. Water swirled into the hole, drawing Simon toward it. The cracks spread, and the tower groaned. Then, with a great roar, it started to tilt towards him. He was consumed by its shadow. His upward look was met by the falling mass. It drove him and Mihalis to the bottom of the bowl. He felt himself rising through the stone. He was floating, high above, watching as the water pushed the fragments of the broken tower into the pit.

⊱⊰

Pete saw it fall as he shot off the lip of the bowl. It was falling toward him. The helmet screen was going crazy but he stopped reading it. He was sick. He knew his son was dying below. He closed his eyes and suddenly felt the override take him.

⊱⊰

He woke with sand in his mouth. Gagging, he tried to spit it out. It was hot. Everything was hot. His vision was returning. He saw the lip of the bowl dark against the nighttime stars. Still in his Augsburg, he couldn't feel his legs, The kayak was twisted and he was paralyzed from the waist down. Then he knew. The helmet had done an override and transported him away from danger – depositing him in a time when the bowl was dry. He had landed in sand and broken his back. The bowl was almost full of sand. The hot wind blew sand at him.

Simon was dead.

"Mihalis!"

i am here

"Where?"

where you found me

"Why? Why have you done this?"

it is what I do

"My son?"

simon is dead his soul perished

Pete's anger was over whelmed by sorrow. Simon! His son. His darling. His hope.

"But why didn't you take me, and leave him be?"

you know the answer you felt it in Bwuy
you failed too many times
your soul is contaminated, decadent
you could not achieve what the task required

"I made it here, didn't I?"

yes but not to destroy the tower

Pete was tired of Mihalis' logic. "What will happen now?"

you will die here
some day the tower will be constructed anew

you will be reborn and find me again

"Fuck You."

your life has been rich

"It was, until you took away all that mattered to me."

it will be rich again
the life of the pilot soul cannot be equaled

"Zul has released me."

that cannot be true

"But it is. I will no longer play your game Mihalis." Pete reached for the pistol beneath his life jacket.

you may not do this
your soul is invulnerable to everything except this

"Thanks for confirming that for me."

wait
if you destroy your soul
your careless meddling with fortunes
will produce profound changes
you must conform

Pete removed the helmet and raised the pistol to his temple.
"Too bad, Mihalis."
The shot echoed in the bowl.

EPILOGUE
X
HOWARD

November 14, 2002

The awards ceremony and the reception were over. Now he was alone back in his Stockholm Regency suite. Howard sat back in his chair and stretched his legs. He felt a sense of Satisfaction. Finality.

It had been a long ordeal. There had been no trial, just endless depositions and plea bargaining. The government's case had been weakened by the disappearance of key witnesses. Anders Lieb's death had been a blow to the prosecution. Anders and Howard had both known that his prostate cancer was inoperable. He had died with resolve and dignity. Unfortunately for the government, he had been a key element in the case. Without Anders' testimony, there was little linking Howard to the plutonium from Northern Dynamics.

Farid Krioche had turned up murdered in Algiers.

The FBI investigation of Howard Calvert/Joe Morton had become a quagmire. The upshot was that if the FBI evidence was to be admitted at all, it had to be admitted in its entirety. That would have put Howard in two places at one time; the government would be supplying him with an iron clad alibi.

Then the government had threatened to charge him in the disappearance of CIA agent Elliot Carlson. The defense team then produced affidavits from a dozen witnesses in the Great Falls parking lot who had seen Elliot depart moments before Howard's arrest.

The other key witness and codefendant had never reappeared.

The defense team had plea bargained away all but one customs charge, a misdemeanor, and Howard had spent six months in federal prison in Julietta, Pennsylvania. It hadn't been too bad. He had been denied any access to computers and all phone calls had been strictly monitored. And, of course, no kayaking.

It had been expensive. He had paid close to a million in legal fees. After all that, the Department of Energy had sent some high ranking officials to sheepishly ask if he would be willing to head up a commission on crystal energy. He declined, saying once again that anything related to that was not his original work. He, and they, already knew that crystal energy was still out of reach, unsustainable, and undirectable.

But now it was over. All behind him. And, strangely, he felt drained. He had been censured and then honored. He had accomplished his personal goal and been involved in an impossible imbroglio. The excitement was gone, and he didn't know where he would find motivation for more.

He went to the fridge under the bar and popped a cold Budweiser just as someone knocked.

He set down the beer and straightened his tie. When he opened the door, an attractive woman and a bell boy with a luggage cart stood outside. There was an oversized trunk on the cart.

"Dr. Calvert?"

"Yes."

"Dr. Calvert, my name is Amelia Ward. I know this sounds strange, but may I come in?"

He looked at her. Mid thirties, well dressed. Her eyes held a sparkle he had seen before.

"Yes. I don't see why not. Please."

The bell boy wheeled in the cart. She tipped him, and he left.

"Dr. . . ."

"Call me Howard, please."

"Howard, I believe I have something of yours."

"So?"

"Yes. I'm afraid it's going to be a long story. Do you by any chance have anything to drink?"

"Excuse me for being so rude. It's just, that this has taken me by surprise. Let me take your coat."

He helped her with her coat and laid it over the arm of a chair. There was a bottle of champagne on ice sent by a well-wisher. He popped the cork and poured her a glass.

"Thanks. By the way, I found your acceptance speech very interesting."

"So you were there?"

"Under the circumstances, I wouldn't have missed it. I have come from my home in Switzerland, just to see you and bring this." She pointed to the trunk.

"Now, where do we begin?"

He looked at her as she sat down, not knowing what to say.

"This all has to do with my great grandfather. His name was Carl Ward. I never met him. He died in 1952, when he was eighty-eight. My great grandfather had a very interesting life. It seems that somehow he scooped everybody else in the Klondike gold rush in the Yukon Territory. He arrived in 1896 and made a fortune panning gold. He was out and in San Francisco before the rush started in 1897. Then he bought a lot of rundown property there. Everybody thought he was crazy. It all burned in the fires after the earthquake in 1906. But he tripled his investment selling it afterward in the redevelopment. Then he invested heavily in various stocks. Standard Oil. Bell Telephone. Things like that. With those investments, he became incredibly rich. Somehow, he had the intuition to sell everything before the crash of 1929."

The story was interesting. The woman was interesting. Howard had no idea where this was going but found himself listening intently.

"He became reclusive after that. He was always fond of his hobbies and spent his time between them and his children and grandchildren. In his later years, he directed that generation to buy up small parcels of beach properties on the southeast and west coasts and farmlands in areas ringing large cities. They were all worthless at the time, and the family thought he was losing it. Of course, that changed, back when I was young. The properties, all together, were worth billions."

Howard still had no idea where this was leading.

"When Carl died, he left each grandchild a series of sealed metal boxes. They had dates when they were to be opened, with investment instructions inside. The instructions were precise, however unbelievable. Investments in communications, computer chips, things he could not have known about. To my father, Jonathan Ward, he left instructions over the future disposition of the sealed box in this trunk. My parents were killed in an automobile crash two years ago. I was their only child, and this was left to me. There was a key and a short note inside that said nothing more than to deliver the metal box to Dr. Howard S. Calvert. Well, I thought surely you must be in your eighties or nineties, but I checked and found out who you were. And that you would be in Stockholm to receive a Nobel Prize in physics. I find this all very, very strange, but, my great grandfather was not to be second-guessed."

Howard was speechless.

"Howard, I am dying to know what is in that box. I feel it will finally disclose Carl Ward's innermost secrets."

"Well, let's open it."

Together, they lifted a square metal box from the trunk by its handles. The key Amelia produced from her purse opened the old padlock. There were two ingeniously made latches camming the lid firmly shut. Howard lifted one and Amelia the other. Air hissed entering the box. They looked at each other and Howard lifted the lid. It was full of rice. White rice.

Rice to absorb moisture, he thought. His mind raced.

Howard sifted down in the rice and came up with an envelope. It was stiff with age, but hadn't yellowed. He opened it.

Washington D.C.
March 11, 1942

Dear Howard:
Dig a little deeper in the rice and I think much will be explained to you and my grandson Jonathan.

Howard dug deeper and felt something hard. He slowly brought it up out of the box. It was the helmet he had given Elliot Carlson. In perfect condition.

"What is it, Howard?"

"Amelia, I don't know how to explain this to you. Your great grandfather was a friend of mine. I last saw him just four years ago."

There was another letter in the helmet. Amelia read it out loud:

Dear Howard,

    Some years have passed for you. For me, a lifetime. A lifetime rich and full of incredible experiences. However, it was a lifetime safely locked away from you and all that I had known. Though I am not at liberty to tell you everything, I will pick up the tale by saying I never did catch up with Pete Dornblaser. I did have the pleasure of meeting his son Simon. We traveled through time and space together and kayaked to the city in the desert, and though I had to make an early exit, I have every reason to believe that he was able to destroy the tower. I woke in a deep well of sand in the desert. Upon ascending a spiral staircase made of sand with your kayak on my shoulder I found myself on the surface with the wall collapsing behind me. An hour later marked the fortuitous arrival of a camel train en route to Timbuktu to buy salt. The Dornblaser's $20 bought my passage out of desert. I then paddled the Niger River to the Atlantic where I found out that I was in 1895. I worked passage on a schooner around Cape Horn to San Francisco where I convinced a benefactor to grubstake my travel to the Klondike. From there, my family knows the rest of the story. It was a burden at times, knowing when disasters and world wars would plague humanity, yet knowing the potential costs of intervening and thus saying nothing. What I will risk saying to you is that awful changes are in store for our country and the only remedy for you will be to choose somewhere else to live out your life. The helmet, while being a unique tool, was unable to tempt me to ever use it again. You in your wisdom will know what to, and what not, to do with it

    Thank you, my friend and mentor, for all of your kindness in preparing me for what has been an incredible journey.

    Sincerely, Elliot

Howard was blown away. He sank into his chair and absorbed what she had read to him. So there would be no more. He would never know what had become of Pete. Or would he?

"Howard, it seems we have much more in common than we knew. How would you like the idea of coming to my home in Switzerland for some rest and relaxation? I think it could be just what you need." The sparkle in her eyes made saying "no" out of the question.

Y
SANA

October 28, 922

Sana was walking through the forest toward the river, as she had every morning since the attacks. The river was as it always had been. Serene, beautiful, eternal. The morning sun lit the canyon wall on the far side. Colors of fall painted the world a patchwork of red, orange, yellow and auburn. A kingfisher chattered by in the chill air.

Men had so much to learn from the river. She wondered how they could be so cruel. Whence the ability to kill and destroy? Did they not feel as did the mothers of their victims when they destroyed hopes and dreams, lives? Women bore the sorrow. The world must change. Something must change it. Someone. She would change it. If she could.

She looked out at the river sweeping by. She fell under its spell. It sang with delicate tones. It was speaking to her, and she fancied that she could hear her lost husband, whispering. Then she saw a shimmering and her son.

She was running across the sand. She dropped to her knees and cradled his head in her lap, and ran her hand through his wet curls. Her tears fell to his face. Though his eyes could not see yet, he felt her pain.

"Mother, please do not cry."

Sana gently pulled on a string around his neck, and a crystal disc came from underneath his life jacket. It slowly spun in the morning light.

Z
A NEW WORLD

December 4, 2004 -- Baaktun 2, Katun 11, Diurna 16

Damn, another flat.

Oma Totclac pulled over to the side of Chichen bikeway. Rain had started to fall. Normally, it would just be a nuisance, but today she carried a precious load on the cargo rack. She checked the binding to be sure it was tight.

In twenty minutes, with the aid of a couple of other commuters on the bikeway, she had changed the latex inner tube and was on her way. Neither had recognized her, mainly because the hood of her poncho partially hid her face. That was fine with her. She was serving her quarter-katun term as Western Hemisphere Chairperson, but like all leaders she insisted on equality of all people. She pedaled past the hospital park and turned down a lane to the museum, parked her bike and carried her parcel inside to the director's office. She hurried because there were only two hours left before dark. She was dying to show Charles Ulabta, museum director, the volume she carried.

"Charles, they found it!"

"You're kidding, aren't you?"

Charles Ulabta had heard the rumors from the Old Chichen Archeological Park confirming the discovery of the vault, but he hadn't dared to hope that they might have found the Book. Oma was already busy unwrapping the waxed paper from the large volume.

"Will you look at that!"

It was in good shape. The legendary voyages of diplomacy had been inspired by this volume. It had been to Europe and back. What foresight and courage those people had had. Fleets of trimaran dugouts sailing to Europe, fanning out across the continent, spreading the message of hope to a world on the brink of disaster. There had been early triumphs: separating church and state, promotion of family planning, world wide surplus sharing, voluntary abdication of kings in favor of democracy throughout Europe and Asia. All these and more had been brought on by this book carried from the 20th century to the 10th, from North America to Central America. What a wondrous time indeed it must have been. The old learned society, the Shawnee woman with her soft spoken son sailing to Europe with a shocking message of what might happen without change.

"Just think, Oma. This one book did so much."

"All these people and places. Montezuma, Missouri, Maryland. Charles, is it true that because history was changed they don't exist and hence never existed?"

"I like to believe that they did and do exist. Their history is separate from ours but just as real." Charles thought about the world described in the book, a history of great technological advances followed by bloodshed, violence, environmental degradation, extinction of whole species for convenience of humanity who didn't think about the consequences of their acts. What a nightmare!

"Dornblaser. Was he evil? He was, wasn't he?"

"We can't judge because we don't understand the play of consequences."

"Charles, it's getting late. I'd better get home." Rain was tapping on the skylights, and the light was failing in the room. Oma could sense a longwinded lecture coming on.

"Okay, Oma. Thanks for bringing it over personally. Stop by when you have time."

"I will. There's lots I want to see in there."

When she was gone, Charles continued to leaf through the volume until it became too dark. Then he carefully wrapped it in the waxed paper and put it in the desk.

He left the building and started biking home. On the bikeway bridge over the grand canal, he stopped. The rain had let up and the moon was breaking through the clouds, lighting up old Chichen. The pyramids stabbed into the night sky like ageless sentinels. He was due to volunteer a shift on the maintenance crew this tenth day. Everyone gave one day out of the ten to some kind of community volunteer service. He was looking forward to this one. He would have a chance to think and live in the past.

The discovery of the volume was important, but it wouldn't reveal anything new about Dornblaser. It had been 1062 years since he had changed the world. History had been hard on him. Charles looked across the expanse of the ruins and thought about the people.

They owed their existence to him. Without him, their blood would be carried by people without dreams. Without hope. Living in poverty in a devastated world. A world that wasted resources like there was no tomorrow. A world that could not continue to provide for a population growing out of control.

Yes, history had been hard on Dornblaser, but who knows? Perhaps the society he left behind in the other 1998 would soon be ruins, consumed by the jungles.

the end

ॐ◌

Made in the USA
Lexington, KY
29 May 2015